MALONE'S FATE

LAYLAH ROBERTS

Laylah Roberts

Malone's Fate

© 2024, Laylah Roberts

Laylah.roberts@gmail.com

https://laylahroberts.com

ALL RIGHTS RESERVED. This book contains material protected under International and Federal Copyright Laws and Treaties. Any unauthorized reprint or use of this material is prohibited. No part of this book may be reproduced or transmitted in any form or by any means, electronic or mechanical, including photocopying, recording, or by any information storage and retrieval system without express written permission from the author / publisher.

Editing: Woncas Creative

Photographer: Golden Czermak; FuriousFotog

Cover Model: Andrew James

Cover Design by: Allycat's Creations

❦ Created with Vellum

LET'S KEEP IN TOUCH!

Don't miss a new release by signing up to my newsletter. You'll get sneak peeks, deleted scenes, and giveaways: https://landing.mailerlite.com/webforms/landing/p7l6g0

You can also join my Facebook readers' group here: https://www.facebook.com/groups/386830425069911/

BOOKS BY LAYLAH ROBERTS

Doms of Decadence

Just for You, Sir

Forever Yours, Sir

For the Love of Sir

Sinfully Yours, Sir

Make me, Sir

A Taste of Sir

To Save Sir

Sir's Redemption

Reveal Me, Sir

Montana Daddies

Daddy Bear

Daddy's Little Darling

Daddy's Naughty Darling Novella

Daddy's Sweet Girl

Daddy's Lost Love

A Montana Daddies Christmas

Daring Daddy

Warrior Daddy

Daddy's Angel

Heal Me, Daddy

Daddy in Cowboy Boots

A Little Christmas Cheer (crossover with MC Daddies)

Sheriff Daddy

Her Daddies' Saving Grace

Rogue Daddy

A Little Winter Wonderland

Daddy's Sassy Sweetheart

Daddy Dominic

Daddy Unleashed

MC Daddies

Motorcycle Daddy

Hero Daddy

Protector Daddy

Untamed Daddy

Her Daddy's Jewel

Fierce Daddy

A Little Christmas Cheer (crossover with Montana Daddies)

Savage Daddy

Boss Daddy

Daddy Fox

A Snowy Little Christmas

Saving Daddy

Daddies' Captive

A Foxy Little Christmas

A Little Easter Delight

Harem of Daddies

Ruled by her Daddies

Claimed by her Daddies

Stolen by her Daddies

Captured by her Daddies

Kept by her Daddies

Haven, Texas Series

Lila's Loves

Laken's Surrender

Saving Savannah

Molly's Man

Saxon's Soul

Mastered by Malone

How West was Won

Cole's Mistake

Jardin's Gamble

Romanced by the Malones

Twice the Malone

Mending a Malone

Malone's Heart

Malone's Pride

Malone's Fate

New Orleans Malones

Damaged Princess

Vengeful Commander

Wicked Prince

Men of Orion

Worlds Apart

Cavan Gang

Rectify

Redemption

Redemption Valley

Audra's Awakening

Old-Fashioned Series

An Old-Fashioned Man

Two Old-Fashioned Men

Her Old-Fashioned Husband

Her Old-Fashioned Boss

His Old-Fashioned Love

An Old-Fashioned Christmas

Crime Boss Daddies

Daddy's Obsession

Papi's Protection

Papi's Savior

Bad Boys of Wildeside

Wilde

Sinclair

Luke

Rawhide Ranch Holiday

A Cozy Little Christmas

A Little Easter Escapade

Standalones

Their Christmas Baby

Haley Chronicles

Ally and Jake

TRIGGER WARNING

This book contains mentions of physical and emotional abuse and some violence. The heroine has some issues with food.

1

Six months ago . . .

THE DART FLEW through the air, hitting just to the right of the bull's eye.

"Ooh, nice shot. Wait, do they call it a shot in darts? Probably not, right? Nice throw, I guess."

Turning, Tanner looked down to see a short, curvy redhead standing beside him. She smiled, her blue eyes dancing with humor.

Well, hello, gorgeous girl.

She was wearing a white top with the bar's logo on it. The top was stretched tight across a pair of magnificent breasts. A short apron was tied loosely around her waist. A pair of well-worn jeans finished off the outfit.

Nothing remarkable, but she wore it well.

"Well, thanks, darlin'. Yeah, I think you'd call it an excellent throw."

"Excellent, huh?" she said dryly.

"Stupendous? Wonderful? Absolutely mind-blowing. I'll take any of those."

Her grin widened. "That's good of you."

He shrugged. "I'm just that sort of guy. Always willing to take on feedback."

"As long as it's good feedback?" she asked.

"Exactly."

"Can I have a go?"

"You don't have to work?" he asked.

She shrugged, looking around. "Things are quiet right now and I'm owed a break. Give me a second to tell Harry."

Tanner watched her stride over to the bar, where an older bartender nodded as she said something. Damn, she filled out those jeans well. When she returned, she smiled up at him.

"You ever played darts before?" he asked her.

"Doesn't seem too hard. You just throw the pointy end at the round board and hit the middle, right?"

Oh, she was cute.

Tanner grinned. "Right."

She took the dart and threw it. It landed against the wall about a foot to the right of the dartboard and fell to the floor.

"Huh. That looked easier when you did it." She frowned, looking puzzled. As though she'd immediately expected to be an expert.

"Would you like some pointers?"

"Sure! That would be awesome." She ran over to pick up the dart and brought it back.

She seemed out-of-place in this seedy bar—like a ray of sunshine and sweetness.

It made him feel... protective.

He took the dart from her. "Okay, watch me."

Tanner showed her how to throw it as she watched with deep concentration, biting her lower lip.

After he threw it, he reached out without thought and freed her lip. "Careful, darlin', you don't want to hurt yourself."

Another big smile.

Damn. He wasn't looking for a hookup tonight. He'd just come here for a drink and to decompress.

But, hey, he wasn't going to turn her away.

"All right, I'll try." She retrieved the dart. Another throw. Again, it hit the wall and fell to the floor.

"Well, hell. This is way harder than it looks." She bounced her way over to the dart on the floor again.

And, yeah, he looked at her ass again.

It would be hard not to. Round and pert and when she bent over. . . okay, now he was feeling like a dick. He raised his gaze back up, looking over to see his brother, Raid, watching in amusement from where he sat at the bar.

Asshole.

"Here. Can you show me again? Please?"

She smelled so good.

Shit.

He needed to clear his head a bit. But with the way she was looking at him . . . yeah, he was pretty sure that she liked what she saw.

Well, who could blame her?

As the youngest Malone brother, he really had gotten all the good looks, charm, and intelligence.

Moving in behind her, he held her hand, his other hand on her hip to keep her in place. She tensed and he immediately stepped back.

"Everything okay, darlin'?" Shit. Had he overstepped? Scared her?

She took a deep breath, then shook it off. "All good. Sorry. Where were we?"

Hmm. Tanner wasn't so sure that she was all good, but he moved in behind her when she smiled encouragingly back at him.

Then he helped guide her arm back. Fuck, her ass felt so good against him.

Don't get hard.

Don't be a dick.

As she let go, the dart flew and actually hit the dartboard this time.

"Yay!" she cried out, jumping up and hitting the top of her head against his chin.

Tanner let out a grunt of pain.

"Oh my God!" she cried, turning to stare up at him in shock. "I'm so sorry! I didn't mean to hurt you. Are you all right?"

He smiled. "All good."

"You're bleeding. Oh shit. Oh hell. I'm such a dumb klutz." Tears filled her eyes.

Tanner frowned at her, not liking the way she just spoke about herself. "You are not dumb or a klutz."

She drew a tissue out of her pocket and dabbed at his lips. "Where is the blood coming from?"

"My tongue. I think I bit it when —"

"When I whacked your chin," she moaned. "Dumb. So dumb."

"Stop," he said sternly. "You are not dumb. Do not speak about yourself like that."

The girl nodded, still looking miserable. "Ooh, what about ice? Ice can help." She reached for a glass on the table beside them and scooped out some ice.

That wasn't even her drink, was it?

"Is that your drink?" he asked.

"What? Uh, no. Ice?"

"No, thanks."

She stared down at her hand, then groaned. "I didn't even think about cleaning my hand first. What is wrong with me?" She put the ice cubes back. "I'll go get some clean ice. Wait here."

Clean ice?

Tanner watched as she moved through the crowd of people to the bar, flagging down the bartender.

Raid shot him a questioning look, but he just smiled back at him. He was good.

He thought.

When she returned, she held a glass of ice. "I am so sorry."

He shook his head, then popped some ice into his mouth. "It's all good, darlin'. Just an accident. They happen."

She sighed. "With me more than anyone else. Can I get you anything else?"

"How about you tell me your name?"

"Oh, it's Lilac."

"Hey, Lilac, I'm Tanner." He held out his hand to her.

"Nice to meet you, Tanner. Are you here in Hopesville for the rodeo?" she asked.

"Yep."

"Are you entering?" she asked.

"Yeah. Tomorrow afternoon."

"I have to get back to work. Will you come back tomorrow night?" she asked, looking hopeful.

"You working?"

"Yep."

"Then I'll be here, darlin'."

2

Two nights later...

"Hey, there, cowboy. What're you doing in a joint like this?"

Happiness filled Tanner as Lilac slid into the chair next to him. "Well, I heard it has this really gorgeous, amazing, sweet... beer."

"Beer! What?"

"Why? Were you expecting me to say something else?" he teased.

"Yeah. I thought you might've been talking about Harry."

Tanner glanced over at the bartender, who had a huge beard that finished halfway down his chest and not a single hair on his head. He had that look of a man that had seen a lot, done a lot, and could only remember half of it. "Hmm, strangely, facial hair doesn't do it for me."

"No?" she said in surprise. "Darn. And here I was going to let mine grow out. I'm sick of shaving it every morning." She touched her chin, giggling.

"For you, I'd make an exception."

"Yeah?" She looked excited but also nervous. Slightly tense.

He felt like he was getting mixed signals. She seemed into him, but skittish.

Yeah, that was the word he'd use.

"Yep." They'd spent all of last night chatting and flirting while she worked. She was easy to talk to. Tanner wished she had tonight off as he wanted to spend the entire night with her.

"What time are you working to tonight, darlin'?" he asked.

She wrinkled her nose, which might be the most adorable thing he'd ever seen. "Midnight."

Fuck.

"When's your next night off?"

"I finish early this Saturday and then I have Sunday off."

"Yeah?" It was only Thursday, but it was something. "Well, save your Saturday night for me."

"Your wish is my command, cowboy," she teased.

"I'll remember that."

One of the waitresses walked past and shot her a dirty look. Lilac jumped to her feet. "What can I get you?"

"Nothing, darlin'. I have to go soon. I'm in the rodeo tomorrow."

"I wish I could come watch."

"Why don't you? You're not working in the morning, are you?"

"Oh no. Just ... other things going on." She moved off before he could question her.

Hmm. Something going on with her, but it wasn't like he had the right to question her.

Someone else slid into her seat and he glanced over at Raid, who grinned at him.

He groaned. Fucking wonderful. "What are you doing here?"

"Came to look for my baby brother, of course. Three nights in a row, huh?"

"Maybe I just like the beer and atmosphere."

"Right. The atmosphere. Yeah, the atmosphere is really, really nice." Raid glanced over at Lilac.

"Don't look at her." Tanner scowled at him.

Raid held up his hands. "Whoa. Sorry. I didn't mean anything bad."

"I know . . . just . . . don't." He didn't want anyone looking at her. Including his brother.

"Remember that you just met her," Raid cautioned. "You don't really know her."

No. But he wanted to know her better. To spend time with her.

"We're spending Saturday night and Sunday together."

"We leave Sunday afternoon," Raid pointed out.

"We can go on Monday. Right?"

"Sure," Raid said slowly. "I mean, Alec is gonna want to know why and I don't think you falling for the waitress is going to make him happy."

"Her name is Lilac and she's more than just the waitress. She's the girl I'm going to marry."

Partly, he said it to rile Raid up. But also . . . yeah, it didn't feel wrong.

Raid groaned. "Are you kidding me?"

"Nope. She's the one."

Raid started muttering under his breath. "This is just fucking great. You're not supposed to find 'the one' yet. I haven't found mine! Butch hasn't even found his."

"It doesn't have to go from oldest to youngest," Tanner told him.

"It has so far. And I don't want to find my 'the one'."

Tanner just rolled his eyes at Raid. No one said that he couldn't find his girl first. Raid would just have to suck it up.

Because he was going to marry that girl.

"We have to head off soon," Raid said. "It's getting late."

"Fine. I'll just go say goodbye."

"Okay, try not to trip up and, you know, get engaged or something."

Tanner shook his head at his brother. Raid was such a drama queen. Tanner walked over to where Lilac was standing by one end of the bar.

"Lilac." She jumped with a small scream as he put his hand on her arm.

When she turned to him, her face was white and the fear on her face floored him.

"Baby, hey, it's just me."

"Tanner." She put her hand on her chest. "Sorry, I was away with the fairies."

Was that it?

"You're not scared of me, are you, Lilac?" he asked.

Her eyes widened and she swallowed heavily. "Of you? No."

"But of someone?" Okay, now he was feeling even more protective. Who had frightened her?

"No one in particular."

He frowned at her answer.

"I, um, I just had a bad experience once with a man."

"Baby." His heart was breaking for her. "Did he hurt you?"

"Not, um, sexually or anything. Just scared me." She glanced around, looking embarrassed. "I've got a ten-minute break and I need some fresh air. Come with me?"

"You bet." Raid could wait another ten minutes.

He followed her out the back. They used a staff door to head outside to a small staff parking lot.

"Where the hell are the security lights?" he demanded.

"Oh, there aren't any."

"What? But how do you see when you're walking to your car? Do not tell me that you walk out to your car on your own."

If she did, that was going to stop. Even if he had to be here every night when she finished work.

How are you going to manage that when you go home?

"Oh, no, I don't walk out here by myself to my car," she said.

The tension left his shoulders. "Good."

Taking his hand, she led him to a couple of metal chairs where he guessed the bar staff took their break. Wasn't the nicest place to sit down, but he figured it was more private than inside. They sat and she fiddled with her phone and turned on the flashlight.

"That's better, now I can see your pretty little face!" Reaching up, she pinched his cheek.

Relief filled him that she was back to being sassy and relaxed around him. Although he hadn't forgotten what she'd told him. Who the fuck could scare and hurt someone like Lilac?

"I need your phone number," he told her.

"What? No please?"

"Nope. It wasn't a request."

"Fine. Here it is." She rattled off her number as he put it into his phone.

She shivered and he realized she'd come out here without grabbing a jacket or sweater.

"Baby, you shouldn't be out here dressed in just a T-shirt."

"How dare you!" she said with mock horror. "I also have jeans on."

"I'm going to pick you up," he warned, pleased with himself for not just grabbing her.

Then he lifted her onto his lap. The chair creaked ominously beneath him, but he ignored it.

"Oh my God!" she cried.

He tensed, looking around. "What? What is it?"

"You are so warm." Turning, she snuggled into him. "How did you get so warm? I need you to just follow me around all the time. You can be my personal heater-boy."

"How well does it pay?"

"Not too well. But the benefits are excellent. Wink-wink. Nudge-nudge."

He laughed. "I don't think you're meant to say the words, wink-wink, nudge-nudge, pretty girl."

She grinned at him. "No? Silly me."

"But still . . . those are some damn good benefits. I'm tempted to become your human heating-pad."

"Yeah, it would be way better than being a cowboy," she said. "I promise to remember to feed you every so often. And water you."

He snorted. "So generous of you."

"I thought so."

They fell silent and he just held her.

"I don't want to go back in," she eventually said.

"Me neither, pretty girl."

"Do you ever feel like your life is speeding by and you haven't done any of the things that you wanted? As though you're trapped with no way out?"

Fuck. Where had that come from? No, he guessed he hadn't thought of his life like that. He was actually pretty happy with everything he had.

Especially now that he'd found her.

"Fuck, Lilac. Is that how you feel?"

She stiffened. "What? Of course not. It was just a . . . a question. I don't feel that way. I'm happy as pie. Although I've often wondered how pie can be happy. It can make you *feel* happy. But it's pie. It doesn't have feelings, right?"

She was babbling, which was damn cute. However, he didn't

let it distract him. And when she tried to move from his lap, he tightened his hold on her hips, keeping her in place. He wasn't having that.

"Tell me the truth."

She huffed out a breath. "What makes you think I wasn't telling the truth?"

"I know you weren't."

"What are you? A human lie detector? I wouldn't tell people that. They might lock you up and use you."

"Not a human lie-detector. Also, you've been watching too much TV. Is that the way you feel, Lilac?"

"Sometimes," she whispered. "It's hard not to feel that way."

"Is there something you want to do with your life? Something that's holding you back?"

Whatever she wanted to do . . . whatever she needed in order to do it . . . he'd give it to her.

"I want to be free."

Tanner scowled.

"And that's the end of my break."

"Lilac, we're not finished talking about this," he told her. No way was she walking away.

"I just . . . I didn't think my life was going to end up like this, you know? Figured I'd be doing more by now."

"And what is it that you want to do?"

"Oh, I don't know . . . so many things."

"Lilac," he said warningly.

"You don't want to know what it is I really want. It's . . . it's boring and it sounds silly."

"Nothing you say will seem silly."

"I just want normalcy. A nice guy who treats me well. Family. Kids. I want to get married. I want a house that I can decorate for the holidays. I want to take Christmas photos with my husband and kids in ugly sweaters that I make them wear. I want coordinated Halloween costumes. To cry when I drop my kid off at their first day of school, and when they leave for their first day of college. I want it all."

"Lilac, baby, you can have all that. You're only twenty-three. Your life isn't over." He'd made certain to ask her age the second night they'd spend together.

"Yeah. You're right. Don't know what I'm stressing over."

"Well, it's probably because you hadn't met Mr. Right. Luckily, he's right here."

"He is? Where? Can you see him?" She peered around.

"Brat!" He started tickling her until she was laughing so hard that she snorted.

"Oh my God. That's embarrassing." She slammed her hand over her mouth. "You did not just hear me do that."

"What? I thought it was cute."

"You have a thing for pigs, huh?"

"You did not sound like a pig!"

She snorted again, then groaned. "God, now I can't stop. It's an affliction."

"It's adorable. Just like you."

Tanner stood and carried her to the back door.

"I don't want to go back."

"You could run away with me," he suggested.

"Believe me, that's tempting but not possible."

One day, he'd make everything that she thought impossible possible.

3

Three nights later...

TANNER PICKED her up and carried her along the hallway.

"Careful," she muttered in between kissing him.

"Don't worry, darlin'. I won't drop you."

"Was more worried about you putting your back out," she joked.

He shifted her so she was supported with one hand while he swatted her ass with the other.

"Hey! What was that for?" she asked as he reached the door to the hotel room. He grabbed his key card from his back pocket.

"Misbehavin'," he told her as he swiped the card and opened the door.

"Hmm, maybe I'll have to misbehave more often."

"I'll spank you any time you want, darlin'. You just have to ask. But if you earn yourself a punishment, you're not gonna enjoy the consequences." He threw her carefully on the bed as she gaped up at him.

Too much?

Was she going to tell him to get lost?

Fuck. He wasn't scaring her, was he? She hadn't told him any more details of what had happened to her yet. But he was conscious of the need to be careful around her.

The more time they spent together, the more relaxed she grew. But he didn't want to take any chances.

They'd spent the last couple of nights together at the bar where she worked. Raid had been giving him shit about it. Today, he'd had enough and punched him in the nose. Now the bastard was walking around with a swollen nose and a scowl.

Thank fuck, the hotel had a free room tonight. The last thing he wanted to do was take her back to the horse trailer. Sure, it had a couple of beds, a small kitchen and a bathroom.

But it wasn't the sort of place you wanted to take a woman back to. Plus, Raid was there. That bastard likely wouldn't give them any privacy.

And Tanner didn't share. Ever.

If a woman was with him . . . then she was his. Not that he yucked on anyone else's yum. Plenty of people back home shared. Including two of his brothers.

Scarlett should be given a medal for putting up with Beau and Maddox.

Just as he was thinking of apologizing, Lilac rolled off the bed, grinning at him. "You'd have to catch me first."

Excitement filled him.

Now, this he could get into.

"That so, pretty girl?" he drawled as he undid the buttons on his shirt. Her gaze was caught by his actions, and he saw the lust there. The need.

Tanner knew it was likely reflected in his own gaze.

"Yep."

"Feeling brave?"

"Pfft. I got skills." She folded her arms under her breasts.

"Oh, yeah?" he teased. "What are those?"

"You look like you don't believe me. You don't know . . . I might be a secret ninja."

"Hmm, I'd like to see you in something black and tight."

She blushed. "Tanner!"

"Do ninjas blush?" he asked.

"Maybe I'm an undercover police officer."

"Yeah? You here to arrest me, baby?"

"Could be."

"Did you bring your handcuffs?" He slid off his jeans. Her gaze flickered down again. Was there a hint of nervousness there?

You need to take this slower.

"Lilac? You okay?" he asked. "We don't have to do this."

"I know," she whispered. "I really want this. I find it hard to be touched unless I know someone well. But I feel so at ease with you."

"I'm glad, baby."

"Now, handcuffs?" she asked.

"Seeing as you're a cop, I'm guessing you're here to arrest me. So, you'll need some handcuffs. Bring them out." He moved slowly toward her.

"You want me to use them on you?" she asked, taking him in.

By now, he was dressed in just his boxers.

Tanner knew women found him attractive. But he didn't think he'd ever enjoyed a woman staring at him as much as he liked the way Lilac watched him. He wasn't going to lie.

She licked her lips.

"No, baby. They won't be used on me." He grew closer and she let out a squeal, jumping onto the bed.

Concern filled him. He knew she was a bit of a klutz. "Careful, pretty girl. We don't want you getting hurt."

He drew off his boxers. Her mouth dropped open as she stared at his cock

"Lie on your back on the bed," he commanded.

Lilac lay down on the bed. Then she stared around as if she couldn't believe she'd just done that.

She scowled. "Hey! That's cheating!"

Damn. She was just so cute. And totally put out. He lay down next to her on his side.

He chuckled. "I cheated?"

"Yes, you distracted me with your... um... with your..."

"With my dick? It's all right, you can say it, pretty girl."

She drew in a sharp breath. "I don't usually do this."

The note of vulnerability in her voice had him leaning up on one elbow to stare down at her. "Hey, what's wrong?"

"I just don't want you to think... I mean, I've known you less than a week... and now we're... you're naked in a bed with me. And I don't want you to think badly of me."

He scowled. "Why the hell would I think badly of you?"

"I don't know if this is a good idea. What am I doing?" She tried to get up, but he wouldn't let her. A flash of fear filled her face.

Fuck!

"Sorry, baby. But please just listen to me a moment." He grasped hold of her chin and turned her face toward him. "I would never think badly of you. As long as you don't think badly of me?"

"What? No! Of course not."

"What we choose to do together is our business and no one else has a fucking say. I do not want you thinking badly about yourself either or you'll get one of those not-fun spankings."

"That's not nice. I only want fun spankings."

The tension in his stomach started to ease as she relaxed slightly.

"Then you'll have to behave."

"That sounds boring." She grinned up at him.

He leaned in and brushed his lips over her cheek. Then he cupped the side of her face, kissing her. "You taste so damn good."

"Tanner," she groaned.

"We don't have to do anything. We can just lay here and cuddle."

"I . . . that sounds nice. But I don't think I want to just cuddle. I want this. I want you. I just want a bit of happiness while I can grab it. That's not a bad thing, right?"

"Baby, you're worrying me now. What's wrong?"

She gave him a sad smile. "Nothing you can help with."

"Lilac," he said in a low, warning voice. "If there's something wrong, you need to tell me. Now."

She ran a finger over his face. "I like how protective you are. But you can't help me. Save that for someone who deserves your protection."

"Oh, you're really asking for a spanking now."

"How about you kiss me instead?" She threaded her fingers through his hair and dragged his mouth down to hers.

Okay, she didn't have to drag him. He wanted to kiss her. Fucking needed to taste her again. A groan erupted out of him.

Fuck.

She tasted like strawberries. And he wanted more.

Her small hand grasped his dick, and she ran her hand up and down the shaft.

"Fuck, baby. You have no idea how good that feels."

"I want you," she said, her breath coming in sharp pants. "Please."

"There's no rush." He sat up, leaning against the headboard. Then he patted his thigh. "Come here."

She eyed him suspiciously as she got up and straddled his lap.

"Good girl." He kissed her again until she lost that suspicious look.

"God, you can kiss," she muttered when he drew back. She tried to follow him. "Come back here."

"Uh-uh. I need you to listen to me for a moment."

"Less talking. More kissing."

"While I am down with that plan, there's something I want to make clear. If you need me to stop at any time you say so. Since I don't know your triggers or limits and I know you're still slightly scared over me touching you, I want you to know that I will always stop if you need me to."

"All right."

"You can trust me."

There was a flash of something in her face. It disappeared so quickly that he thought he might have missed it. She was probably thinking that it was all very well to tell someone that you could trust them . . . but you also had to show them.

"I won't hurt you, baby."

He placed his hand around the back of her neck. With his other hand, he cupped her full breast.

Fuck, yes.

He wanted to get his mouth around her tit. To suck her nipple into his mouth. To drive her as insane as she made him.

"So, no spankings?" she said hopefully.

"No promises. Good girl spankings are fun. Bad girl spankings . . . well, if you want to avoid them, then you know what you have to do."

"Run?" she said with a grin.

"You can run. I'll follow. And when I catch you, then you'll be in a world of trouble."

Her mouth parted slightly.

"Fuck, you are beautiful."

A blush filled her cheeks, and she glanced down as though uncomfortable at his words.

He didn't understand that.

Couldn't she see how gorgeous she was? It was so fucking obvious to him ... and every other man in that bar tonight. And all of the other nights.

But she was with him.

He cupped her chin with his hand, raising her head. "Uh-uh, eyes on me, pretty girl. I don't know how you can't see it. But you're the most beautiful person I've ever seen. When you spoke to me the other night ... I couldn't fucking believe my luck."

"But you ... you're you." She ran her hand through the air between them. "You look like this. Women must hit on you all the time."

"You calling me easy now, darlin'?" he drawled.

"What? No!" Her eyes were wide with horror.

He couldn't hold back his grin.

She slapped his chest. "You're so mean."

"Poor baby. How can I make it up to you?"

"Hmm." She tapped her chin with her finger. "I'm thinking that you could let me go down on you."

"That's me making it up to you? Sounds like I'm the one who should be going down on you."

She blushed, shaking her head. "I want to ... please."

"You can go down on me, pretty girl," he told her, stilling her as she tried to slide off him. "But first, I want you naked."

There were a few seconds where she hesitated. If she started spouting off crap about the way she looked, then he was actually going to spank her. Which was probably a quick way to end tonight's fun.

But if there was one thing he'd learned from his brothers, it was that they didn't let their women talk shit about themselves.

And he wouldn't let Lilac do that either.

However, she surprised him by climbing off him to stand on the floor by the bed. Reaching over, she switched off the main light, leaving just the bedside lamp on.

He didn't mind, though. Not if it made her feel more confident.

There would be plenty of time for him to properly take her in.

Then she took a deep breath and stripped down to her underwear.

"Fuck, yes," he muttered as she revealed all those curves to his gaze.

She was pale, her skin smooth and creamy. Her tits were barely encased in a black lacy bra, and she wore matching black panties.

"Love the sexy lingerie, baby." Had she put it on hoping he'd get to see it? Or was this what she always wore?

He wasn't sure what he was hoping for most.

"Yeah?" she asked with a shy grin. "I like pretty things."

"So do I," he replied.

A giggle escaped her. "That was terrible."

"Terribly good?" He wriggled his eyebrows. "I agree."

She climbed onto the bed, crawling over to him. Her breasts were still encased in that damn bra though.

Just.

The bra looked like it was a few sizes too small. Not that he was complaining. Nope. He didn't care if they popped out.

"Baby, take your bra off," he commanded as she slid between his legs.

Ignoring him.

He frowned until she ran her tongue along his shaft.

Fuck. Him.

As a distraction that worked a bit too well. He groaned as she took the head of his dick into her mouth, sucking strongly.

Damn. She was good at that. She took more of him, swallowing.

"Baby! Christ." She almost made him embarrass himself.

She licked her way back up his dick, running her tongue over the head.

His breathing grew faster as he placed his hand on the back of her head. "Take me deep again. That's it. Good. That feels so fucking good. You don't know what you're doing to me."

She was making his head spin. The room grew hazy.

"That's it. More, baby. Good girl."

Lilac slid up and down his shaft, driving him higher and higher. Her hand grasped the base of him, holding him still so she could lap at him like he was a fucking ice cream.

He saw the bliss on her face. "Do you like sucking my dick, pretty girl?"

She didn't pause. It was almost like she was in a trance. Off somewhere else.

Yeah, he wasn't having that.

Reaching out, he took hold of her chin, drawing her away from his dick.

A whimper escaped her, and she tried to move her face away from his hold.

"Look at me," he commanded.

Her gaze shot up to his. Irritation filled her face. "Why did you stop me?"

"Just wanted to be sure you knew whose cock you had in your mouth."

Red filled her cheeks. "If you didn't like it . . ."

"Oh, I liked it, baby," he murmured. "But you looked . . . distant. As though you weren't here."

"Shit," she muttered. "I'm sorry." A groan escaped her.

"Come here," he murmured.

He longed to grab her, to tug her toward him. But she looked like she was seconds from losing it and the last thing he wanted was to freak her out.

She gave his dick a sad look. "I was enjoying myself, though."

A surprised bark of laughter escaped him. "You can go back to sucking my dick soon. I just want to know that you know who you're with. And that it's *my* cock you want."

4

Lilac grimaced. "Sorry."

"No more sorries. Come here." This time, he put more command into his voice, and she crawled over him, straddling him once more.

Cupping her face between his hands, he kissed her. It started off light, then grew deeper. He let his hands drop, one going to her tit. He massaged it through her bra.

She drew back, her face flushed, her lips swollen and wet.

"I want to see you." Without any more warning, he reached behind her and undid her bra.

Tanner only had a few seconds to take her in before her arm came over her boobs, hiding herself from him.

"Uh-uh, no hiding from me. Not by going somewhere in your head and not by covering yourself. Show me."

"They're . . . they're not that attractive."

"Lilac, I've already warned you. No more warnings. The next time, you're going over my lap."

Her eyes widened as she dropped her arm. He had no idea what she was talking about. Her breasts were gorgeous. Heavy and lush, tipped by delicious-looking nipples he couldn't wait to taste.

He moved them so that she was sitting up, leaning back against the headboard and he was between her legs.

"Tanner! What are you doing?" she asked.

"My turn to taste you, pretty girl."

She shook her head. "No, I want to be the one to do that."

"Well, sometimes you don't get what you want. Sometimes, you have to do as you're told."

"Maybe I want to be the one in charge." She glared at him.

"Hmm, do you? Do you want to call the shots, pretty Lilac? Tell me what to do? Or do you want to let me be in charge?"

He could see her thinking. Perhaps she did want to be in control. He'd give that to her if she wanted it this first time.

Sure, he preferred it the other way around.

However, if it helped her become more at ease with him . . . with this . . . yeah, he'd give her whatever she asked for.

It should worry him how deep he was getting with this girl in such a short amount of time. How much he desired her.

"I don't . . . I don't know."

"It's all right to be hesitant. You don't know me that well. But just know every inch of you is beautiful. That I want you to feel pleasure. And to feel like a fucking goddess."

"And you think you can do that by eating my pussy?" she said dryly.

He barked out a laugh. "Well, how about we find out?" Moving back, Tanner grasped hold of her thighs and tugged her until she was lying flat on the bed.

She let out a cry of surprise and he grinned down at her. "Prepare to have your world rocked, baby."

Lilac rolled her eyes. "Think much of yourself?"

"I don't think it. I know it."

"We'll see. You might be all talk and no action."

"Those there are fighting words if ever I heard some." Leaning over her, he placed his hands on the mattress before bending down to kiss her lightly. "Prepare to eat your words."

"Yeah? You gonna keep talking or put that tongue to other uses?"

"Someone found their sass."

A strange look crossed her face. Almost . . . regret? Worry?

"I like it," he quickly reassured her.

"You do?"

"Yeah, baby. I mean, you're wrong. And you're gonna go down. But I like the bravado."

"Um, actually, I think you're the one who is gonna go down."

He threw his head back with a laugh. "Why, yes, I am. And you are going to lie there with your hands above your head. No moving them."

Her breath hitched. "Really?"

"Really. Put your hands up."

Slowly, she raised her hands above her head.

"That's my brave girl."

She made a scoffing noise. "Hardly."

"You don't think you're brave?" He licked his tongue over one tight nipple.

Fuck. Him.

So gorgeous.

"I've been a coward for most of my life," she muttered.

"Don't like you talking about yourself like that," he told her before sucking on her nipple.

She let out a low moan.

"Although we do have to talk about you being so friendly to strangers. What if I'd been a creep?"

"Hmm, the jury is still out on whether you are or not," she teased as he moved to her other nipple.

Tanner looked up at her. "I'd never harm you, baby. Ever."

He swore he saw her eyes glistening with tears before she blinked, and they were gone.

"I wouldn't let you."

"Good girl." He started kissing down her stomach, noticing the way she sucked her stomach in. But he didn't comment on it; he just kept touching her and gradually she relaxed.

Reaching the top of her panties, he kneeled and drew them off. He took a moment to study her.

"Is . . . is everything all right? I don't . . . I mean . . . are you . . . crap!" She attempted to close her legs, but he put pressure on the inside of her thigh.

"Stop," he said firmly as she attempted to roll away. "I want to look at you."

Lilac was breathing heavily. "Why?"

"Because you're beautiful and I want to take my time."

"Usually, men just roll on top and get on with it."

He lightly smacked the inside of her thigh. "No talking about other men when you're with me."

It made him feel murderous. Those other assholes didn't deserve to look at her . . . to touch her.

She was his.

Bending over her, he kissed her again. "Girls who say bad things about themselves find their ability to talk restricted."

Her eyes widened. "What does that mean?"

"It means I might gag you."

"With your cock?" she asked.

He grinned. "Somehow, I think you might like that too much."

Before she could come up with a sassy answer, he drew her legs farther apart and lay on the mattress between them. Parting her lower lips, he took a long lick of her pussy.

Fuck. Yes.

He wasn't sure what tasted better. Her pussy or her mouth.

Or her nipples.

He teased her clit with his tongue, flicking it lightly as he drove two fingers into her pussy. God. She clenched around him. She was going to feel good once he was inside her.

Then he realized that she was being weirdly silent. Fuck. Was she upset because he said he'd gag her?

Had he gone too far?

Moving his mouth away from her pussy, he glanced up at her. "You've gone all quiet on me, baby. Make noises, tell me what's going on. What you want."

"Oh, uh . . . you want me to?"

"Yeah. I didn't mean you had to be silent when I said I'd gag you for talking badly about yourself."

Her cheeks grew red. "No, it wasn't that. It's just . . ."

"Just what?"

"The, uh, the guy I slept with didn't like me to make noises while he . . . um . . ."

Yeah. He didn't like hearing about another guy touching her . . . but he pushed that feeling to one side. He needed to know.

"While he ate you out?"

"Oh no, he didn't do that. I meant, while he was, uh, fucking me. He liked silence."

"Well, I want you to make noise."

"I don't know if I can."

Fuck. She was wound up so tight that there was no way she could enjoy herself now.

"Just relax, pretty girl. There's no right or wrong way to do this." He placed kisses on the inside of her thighs. Then he lightly moved his tongue over her clit. Over and over until her breathing grew faster and her thighs were trembling.

But she still wasn't making any noise.

He moved his tongue lower, thrusting it into her passage. She cried out. Better.

But it wasn't enough.

He drew back and a whimper escaped her. "Please, don't stop."

"Good girl."

That was better. Much better. Grabbing her legs, he pushed them back against her as he ate her pussy. She was trembling, her breathing growing faster.

Fuck.

So good.

Until he realized she'd gone silent again. He pulled back.

"Nooo," she cried out. "I was so close!"

"Then you better make some noise."

She moaned. "Oh, Tanner! Take me! Fuck me! Make me yours!"

"Don't be a brat." He smacked the side of her thigh. "But, yes, just like that."

Returning his mouth to her pussy, he was gratified to hear her moan. That was better. A man liked to know he was doing a good job eating his girl's pussy.

She shuddered, her breathing growing faster and he knew she was close.

"Please! Oh, please! It feels so good."

Good girl. Come for me.

She cried out as she clenched down around him and came.

Damn. He couldn't hold back any longer. He needed to be inside her.

Pulling back, he rolled over to where his jeans were lying on the floor and drew a condom out of his pocket. Kneeling between her legs, he rolled it onto his dick while she watched him, her face flushed, mouth parted.

"You good, baby?" he murmured. "Still want this? Want me?"

"Yes. God, yes. Please fuck me."

"Actually. I think you should fuck me."

"What do you mean?"

He grabbed hold of her, then rolled them both so he was lying on his back, and she was on top.

"Tanner!" She scooted off him, kneeling next to him.

"Ride me."

Her eyes widened. "Ride you?"

"Yep."

She grinned. "I thought you were the cowboy."

A bark of laughter escaped him. "I am. Doesn't mean that I don't like to be ridden once in a while."

She bit her lip. "I've never . . . I mean . . . I don't know how . . ."

Tenderness filled him. Mixed in with a fierce possessiveness. "You've never ridden a cock before, pretty girl?"

"No." Her shoulders were hunched. "Are you sure you want me to?"

More than he'd wanted anything in his life.

"Yeah, baby. I want you to. Come here. It's not rocket science. Put your legs over me. Line my dick up with your pussy, then sink yourself onto me."

She bit her lower lip but let him help her straddle him. Reaching down, she grasped his dick and slowly started lowering herself onto his cock.

"Oh God."

"Not God. Tanner. Say it. Say my name."

"Tanner," she moaned.

"That's it, baby. Good girl. Fuck me."

She slid up and down his dick. Fuck him. She might never have fucked someone in this position before, but she quickly picked up what to do. Placing her hands on his chest, she moved up and down faster. Harder.

Until he was breathing heavily, straining to keep control of himself.

"God, baby. You look so damn good riding me." Reaching up, he played with her tits, pulling on her nipples. "Keep moving. That's it."

"It feels so good," she moaned as her red hair flowed around her.

His hands went to her hips as he guided her, fucking up into her.

"I'm so damn close." Moving one hand from her hip, he played with her clit, and she froze.

"What ... what are you doing?"

"I want you to come with me."

"Come with you? Come again? I can't come again."

"Sure, you can."

She shook her head. "I've never ..."

Placing one hand behind her head, he drew her down into his kiss. "First time for everything, isn't there?"

As she started moving again, slower, then faster, he moved his finger over her clit, driving her up higher and higher until she screamed, clenching down on his cock.

He reached his own release, his yell drowning out hers as he found his release.

Breathing heavily, he grabbed her, pulling her into his embrace, still buried inside her. He knew he had to pull out, to take care of his condom, but he just needed to hold her for a moment while they both calmed down.

"That was the best fucking orgasm I've ever had," he whispered to her as he ran his hand up and down her back.

She stiffened. "You don't have to lie to me."

"Baby girl, I don't lie. Ever. Fucking hate liars."

If possible, she grew even more tense. He slid out of her and rolled them both onto their sides. "Something wrong?"

"It's just ... sometimes a lie isn't a choice, you know?" she whispered.

"Uh, no. I don't know. A lie is always a choice. And it's wrong."

What was she talking about?

Then she shook her head and smiled up at him. "Of course. You're right. Lying is always wrong."

"Got to take care of this." He walked into the bathroom and got rid of the condom, glancing back as she moved up behind him, wrapping her arms around his waist.

"Sorry. I didn't mean to make anything weird."

"You didn't." He turned and hugged her against him tight. Something felt off, but he shook that thought away. He noticed that she'd pulled his top on.

Fuck, he liked that.

"Come on. Come back to bed." He slid away and grabbed her hand to lead her back to the bedroom.

"I can't."

He frowned.

"I've got to pee," she whispered.

"I'll wait for you in bed, then."

When she climbed in a few minutes later, he tugged her to him, pulling her against him so her head rested on his chest.

"You okay, baby? None of that was too much?"

She sighed sadly. "Where did you come from, Tanner Malone?"

He laughed. "A strange place called Haven."

"Really? That's the name of the town?"

"Yep. And it lives up to its name. It really is a haven for the majority of the people that live there."

"You too?" she asked.

He ran his hand up and down her back. "In a way, it was for my family too. My oldest brother had to get us out of a dangerous situation. We moved to Haven, where he bought a ranch. I still live and work on the Ranch along with some of my brothers."

"How many do you have?"

"Too many. So many, I lose track."

She snorted. "Really?"

"Yeah."

"Tell me about them."

"Why would you want to know about my brothers? You've got the best Malone in your bed right now."

"Good Lord," she muttered. "Are they . . . are they good men?"

An odd question, but he figured she just wanted to know more about him. Or perhaps she was thinking that one day she might meet them.

Which she would, because they were going to be her brothers.

"They are. I mean, some of them are dicks. Like West."

"How is he a dick?"

"Eh, he's a grumpy ass. Thought he might get better after meeting Flick, but he's still a dick."

"He's a dick to Flick?"

"What? No! Fuck, no. We'd all kick his ass if he was mean to her. Nah, he's a big teddy bear for his girl. It's the rest of us that have to suffer his less-than-stellar personality."

"You said your oldest brother had to get you out of a bad situation?"

"Hmm. Probably a story for another day."

"So, moving to Haven was good for you?" she asked.

"Yep. Best move ever. Haven is a special place. You'd like it."

"How do you know that?"

"Because women are taken care of there. We protect them. Look after them."

"It sounds . . . different. I've never heard of a place like that."

"Yeah. Well, it's not just about keeping women safe. It's about having a place where people can be themselves. We have lots of different sorts of relationships."

"Like what?"

"Hmm, well, two of my brothers share a woman."

"What?"

"Yeah. And no one bats an eye because they're not the only ones in a relationship like that. We have an active BDSM community with our own BDSM club in Haven."

"Are you a Dom?"

"No. But when I find someone special, I will look after her just like my brothers look after their women. She'll be taken care of, safe, healthy, and happy. I'll make sure of it." He yawned. "I'm beat. Someone wore me out."

"Who was that?" she asked with mock-innocence.

"Brat." He tickled her sides.

5

The following morning, Tanner woke up to find the bed empty. Thinking that Lilac had to be in the bathroom, he lay there for a while.

Then he realized that the hotel room was too quiet. Getting out of bed, he rushed to the bathroom.

What the hell?

Where had she gone?

Grabbing his phone, relief filled him as he saw a message from her.

LILAC: *Sorry to run out on you. I had an appointment I couldn't miss. And you looked so peaceful sleeping.*

Tanner: *Next time, wake me.*

HE WAITED but there was no reply. After showering, he made sure he had everything and headed out. The rodeo was finished, but he'd decided he was going to stay on for a while.

Because of Lilac.

His phone beeped.

LILAC: *You looked tired. I thought you needed your sleep. Can I see you tonight?*

DISAPPOINTMENT FILLED HIM. He'd thought they were going to spend the day together.

TANNER: *Yeah. Where should I meet you?*

Lilac: *At the bar at eight. I have something I need to talk to you about.*

WORRY FILLED HIM. What could she possibly have to tell him?

TANNER: *You could tell me now.*

Lilac: *I would rather do it in person. See you at eight.*

~

TANNER WALKED into the bar just before eight and looked around for her. There were a couple of other waitresses working tonight.

He sat down at the bar and ordered a beer.

Getting out his phone, he sent Lilac a text. She didn't reply, but he didn't let it get to him.

Not until half an hour passed.

Where was she? Fuck. What if something had happened to her?

He tried to call her, but it went straight to voicemail.

Where was she?

"Hey!" he called out to the Harry, the bartender.

"Yeah? You want another one?"

"No. Do you know where Lilac lives?"

The guy frowned down at him. "What's it to you where Lilac lives?"

"I'm her friend."

"Yeah? You'd think her friend would already know where she lives."

He sighed. Fucking asshole. Although he did understand.

"Look, I get you're trying to protect her. But I was supposed to meet her here tonight at eight; however, she's not here and she's not answering her phone."

"Sounds like she stood you up."

"She wouldn't do that. Haven't you seen her with me lately?"

Harry gave him a skeptical look. "Maybe. But that might be that you're hassling her. Lilac has only worked here for two weeks. Don't exactly know her that well."

Two weeks?

Really?

He'd thought she'd lived here all her life. Although, now that he thought about it, he realized she'd never said that.

And you never really asked.

A strange feeling developed in his stomach. But he was being ridiculous. He and Lilac had shared something.

They'd had a connection.

Harry eyed him for a moment, then waved over one of the waitresses. "Hey, Shelley, you know when Lilac is back on?"

"She's got a shift tomorrow night, but Julie tried calling her to see if she could work tonight and it went straight to voicemail."

"Do you know what kind of car she drove?" he asked desperately.

"Why would I know that?"

"Uh, because you walked her to her car every night she worked," he said. Jesus. Surely, he had to notice what she drove and maybe what the plate was if Tanner was lucky.

He didn't know how he'd track her using her license plate, but Tanner was a resourceful guy. He knew he could use his charm to get his way.

"I don't know what Lilac's been telling you, but I never walked her to her car. Offered to, but she always took off in a different direction."

"I don't think she even had a car," the other waitress said.

What the fuck? She didn't have a car? But she'd told him . . . no wait. She hadn't exactly told him. Had she?

Fuck. How much had she left out or not told him?

He was going to spank her ass until she couldn't sit for a week once he found her.

If you find her.

"If you see her, can you call me?" Tanner asked.

"Sure." Harry grabbed a pen and a piece of paper, and wrote his number and name down. He gave Tanner another pitying look before turning away to serve someone.

Yeah, he got it. He didn't think that Lilac wanted to see him. Or talk to him.

But she did.

He knew she did.

∼

Tanner went back to the bar the next night.

But she didn't turn up for work. No one had heard from her.

And the look on Harry's face told him that they didn't expect her back.

That's when he knew that their connection had been all one-sided. There hadn't been anything there.

He'd been fooling himself.

She'd been using him. And now she was gone.

6

Present day...

Lilac stared down at the single piece of toast on her plastic plate. She should eat it, but she knew that if she tried to she was going to choke on it.

She'd lost weight in the last six months. A lot of weight.

Her brother would be so proud. For the first time. He'd always tried to starve her into being a size two. Unfortunately for him, his staff had always liked Lilac better than him, so they used to sneak her food when they could.

So, she'd always kept some pounds on her. After her escape, well, she'd eaten whatever the hell she'd wanted and she'd enjoyed all of it. Even though she hadn't enjoyed having to buy new clothes.

Now, nothing fit her.

Who knew that meeting the love of your life and having to leave him was what she needed to drop fifty pounds?

So, instead of eating the toast, she slid it onto Ryleigh's plate.

Ryleigh needed it more than she did anyway. Lilac wasn't important. Ryleigh and Opal were.

She watched Opal and Ryleigh share a look. She knew they were concerned about her. If she was in their place, she probably would be too. Yesterday, a chunk of hair had fallen out while she was washing it.

She was pretty sure that wasn't a good sign.

"You need to eat, Lilac," Ryleigh told her worriedly.

She hated that Ryleigh was worrying about her. She had enough going on. But Lilac couldn't seem to shake this depression. Only one person brought a smile to her face anymore.

Ryleigh slid off the end of the bench seat across from Lilac and kneeled next to her on the floor.

Lilac stiffened while Opal let out a shocked noise. "What are you doing?"

Ryleigh stared up at her. "I'm so sorry, Lilac. This is all my fault. I never should have asked you to search them out. To speak to them. I should have been braver, should have done it myself."

Lilac glared back at her. "You listen to me. I wanted to do it. I volunteered."

"I shouldn't have let you. Look what's happened. You're . . . you're fading away before our eyes. You don't eat. You don't smile. I'm so scared."

Fuck. What was she doing? She was being so fucking selfish.

"Get up, Ry." Reaching for the other woman, she attempted to lift her. But she barely had the energy to move herself around.

Wow. She really was in a bad way, huh?

Ryleigh took pity on her and climbed up onto the seat next to her. Lilac wrapped her arms around her, running her hand over Ryleigh's dark blonde hair. She glanced over at Opal, who was staring at them both worriedly.

"I'm fine. I'm sorry I've been worrying the two of you. But none of this is your fault, Ry. I was the one who decided to . . . to sleep with Tanner."

To fall in love with him.

"I can't believe *he* found us in Hopesville," Ryleigh said, looking pensive. "And that it took us so long to lose his goons again."

When she'd spotted Stefan's goons in Hopesville, they'd hightailed it out of there. They'd been on the move for months, too afraid to settle in one place.

But things were different now. They couldn't keep running like this.

Regret sat like a brick in her tummy. What must Tanner think of her? She hadn't even been able to text him goodbye. Had he turned up at the bar only for her to stand him up?

Yeah, he had to hate her.

"Stefan's going to find us again," Lilac said. Fear filled her. Not for herself. But for Ryleigh and Opal.

And Kye.

"He can't get his hands on Kye," Ryleigh whispered.

"There's no fucking way we're letting him fucking touch Kye," Opal said with a scowl.

"What shall we do, though?" Lilac asked.

The other two women, her best friends, shared a look. And she knew what their answer was going to be. She could feel it. They'd been heading down this track ever since she got a job at that bar, hoping to meet one of the Malones.

"We've got to go to them," Ryleigh whispered.

Yeah. They did.

Or at least, Ryleigh did. They'd help her and Kye. Lilac was sure of that. If she'd learned nothing else, she knew the Malones took care of women and children.

At least, ones that didn't cross them.

"Do you think they'll accept us?" Ryleigh asked her.

God. This wasn't what she deserved. None of it. Right now, Ryleigh should be enjoying this stage of her life. Not on the run, scared, worried about the future.

Worried about you.

Lilac had to pull herself together. At least long enough to get them to Haven.

And then she could leave.

"We're nearly out of fucking cash," Opal stated. As usual, her hair was teased up to about five times its normal volume. She liked her skirts short and her shoes high. Her make-up could best be described as loud. A lot like the woman herself.

And she was the kindest person Lilac had ever met.

Loyal to a fault. There was nothing that Opal wouldn't do for them.

"We've got to do something, and we all know it," Opal stated. "So, is this the best fucking option?"

Lilac stared at Ryleigh who was staring out the window. They'd found a place to park up last night, but they'd have to head out soon before someone came along and called the cops on them.

There was a toilet in the vicinity but no showers, so they'd all washed up as best they could with the cold water from the sink.

But Opal was right . . . they had to do something. They were running out of cash and options.

"We're going to Haven," she said.

Ryleigh took hold of her hand. "You're sure? Maybe we can think of something else."

Lilac let out a breath. "No. We probably should have gone there months ago."

Maybe they would have if it wasn't for Lilac and her broken heart. Perhaps, even now, they could have been safe.

"Nope," Opal said. "We did the fucking best we could. We had to get rid of those assholes, then lie low for a while until things died down. Still don't fucking believe all that hype. It can't be real. Women being looked after and cared about." She made a scoffing noise. But Opal was probably the most cynical of them all. "We still need to be sure that they can protect Ryleigh and Kye."

"And you guys." Ryleigh's head shot up, looking over at them both in alarm. "You two are staying with me. Right?"

Lilac glanced over at Opal. The other woman looked uncharacteristically unsure.

"You have to stay!" Ryleigh cried.

"They won't want us to stay," Lilac said. "Or me, at least."

"Well, they don't get a say, right?" Ryleigh said. "All for one and one for all. Right?"

"We ain't no musketeers," Opal told her. "This hair isn't going under no hat. That would be a crime." She fluffed her hair. Lilac hated to think about how much damage all the hairspray it took to keep her hair like that was doing to the environment.

But right now, she didn't have time to worry about the environment. She was busy trying to keep them all alive.

"Okay, so we're not the musketeers," Ryleigh said. "We're like Shrek, Fiona, and Donkey."

"I'm Donkey!" Opal said.

They stared at her.

"What? We all know it's true. I'm the funny, likable one."

"So, which of us is Shrek?" Lilac asked Ryleigh.

"Pretty sure it's me," Ryleigh replied. "Maybe Alvin and the Chipmunks."

"I don't think so," Opal replied. "Not unless I'm Alvin. Someone like me has to have a leading role. At least a name."

"The other chipmunks had names," Ryleigh protested.

"Yeah? What were they?" Opal challenged.

"Well, hell. I don't remember."

Lilac sighed and they both looked at her.

Ryleigh took one of her hands and Opal reached over to grab the other. "You going to be okay, Lilac?"

"He's going to hate me." She had to fight back her tears. She'd cried enough.

It was getting ridiculous.

She'd left him. He might hate her, but she could handle it. As long as her friends were safe.

"If he does, I'll set him straight," Opal said.

Oh hell.

"No, don't do that," she said quickly as Ryleigh attempted to hide her grin. "I'll talk to him myself."

"Right. We have a plan then." Ryleigh looked happier.

Dread filled Lilac. She hated living like this. Never knowing where they were going next. Not having a proper place to call home. So, she should be ecstatic that they had a plan. A place to go.

But all she felt was this sense of doom. Would the Malones actually help?

Tanner was a good guy. She'd met Raid briefly, and he'd seemed like a good guy too.

But the town . . . it sounded too idyllic.

"I'm going to go to the bathroom and then we'll leave," Ryleigh said.

They both nodded, watching as she left.

Kye started to cry, and Lilac walked over to where they had set up his bed. It was a wicker basket with a mattress. She had found it in a thrift store. It should hopefully do until he was three months old. If he didn't grow too big too quickly.

Picking him up, she held him against her chest. Turning, she nearly slammed into Opal.

"Jesus, woman."

"You're worried," Opal said.

"I'm sure this is the best thing to do," Lilac lied.

"No, you're not. You're worried she's pinned all her hopes on a town that sounds too fucking good to be true. On stories that her fucking useless old man sold her. We barely know these Malones."

"Tanner is a good guy," Lilac protested.

"Yeah, but we don't know the rest of them. And we don't know how they'll react to all of this. You and I both know that Stefan isn't going to just let us go. No matter who we've got on our side."

"We need somewhere safe for Kye, though," Lilac said. "And this is the best option we have. Plus, you know who their cousin is from that research you did."

"Yeah, well, maybe we should go to him," Opal suggested.

"To Regent Malone?" Lilac asked, fear filling her. "I don't think that's a good idea. He could be just as bad as Stefan."

"No one is as bad as Stefan," Opal replied.

They both shuddered.

"We need to do something about Stefan."

"Yeah? And what are we going to do?"

Lilac let out a deep breath. "I don't know that part yet."

That was a lie. She had a plan. Well, more like a rough outline. But if it worked then she hoped she'd save Ryleigh and Opal.

Opal eyed her. "Uh-huh. Well, when you know you need to tell me so I can help."

Lilac shook her head. "It would be safer for me to do it alone."

"Safer for who?" Opal asked.

"For you and Ryleigh and this sweet baby." She breathed in the scent of him. God, she loved him. She'd do anything for him. "He's innocent in all of this, Opal. I have to protect him."

"And risk yourself? That's not the way this works, Lilac."

"Sure, it is. Ryleigh and Kye have to get through this."

"And so do you," Opal said. "We didn't go through all of this to lose one of us."

"I'm not planning on dying." But she wasn't sure if she cared that much if she did either.

"Glad to hear it. Whatever this plan is, I'm in, provided it isn't a fucking suicide mission. I didn't get out of that mess to dive back in. But I'm not letting you die either. So, you just figure out a way to get us out of this fucking mess that doesn't involve someone other than Stefan dying."

Yeah. She'd get right on that.

"We both know that Ryleigh is the optimist," Opal said. "The one who has her head in the fucking clouds. We have to look out for her and this one. But you never fucking know, Haven might just be a haven for all of us."

7

"Son of a bitch!" Lilac swore as smoke billowed out of the RV's engine.

Why? Why did life keep sending shitty things her way? She wasn't a terrible person. All right, so she could be better. But still . . . she'd never hurt anyone deliberately. Sure, sometimes she'd had to do a few dodgy things.

However, when you were trying to keep yourself and your friends alive, the lines between right and wrong could grow a bit blurred.

Still . . . she didn't think that was bad enough for the world to keep sending shit her way.

Look at Stefan and all the terrible things he'd done. And yet he lived in the lap of luxury doing whatever the fuck he wanted. She gritted her teeth and kept driving.

"This is a fucking problem," Opal said.

"Tell me about it."

"Oh my God!" Ryleigh cried out. "Is the engine on fire?"

"Well, not yet."

"Shouldn't we pull over?" Ryleigh asked.

Lilac shared a look with Opal. If they pulled over now, they were gonna be walking to Haven—with all their stuff and a three-week-old baby.

Not fucking happening.

And worse still, they'd have nowhere to live since they had no money to tow or fix this thing. They just had to get it to the outskirts of the town.

At least Kye was asleep. They'd been hoping to get to Haven and settled before he woke.

"We've got to keep going," Lilac said.

"It's smoking!" Ryleigh cried.

"I know. But . . . we don't have much choice."

They passed the sign announcing that they'd reached Haven, Texas.

Thank God.

"Someone find me a park or somewhere to stay," she said urgently.

They were at the outskirts of the town. She could see houses.

"Pull off here," Opal said. "Take the next right. Then left."

She drove into a large sports park. This wasn't ideal, but what other choice did they have?

Stopping the RV under a big tree, they all climbed out. Ryleigh unbuckled Kye's car seat and carried the whole thing out, so she didn't wake him.

"Well, this ain't no fucking good," Opal said.

Lilac felt the stress building up inside her. What were they going to do now? They couldn't go anywhere. This park wasn't exactly a good hiding spot.

They had no money. No vehicle. No home.

A sob built inside her, but she pushed through it.

"Lilac? It will be all right." Ryleigh wrapped her free arm around her shoulders, giving her an optimistic smile. That was

Ryleigh. She always found something good even when it was all bad.

Lilac took in her tired, pale face. She looked drained. Though even with dark marks under her eyes and messy hair, Ryleigh was a knock-out.

Unlike Lilac who knew she was just okay looking. Kind of plain. Opal and Ryleigh were the ones who drew looks. And Lilac was good with that. Although it meant that she was often the one who had to deal with people because she blended in the easiest.

"I know. Of course it will be." She gave Ryleigh a wobbly smile. "I mean . . . what else could possibly go wrong? We must have had all of our bad luck."

"I was born with bad luck," Opal said wryly.

"Not helping, Opal," Ryleigh said.

"Right." Lilac had to keep them on track. This is what she did. She problem solved. "It's Sunday and it's getting dark. We can't do anything tonight. I'm going to try and figure out what is wrong, and tomorrow, I'll walk into town and find what I need."

Easy-peasy.

Right?

~

LATER THAT EVENING, Lilac was still feeling stressed. Tears blinded her, making everything turn blurry. She'd searched on the internet for information. She thought she had an idea of what was going on, but she could be wrong.

She could get it all wrong and then what?

What if she made things worse?

Grabbing her phone again, she brought up another search.

"No!" she groaned. She was out of data. Fuck. That meant more money.

That they didn't have.

And Kye needed diapers. Opal and Ryleigh had to eat.

Everything was too much . . . it was too much.

"Lilac?" Ryleigh called out from the bus. "You okay?"

She took a deep, steadying breath. "Uh-huh. I think I know what we need."

"Hey, that's great! See? I knew you could do it."

Yep. Totally. She could do anything.

"Why don't you come eat some dinner?" Ryleigh asked.

Dinner. Right. Food. She should probably eat something. She was shaking. Her blood sugar was likely low. But she couldn't do it. If she ate, she'd likely just vomit it straight back up. And that was food that someone else needed.

"Um, actually. I think I'm going to go for a walk. I have all this energy," she lied.

There was a beat of silence. She could feel Ryleigh's worry beating down on her.

Please don't argue with me. Please.

"All right. But be careful. We don't know this place and it's dark."

Well, hopefully Tanner hadn't been lying about the way that people in Haven looked out for women.

She had her doubts. She wasn't sure she should be here at all. When he saw her . . . well, she wouldn't be sticking around, anyway.

Taking the flashlight, she set off, walking down quiet streets. This place seemed so pretty, even at night when it was difficult to see. Although at least there were plenty of streetlamps.

Music in the distance caught her attention and she found herself walking toward it without thinking.

It sounded like a bunch of people having fun. Laughing. Drinking. Probably dancing.

God. Had she ever been so carefree? Had she ever been able to laugh and dance without a worry?

Stopping in front of the house having the party, she stood and watched. She could see a bit of what was going on in the backyard from the street. Looked like there were a lot of people back there. Fairy lights. Tables. A bar.

A real party.

Longing filled her and she wished she could join them. Unable to tear herself away, she just stood there and daydreamed about a different life.

Suddenly, a man stepped out from the side of the house. Tension filled her.

Was it . . . no, it wasn't possible, right?

No way that could be Tanner. She knew she was going to have to see him eventually. But not tonight, when her shields were so low. When there was no way that she could protect herself from pain.

So, she slid back into the shadows.

Lilac was good at doing that.

At being invisible.

Rushing away, she headed back to the RV and her friends. Tomorrow was a new day.

She just had to hope it was going to be better than today.

8

Tanner Malone watched all the happy couples on the dance floors.

"Assholes," he muttered.

The baby lying on his chest shifted around before letting out a fart.

"Yep, exactly, Mitch. I knew you'd agree with me." He glowered at them all as he lifted his drink and took a sip. It was just soda since he was on baby duty. Once someone else took over, he'd get something with more bite.

The one good thing about a wedding was the free booze.

That was pretty much the only good thing.

"Fucking Butch," Raid muttered as he sat next to him. "The asshole is a fucking genius."

"How do you figure that?"

"A birthday party that's also a surprise wedding? With no engagement party necessary? That's fucking genius. Do you know how many conversations I've had this week about what flowers should be in the centerpieces on the tables at our wedding reception?"

Tanner sighed but didn't answer because he knew Raid was going to tell him anyway.

"About twelve," Raid said. "That's twelve too many. Who the fuck cares about flowers? Or centrepieces?"

"So, elope? Do what Butch did and just surprise everyone. How did you not know about this anyway given that it's happening in your backyard?"

"All I said yes to was a birthday party. Apparently, Lara roped Hannah in and swore her to secrecy. Need to have a word with her about keeping secrets from me."

A word, huh?

Tonight was meant to be Lara's birthday celebration and instead it had turned into a surprise wedding.

It was damn . . . romantic.

Or at least that's what he would have thought if he hadn't hardened his heart to anything romantic. Tanner no longer cared about any of this shit.

Not since *her* . . .

"And I can't elope!" Raid said. "Hannah loves this stuff. I'm not taking this away from her."

Tanner rolled his eyes. For fuck's sake. "So then stop complaining."

"Why would I want to do that?"

"Maybe because I don't want to hear it?"

"If I have to live it, then you have to hear me complain about it," Raid grumbled.

"That's ridiculous."

"It is what it is," Raid replied. "My girl wants the big, white wedding, so that's what she gets. With all the hoo-ha that comes along with it."

"Even if you don't enjoy any of that?"

"What's my enjoyment got to do with it?" Raid gave him a bewildered look.

"You're ridiculous," Tanner told him, shifting Mitch on his chest. The baby was handling all the noise like a pro.

He was a Malone, though.

Malones thrived on chaos.

"And you're turning bitter and twisted," Raid told him. "Never thought you'd end up grumpy and anti-social. You're making West look good."

"What are you talking about?" He was not grumpy and anti-social.

"You're sitting here, scowling at anyone who looks like they're having fun. You're like the dark gloomy uncle, living under a thundercloud, sucking the fun out of everything."

"Ouch."

"Someone has to give it to you straight. Tanner, I know Lilac broke your heart—"

"She didn't break my heart," he interrupted Raid, turning to glare at him. "Shut the fuck up. You know nothing about it."

"I know you fell in love and then she left. She didn't tell you she was going. She never answered her phone or texted you. There were things she didn't tell you. And now she's gone, and you'll likely never see her again. I get that fucked with your head, but you have to get over it. There are plenty more women out there."

"Yeah? What would you say if I said that about Hannah, huh? If you lost her?"

Raid stood up slowly and glowered down at him. "If you weren't holding my baby nephew . . ."

"Yeah," he said bitterly. "Plenty more women, huh?"

"Fuck, Tanner. It's not the same."

Tanner just stared up at him.

"You cared about her that much?" Raid asked, looking pained. Even though evening had fallen, the fairy lights strewn everywhere lit up the darkness. They were in all the trees.

Around the tables that were set out around the makeshift dancefloor.

Hannah and Raid's backyard had turned into something magical. Well, that's what he might have thought if he'd still had some softness in him.

He patted Mitch's back lightly as the baby grumbled.

"I did. But don't worry, I'm over it."

Raid sighed. "We can find her."

"No," Tanner said abruptly.

Mitch let out another small noise. Great, the kid slept through a party, but he was waking him up with his anger.

Breathe in. Breathe out.

"I'm fine."

"Sure, brother." Hannah waved, gesturing to Raid. "Come out on a date with us."

"With you and Hannah? Sounds awkward. I'm not into threesomes, man."

"Not suggesting that. I'd never let you touch Hannah. No, a double date with her friend Carlie."

Tanner groaned. He knew Carlie. She was a nice girl, but they had no chemistry.

"Doesn't have to mean anything. Just friends getting together, but it will get you off the Ranch and back out there. I kept my promise not to say anything about Lilac to anyone. That means you owe me."

It didn't mean that at all. It just meant that for once he'd kept his big mouth shut. "If I say yes, will you shut up about Lilac?"

"Yep."

"Fine. I'll go. Now, you better go. Hannah wants you."

"You sure?"

"Go," Tanner said with a forced smile. "I'm fine."

"It's okay to not be fine," Raid said.

Tanner groaned and stood, rocking with Mitch. "Just because

you found a good woman doesn't mean we need to get all touchy-feely and in touch with our fucking feelings."

Suddenly, Raid's eyes widened, and he took a step back.

Tanner tensed and half turned, ready to shield the baby against whatever threat he saw. However, he realized too late that Raid wouldn't have stepped back if there had been a threat to Mitch.

Nope, this threat would defend the baby in Tanner's arms with his life.

"Did you just swear in front of my baby?" West snarled.

"You couldn't have warned me he was standing there," Tanner said to Raid.

Raid grinned. "Nope. Bye."

"Give me my baby," West demanded.

"Ahh, no, I think I'm gonna keep him until you've calmed down."

West's gaze narrowed. "Give him to me now."

"Hey! What's going on?" Flick asked, walking up. She smiled at Mitch. "Aww, look he's still sleeping. You've got the magic touch, Uncle Tanner."

"He's a good baby." Tanner kissed the top of his nephew's head and watched West relax slightly.

The guy was wound up tighter than usual, which was saying something since he wasn't the most relaxed individual.

"He sure is. Come on, West. Dance with me!" Flick tugged on his arm.

West? Dance? He'd like to see the day that happened.

"No dancing," West replied. "Tanner needs to give me my baby."

"Why? He's happy," Flick told him. "If you won't dance, you can just stand there while I dance around you. That's what he considers dancing anyway." She grinned at Tanner.

"He swore in front of Mitch," West grumbled.

Flick sighed and shook her head. "We've had this conversation, West. People are going to swear in front of Mitch."

"They shouldn't."

"It happens. I stubbed my toe the other day and I said a bad word. Are you going to punish me?"

West turned to look at her. "You stubbed your toe? You didn't tell me!"

Flick sighed. "That's not the point of this. The point is—"

West pointed a finger at her. "You tell me if you hurt yourself. That's the rule."

"Darn it, West!" Flick stomped her foot.

West swooped down and picked her up, cradling her against his chest.

"Tanner, watch Mitch."

Flick groaned as he carried her away, scolding her. Tanner grinned.

"Your father is nuts, Mitch. Thank God the Malones pretty much always have boys because imagine him with a baby girl. That poor child would never get to leave the house. He'd probably put her in a bubble."

Tanner shook his head at the thought. His cousin, Lottie, was the only Malone girl to be born in years.

There had to be a reason for that.

Swaying with the music, he headed toward the bar to get another soda. Seemed he wasn't going to be drinking for a while. The bar was set around the side of the house to leave more room for everyone out back. Seemed like most of the town was here.

He froze as he spotted someone in the distance, watching from the street. There was no way he was seeing what he thought he was seeing. He shook his head and stepped farther forward. Just then, the person disappeared.

"Fuck, Mitch, now I'm seeing things," he muttered. "There's no way that was Lilac."

He was definitely losing his mind.

9

Lilac looked up at the name of the bar.

Dirty Delights.

Okay. Interesting name. Didn't have to mean that anything dirty or dodgy went on inside.

And really . . . what choice did she have? There were several businesses in Haven, which was surprising considering it wasn't a large town, but only one bar.

She couldn't get a job at the nice restaurant. But maybe she could find a job at the diner. However, waitressing at a bar was really her only experience. Plus, she felt like the owner of a bar was less likely to ask questions. Or want pesky things like a social security number.

You can do this.

You guys need the money.

Especially now since she'd spent most of their remaining money on coolant for their RV.

Please let it work.

It had taken her longer than she'd thought to walk into town and buy the coolant. So now she had to make the walk back when it was getting decidedly warmer.

She wasn't dressed to go job hunting. Her jeans were old and worn and she'd had to secure them with a belt, or they'd fall right off her. But it wasn't like she had any other clothes that fit her any better. Buying clothes for herself was the last thing on her list to do.

"While you're here, you might as well go in," she muttered to herself.

"Hey, are you okay?"

Jumping, she glanced over to see a beautiful blond woman smiling at her. She had a double stroller that held two gorgeous baby girls. God, Lilac would love to be able to afford a stroller for Kye.

Maybe if the universe would stop punishing her, then she could.

"Um, yeah, I was just going in here."

"I don't think it's open yet." The woman gave her a curious look as she pushed the stroller back and forth.

"Right, of course. Silly me. I was, um, hoping there might be a job available."

"Oh!" The woman looked surprised, but quickly hid it. "You live here?"

"Well, um, I thought I'd stop here for a while. Is that not okay?"

The other woman shook her head with a laugh. "Of course, sorry. Small town. Everyone knows everyone else, you know? I just assumed you were passing through. Sorry."

"It's all right. I'll, um, come back later when it's open."

"Actually, Devon is probably in there. Let's find out."

"Oh, you don't have to . . ." she trailed off as the other woman reached up and knocked on the front door.

They waited, but nothing happened.

"Thanks for helping, I'll come—"

The door to the bar opened and an attractive, muscular man stepped out. He frowned down at Lilac and she felt her insides shrivel.

Yeah. She should have come back when the bar was open. In more appropriate clothing. Now he was annoyed with her.

Not a good start.

Then, his gaze moved to the blonde woman and his whole demeanor changed. His face softened and he smiled.

"Savannah! What are you doing here?" His gaze dropped to the babies sleeping in the stroller. "And you brought two of my favorite people with you."

Okay, that was kind of sweet. And not at all what she'd been expecting from the grouchy-looking man.

Savannah smiled up at him. "Hey, Devon."

"What are you doing here this morning, darlin'?" he asked.

Crap. That darlin' reminded her of her Tanner.

Stop thinking about him. He's not yours.

Devon gave Lilac an assessing look.

At least he'd stopped frowning at her. So that was a bonus.

"Sorry to interrupt. It's just that, uh, drat, I didn't catch your name," Savannah said to her.

"It's Lilac. Lilac Masters." It wasn't her real last name, of course. Opal had gotten them all fake IDs and she'd chosen her last name for her.

"Lilac is looking for a job and we thought you might have one open," Savannah said.

Lilac glanced over at the other woman, wondering why she was trying to help her. Why she cared. What was her ulterior motive? She had to have one, right?

"Is that so? Well, Lilac, you better come in, then."

Awesome.

This was such a stupid idea. What if she went in there and this guy hurt her? No one would know she was in there except this woman, who was a stranger.

But she couldn't back out or she might miss out on a job. So, she shot Savannah a tight smile.

"Thanks for the help."

The other woman gave her a cheery smile and wave. "No worries. I better get going. Logan will be waiting for me. Bye!"

She followed Devon into the bar. It was quiet and slightly dark. But surprisingly, there was no smell of stale beer. No mustiness. Or body odor.

Whenever she entered a bar, those were the main smells. Sometimes cigarette smoke too.

In fact, there was a pleasant smell of gingerbread. How odd.

"You okay?" Devon asked her as she paused, looking around.

"It doesn't stink."

"Uh, thanks."

She grimaced. "Sorry. I didn't mean that to sound rude. It's just that all the bars I've worked in have had a definite odor to them even when no one was in them. Maybe especially when no one was in them."

"Yeah. I have burners with different scents I like to use. Plus, I have a cleaner that comes in early each morning. Come into my office."

All right.

She followed him out the back into an office, which was the total opposite of the clean and orderly bar.

It was a complete mess with stuff everywhere. Papers and folders covered the desk. There were boxes on the floor and the sofa. Devon moved around behind the desk.

"Have you just bought the place?" she asked.

"Nope. Why?"

"Oh, I thought maybe you were moving in. Moving out?"

"Ah, no. I just . . . haven't worked out a filing system yet."

"How long have you owned the place?" she asked, taking a seat.

"Seven years."

Her mouth dropped open before she could feel herself smiling, unable to help herself.

"I know it's a mess. It's just . . . everything has its place, and I don't want anyone messing with my system."

Somehow, that admission made her relax around him. He seemed more approachable.

Normal.

"So Lilac Masters, was it?"

She nodded as he sat back and stared at her. "How do you know Savannah?"

There was no point lying, he'd be able to ask Savannah for the truth.

"I don't. She came up to me as I was standing outside and for some reason, decided to help."

Devon sighed. "Damn it. She's got to stop talking to strangers like that. I'm gonna have to tell Logan."

She frowned, a wary feeling inside her growing. "Who is Logan?"

"Her man."

"Will he get mad at her?" she asked with concern.

"If you just met her, why do you care?"

She didn't know. But she wasn't going to just sit here if the other woman was being abused. "I thought this was a safe place where women were taken care of. Obviously, I was wrong. Where does she live?" She jumped to her feet.

"Whoa, firecracker. Take a seat again." Something changed

in Devon's expression. She got the strange idea that he approved of her.

Weird.

"Logan won't harm her. He'd never hurt any woman. Neither would Max."

"Who is he?"

"Her other man."

Lilac's mouth dropped open. Okay. Tanner had mentioned that, but part of her hadn't believed him.

"Savannah is well loved and taken care of. No man in Haven would hit a woman. Spank them, maybe. Hit them, no."

Her body grew hot. "He'll spank her?"

"I can't say. But whatever happens, it will be with Savannah's consent."

Tanner had threatened to spank her . .

"You still want a job here?" he asked.

"Yes. If you have one."

"Turns out I do." He tapped his fingers on the desk. "You're living in Haven?"

"For . . . for the time being."

"So, at some stage, you might just take off on me?"

"I'll try not to. We want someplace safe to live. If that's here, we might stay."

"We?" he asked.

"I have some friends with me."

"Men? Women?"

She didn't answer. "I think I better go." She hadn't been expecting people to be so nosey.

"Sit down, Lilac."

There was such command in his voice that she found herself sitting before she even thought about it.

Darn it.

"Are you in trouble?"

"What makes you ask that?" she asked.

"Many women have come to Haven because they were in trouble, and needed protection."

"I can protect myself," she muttered. Crap. She wasn't getting this job.

He eyed her for a long moment. "It's eighteen an hour and tips are split evenly at the end of the night."

Relief filled her.

"That's fine." Eighteen was better than she'd ever been paid before. "Do you need me to do a trial?"

"Can you come back tomorrow at five?"

"Yes."

"We'll do a trial then. Hours will normally be from five until close, Tuesday to Saturday."

"That's fine. I can also fill in if you need me to help on any other days."

"No working more than five days a week," he said firmly.

"All right. Thanks. I'll be back. Is there anything I should wear or..."

"Just whatever is comfortable. I'll order you a shirt if things work out. We don't have anything small enough for you in stock." He frowned slightly as he said that.

And she told herself she didn't care if he didn't think she looked good.

But she was lying.

"Have you spoken to the sheriff?" he asked.

Lilac straightened. "About what? Why would I talk to the sheriff? I haven't done anything wrong."

By the time she'd finished talking, she could feel herself breaking out in a sweat, her heart racing.

"Easy," Devon said in a low voice. "I wasn't suggesting you'd done anything wrong."

She swallowed heavily. He rose and grabbed a bottle of water, handing it over to her.

Lilac just stared at the water. She wasn't used to being offered things without an ulterior motive. Not from men, anyway.

Unless it's Tanner.

Because for some reason she'd trusted him.

God. That one night they'd spent together had been such a foolish risk. He could have hurt her. Could have done anything to her and no one had even known where she was.

Sleeping with him had been both stupid and amazing.

"But he can help you if you're in trouble."

"I'm not in any trouble." She smiled. He didn't look like he believed her, though. Crap. She didn't have Opal's ability to lie with ease.

And this guy was good. He knew when to back off and when to press.

"Right. But you want to be paid cash. Because you don't believe in banks. Is that it?"

Double crap.

"All right. My brother isn't very nice, and the truth is, I don't want him to find me. He's . . . he wants me to do something I don't want to do. But I'm not in immediate danger."

Devon watched her. "Jake, that's the sheriff, he's gonna want to talk to you. If you're staying in Haven, you need a guardian. Jake will be that for you if you don't have anyone else."

A guardian? They'd heard about this . . . but like other things she'd heard about Haven, she hadn't been sure whether to believe it or not.

"I can take care of myself. And I might not be here long, um, sorry." Probably not the thing to tell the guy that had just hired you on.

"I get the deal, Lilac. But if you're in trouble, you've landed in the right place. And if you need help, then you talk to Jake. We take care of our own here."

That sounded amazing.

But she still couldn't quite believe in it. And she knew, deep down, that she'd never belong in a place as beautiful and clean and nice as this.

Because at heart, all she was . . . was trash.

10

By the time she got back to the RV, Lilac was sweaty and trembling. Her heart was racing, her head thumping, and she didn't feel good.

"Really should have taken that bottle of water."

Yep. She'd had that thought a lot on her trek home. Walking into town hadn't felt so bad in the early morning with an empty backpack. But walking back in the midday heat with a backpack full of coolant and diapers.

Yep. Not good at all.

So, when she stepped into the park and saw a deputy sheriff's car sitting next to the RV, Lilac considered turning around and running.

But she couldn't.

Put your big girl panties on.

Taking a deep breath, she headed to the RV, alarm filling her as she heard Opal talking.

Oh God. Why was Ryleigh letting Opal do the talking?

"Hello!" she called out.

A nice-looking man turned toward her, eyeing her as she moved closer.

Damn. Were all the people in this town good-looking? The deputy sheriff had a fit build and dark hair. He looked like he was in his midthirties.

"Hey, doll," Opal called out. She was dressed conservatively today. At least for her. Her jeans were skin-tight with rhinestones up the sides, paired with a short-sleeved tight top that was low-cut. "This is deputy Linc. He just wanted to check we were okay. I told him we'd be fucking peachy once you got back."

"Yep. And I'm back." She gave Linc a big smile.

He didn't look convinced. Awesome.

"I'm Lilac."

"Lilac." He held out his hand and shook hers. Nice handshake. Not sweaty and clammy, but not too hard either.

Stefan used to shake hands with people like he was trying to break them.

Mind you, he often did go on to break them.

"I was just telling your friend here that we can't let you park here overnight, I'm afraid."

"Oh, we won't be. We just had a bit of engine trouble last night, but I just got some stuff to fix it. So, we'll be moving on."

Nothing to see here.

Everything is fine.

Please don't put our names in the system.

They all had fake last names. But she was worried their identities wouldn't hold up if someone looked into them.

"Again, I'm really sorry. We'll move on as soon as we can," she said. "I just got a job at Dirty Delights, but we don't have to stay if you'd rather. We can go to another town."

She didn't know why but she felt like she was on the cusp of breaking down, of just giving in and crying. She was aware of

Opal giving her a shocked look as she shook her head, trying to tell her to stop talking.

Right. They weren't leaving. Because this was their last option.

"Hey," Linc said, holding his hands up. "No one is going to hurt you, okay?"

Why would he think she was worried about that? She hadn't mentioned anything about anyone hurting her.

"Lilac? You okay? Nobody gave you trouble, did they?" Opal demanded, striding over to her. "I'll fucking kill them."

"She didn't mean that," Lilac told the deputy quickly.

He gave her a faint smile that didn't dispel the worry in his gaze. "I didn't think she did."

If only he knew what Opal was capable of . . . he probably wouldn't say that.

"Did anyone give you trouble in town?" he asked.

He really looked like he actually cared.

"No, everyone was nice. I'm just a bit stressed out because of the van breaking down."

Linc gave the old RV a doubtful look. "Did you say you got something to fix it?"

"Uh-huh. Coolant."

"Did you get Matt at Haven Mechanical to come look at it?" Linc asked. "Why didn't he bring out the coolant? Did you walk all the way into town on your own?"

She blinked at him. That was a lot of questions.

"Oh, no, I know what to do," she reassured him. "Don't worry. And I didn't need to bother anyone. It wasn't that far to walk into town."

Linc gave her a doubting look, then glanced around the park. "You stayed here last night?"

"Um, yes. I'm really sorry. Is there . . . is there a fine or something? It was late and we didn't want to drive it any farther so we thought this would be all right?"

Please don't fine us.

"No fine," Linc told her. "It's just not a safe place for two women."

"I know." Lilac nodded. "Which is why we'll be moving to a camping ground as soon as I get old Sugar going."

"Sugar?"

"The RV," Opal said. "I named her. It suits her, huh?"

"Um, yeah, sure." Linc looked doubtful. "So, if you got a job at Dirty Delights, I'm guessing you're planning on staying."

"We were, yes," she said.

"Thing is . . . there's no camping ground here in Haven."

What?

Fuck. Why hadn't they looked that up? She'd just assumed . .

"Oh," she said, trying to hide her disappointment. "Right. I guess we can find somewhere else to go."

"You're living in this full-time?" he asked them.

Crap. He had so many questions.

"No, honey," Opal said, laying on her charm. "We're doing some sightseeing, but we need to earn money along the way. Especially with Sugar here acting up."

"Right. Well, I guess the first thing to do is to get Sugar working again," the deputy said.

"We'll do that now. Thanks for checking on us." Lilac smiled up at him.

Linc eyed her for a long moment. "Why don't I help you?"

"I don't want to get you dirty," she told him. "And this could take a while."

"I've got time."

Just awesome. Now he was going to see that she had no idea what she was doing. She needed to watch the video first to follow the instructions. At least she had more data on her phone now.

Suddenly, his radio crackled, and he moved to his car. "Excuse me a moment."

She turned to Opal. "Ryleigh and Kye?"

"Thought it was better to hide them." They tried not to make it obvious that there were three women traveling together. And people always remembered a baby.

Although it was usually better for Opal to say hidden since she was the most memorable of the three.

"Do you think he's really gonna stay while you try to fix poor Sugar?" Opal asked.

"I hope not," Lilac said. "Since I have no clue what I'm doing."

Opal shot her a warning look as the deputy walked back over. "Sorry, I have to go. I'm going to come back and check on you after, though. If you need help, I want you to call me." He handed Lilac his card. "And if you're planning on staying for any length of time, you're going to need to talk to Jake, the sheriff."

"We haven't done anything wrong," Opal protested.

"Not saying that," Linc said soothingly. "Around here we take care of our women. If you're staying for any length of time, you'll need a guardian. Just someone who watches out for your best interests, and Jake often acts in that capacity for women on their own. I know it sounds odd, but it's for your safety. I'll be back soon. Be safe."

When he left, Lilac slumped down onto the ground, unable to keep herself up.

Ouch.

"Lilac? Fuck, Lilac! Ryleigh," Opal yelled.

"What is it? Oh God, Lilac! What happened?" Ryleigh asked frantically.

Then Kye started crying.

Shit. She had to get herself together before they all lost it.

"I'm okay. I'm fine." Close to passing out . . . burned out, exhausted and thirsty.

But. Yeah. Fine.

"Water," Opal said. "She needs some water."

Someone pressed a bottle of water into her hand and guided it to her mouth. She sucked it down. God, she'd been so thirsty.

Idiot.

"Lilac, are you sure you're all right? Do we need to call an ambulance?" Ryleigh asked.

"No! No ambulance." She managed to stand with Opal's help. They couldn't afford an ambulance. She had to get herself together. "I just got a bit dehydrated, is all."

"Not to mention you haven't fucking eaten in six months," Opal said. "Surprised you haven't fainted before now."

"Opal," Ryleigh said softly as she swayed back and forth with Kye pressed to her chest.

"Got to be said, you don't fucking eat soon, and we will be calling an ambulance for you."

"Yeah, well, I think we have more important things to worry about right now," Lilac replied. "Like getting Sugar up and running before he comes back."

"Where are we gonna fucking go?" Opal asked, pacing back and forth. "We can't stay here, not if we have to meet with the fucking sheriff."

"What?" Ryleigh asked.

Lilac filled her in on her conversation.

"So that's it? We have to leave?" Fear and sadness filled Ryleigh's face.

Opal and Lilac shared a look.

"No, we don't have to leave. But we also can't have the sheriff looking into us," Lilac said. "I told Devon, the guy that owns Dirty Delights, that my brother was trying to force me to do something I didn't want to, but that I wasn't in immediate danger."

Opal snorted. "Sort of true."

"I'll just convince the sheriff not to look into us." Somehow. Fuck.

"But where will we stay if there's no camp ground?" Ryleigh asked.

That part was more complicated. "We'll move around. You guys can drop me off close to town when I have to work, and I'll walk the rest of the way. Then you can go further out to park."

"Or . . ." Ryleigh let her voice drop off as she chewed at her lower lip.

"Or what?" Opal asked.

"We go straight to the Malones. Ask for their help," Ryleigh said.

Part of her desperately wanted to see Tanner again.

And an even bigger part of her was dreading it.

But that wasn't even her biggest worry over going to the Malones. What if she'd gotten it wrong and they weren't good people? What if they didn't want to help? Hell. She couldn't even blame them . . . they were in such a mess that no ordinary people would choose to help.

But if they turned them away . . . there was no other plan other than her shaky one. And to do that, she had to ensure that Ryleigh, Kye, and Opal were safe first.

And then there was Ryleigh . . . she was counting on them. She believed in them. What if they let her down?

"Are you . . . is that what you want to do?" Lilac asked.

Because it was up to Ryleigh.

"I don't know. I don't . . . I'm scared. If we go there and they reject us, then we've got nothing." Ryleigh looked so terrified. Lilac hated it.

"We haven't got nothing," Opal said, wrapping her arm

around Ryleigh. "We got the three of us. Who needs anyone else? Not me."

"The A team," Ryleigh said.

"Right," Lilac said. "The three of us can handle anything."

"I just think maybe we should . . . we should get the lay of the land first, you know?" Ryleigh bit her lip. "I mean, I know you said that Tanner and Raid were good guys, and I'm sure you're right. But . . ."

"But that doesn't mean the others are," Lilac finished. "So, we try to find out what we can about them. Then we come up with a plan. First, Sugar. Second, we drive out of this park. Third, find somewhere to park until tomorrow night when I can go earn us some money."

Even if she didn't get the job, at least she'd get some tips tomorrow night. That should buy them some more food and time.

Optimism filled her.

They had this.

11

She didn't fucking have this.

Lilac kicked Sugar's tire.

Pain shot up her leg and she hopped around with a cry, holding her foot between her hands. "God damn it! Stupid! Useless!"

"Things aren't going well then," a male voice said.

Fuck.

How had she missed him driving up? Well, she did have the music up and was nearly in tears from breaking her toe.

Such an idiot.

"Um. No. It's not. Sorry." Turning, she looked up with a forced smile at the deputy, who didn't look all that amused.

"Did you hurt yourself?"

"I'm fine."

"What happened?" he asked.

"Nothing. I'm all good."

Linc's gaze narrowed. "I don't like being lied to."

Shit. What was with the men around here? They all seemed

so dominant. Tanner had moments of being like this . . . commanding. She shouldn't like it . . . not after the way she'd been raised. Being controlled was something she'd fled from.

Yet, not once had these guys tried to bully or threaten her.

"I just kicked the wheel in frustration," she confessed.

"Don't do that again."

She swiped at her eyes as he turned to look at Sugar.

"The coolant didn't work?"

"Um, no. Didn't seem to."

"Do you really know what you're doing?" he asked.

"Not really. No." What choice did she have but to tell him the truth?

"Another lie." He folded his arms over his wide chest. "Stacking them up."

"Sorry," she said. "I just . . . I thought I could fix it, but she won't start, and I don't know what I'm going to do." She rubbed her chest, feeling the panic well again.

"It's all right, we'll figure this out."

That shouldn't reassure her when she didn't know this man *and* he was a cop.

"Where's your friend?" he asked.

"They went for a walk." Ryleigh had needed to stretch her legs and Opal had gone with her for company. Kye was sleeping in the RV, and she was keeping an eye on him

"They?" he queried.

Shit. She was so tired that her tongue was getting loose. Instead of replying, she just sent him a look.

The deputy grunted. "I'm not going to like all the secrets you're keeping, am I?"

"I haven't done anything wrong," she said hastily.

"Easy," he said soothingly. "I'm not accusing you of anything."

Great. She probably looked guilty by protesting her innocence.

"But you guys can't stay here. It's not safe. And there's nowhere for you to hook up for electricity or water. So, we have to get Sugar going or get her towed and then settle you guys into the hotel or B&B."

"Right." She was going to be ill.

"Guessing that's a problem."

"Just a bit," she replied.

"Money?"

"Yeah," she whispered.

"Let me make some calls." Linc disappeared into his car.

"Lilac! Look what we found!"

She glanced over as Ryleigh raced up with her arms full of plums.

Uh-oh.

Her friend came to a stop as she saw Linc. "Oh, shit."

He glanced out of his car and looked from her to Lilac pointedly.

Lilac groaned. "He's going to think I do nothing but lie."

"Sorry," Ryleigh told her. "I didn't see his car until it was too late. Oh no, and I'm holding an armful of forbidden plums."

Forbidden plums?

Lilac snorted. "Don't worry. The plums are the least of our worries."

"Christ, this fucking walking thing is a joke," Opal complained as she strode up to them. "Why do people do it?"

"To get to places," Lilac said dryly.

"That's why cars were invented," Opal said.

"Well, you did go for a walk in five-inch heels," Ryleigh pointed out.

"These are the lowest heels I own."

Lilac felt her lips twitch.

"I see Deputy Hottie is back," Opal said. "And that Sugar ain't runnin'."

"Your powers of observation are astounding," Lilac said sarcastically.

"I'm just gonna put these plums away and check on Kye," Ryleigh said as Linc opened the car door.

She scurried inside and Linc's gaze followed her.

"Slipped up when you said 'they,' huh?" Linc said.

She shrugged.

"Do I want to know why?" he asked.

Sighing, she shook her head.

"Hey there, Deputy Hottie," Opal said loudly.

Linc narrowed his gaze as he turned to look at Opal. Lilac knew her friend was trying to divert his attention from Ryleigh. But if she didn't tone it down, she was going to end up in trouble.

"So, um, thanks for checking on us, but I need to talk to my friends about what to do," Lilac told him. "Do you think it would be okay if we spent another night here?"

Please. Please.

Desperation filled her.

Linc shook his head. "I'm sorry, no."

Suddenly, a cry filled the air.

Fuck.

Linc scowled. "Is that a baby?"

The crying stopped, but it was too late. Crap. Now he was going to wonder why they'd also kept Kye a secret from him.

"Yeah, that's Kye," she said. "Ryleigh? Everything okay?"

"Yep. Fine." Ryleigh appeared in the doorway, holding Kye. She looked slightly pale and worried, but someone would have seen Kye eventually. So it might as well be the deputy.

"Sorry, we weren't keeping him a secret or anything," Lilac said. "It's just . . . we don't know you."

"He's not very old."

"Nearly a month," Ryleigh said.

Linc gazed down at her, his face softening. "You shouldn't be here with a baby."

"We're fine," Ryleigh said. "Lots of people raise children in RVs."

"With electricity and water hooked up. Look, I made some calls. Matt is gonna come and tow Sugar to the garage."

"We can't do that," Lilac said. "We can't afford it." God, she hated admitting that.

"Don't worry. Matt knows that and is willing to let you pay it off."

"But why would he agree to that when he doesn't know us?" Ryleigh asked.

Linc kept his gaze on hers. "Because around here, we look after our women. And children. This changes your accommodation needs though. Can't send a baby to the bar."

Huh?

"Devon has a one-bed apartment above Dirty Delights," he explained. "Would have been a tight fit but bigger than Sugar. You can't have a baby in a bar, though."

"I'm sure we could make it work if Devon is okay with it." Would he be? Would he really want them there? And how much would he ask for rent? "We'd only have to stay a night or two until Sugar is ready. And we could offer to do other things around the bar, like cleaning."

Both Ryleigh and Opal nodded.

"No, no." Linc shook his head, making her stomach drop in disappointment. "That's not gonna work. But I have another plan. I have a guest house."

"A guest house?" Ryleigh asked.

What sort of property did he own that he had a guest house?

"It has two bedrooms. You could stay there. When I bought

the property, my ma was gonna come live in it. But she, uh, she died."

"I'm so sorry." Ryleigh walked up and placed her hand on Linc's arm. She was the sweetest of them all. The most empathic.

The least fucked up.

"I know it's not ideal. I mean, if you wanted, you could sleep in the main house, but I'm guessing that might make you uncomfortable."

"Um, yeah, thanks for the offer, but—"

"Can we have a key to the place that no one else has?" Opal interrupted Lilac.

"Yes, of course. I have two keys. You can have them both."

"It's got a bathroom?" Opal asked.

"Fully self-contained."

"What's the cost of rent?" Opal queried.

Was she seriously considering this? They didn't know this man. They couldn't live with him. Plus, he was a cop.

But then again . . . wouldn't it be safer to stay with someone in law enforcement? And they really needed somewhere.

"Free," Linc said.

"Wow, that's so nice," Ryleigh said, smiling up at him.

"We can't stay for free," Lilac said. "We'll have to do something in return. We can garden or clean or something." The scales couldn't be in Linc's favor. Well, they would be since cleaning and gardening didn't equate to rent. But it didn't sound like he rented the place out anyway.

Opal nodded. "Yes. We'll do that."

"All right. It's a deal, then. But I need to know if any of you are in danger."

Shoot.

She couldn't tell him that.

"You don't have to give me the details until you get to know me better, but is someone gonna come and try to hurt any of you?"

"My brother isn't a good man," Lilac said. "We don't want him to find out where we are."

Linc eyed her. "All right. But when you trust me more, I want the full story."

Yeah. That wouldn't be happening.

12

Dirty Delights wasn't a bad place to work.

It was Thursday night and she'd easily gotten into the swing of things. Devon and another guy called Darne were bartending tonight. They also had three waitresses on since tonight was going to be busier.

The other waitresses were friendly. Cherie had shown her all the ropes over the last two days, while Lemon seemed quieter but still kind.

By around ten, she was exhausted. Her adrenaline buzz was disappearing and she was fading fast.

"Go for a break, darlin'," Cherie called out.

"Oh, but I've got full tables."

"Yeah, but we all get a break. Devon's orders. And he's been giving you 'the look' for a while."

Oops. Lilac had noticed 'the look' earlier but had done her best to ignore it. Now, when she turned to him, he was glowering at her.

Probably not a good idea to annoy your boss on your third night on the job.

The pay was good, but it was the tips that blew her away. People around here were generous. And respectful. So far, she hadn't had any trouble with anyone trying to grope her or making lewd remarks about her.

Of course there was still time for that to happen.

However, Devon seemed to have a close eye on his bar and workers. Case in point . . . right now he was pointing to the door behind the bar, which led to the office and staff area.

She sent him a salute and he rolled his eyes. But she headed back. There was a full carafe of coffee, along with creamer and sugar.

She poured some into her mug with a sigh. Sleeping was becoming increasingly hard for her.

"Lilac?"

Shocked, her hand jolted and she splashed some coffee on the floor. "Shit! Sorry!"

"Did you burn yourself?" Devon strode into the room and grasped her hand.

She immediately wanted to wrench it away from his touch. It wasn't that she didn't like Devon. She did. And he'd never given her any indication that he'd hurt her.

But Lilac wasn't used to being touched with kindness or caring by a man.

There was only one man she'd ever wanted to touch her. Who had made her feel good. Who she'd finally felt like she could relax with.

"Easy," Devon said. "Not going to hurt you."

"I need to clean up the spilled coffee."

He snorted. "Nothing this floor hasn't seen before. It's fine. Are you?"

"Yep. You just gave me a fright." She offered him a big smile. Shit. He was probably wondering if she'd act like this every time she went out into the bar, and someone tried to touch her.

But out there, she knew to wear her armor. In here... she'd let her guard down.

Not a smart idea, Lilac.

"Really don't like this brother of yours."

"You know him?" She stepped back, her heart racing. He knew Stefan? How?

"Nope. I don't." He eyed her sternly. "Doesn't mean I can't hate his guts for the way he's obviously treated you."

Oh.

Shit.

She was giving too much away. She smiled brightly. But she could tell from the look on his face that he wasn't buying it.

Devon pointed a finger at her, a stern look on his face. "When you're due for a break, you have a break. Understand?"

"Yes." Damn. She felt a bit sorry for whatever woman or man he ended up with. She didn't know what his preference was, only that he would be a force to be reckoned with.

"Good. You got something to eat?"

"I ate before I came."

With a grunt, he turned and left the room.

She glanced down at the minor burn on her hand that she'd managed to keep hidden from him by turning her hand into the cup. Hadn't helped the throbbing pain, but she didn't want his help or touch.

There was only one person she wanted that from... and he likely hated her guts.

13

Tanner was bored out of his mind.

It wasn't Carlie's fault. She was funny. Full of energy. Gorgeous and engaging.

But she wasn't a sweet redhead. With big blue eyes. And curves that didn't stop.

Fuck.

Was he ever going to get over her?

Raid leaned into him as the girls disappeared to the bathroom. "Dude, you need to at least be friendly."

Fuck. "That bad, huh?"

Raid sighed, shaking his head. "You're not being rude, just quiet. What's the problem?"

"You know what the problem is."

"That girl ghosted you. How long are you going to pine after her? Look, Carlie knows this is just a friendly date, but you have to at least talk to her."

Guilt filled him. He wasn't being fair to Carlie. The four of them had been out to dinner and now they'd grabbed a table at Dirty Delights. It was pumping tonight.

Generally, he enjoyed being here.

"You're right." He made an effort to smile at Carlie as she reappeared. Getting up, he drew out her chair.

She laughed. "Such a gentleman. I think all those rumors about those Malone boys must have been exaggerated."

"They weren't," Tanner said with a grin. "Tell me what you've been doing this week."

Raid and Hannah were staring at each other with lovey-dovey eyes. It was kind of sickening, so he moved closer to Carlie as a distraction.

Reaching out, he tucked a piece of hair behind Carlie's ear. She smiled up at him.

Someone jostled her and she slid into him as he turned to glower at the asshole who had already walked past. He helped her sit up.

"Are you all right?"

She smiled up at him, her hand still on his thigh where she'd put it to keep her balance. "I'm good. Thanks."

"What a jerk. Must be from out of town."

The sound of glass smashing had everyone's attention turning. His gut instantly soured as he spotted the waitress who'd just dropped a glass on the floor.

It couldn't be . . .

His breath caught as he studied the pale woman. She was thinner than his Lilac. In fact, she was way too thin—to the point of being unhealthy. Her skin was pale. Her hair, which she'd drawn back from her face into a ponytail, was lank and dull.

But still . . . it was his Lilac.

What the fuck was she doing here? How did she come to be working here?

He watched as she seemed to come back into her head and

looked down with a gasp. Then she kneeled right in the fucking glass and started to pick up pieces.

What the hell was she doing?

Sliding from the booth, he stood.

"What's going on? Tanner?" Carlie asked.

"Fuck, is that Lilac?" Raid said with shock as Tanner rushed toward her.

Around her, people were trying to talk to her, to convince her to put the glass down. She was going to fucking cut herself.

"Lilac?" Devon said, reaching her at the same time Tanner did.

Tanner shot the other guy a dirty look, not liking the way he said her name.

Yeah, he knew he was being irrational. But he couldn't help it. Lilac was his.

Except . . . she left you. Ghosted you. She didn't want you.

So, if she didn't want him, what was she doing here? Why come to his town?

Was it for him?

"Lilac, drop the glass, honey. You're going to hurt yourself," Devon told her.

"Don't call her honey," Tanner said in a low growl.

Devon gave him a narrow-eyed look.

"I've got to clean it all up," Lilac said, sounding almost frantic as she grabbed another piece of glass. She hissed and worry flooded Tanner as he saw a drop of blood land on the floor.

"Fuck. Lilac, release the glass. Right now."

Lilac froze, her gaze rising to his.

"Lilac," he said warningly, putting as much command as possible into his voice.

She placed the glass down, glancing around. Her face grew red, and he swore he could see her eyes glistening with tears.

"I'm so sorry, Devon. I'll clean it up. I just . . . need . . . a minute."

"I've got this. Go clean up," Devon reassured her.

"Wait right there, Lilac." Tanner got to his feet, but by that time she was pushing her way across the room.

Fucking hell.

This girl had to stop running from him.

"Tanner? Everything okay?"

Fuck. He'd forgotten about Carlie. Turning, he gave her an apologetic look.

"Do you know her?" she asked.

"Uh, yeah. I met her about six months ago. But I wasn't expecting to see her here."

"I think she hurt herself," Hannah said worriedly. "Maybe I should go check on her."

"I'll go," he said sharply.

Both women stared at him in shock while Raid scowled at him.

"Watch your tone," Raid warned, wrapping an arm around Hannah.

"Right. Sorry. Carlie, I'm really sorry—"

"Go. It's all right." Carlie smiled at him.

He felt rude, but he *had* to check on her.

"I'll be back soon." Turning, he rushed off out the back. Devon had already tidied up the glass and disappeared.

A sense of urgency filled Tanner. What if she disappeared on him again? What if she was badly hurt?

He heard some voices coming from farther down the hallway. A door was open, and he looked in to find Lilac standing at a sink, with fucking Devon standing next to her.

He was way too fucking close, and Tanner saw red. "Get away from her."

Both of them turned to look at him. Lilac's mouth dropped open as she gaped at him in shock.

Devon just folded his arms over his chest, glaring at him. "This is the staff area, Tanner. Last time I looked, you weren't on my payroll."

Tanner scowled. He didn't give a fuck if this was the President's private toilet; if Lilac was here so was he.

He strode over to her. "Let me see."

"T-tanner," she stuttered.

"Let. Me. See." He couldn't handle any bullshit right now.

"Obviously, the two of you know each other," Devon said. "But, Lilac, if he's making you uncomfortable, I will kick him out."

"No, you won't. Because she's mine," Tanner snapped.

Lilac sucked in a breath and Devon narrowed his gaze at him. "That's news to me. Seems like it might be news to her too. Lilac, are you Tanner's?"

"I . . . we met six months ago. Then I . . ."

"Disappeared without a word. Never even left me a message. Then you turn up in my town. I think that means you owe me an explanation."

Before she could answer, someone called out for Devon.

"Shit. I need to get out there. Lilac, want me to get rid of Tanner?"

Tanner growled at Devon. Fuck, he'd never made a noise like that in his life, but he was unable to help himself.

He wasn't going anywhere.

LILAC LOOKED from Devon to Tanner. Devon would actually kick out Tanner for her? She assumed they knew each other. And Devon barely knew her.

But he was prepared to do what was needed to protect her?

That never happened. The only people to ever protect her were her friends.

"I'm all right with him," she said quietly. "Tanner won't hurt me."

She hoped.

Devon seemed unsure but nodded. "There's a First-Aid kit under the bench. Make sure you get her cleaned up. And if I hear that you've been mean to her, I will not be happy."

She winced at Devon's words as he left.

What was she doing? Why had she told him that she'd be all right with Tanner?

Tanner was mad, upset, and he had every right to be.

She couldn't blame him for that. She knew that seeing him again would be hard. Why hadn't she gone through all the possible scenarios?

Instead, she'd buried her head in the sand and just thought she'd figure it out when it happened.

But seeing him with another woman tonight . . . it had nearly broken her. Watching him touch her . . . she hadn't been able to think, to act. Then the glass she'd just picked up had slipped from her hand and fell onto the floor.

She needed to offer to pay for that glass.

Lilac had known there was a chance he would have found someone else, but she guessed she'd been hoping that he might still want her.

You idiot.

You don't deserve him.

She knew that. Just as she'd figured that he would want an explanation about why she'd disappeared.

You have to tell him something.

What she hadn't expected was for him to chase her down like this.

"Show me your hand." Tanner's voice was low, quiet, but the command in it was clear.

She held her hand out to him; aware it was shaking. He took in a sharp breath.

"What were you thinking?" he demanded as he took hold of it, placing it under the tap before turning on the water.

Clearly, she hadn't been.

Lilac wasn't sure she'd been thinking all that well for a long, long time.

"It's fine," she whispered as the water cleared the blood away.

"No, it's not fine. It's bleeding. What were you doing picking up the glass like that? That was reckless. Have you got no sense of self-preservation?" he ranted as he let go of her hand to reach into the cupboard under the sink.

Lilac blinked at the words, barely able to comprehend them. He was angry over her cutting herself? She thought he was mad at her for leaving the way she had . . . then for reappearing without a word.

Well, she guessed he was likely angry about those things too. But why did he care that she had a small scratch on her hand?

"Let me find you a Band-Aid," he muttered, searching through the kit.

"It's just a scratch, though. It doesn't need one."

"Yeah, well, you're getting one. It's that or I call Doc."

"You can't call a doctor over a scratch!"

"Watch me," he growled. Finding some antiseptic, he gently put it on the cut, then placed a Band-Aid over it. "What's this red patch?"

"Oh, it's nothing," she dismissed.

"Looks like a burn."

"It was just from a coffee spill."

He muttered to himself as he grabbed out some burn cream and slathered it on. Actually, that did feel good.

"You need to keep that cut dry and watch it doesn't get infected," he ordered, putting the First-Aid kit away.

"It's a scratch." She knew she sounded like a broken record, but she couldn't stop saying it. No one had ever fussed over her like this before.

It was bizarre.

It felt like her mind just couldn't comprehend what was going on.

"You need to take care of it, or I will have you at the doctor's so fast that your head will spin," he told her.

"Why do you care?" she asked.

Crap.

He froze as she asked him that. She shouldn't have said it. What did she say now?

Was he going to get angry at her?

You deserve it.

"Just because I'm upset with you, doesn't mean that I want you hurt or suffering," he told her. He didn't look at her as he spoke. Instead, he gripped the bench tightly, staring at the wall. "I've spent the last six months wondering what happened to you. If you were harmed. Scared, sick, worried. Until I had to stop wondering. Until I started to forget about you."

Ouch.

She'd thought he'd yell at her. She hadn't been prepared for this.

"I ... I'm so sorry, Tanner."

"Why did you leave?"

"I ... I ..."

"Why, Lilac? You can tell me sorry until you're hoarse, but it means fucking nothing unless you tell me why. So why did you leave? Without an explanation? Without even a text message?"

"I . . . I . . ."

"I mean, I get that we didn't promise anything to each other, but to just fucking leave like that wasn't right. You stood me up. I didn't know where you were. I was concerned about you. Then, after a while, I realized that you obviously didn't have much respect for me if you could leave me without a word like that. And now that I'm asking for an explanation, you can't even give one. Yet, you've turned up in my town. Want to explain that? And don't tell me it was a fucking coincidence."

"It . . . it w-wasn't. I didn't mean to . . . I never wanted to hurt you, Tanner."

"Who said you hurt me?" he said coldly. "I mean, sure, in the beginning, I was worried about you. But it was a fling and once I put you out of my mind, well, I didn't think of you again. I moved on."

"With that girl out there?" Why was she still here having this conversation? Hurting herself? She knew he'd be upset with her. What she hadn't expected was that his anger would be cold.

That he would have completely put her out of his mind . . . that he no longer cared about her.

How arrogant were you to think he'd still care?

"Carlie has nothing to do with this conversation."

There was something in his voice? Protective? Did he think that she would try to come between them? To harm what they had together?

She wouldn't.

"Why are you here, Lilac? If you won't tell me why you left me like that, then you can damn well tell me the real reason why you're here. Did you come back here for me?"

He spun toward her. She reacted instinctively, fear filling her as she shied back, falling on her ass. But she didn't even feel the pain through the panic flooding her. She put her arm up to protect herself.

A whimper broke free as she waited for him to hit her, hurt her.

"Lilac?" His voice was a rough whisper. Filled with regret and pain.

But she couldn't deal with his feelings right now. She'd gotten her initial panic under control. Only now, she had to deal with the humiliation of what had just happened.

What was she going to do? Say?

"What the fuck is going on in here?" Devon demanded.

Oh God. Oh God.

Now her new boss was here to witness her complete humiliation.

"Lilac? Fuck. Did you think I was going to hit you? Baby, I would never hurt you."

"I . . . I don't know what you're talking about," she muttered. "I just tripped and fell. Excuse me, I've got to go back to work."

Pulling herself up, she slipped past him. She half-expected him to reach for her, to try and touch her. And she wasn't entirely sure how she'd react.

But he didn't.

And she wasn't sure whether that upset her more.

Lord. She was losing her mind. But she just couldn't deal with anything more.

She rushed past Devon, who didn't stop her either, and headed out to the bar. And nearly bowled someone over.

The person grabbed her, steadying her, and she looked up to see the woman that Tanner had been sitting with.

God. Of all the people, why did she have to crash into her?

"Hey, are you all right?" the other woman asked.

And nice too.

"I'm fine. I'm sorry. Are you all right? I didn't hurt you, did I?"

"Hardly. You're tiny." The other woman eyed her curiously. "I'm Carlie."

"Lilac," she said. "Sorry, I have to get back to work before I'm fired."

"Sure. I hope you're all right, Lilac."

"Of course. Why wouldn't I be?" What did she know? Had Tanner told her something about her?

"I meant your hand."

"Oh yes, it's fine. Thank you. Nice to meet you. See you soon." As she walked off, she winced.

Seriously!

Nice to meet you? See you soon? Could she have embarrassed herself anymore?

She decided the only thing she could do was throw herself back into work and try to forget about this entire disaster of a night.

Easier said than done.

∼

"What did you do to her?"

Tanner turned to look at Devon, who was glowering at him. "Nothing."

Yeah, nothing except act like a total asshole and scare her to death. He didn't care what she'd tried to say after. She'd been scared of him . . . she'd thought he would hit her.

Fuck. He shouldn't have said what he had. He'd been hurt over her leaving like that . . . he could admit that to himself even if he couldn't say it to her.

"That didn't look like nothing," Devon said in a low voice. "That looked like you terrified a woman who is already in a fragile state of mind."

Fragile? Lilac?

Was she close to breaking? She'd certainly looked that way just now . . . yeah, he thought she might be.

"She's lost so much weight." It was worrisome. Why would she have gotten so skinny? Was it on purpose? Had she been ill?

"I need to talk to her again."

"No." Devon blocked his path. "You're not. You're going to go collect your stuff and your fucking date and leave."

"You have no idea what you're talking about. I know Lilac. She's mine."

"She's not yours. If she was yours, then she wouldn't have been on the floor, staring up at you in utter fear."

"That . . . I didn't mean to scare her. I'm not sure what happened."

Devon sighed. "I know you're a good man, Tanner. But if you go after her right now all you're going to do is make her more skittish. I don't want her running."

Fuck. Neither did he.

Now he was going to worry about her running off again.

"Why do you care?" Tanner asked.

"Because it's obvious that Lilac hasn't had an easy life. I hired her on because she needed this. A job. Someone to give a shit about her. That's what I'm going to give her."

Tanner clenched his hands into fists, battling back his jealousy. "You want her?"

Devon sighed. "I can't do something nice for a woman without wanting her? I have to have an ulterior motive? You don't think much of me, do you?"

Great. He was being a complete ass all the way around.

"Fuck, sorry, man." Tanner ran his hand over his face. "It was just a shock seeing her. We didn't part ways under the best circumstances. She just left. Didn't message me, didn't answer her phone, and all this time I had no fucking idea whether she was dead or alive."

"I get that must have been awful. Not excusing what she did, but did you ever think she might have had a good reason?"

Had he?

Or had he figured that no reason would have been good enough?

"And did she actually promise you anything? Did you tell her how you felt about her?" Devon asked.

No. But it was unsaid. Or at least on his side, it was. He knew he'd just told her it'd been nothing more than a fling. But he'd been lying, since that certainly hadn't been true for him. Had it been for her, though?

"I worried about her . . . she ghosted me. I deserve an explanation."

"Maybe. But you don't need to terrify her to get it."

He'd done that, hadn't he?

Scared her.

Fuck. What was wrong with him?

"I'll go apologize."

"Like I told you, not now. Just . . . go get some air and sleep on it. She's had enough tonight. I don't know what she was like when you first met her, but she seems like she's close to the edge. And you don't want to be the one who pushes her."

Yeah. He nodded and walked out, aware of Devon walking behind him. When he entered the bar, his gaze instantly went to her. He couldn't help it. She was like a beacon pulling him in, tugging him home.

But he finally took the time to take stock of her.

Fragile.

Yeah . . . now that he could think clearly, he saw it.

So thin. Painfully so. Why? She'd been curvy and gorgeous before. Smiling. Happy.

Or was that what she wanted you to see? What if it was all an act?

How would he know? He was beginning to see that he hadn't known her at all.

"She's gorgeous."

He startled, staring down at Carlie, who had come up beside him.

Fuck.

"I'm two for two on the asshole charts tonight," he muttered.

"Are you?" She raised her eyebrows.

"I'm so fucking sorry, Carlie. I understand if you're completely pissed off with me for leaving you like that. It's just . . . I haven't seen her in six months. It was like seeing a ghost. But that's no excuse for being a dickhead."

"Don't be so hard on yourself, Tanner. Yeah, if this was a regular date, I'd be hurt. But we both agreed to do this to keep Raid and Hannah from nagging us." She winked at him.

He blew out a sigh of relief. "I don't deserve you being this good about it all, but thank you."

"What are you going to do? She seems like . . . like she's in trouble."

He ran his hand over his face. "You could sense that, huh?"

"You'd have to be blind not to see it."

Fucking hell.

She walked off after squeezing his arm.

Looking around, Tanner spotted Devon giving him a dirty look.

Fine. He was leaving.

But he wouldn't be going far.

14

"Come on, honey. Time to head home."

Lilac jolted awake. Shit. Had she fallen asleep? How had that happened?

She was still in the staff room at Dirty Delights. Devon had asked her to wait for a few minutes so he could drive her home.

Oops.

At the end of her first shift, Devon had insisted on walking her to her car. Instead of telling him she didn't have a car, she'd chosen one at random.

As they'd gotten closer, he'd beeped the locks.

Yeah . . . to her embarrassment she'd chosen his car.

So now he insisted on driving her home until she had her own mode of transport.

She felt terrible that he kept having to drive her home after every shift.

"Sorry I kept you waiting, honey," he apologized as they walked out to his car.

A chilly wind hit her. Soon, it would start getting colder and she didn't have the wardrobe to cope with cooler weather.

"You don't need to apologize, Devon," she said. "I feel awful that you're driving me around. You really don't have to. I'm fine walking home."

He opened her passenger door. He really was a gentleman.

"One thing you need to learn about living in Haven is that no man here is going to be comfortable with you walking around at night. If I don't take you home, anyone who sees you is going to offer you a ride. Or they're going to call Jake. Did you have a meeting with him yet?"

"Um, no."

He shut her door and walked around to the driver's side. His car was fancy, with leather, heated seats.

Ahh, heated seats. So deliciously decadent.

"You're going to have to."

"Because of that whole silly guardian thing?" she asked.

"It's not silly," he told her sternly.

Right. Maybe it wasn't, but it seemed awfully unrealistic. People just weren't this nice.

Mind you . . . everyone she'd met so far had been pretty nice. But surely there was an ulterior motive to it all. Opal had suggested that maybe the entire town was like a giant cult.

To be honest, it made the most sense.

Both she and Ryleigh had warned Opal not to say that out loud anywhere that anyone in this town could hear her.

With Opal, it was a fifty-fifty chance of whether she'd listen to them.

"Linc will probably act as your guardian if you ask him, since you're staying in his guesthouse."

"I can't ask Linc to do anything more for us."

"Us?" Devon asked.

Shit. Had she not mentioned the others?

"I've been traveling around with my friends."

"You didn't say anything about them," Devon said.

"I must have forgotten. Thanks, Devon," she said as he pulled up outside Linc's. She undid her seatbelt.

"Before you go, there's something I want to talk to you about."

She tensed. Great. Was he going to tell her that she couldn't work there anymore? Shit. That would be a blow. Still, she'd get it after everything that had happened during tonight's shift.

"I'm sorry about tonight. I won't break anything else. I just got a shock, seeing Tanner—"

"Hey, you're not in trouble."

"I'm not?" She was jittery with nerves. Her heart felt like it was beating too hard.

"No. Of course not. I just wanted to let you know that if Tanner is upsetting or bothering you, you can let me know. I'll ban him from the bar if I have to."

She sucked in a breath. "You'd do that?"

"You work for me now, Lilac. I take care of my own."

"But you barely know me. And I'm guessing Tanner is a good customer so isn't he one of your own?"

"Nope. All of my staff are like my family. I protect them. So, you will let me know, yeah?"

"Yes, thanks, Devon."

He grunted. "For what it's worth, the Malones are all good men. Just fucking crazy. Particularly, the younger ones. Get some sleep, honey."

"Thanks. Night."

∼

W HY WAS she spending so much time in his car?

And why was Devon driving her home?

Tanner stood in the shadows of a tree as he watched them. He'd parked his truck a few blocks back when he'd seen Devon's car stop and jogged the rest of the way, not wanting them to know he was watching. But he was starting to get pissed off.

Had Devon warned him off because he wanted Lilac for himself?

He couldn't see what they were doing. Why had they stopped outside Linc's house?

Stepping forward as Devon's car sped off, Tanner followed her around the back of Linc's house to his guest house. He'd been to Linc's a few times. He was a good guy. But Tanner didn't like that Lilac was staying in his guest house.

He found a spot to stand in, ignoring how cold it was getting. It was after one in the morning, and she was just getting home.

He didn't like that either.

Fuck. What was wrong with him? He'd he become some sort of stalker. He needed to go home. She wasn't running. Hell, it seemed like she didn't even have a vehicle.

None of this was adding up.

Maybe he should pay Linc a visit.

Or perhaps you should just leave since this isn't any of your business.

Tanner turned to leave when an unexpected noise had him stilling.

Was that a baby crying? He looked over at the guest house. A soft light turned on in the living area and he saw her walk in front of a window. It had to be slightly open because he heard that cry again coming from the bundle of blankets she held against her chest.

Was that a fucking baby?

His stomach dropped as he did the math. No. No, there was no way it could be his. But that meant that she had to have been pregnant when she was with him.

Why the fuck hadn't she told him? How hadn't he noticed? Then again, she might not have been showing.

He just . . . he didn't understand this.

Was the baby the reason she'd run? Had she been worried that he'd notice? Or was there some other reason?

Then the crying stopped and the light turned off.

Wait. Who had been looking after the baby while she was out? Had she left it alone?

Fuck. He had too many questions and not enough answers.

But he was going to get them.

15

"A baby?" Raid repeated. "What the fuck?"

"I know." Tanner leaned an elbow on the table in Raid and Hannah's kitchen.

He'd stayed here last night, not wanting to drive back to the Ranch. Besides, the bunk house was kind of quiet and lonely now that all of his brothers had moved out. It was just him. Sure, Alec and Mia were close by in the big house. And Flick and West weren't far away. Neither were the others, really. Only Raid and Hannah had moved into Haven.

But he'd always been closest to Raid. And Alec.

"Fuck, it can't be yours, right?" Raid asked.

"No, but she must have been pregnant when I met her."

"She didn't look it."

"But neither did Flick until she was further along, right? I just can't believe I didn't know . . . that she didn't tell me." He felt sick. "And what is she doing working nights and leaving the baby home?"

"She must have had someone watching the baby. She's really in Linc's guest house? How does he know her?"

"I dunno. But I'm going to find out."

"Are you sure you want to do that?" Raid asked.

He frowned. "Why wouldn't I?"

"Because she fucking ghosted you, man. You were upset for ages about it."

"I wasn't upset."

"You were. You cried like a baby each night. Moped around like a dog without a bone."

"I did not, you asshole!" Tanner grabbed Raid in a headlock right as Hannah walked in.

She shook her head at them. "Do not break any of my furniture."

"No, ma'am!" Tanner winked at her.

"Or my man," she added.

"He can't break me, I'll break him." Raid elbowed Tanner. Hard.

"Ouch, fucker," he muttered as he let him go.

Raid moved to Hannah and took her face in his hands, kissing her deeply.

When he drew back, Hannah was staring up at him with a dreamy look on her face.

Tanner wanted that.

Fuck. What? No, he didn't, right?

He didn't need a relationship.

No? Then why the hell are you back to being obsessed with Lilac?

It was only that he wanted an explanation.

"Sorry the date didn't work out last night, Tanner," Hannah said sweetly.

"Nothing for you to apologize for, darlin'," he told her. "We just make better friends."

"So, you going to tell me about the girl in the bar?" Hannah asked.

"I met her six months ago in Hopesville," Tanner told her.

"We spent some time together and then she just left without a word."

"What? Not even a text?" Hannah asked, looking shocked.

"No, I was supposed to meet her that last night, but she never turned up. Never answered my calls or texts."

"That's so rude! And then she just turns up where you live? That's a weird coincidence." Hannah frowned.

"Or not a coincidence at all," Raid said.

"You think she came back for you?" Hannah asked Tanner. "Maybe to apologize?"

"No." He shook his head, thinking it over. "I don't think that's it. I told her about Haven, so I don't see how it can be a coincidence that she's here. And if she came to apologize, she'd have searched me out immediately, right? She has my number. Why not just text? Why get a job here?"

Hannah frowned. "That's true. Do you know where she's staying?"

"Linc's guesthouse," Raid said. "And she has a baby."

"What?" Hannah gave Tanner a shocked look.

"Not mine," he said quickly.

"Linc's?" Raid guessed. "Since she's staying with him?"

He frowned at that idea. But no . . . Linc wouldn't have his baby in the guesthouse.

"No. I don't think so. I don't know how he fits into this."

"But you're going to find out," Raid said.

"Yeah, but I don't think she'll be receptive to telling me," Tanner said as he poured himself another coffee.

"Well, why not?" Hannah demanded. "She owes you."

"Because she's scared of me."

"Why would she fear you?" Raid asked.

Because he'd been a bit of a dick. But he'd thought he was going to marry that girl . . . and then she'd left him.

"I don't know . . . but perhaps I should give her some time to get settled."

But what if she left again?

Fuck. He didn't know what to do.

"I'm gonna head to the Ranch," he said. "Thanks for the coffee and for letting me crash last night. I'll see you later."

He needed some time to think about this.

~

"You know, Tanner is a good man. And he doesn't deserve you treating him this way."

Lilac jolted, dropping the packet of cold medicine. She turned to look at the woman speaking to her. She looked familiar.

Then she realized she'd been with Tanner at Dirty Delights the other night. Not the woman he'd been with, the one sitting with Raid.

Just then, the other woman raised her hand and Lilac spotted a large rock on her ring finger.

Raid's fiancée?

"I know he is," she replied quietly, bending down to pick up the cold medicine.

Ryleigh wasn't feeling well, which was worrying. Because when Ryleigh got ill, she usually got *really* ill.

At least they had a warm, dry place to stay thanks to Linc. He'd been working night shifts, so they hadn't seen him much. Which Lilac was kind of relieved about. She didn't need him asking too many questions.

She'd really thought that Tanner would turn up at Dirty Delights last night. When he didn't appear, she'd had to battle with her disappointment and relief.

Maybe he really had thought of her as a brief fling. It was better that way, right?

It wasn't like she'd come here for him . . . to rekindle things with him. All she was here to do was to find a safe place for her friends. For Kye.

Then she was going to take care of Stefan.

"Then why did you ghost him?" the woman asked.

Wow. Okay. This wasn't what she'd expected. She pushed back a wave of fatigue. They'd sequestered Ryleigh in one bedroom, then Opal and Kye had the other bedroom while she was on the sofa. Opal looked after Kye while she was working, then when Lilac got home, she took over.

Which would generally be fine since Kye was a good sleeper. But these last few nights, he'd been really unsettled. It could be because he missed Ryleigh. Or just a stage. Or it could be that he was feeling under the weather too.

Please don't let him get sick.

She didn't know if there was anything you could do if a one-month-old baby got ill. She'd have to ask the pharmacist.

"Look, I get that you're just trying to look out for Tanner, and I'm glad he's got good friends and family. However, it's none of your business," she told her.

The other woman stared at her in shock as if she hadn't expected Lilac to tell her to butt out.

God. She just wanted to sleep. But even if Kye was doing okay, sleep was hard for her to come by.

Maybe it would help if you ate something.

Shut up, brain.

"You need to tell him why you ran off. And why you're here. It's not fair to leave him wondering. Why *are* you here?"

"Wow, you're nosy, huh?" Opal asked as she walked up, carrying Kye.

Shit. This was just what this situation needed.

The other woman blinked at Opal. Today, she was wearing thigh-high boots with a pair of daisy dukes and a tight corset-like top.

"Who're you? And why are you giving my best friend here the shake-up?" Opal asked.

"Shake-up?" the other woman said.

"She means shake-down," Lilac explained. "This is my friend, Opal. And this is . . ."

"I'm Hannah."

"Well, Hannah, if you don't mind, we got some shopping to do. This place is fucking stocked, considering we're in small-town Texas, huh?" Opal said loudly. "This town is too cute. Did you know they even have a sex toy shop?"

Lilac sighed as everyone in the pharmacy turned to look at them in shock. Reaching over, she took Kye from Opal, pressing him against her chest. She kissed the top of his head, then glanced up to see Hannah staring at Kye softly.

"You should have told him," Hannah said. "He's a good guy. If you were in trouble, he could've helped you."

Turning, she left.

"Well, she's lots of fun, huh?" Opal said.

"I'm going to grab this stuff. Can you go to the grocery store?" She needed another job.

"You bet, sugar. Damn, there's some real eye candy around this place." Opal eyed an older man who was walking down the aisle.

He gave her an admiring look back.

Lilac had to smile. There was no one quite like Opal.

∽

LILAC MOVED THROUGH DIRTY DELIGHTS, fatigue making every movement hard.

She could do this. Tomorrow was Sunday and she had the day off. Perhaps she'd see if she could find a second job.

"Lilac, sit down," Devon ordered.

"I'm fine. I've got another order to take out."

"Sit. Down."

Her eyes widened at the stern words, and without thought, she took a seat on a bar stool next to Jeremy, who sent her a smile. Jeremy was a regular customer who was here every night the bar was open. Which kind of made her sad. She wondered about his home life, but he never seemed down or upset. He always had a smile for her and the other girls.

"Hey, girlie."

"Hey, Jeremy," she said.

"You look like you've got the weight of the world on your shoulders."

"I'm fine. I didn't need a break," she complained to Devon, who just gave her a stern look back.

"If you don't take your breaks, then you'll get tired and make mistakes. This is for me, not you."

Uh-huh.

Devon disappeared out the back and returned with fish bites sitting on a bowl of fries and some mayo and ketchup. Damn, that smelled good. They didn't offer meals at Dirty Delights, but they did have bar snacks.

Devon placed the bowl of food in front of her. She frowned. "Oh, you want me to deliver this? Where is it going?"

"It's for you," he replied.

She couldn't afford this and they didn't get food with their wages.

"I'm fine. Thank you, though."

"Eat the food, Lilac," Devon said sternly.

"I didn't order it, though."

"But you're eating it before you go back to work." Devon disappeared down the other end of the bar.

How rude.

Who did he think he was?

"Better do as he says, Lilac," Jeremy advised. "Devon's got a real stubborn streak, and he means what he says."

She sighed and pushed the bowl toward him. "Want some?"

"I'm not eating until you do."

She picked up a fry and forced it down. Her stomach grumbled. When was the last time she'd eaten? Shit. She couldn't even remember. Her hand was shaking; in fact, she felt incredibly weak. Fuck. Maybe she should eat something.

After a few bites, though, she was feeling uncomfortably full.

"I've eaten. I'm heading back to work."

Devon frowned, taking in how little she'd eaten, but he nodded.

Getting up, a wave of dizziness hit her, but she ignored it. She had to keep moving forward.

There was no going back.

16

Shit, it was busy tonight. Far busier than last weekend. Apparently, there was a stock sale on in the next town over and people had spilled over to Haven.

Which wouldn't be so bad, except it seemed like a lot of the locals had been scared away. And she was left dealing with people that weren't as nice.

Lilac had been working here for a week and a half and she still felt like she was waiting for the other shoe to drop. For people to show her that they weren't as nice as they appeared. That they didn't look out for each other.

People weren't like this anywhere else. Even the sheriff, who had come to talk to them the other day, seemed like a good guy.

Although his talk of needing to have a guardian was unwelcome. He'd given them another week to think it all through. But what was there to think about? She didn't need anyone telling her what to do. Not even Linc, who'd offered to act as their guardian.

No, thanks.

A wave of fatigue hit her as she delivered a tray of drinks to a table full of rowdy guys.

God, she hoped she wasn't getting whatever Ryleigh had. She was still feeling unwell.

Well, you can't get sick, so just push through it.

She couldn't afford time off. Yesterday, she'd received the bill for Sugar, and she'd nearly cried. It was far more than they could afford, and she didn't know what they were going to do.

At least she started her first shift at the diner tomorrow. She'd already done some training.

"Hey, sweetie, get us another round, will you?" A middle-aged guy called out from another table as she moved past. He had a potbelly and sweat patches under his arms.

"I'll let your waitress know," she said. They were in Lemon's section.

He scowled. "No, I want you to fucking get them, understand?" Reaching out, he grabbed her wrist and squeezed it. Hard.

Lilac's heart started racing as her stomach rolled nauseously.

Do as you're told, Lilac.

You're just a stupid, ugly bitch.

Her breath heaved in and out of her lungs.

Shit. Fuck.

"Hey! You paying attention? Silly bitch!" The hold on her wrist tightened and she was drawn closer to the disgusting man as his hand came up to grope her ass.

Fight back.

Do something!

Fuck. How could she expect to take Stefan on if she couldn't even defend herself from this asshole?

"What the fuck? Get your hand off her!"

Tanner appeared and she was released so suddenly that she stumbled back, falling on her ass.

What was happening? Where had Tanner come from? She hadn't seen him since that night she'd broken the glass.

Tanner had the guy up out of his seat and was shaking him. "Don't you fucking touch her!" he roared.

She gaped up at him. Her heart was still racing, and she couldn't move.

Fear had her frozen in place.

Then, all the guys at the table stood. There were several of them. Tanner couldn't take them all on!

Scrambling to her feet, she curled her hands into fists as she moved to back him up.

"Let go of me, motherfucker!" the guy who'd groped her demanded.

Glancing around, she didn't see any friendly faces. In the distance, she could see Devon and Carlisle, the bouncer, dealing with another issue.

"Don't touch what doesn't belong to you," Tanner snarled.

"I'll touch whatever I like." One of the other guys swung his fist toward Tanner and she threw herself at him, taking both of them to the floor. She lay there, feeling a bit winded.

Someone let out a roar filled with fury, and it shocked her to realize it was Tanner.

The place erupted into a fight. More people joined in, and she couldn't tell whose side they were on until she saw Raid punch the guy she'd tackled. Someone kicked her, hitting her right in the side.

Ouch.

She needed to get off the floor.

Someone grabbed her, lifting her up into their arms. She tried to fight them, even as pain made her cry out.

"Easy, darlin'," a voice soothed. "I'm just getting you out of the way before you get hurt."

She glanced up into an attractive-looking man's face. He

grinned down at her. "Come on, let's get you out of here. If someone punches my pretty face, then my Snow is gonna be super angry. I won't be allowed out of the house for a week."

"Who . . . who are you?" she asked as he carried her to the bar. And who was his Snow? She saw Lemon and Cherie huddled back there with Jeremy standing over them.

"Name's Beau Malone. Guessing you know my brother, Tanner."

"Oh, you're a Malone?"

"Darlin', you say that with such enthusiasm." He winked at her as he set her down behind the bar. "Now, stay here with Jeremy until Tanner comes and gets you."

"I'm not . . . Tanner and I aren't anything."

"Uh-huh. Well, anyway. Stay."

This guy was unbelievable. But then he stepped away.

"Wait, where are you going?"

"Why, to back up my brothers, of course." He grinned.

"I thought you couldn't let anything happen to your pretty face."

"Aww, you think I'm pretty? I'm flattered, but I have a wife. I share her with my brother, but I don't think she's looking for a sister-wife."

"That's not . . . you called yourself pretty!"

"Stop flattering me," he yelled back. "I've got to go fight."

He was insane. She watched as he let out a whoop, then forced his way into the fight with a grin.

"Don't worry, the Malones can take care of themselves," Cherie told her, taking hold of her wrist to tug her down.

She winced, hissing in pain.

"Shit! I'm sorry. Oh God, look at your wrist!" Cherie said in horror.

"It's fine." She glanced down at her wrist which was already swollen.

But Lilac had experience with ignoring pain. What she couldn't do was ignore the fight happening around her.

This was all her fault.

She should have just gotten the damn drinks. If she hadn't frozen like that...

Fuck.

She was going to get fired, and then how would she pay the bill for Sugar? How would she buy medicine for Ryleigh? And the stuff that Kye needed? Or food?

And what about Tanner? He'd come to her rescue when he hated her. What if he got hurt because of her? She'd never forgive herself.

Getting to her feet, she attempted to stumble to the end of the bar. But Jeremy got in her way as Cherie reached for her.

"What are you doing, Lilac?" Cherie demanded.

"I have to make sure Tanner is all right. He could get hurt, and it will be my fault."

"It's not your fault, girl. Tanner will be fine. Been in more bar fights than you've had birthdays. Don't you worry about him," Jeremy told her.

Sounds of sirens filled the air.

"Oh, thank God," Cherie muttered as she tugged her back.

Soon, several deputies entered Dirty Delights. People started to clear out and Devon slid behind the bar, his eyes moving over the three of them worriedly.

"Fuck. You're all okay?"

Cherie and Lemon both nodded, standing with her. They all took in the destruction of the bar. She put her hand over her mouth in horror.

"Oh God, Devon. I'm so sorry."

"Nothing for you to be sorry about, honey," Devon replied, sounding tired. "Are you all right? Someone said that you were in the middle of it all."

"There is something for me to be sorry for," she replied, taking in everything. "This is all my fault."

"Doubt that, honey."

"It is. That table of guys . . . one of them called me over, wanting me to get drinks for them. I said I'd tell their server, but he got mad and grabbed me."

"He what?" Devon growled.

She failed to notice the anger in his voice. Instead, she moved out from behind the bar, stepping around broken chairs.

"And when I froze, he got angry and pulled me toward him. That's when Tanner appeared. I fell as he let me go, and then one of the other men at the table tried to punch Tanner. I shoved him to stop him and we landed on the floor."

"Then what happened?" Jake asked.

She startled. When had he entered the bar?

"Where's Tanner?" she asked urgently. "Is he all right?"

"He's been taken to the station for questioning," Jake told her grimly. "I'd like you to come as well."

"Questioning? No, no, no, I can't." She shook her head, wincing as it throbbed. Nausea bubbled. Shit, she was going to be sick. "I can't."

"Okay, it's all right. We can just talk here," Jake soothed.

"I can't have my name on anything." Crap! She was revealing too much.

Jake eyed her for a long moment. "Then your name will be left off. Just tell me what happened."

"You . . . you promise?" She shouldn't trust anyone. She knew that. But if she didn't tell him what happened, then would Tanner be arrested? What about his brothers?

"I do. I want you to sit down and tell me what happened."

Taking a seat in the chair that Devon found for her, she went over everything that happened for Jake.

"Right," Devon said. "You need to get checked over. Linc is helping deal with all of this, so he can't take you to the hospital."

"I can," Devon told them.

"I don't need the hospital," she protested.

"Your wrist looks swollen," Jake said. "And you might have a broken rib."

"I don't. I'm fine. Honestly. I've had far worse."

She saw Jake and Devon share a look. Fuck, she had to stop oversharing.

"I'm good. Just . . . you're not arresting Tanner, are you? He was only helping me."

"Tanner Malone is a big boy. He can take care of himself. You are the one who needs looking after right now," Jake told her.

See?

These people were so weird. They didn't really know her. So why would they care?

"I'm not going to the hospital," she said firmly. "I can't."

"I'll call Doc and see if he can come out," Devon said.

She opened her mouth to protest, but they both shot her looks.

"It's this or the hospital," Jake told her firmly.

"But Doc will do it off the records," Devon added.

Great, just what she needed. To spend more money that she didn't have. But she knew they wouldn't to listen to her, so she nodded.

17

Tanner looked up as the door to the interrogation room opened and Jake stepped in.

"Fuck. Finally. Am I free to go?"

"We interviewed some witnesses. They all said that you grabbed that guy, Tanner."

"Because he touched my girl."

"Your girl?" Jake sat across from him. "She said nothing about being yours."

He ran his hand over his face. "Fuck. Fine. She's not mine. But I know Lilac. We met six months ago. I'm not going to stand by while some asshole puts his hands on her. Fuck. I wouldn't do that for any woman in Haven. I can't believe you'd expect me to."

"Of course I wouldn't. But I also don't need you to escalate the situation. That was a full-on bar brawl. The two Docs had to get out of bed to come and patch people up. Do you know how fucking mad Curt is that I got Jenna up at one in the morning?"

"Is Lilac okay?" Worry filled him. He'd been so angry seeing that asshole touch her that he hadn't seen anything but him.

"She got checked over and went home."

Relief flooded him. Thank fuck.

"My brothers?" he asked.

"They're waiting for you. Listen, I'm not charging you since that guy grabbed Lilac and you defended her. But you need to get yourself under control. Throwing punches and getting mad isn't always the best way to deal with things."

He wanted to tell Jake where to stick his advice. What did he know about shit? But the truth was, he kind of had a point. Tanner had spent most of his life doing whatever he wanted. Shoot out the tires of a car on his property, sure. Get banned from most of the bars in the county, yep.

But this time, he actually wondered if he'd made the right choice in his actions because . . . what if something had happened to her while he was busy fighting?

Thank fuck she was all right.

Walking into the main area, he saw Raid and Beau waiting on him.

Beau grinned when he saw him. "Aww, I told Jake he should just lock you up and throw away the key. But then he threatened to lock me up if I didn't shut up. Not that I wouldn't do well in jail. Everyone would love me."

Tanner just scowled at him as they walked out. "Love you? Do you want criminals to love you?"

"Why not? Criminals are people too, Tanner."

"Come on, I need to get home. You staying with us tonight?" Raid asked them both.

"I better go home before Scarlett hears about tonight. Is your girl okay?" Beau asked.

"My girl?"

"Don't play coy with me. The girl you just defended in there? She was about to get trampled on when I got to her."

"What?" Tanner felt ill. "Jake said she got checked over and went home."

"Must be all right, then. She looked a bit pale and frightened when I picked her up and carried her away. She seemed like she'd hurt her side."

"Fuck!" She had? "I need to go make sure she's all right." He'd go there right now. Maybe he should take her home with him. Make sure she was properly looked after.

Yep. That was the best idea.

But as he stormed off, Raid wrapped an arm around him.

"Let me go."

"You need to stop," Raid warned.

"Let. Me. Go."

Beau moved in front of him. "You can't go to her now, Tanner."

"Why the fuck not?"

"Because she's likely asleep, asshole. You want to go terrifying her?" Raid snarled.

No. Of course he didn't. "But I need to know that she's all right. She could be alone and hurting."

"Hannah saw her with a woman the other day," Raid told him.

She had? Who was she?

"She seemed fine, just a bit shaken," Beau told him. "She'll still be there in the morning. But you go there now, and you'll scare her."

Fuck. They were right.

But in the morning, he was going to check on her.

∼

"WHAT DO YOU MEAN, she's not here?" Tanner's heart skipped a beat. Had she left? Where had she gone?

How was he going to find her?

"I mean, she's not here." The woman in front of him had her

hair teased up so much it almost stood on end. She was in a pair of silky pajamas that clung to her generous curves. Was she a friend of Lilac's? "She's at the diner."

Lilac must have gone to get breakfast. He heard a baby cry in the background and the woman at the door turned away. "I've got to go."

The door slammed shut in his face before he could ask any more questions.

Frustration filled him, but he knew he had to talk to Lilac.

Turning away, he stormed down the path to head around the main house. Linc had a large house with a wraparound porch. He didn't know how the deputy could afford a place like this on his salary, but it wasn't his business.

Except for the fact that he was helping Lilac. Why? Linc was a nice guy, but to put up two strange women and a baby in his guesthouse? That seemed . . . odd.

"Tanner." Linc walked out of his house onto the back porch. "Didn't expect you here this morning. You here about last night?"

"Sort of. Did you really have to cuff me?"

"Just doing my job. Why're you here then?" Linc asked.

"Really? That's all you've got for me? No, sorry for being a dick and arresting you?"

Linc sighed. "You didn't get processed. From what Jake said, some asshole grabbed Lilac and you waded in to help her."

"How do you know her?" he demanded.

"Lilac?"

"Yeah. Why is she staying in your guest house?" Tanner asked.

"Don't think that's any of your business."

"That's where you're wrong," Tanner replied. "Lilac is my business. Or she's going to be my business."

He'd done some thinking last night. And while he understood Raid and Beau's reasoning when they'd told him to pull back and put some distance between them . . . he'd decided it was bullshit.

He'd thought about her for months.

Grown bitter over what happened.

Would he have done that if he hadn't cared? Nope. If she'd never meant anything to him, then he'd have quickly forgotten about her. He'd planned to marry her. And he figured the fact that she had turned up in his town was a sign.

That he was supposed to have her.

So, he didn't care who got in his way nor her reasons for ghosting him. The simple fact was, if he had to lock her up in the bunkhouse to keep her, he would.

Or even put a tracker on her . . . yep, he liked that idea.

He wasn't letting her go. And he wasn't stepping aside so Linc or Devon or any other prick interested in her could have her.

"You can't just declare someone is yours. They have to agree."

"Don't see why."

"Free will?"

He snorted. "She wants me."

"So many red flags," Linc muttered. "You know I'm sworn to protect the people in this town, right?"

Tanner folded his arms over his chest. "Yeah. I'm one of them. Remember?"

"You can protect yourself."

Damn right, he could.

"You don't need to protect Lilac from me," he said, knowing where Linc was going with this.

"I better not, Tanner. Because, believe me, I'll pick her over you. Not because I don't like you, but because she needs help. You have a whole fucking huge family behind you. As far as I can tell, those women have nothing." He nodded over to the guesthouse. "Nothing but the clothes on their backs and a shitty RV that's probably going to cost more than it's worth to fix. So, you give her any grief and I will protect her. That's my job as her guardian."

"You are not her guardian."

Linc was right, though. She needed someone to protect her.

Him.

"Not yet," Linc replied. "But she's living on my property. I put a roof over her head. She knows it's Jake or me, and she trusts me more. So, guess who it is going to be."

Linc knew just how to push his buttons.

If it wasn't for the fact that he did not have time to spend in fucking jail, he'd lay him out flat.

"I'm the only person who is going to be her guardian," he said through gritted teeth.

Linc narrowed his gaze. "We'll see. But if I ask her and she tells me that you're annoying her or trying to push her into something she doesn't want, I won't be happy. Nor will I allow that to happen."

Fuck. He was furious at Linc. Yet, at the same time, he knew that the other man was just trying to look out for Lilac. And it sounded like she had little of that.

Which made him wonder what her life had been like up until now.

"I won't pressure her into anything. I'm not an asshole. But I . . . I want her, and I'm gonna make that clear. She ran from me before, but I'm not gonna let that happen again. I can't."

Linc eyed him for a long moment. "As long as she gives consent, I'll back you. You're a good guy. Crazy and wild, but I know you'd look after her. After them."

"I would. Her and the baby."

Linc gave him a strange look.

"Where did you meet them? Why are they staying here with you?"

"Probably something for her to tell you."

"Why do people keep saying that," he muttered. "No one wants to give me a straight answer."

"Guess you'll have to discover the answers yourself. If Lilac is willing to share, that is."

"You said they had an RV that needed fixing. Where is it? With Matt?" he asked.

"Yep. And that's all I'm going to say. I'm going to go check on them."

"Lilac's not there."

"That's okay." Linc whistled as he walked away.

Huh. Perhaps he was into the one with all the hair. That would certainly make things easier for Tanner.

18

Breathe through the pain.
Don't let it get the best of you.

Last night, an older doctor with kind eyes had checked her over. He'd wanted her to get an x-ray of her side, but she'd assured him that she knew what a broken rib felt like and that it was only bruised.

Doc had given her a horrified look that she'd pretended not to see. She didn't want to answer questions about how she knew what a broken rib felt like.

But the painkillers she'd taken before her shift this morning were wearing off. Her head was thumping, her wrist ached, and every time she moved, her side let her know that it wasn't impressed.

But while she'd thought that she could get through anything, could push aside any pain, she had never worked a full-on shift at a diner after suffering a blow to the ribs, as well as a bruised and swollen wrist.

Thankfully, she'd managed to leave this morning before

Opal or Ryleigh woke up and saw her. She just hoped they didn't go out today and hear about the brawl.

Well, Ryleigh wouldn't be. She still wasn't feeling well.

Worry filled Lilac. Ryleigh didn't have the best constitution. She often got bronchitis during winter. But it wasn't winter. Surely, she'd feel better soon. Right?

The door dinged as someone entered, and she forced herself to move to the front of the diner to direct them to a seat. Well, there weren't any tables or booths left. So, hopefully, they were okay sitting at the bar. Most of the locals didn't mind, but there were still a few people here for the stock sale who'd gotten huffy when they'd seen how packed the place was.

She froze as she saw who was standing there, staring at her.

He grew tense as his gaze ran over her body. She wore dark yoga pants and a long-sleeved white top with the diner's name on the back. A small apron was around her middle. She'd covered up her wrist as much as she could with the sleeves.

"What the fuck do you think you're doing?" he boomed.

Everyone stopped talking. And she meant everyone.

Instant. Silence.

She could feel her cheeks growing heated as she looked around.

Peggy walked over from out the back. "I don't want no trouble, Tanner Malone. This isn't Dirty Delights."

"That's the asshole that attacked Ronny last night." A guy stood up from a booth.

Oh. Shit.

She hadn't recognized him from last night, but perhaps he'd been there. Or just heard about it.

Either way, she tensed.

"He touched a woman without her permission. Hurt her. You got a problem with me dealing with him? Do you like to touch and hurt women too?" Tanner asked the guy.

The other guy started to bluster, his face growing red and then purple as people glared at him. Finally, his friends pulled him back into his seat. By this time, her heart was racing, and she couldn't seem to catch her breath.

"Lilac? Lilac, breathe, baby."

She jumped as she realized that Tanner was somehow standing right in front of her. How had he gotten there so fast? She tried to step back, but he placed his hands on her hips, keeping her still.

"L-let me go," she whispered, aware that people were still too quiet. They were watching them . . . waiting for a show.

Well, she was tired of being a fucking spectacle.

"Never," he said in a low voice.

She jolted at that word. It was said calmly, but in a voice that brooked no hesitation. There was weight to that word that shouldn't be there.

Because he had no right to her. No right to think he could hold onto her.

"Let me go. I'm working."

"You don't work here." His gaze was narrowed.

"Yes, I do."

What the hell? Why did he think he got to tell her anything about her life? She was the one living it.

"You work at Dirty Delights. Or are you giving that up?"

"It's not any of your business, Tanner." She attempted to move away again, shocked when he let her.

But even more stunned that she felt disappointed. What was wrong with her? She didn't want him to touch her. Didn't want him near her.

Liar.

"It will be," he said as she turned away. "You're going to be my business, Lilac."

Fuck.

She was trembling as she headed to the counter to pick up an order. She tried not to look over at him, to see those broad shoulders as he sat at the bar, greeting everybody who spoke to him.

Everyone seemed to know him. And like him.

Well, except for the people sitting in the booth of the guy who'd spoken out earlier. And their meals had just come up. Great.

She walked over with their food. The guy who had spoken up sneered at her. "When you want a real man, doll, you come to us. Not to that little cunt."

She dropped their plates on the table and glared at the asshole. "A real man? Really? Well, where is one? Because I certainly don't see one sitting at this table. All I see is a bunch of little boys with equally small appendages."

As the asshole stood up, an arm suddenly wrapped around her from behind. "Get behind me, baby. Now." He shoved her behind him, making her wince as pain shot up her side.

"Right. That's it. All of you are leaving." Peggy walked up and glared at the men in the booth.

Great. She'd just gotten this job. And now she was probably getting fired. Why did this keep happening to her? What was wrong with her?

Or maybe it's not you. It's him. This is all Tanner's fault.

With that thought in mind, she pinched his side while the guys at the booth all complained. Loudly.

But Peggy was standing firm, so they started shuffling out. Tanner turned to give them his back while he crowded her out of the way. One of the guys stopped and she saw him raise his arm. With a scream, she shoved Tanner, making him stumble in surprise and the guy's fist missed where he'd been aiming— likely at Tanner's kidney.

Tanner turned, but a couple of other guys got up from their

tables and hustled the asshole out. Tanner glared after them, clearly angry, his hands in fists.

She should have been scared of him. She'd grown up with a man who'd gotten angry at the drop of a hat. And who had enjoyed turning that anger on other people, blaming them, hurting them.

"Hey, Lilac. It's all right. They're gone. They won't hurt you." Putting his arm around her, he led her out the back.

"You shouldn't be here. This is staff only."

"Peggy won't care that I'm here. She won't kick me out."

"Maybe not." It was obvious that he was well-liked. "But she might fire me. Hell, there's no might about it. After all the issues I've just caused, I'm definitely getting fired." She placed her hand over her chest as she heaved for breath.

"Whoa. Take a deep breath for me. Come on, baby. Just breathe."

"I can't . . . I can't do this anymore. I don't know how to do this anymore."

"Do what, baby?"

She shook her head. She couldn't be taken in by his sweet tone, by him calling her baby. He didn't want her . . . definitely wouldn't want her if he knew it all.

Her life was a complete and utter clusterfuck.

"I'm going to get fired . . . I . . . I need this job."

"Hey, no one is firing you. Come on." He took her hand and placed it on his chest. "Breathe in. Then out. Follow me. In, one, two. Hold, one, two. Out, one, two. That's it. I want you to do it again."

The dominance in his tone cut through her panic. It lent her strength and she found herself following his words until the panic started to fade away.

She could barely keep herself up anymore though. How long could a person go without proper sleep and food?

Had she finally found the limit of her endurance?

Tanner drew her over to a bench and sat her down. He crouched in front of her, placing his warm hands on her thighs.

"Did you take this job because of last night? Are you quitting Dirty Delights? I think that's smart. It's safer to work here."

"I'm still working there," she muttered without thinking. She had to get back out into the diner. She wasn't scheduled for a break yet.

"Wait. You've got two jobs?" He was staring at her like that was the weirdest thing he'd ever heard.

"Yes. Why? A lot of people have two jobs."

"Yes . . . but . . . you're clearly already exhausted. You've got dark marks under your eyes. You're pale. You can't keep pushing yourself like this or you're going to collapse."

It wasn't anything that she hadn't already thought. But she wasn't letting herself linger on those thoughts. Because then she'd start to believe them.

And she couldn't afford to do that. She had to keep pushing forward.

"I'm fine." She attempted to stand, but he refused to move. "Tanner, get out of my way."

"I'm not moving until you tell me what the fuck is going on. Why are you so thin? Why are you working two jobs? You can't tell me that Linc is charging you rent. He better fucking not be, or I'll have words with him." His face grew dark.

She slapped his shoulder. Sharp pain stabbed her wrist.

Fuck.

"Tanner, you cannot get angry like this. You can't just step in all the time to rescue me. Especially when I don't need it."

"Of course you need it."

"I don't. Linc has been nothing but good to me. And you are not going to go have words with him or anything else!" She pointed a finger at him. He lightly grabbed it, tugging her hand toward him.

Too late, she realized what he was doing as he pushed back her sleeve to look at her wrist.

"This is why you need me. Look at your wrist."

"It's fine." She didn't want to look at it. Seeing it bruised and swollen was going to trigger her.

Every bruise Stefan had put on her was ingrained on her brain. They were memories she didn't wish to dig up.

"It's not fucking fine. No one should put a hand on you like this. No one should hurt you."

"You're touching me right now."

She knew it was a low blow because his touch was nothing like that asshole from last night.

He grew pale and drew back, giving her the space she wanted.

Well, what she'd told herself she wanted.

She took in a sharp breath.

"Are you scared of me, Lilac?"

Talk about déjà vu. He'd asked her that same question the night they'd had sex in the hotel room.

A small bark of laughter escaped her. It had a slightly hysterical sound to it. "If I were smart, I would be. A smart woman would stay well away from you, Tanner Malone."

But she wasn't smart. She was so freaking dumb. Because she didn't want him to stop touching her. She wanted more. All of the touches. The kisses. The looks.

The possessiveness.

"Do you want me to stay away from you, Lilac?"

"Yes." She forced the word out. Watching as he shut down. This was it. He was going to storm out of here. Tanner could be so damn sweet and kind and caring.

But he had a temper as well. That was clear.

Besides, he'd told her that what they'd had was just a fling. God, that had hurt.

"I see. Is it Linc?"

"Is what Linc?" she asked, confused.

"Is he the reason you want me to stay away from you?" he asked, looking ill. "You want Linc?"

Shock filled her. "What? No! Why would you think that?"

"You're living with him, and he seems protective of you. So, I was wondering . . . is it him? Or maybe it's me. You're just not into me anymore?"

God. She should tell him yes. That she wasn't into him anymore. But she lie to him. Sometimes, it felt like her entire life was a lie.

"It's not you, it's me."

He made a scoffing noise. "That's such a cop-out."

"It's not," she told him, grabbing his hand to try and emphasize her point. "I'm trouble, Tanner. You don't want to be near me. I'll just . . . I'll just bring all of my bad luck to you. There are things you don't know . . ."

"Then tell me." He leaned forward, placing his hands on the bench on either side of her.

"You don't want to be involved in my life, Tanner. It's a mess." Tears dripped down her face. What would it be like to have someone to lean on? To help her? Of course, she had Opal and Ryleigh. But Ryleigh was fragile. She was always so eager to believe the best in everyone that Lilac felt like she had to protect her.

And Opal? She'd had such an awful life, even worse than what Lilac had experienced. She just wanted to make things better for her. To not burden her further.

Lilac wanted to take care of them . . . but that meant everything fell on her. And she wasn't coping.

At all.

"Lilac. Tell me what's going on."

"I ghosted you. I left without a word. Then reappeared and I've caused so many issues since. Why would you care about my life and what I've been through? I was just a fling, remember?"

He closed his eyes. "I might have said that in the heat of the moment, all right? I didn't actually mean it."

He didn't?

"I care about you, Lilac. And as much as I've tried, I haven't been able to forget you. But I need to know what is going on with you. Why you left. Why you've shown up here now. With a baby."

Had he wanted to hurt her? She couldn't blame him for that. Or for wanting an explanation.

"I know you wanted me. You couldn't fake that," he said. "And I think you want me still."

She sat there, frozen. She couldn't deny it, but she also couldn't move. Tanner wrapped his hand around the back of her neck. "Shall we test that?"

God, no.

Please, yes.

His lips brushed hers and she stayed still. She couldn't participate. Shouldn't encourage him. That would be wrong.

And yet, as his mouth continued to move against hers, she started to cave—so much for self-control. Her hands drifted up his arms as he grabbed her, pulling her onto his lap. Her legs went around him, his arms supporting her as he kissed her like he wanted to eat her. Like he couldn't imagine not touching her.

A sound interrupted them.

Her phone.

It buzzed against her thigh, where she'd placed it into the pocket of her apron.

That was Opal's ringtone.

"Ignore it," Tanner ordered.

"I can't." And she shouldn't be sitting here in the freaking staff area of the diner, letting him kiss her. Fumbling for her phone, she drew it out.

"Opal? What's wrong?"

19

Tanner wanted to snatch the phone off her. But he held back, knowing that wouldn't win him any favors.

She grew pale and climbed off his lap. Worry filled him. He stood, watching as she grabbed a handbag from a locker, pulling the strap over her.

"I'll be right there! I'm coming now. I'll run! Yep! Okay."

"What is it? What's wrong?" he asked as she rushed out of the room.

"That was my friend, Opal. Ryleigh is sick. She's been sick for a while, but she's gotten worse. Linc is taking her to the doctor. And Kye too just in case."

"Ryleigh? Who is Ryleigh?" he demanded. Was he the father of her baby? Why hadn't she mentioned him, though?

"Peggy." She stopped by the older woman. "I'm so sorry. I've got to go. Family emergency."

Peggy eyed Tanner suspiciously as though this was his fault.

"Of course. Go."

Lilac raced out.

"Lilac! Wait!" he demanded.

"I can't. I have to meet them at the doctors."

"I'll drive you."

She slowed, turning. "What?"

"My truck's here." It was right next to her. He unlocked it and she practically dove for the passenger door, opening it with fingers that fumbled.

He opened it for her and lifted her in.

"Go! Let's go!" she said as he got in.

"Seatbelt," he said sternly.

"Tanner, go!" she wailed.

Instead of arguing with her, he decided it was better to reach over and buckle her in.

He drove her to the doctors. She undid her belt, jumping out as he was still parking.

She was in the building before he'd even gotten out of the truck.

Oh, she was in trouble when he got his hands on her.

When he got inside, he found her talking to Hannah. To his surprise, Hannah was frowning at her. Hannah never frowned at anyone.

"Where is Ryleigh?" Lilac demanded. "Kye?"

"I'm sorry, they're in with the doctor."

"Where?" Lilac demanded.

"I can't let you in there."

"Hannah," he said in a low voice, coming up beside Lilac. He wrapped his arm around her trembling form. "Tell her where her son is."

He couldn't believe this.

"Her son?" Hannah gave him a shocked look.

Lilac gaped at him. "Kye isn't my son."

Suddenly, the woman he'd met earlier with the big hair walked out of a room, looking around. "Lilac! Come here."

"Opal!" Lilac rushed forward. The other woman eyed him

for a long moment. "Well, Cowboy, you coming too?"

That was surprising.

But he wasn't saying no. He stepped in, shutting the door behind him. On Doc's exam table sat a tiny, pale woman with dark blonde hair. A baby lay on the table next to her with Doc leaning over the baby, listening to his chest.

Linc hovered next to her as Lilac moved to Doc's other side, her hand reached out to the baby who'd started to cry.

"You can pick him up," Doc said. "Now I need to examine you, Ryleigh."

That was Ryleigh? Ryleigh was a woman. Good.

"I'm fine," the woman on the exam table said. "Just look after Kye."

Lilac had Kye in her arms, bouncing him up and down lightly. Tanner walked over to her, placing a hand on her back.

"Kye is fine," Doc reassured her. "His lungs sound good and he doesn't have a fever. Whatever is going on with you, you've all kept him from catching it."

They all breathed out sighs of relief.

"Thank God," Lilac muttered.

"Perhaps you could all step out while I check Ryleigh over," Doc said.

"I'm staying," Linc insisted.

Huh. Maybe Tanner had read things wrong. It wasn't Lilac he was interested in. Or Opal. It was the pale, sick-looking woman on the table.

"We'll wait for you in the waiting room, Ryleigh," Lilac told her.

As he walked out of the room, he felt Ryleigh's eyes on him. But he only had attention for Lilac.

They settled in the waiting room, Opal sitting across from them while Lilac still held Kye, who had fallen asleep against her.

"He's gorgeous. How old?" he asked.

"Four weeks," Lilac said, staring down at him worriedly. "What if he gets sick, though? What are we going to do?"

"Take him to the hospital," Opal said. "We'll work it all out after."

"Of course. Of course. I'm not thinking. I was just so panicked when you called me."

Opal winced. "Sorry, babe. I didn't mean to scare you. I shouldn't have called until I knew what was going on."

"No, you were right to call me. Do you think Ryleigh is all right?"

"So, who is Ryleigh?" he asked, interrupting their conversation

They both stared at him as though they'd forgotten he was there.

Flattering.

"What do you mean? That's Ryleigh in there." Opal pointed at the room, giving him a look as if she was wondering if he was a few beers short of a six-pack.

"I mean, who is she to the two of you? To him?" He nodded at the baby.

"She's our friend. And Kye's mama," Lilac said quietly.

"He's really not yours?" he said. "You weren't pregnant when we met?"

Opal made a scoffing noise and got up to go look at the pamphlets.

"You thought that? That I hid a pregnancy from you?" Lilac asked.

"I didn't know what to think. That night, you never turned up. You didn't reply to my messages. I thought something terrible had happened. Then I figured you'd used and discarded me. So, what is the truth, Lilac?"

Guilt hit him as a tear dripped down her cheek. "I'm so sorry. I never meant to hurt you."

"The way to make it up to me is to tell me the truth."

She nodded, sniffling. "All right, but not here. Not now."

"Yeah. Not here. But soon." He didn't want her disappearing on him again.

"Either of you know why the receptionist keeps glaring at Lilac?" Opal asked. "She looks like she's sucking on a lemon."

Opal didn't seem to have an indoor voice. Everything boomed through the room, and he glanced up to see Hannah giving him a mortified look.

He sighed. "That's my fault. That's Raid's fiancée, Hannah. I'll talk to her. Stay here." Getting up, he moved to the desk to speak to Hannah.

Lilac glanced over at Opal as Tanner moved to talk to Hannah. "Do you think Ryleigh is okay?"

"I don't know." Opal chewed her lip, looking worried for the first time. Lilac knew she wore a mask around other people. But never around her or Ryleigh. "Linc was really upset that we hadn't taken her to the doctor already."

Guilt had her stomach rolling. God, she should have insisted Ryleigh go to the doctor. What was she thinking?

"Yesterday, she didn't seem this bad."

"I know. Her breathing started to go funny this morning. At least Kye is okay. We've kept him away from her. Sorry to call you. Do you think you'll get fired?" Opal gave her a concerned look.

"Probably." She wouldn't blame Peggy for firing her. Especially after that mess with the guys at that booth. "I'm the worst employee."

"I heard there were some issues last night at Dirty Delights,"

Opal said. "Linc mentioned it when I first saw him this morning. You never said a thing."

"I haven't seen you today."

"Sure. That's the reason." Opal nodded over at Tanner. "What's going on with the cowboy?"

"What do you mean?"

Opal leaned forward. "Why is he here? Are you back with him?"

"No!" she said sharply.

Tanner glanced over. He raised an eyebrow, and she nodded back at him to let him know she was all right.

"Hmm, yeah, you two don't act like a couple at all," Opal said dryly.

"We're not together. He was at the diner when you called and offered me a ride."

And they'd kissed. But she wasn't going to tell Opal that.

Linc opened the door and stepped through, a pale Ryleigh in his arms.

"What is it? What's wrong?" She stood, holding Kye close.

"Ryleigh is very sick," Linc said. "I'm taking her home with me. Can you bring Kye out to his car seat?"

"Um, yes. I need to settle the bill first."

"Already taken care of," Tanner said, walking over to them.

Wait. It was?

Shoot. She needed to talk to him about that.

Linc nodded at him briefly before carrying Ryleigh out. What was wrong with her, though? What was going on?

"Linc? What is it? What's wrong?" she asked as they headed to his truck.

Linc glanced down at her, his face grim. "Why didn't you take her to the doctor earlier?"

She jolted back, feeling as though she'd been slapped.

"Hey!" Tanner growled. "Don't speak to her like that."

It was true, though. Ryleigh often got sick, though, and Lilac hadn't realized that she was feeling this bad.

Was that the real reason she hadn't taken her to the doctor, though? Or was it because she was worried about the paper trail and money?

Had she risked her best friend's health?

Guilt made her feel nauseous, and she was barely aware of the argument going on around her.

"Look! The fact is that Ryleigh is this close to ending up in the hospital because she didn't receive early care. And that's on you." Linc glared down at her.

She stumbled back, nearly falling. Shit. She was still holding the baby!

"Fuck you, Linc!" Tanner snapped. "Ryleigh is an adult. She can make decisions about her own health. Lilac is not to blame for her being sick."

But she was . . . she totally was.

Why couldn't she get anything right? What if Ryleigh got worse?

Oh God.

She couldn't breathe.

Do not panic. You need to keep it together.

"You don't know jackshit about what Lilac has done for us, Deputy Dickhead," Opal snapped at him as Ryleigh let out a small moan.

How she was sleeping through this, Lilac had no idea.

"No, because the three of you are extremely secretive. If you'd asked for help, then this might have been avoided. I need to get Ryleigh back to my place. I'll be taking care of her from now on." Linc grimaced as he glanced at Kye. "Kye too."

"No, you can't take Kye," Lilac said, stepping back.

"Give him to me."

No. If Ryleigh couldn't look after Kye, then she'd want Opal and Lilac to. "No. We'll look after him."

"And how can I trust you to do that?" Linc asked quietly.

But she felt like he'd punched her in the gut. Her breathing grew ragged.

"Because we've looked after him since he was born," Opal said sharply. "You better rein yourself in, boy. Before I do it for you."

She put a hand on Opal's arm. She knew her friend was close to losing her shit on Linc. And it wouldn't be pretty. Opal was pretty easygoing until you hurt someone that she cared about.

Which was a short list.

"Fine. Kye stays with the two of you, but I will be checking on him. I'm taking Ryleigh home now to look after her."

"Fine, but *we* will be checking on her," Opal told him. Reaching into the back of the truck, Opal unhooked his car seat and dragged it out. "And when Ryleigh is better, you can bet she's not going to be happy with the way you spoke to Lilac."

Linc looked tense as he got in the truck and drove away with a sleeping Ryleigh.

"What if she's not okay, Opal?" she whispered. "He's right. It's all on me. All my fault."

Before Opal could reply, Tanner stepped between them, his hand cupping her chin to tilt her face back.

"Did you make her sick?" he asked.

"No, of course not." How would that even be possible?

"Did you tell her that she couldn't see a doctor?"

"No. I asked her if she needed to go, but she said she would be all right. However—"

"No, no howevers, no buts."

"I should have insisted she go."

"How old is she?" he asked.

"Um. Twenty-three."

"How old are you?"

"The same."

"I'm twenty-nine, doll," Opal drawled. "Just in case anyone cared."

Tanner flicked her a look, and to her surprise, his lips twitched. "Would have thought you were the same age."

"Oh, I like him," Opal purred. "Which truck is yours, Cowboy? I'll go get this set up." She held up the car seat.

"Red truck over there." He pointed to it and handed her the keys.

Opal strode away, her legs encased in tight jeans and a pair of thigh high boots with a thick wedge heel gave her some much-needed height.

"She's not going to steal my truck, is she?" he asked.

"Of course not!" Lilac glared up at him.

"Just checking. Back to my scolding."

"It's rude to scold me," she muttered.

"Not when you've earned it. You're being way too hard on yourself and you need to stop."

"Says you."

"Yes, says me."

"You don't have a right to tell me off." Although she had to admit it was helping to assuage her guilt.

"Has my dick been inside you?" he retorted.

"Tanner!" She tried to cover up Kye's ears. "You cannot talk in front of children like that."

Tanner grinned at her. "If he's going to be around me or my brothers, he's gonna hear worse than that."

"Then you should clean up your language. And what does that have to do with anything?"

"My dick's been in you. I've kissed you. Slept with you. Cared for you."

Cared?

So, he didn't anymore?

Pay attention, Lilac. That's not what is important.

It felt like it was, though. Because her heart felt like it was tearing into pieces.

"And here's the thing, I never let you go."

Her mouth dropped open. "What?"

"I never let you go. You left. But I'm thinking now that you didn't want to. I think there's a reason you left which you're going to tell me soon. But that just means you didn't want to leave me. My claim still applies."

"There . . . there was no claim!" What the heck? Was he for real right now?

"Baby, there was definitely a claim. And that claim still exists. So, get your head around being mine."

"How did I not know how arrogant you are?"

He grinned. "You knew. You just liked it before. But now that I'm bossing your ass for your own good, I might add, you've decided it annoys you."

"Of course it does! Arrogance is annoying."

"Nope. Arrogance is me knowing I own you."

"Nobody owns me. Nobody!" She practically yelled the words, her heart racing. It was too close to something Stefan would have said to her.

Kye let out a startled cry while Tanner stared down at her in shock.

"Here." Opal reappeared, taking Kye from her. "I think it's best we all get home, yeah?"

Lilac nodded. She felt more exhausted than she could ever remember feeling before. It was like all of her energy had been drained out of her. Turning, she stumbled again as she tried to walk to Tanner's truck.

Letting out a grunt that she assumed was one of annoyance, he picked her up and carried her over to the truck.

"You don't need to carry me." Even though she knew she should be stronger than this, it was kind of a relief.

"I think you'll find that I do. You're so exhausted that you can barely walk. And I don't want you tripping up. Plus, this means I get hold you. Never a bad thing."

"Really?" she whispered.

"Why would it be, baby?"

"Because when I first arrived here and you saw me at Dirty Delights, you looked at me like you hated me. You said what we had was just a fling."

"I told you I didn't mean that. I wish I hadn't said it because it's not true. I'm mad at you, make no mistake of that. And you're going to get punished. For running from me. For not coming to me if you were in trouble. Oh, and for jumping out of a moving truck. Yeah, your ass is toast."

"What?" She looked up at him in confusion as he placed her in the front passenger seat. "When did I jump out of a moving truck?"

Opal was already in the backseat with a now-quiet Kye. Tanner pulled her seatbelt over and buckled it in. "Earlier, when we pulled up here. Make sure that doesn't happen again."

The door shut and Opal whistled. "Daddy can spank me anytime."

"Opal!" she scolded, looking over her shoulder at her friend.

Opal just grinned. "Don't tell me he wasn't giving you Daddy Dom vibes."

Lilac groaned. "This isn't one of your romance books."

"Why not? It could be."

Tanner got in and Opal leaned forward. "Are you a Daddy Dom, Tanner?"

Tanner's eyebrows rose as he half turned to look at Opal, then at her. "No, I'm not. Is that what you want, Lilac?"

"No." She shook her head.

"Sure? I've never been to Saxon's, but I'm willing to go if it's what you need. Learn how to be a Dom."

"Saxon's?" Opal asked with interest.

"Local BDSM club," Tanner explained.

"I don't need that," she said.

"Sure? I've got no objections to you calling me Daddy."

"Are there any Daddies in this town?" Opal asked. "Who need a bratty sub with a taste for pain?"

Lilac groaned as Tanner stared at Opal in shock. "I suspect there could be."

"Well, now," Opal said. "I didn't think this small town was going to be for me with all these goody-two-shoes, but things are looking up."

"Goody-two-shoes?" he repeated.

Lilac just shook her head at him, swallowing a groan as everything spun. Shit.

She needed some sleep.

But she knew that wasn't going to be possible anytime soon.

"Yeah, everyone here just seems too good to be true, you know?" Opal said as they started driving. "Like, it can't be real. Although that receptionist didn't like the look of you, Lilac."

"Again, that was my fault. She thought she was defending me," Tanner explained as he parked in front of Linc's house.

"Well, I hope you set her straight," Opal said. "Wouldn't want to ruin her nose."

"Ruin her nose?" he asked her after Opal climbed out of the truck.

"Don't ask," Lilac told him. "But Opal has a mean right hook."

Getting out, she moved to the back door to unhook the car seat, dragging it out. Her energy was waning, and for a moment, she was worried that she wouldn't manage.

Then Tanner tugged the baby seat out of her hands and

started walking toward the guesthouse before she could even say anything.

"Well?" he questioned. "Are you coming or not?"

With a sigh, she trudged after him. He really hadn't been this bossy and demanding before.

Had he?

20

Tanner didn't like this.

The guesthouse was all right, but there were only two bedrooms and it looked like someone was having to sleep on the sofa.

And he was pretty certain he knew who that person was.

His girl was far too self-sacrificing for his peace of mind.

She'd totally believed that shit that Linc had said to her. Which reminded him, he owed that bastard a black eye. He'd wait until Ryleigh was feeling better.

He was just nice that way.

People failed to see that he was nicest Malone brother.

It was baffling how they missed it.

Lilac was in one bedroom, getting Kye settled while Opal made him a bottle. As soon as Opal disappeared, he started snooping. Fuck. They barely had any food. A loaf of bread. Some peanut butter. Creamer and coffee.

This wasn't good enough.

Grabbing his keys, he headed toward the door. What the

fuck right did Linc have to go off at Lilac for not taking care of Ryleigh when he was letting them live here with no food?

Well, he'd soon remedy that.

Yes, he'd rather move Lilac in with him so he'd know that she was being looked after.

But he knew that was likely too soon.

He'd give it a week.

The lack of food worried him, though. Was this why she was so thin? He could see her making sure everyone else was fed and taken care of first and forgetting about herself.

That was going to change.

"You're leaving."

He glanced over to see Lilac staring at him with a look of resignation. There was no surprise. Just a hint of sadness.

"I'm going to the grocery store."

"Okay."

"I should be about an hour," he added.

"You're coming back?"

"Yeah. With groceries."

She frowned as though she didn't understand what he was saying. He walked forward, cupping the side of her face. "Baby, you don't have any food."

Surprise filled her face. "You're going to the grocery store to buy us food?"

"Yep. Is there anything you want? Chocolate? Ice cream? Any allergies I should cater for? What about sanitary products?"

"S-sanitary products? Are you seriously asking me if I want you to buy me tampons?"

"Well, I don't know when you guys are due. You might need to restock."

"Tanner!" She slapped his chest, wincing as she obviously hurt her wrist. "You can't offer to buy us sanitary products!"

"Why not?" he asked, genuinely confused.

"B-because it's something personal. I don't talk about things like that. Not with . . . not with you." She glanced away, blushing.

Was she . . . embarrassed?

Nope. He wasn't having that.

Picking her up, he carried her to the sofa and sat with her on his lap.

"Tanner," she said with a sigh.

"If you're about to complain about me picking you up and carrying you around, then just stop."

"Just stop?"

"Yep. I want to do it and you look like you barely have the energy to blink, let alone walk. So just . . . let me take care of you, okay?" He tried to keep the frustration out of his voice but didn't think he fully managed it.

"You don't have to take care of me. We're not . . . you and I aren't . . ."

"Did you forget the conversation we just had about me claiming you?"

She buried her face into his chest with a groan. "I don't have the energy to argue with you."

"Good. Then don't."

"Tanner, I don't know what's happening here."

"Yes, you do. You're just in denial. We'll work on that. As well as your inability to ask for help, your tendency to work too hard, and the fact that you don't seem to be eating."

She tensed in his arms.

Fuck. What if she'd grown so thin because she was ill? Or had an eating disorder?

He drew her back so he could stare down at her. "I know I'm not the most sensitive guy and I should likely handle this differently. But you need to know this. I am not going to let you hurt yourself."

"I-I'm not."

"I'm glad to hear that," he replied, unsure it was true. "But if you were, you can tell me. I'll hear you out. I'll listen and I won't judge."

"Uh-huh. And then what will you do?" She gave him a skeptical look.

"I'll do whatever I think is in your best interests."

She sighed. "Even if I don't like what you choose to do?"

He grinned. "You know me so well. I should have known you couldn't stay away from me, that you'd turn up eventually. I mean, I am freaking irresistible."

Lilac groaned. "You're impossible, is what you are."

"Impossible to resist." He winked at her and lifted her off him before standing. "I want you to have a rest. I'll bring back dinner too."

"You don't have to do that."

"If you're mine, I take care of you. So yes, I do."

"Well, just don't go overboard, all right?"

"Who me?" He put his hand to his chest. "I will be restrained like always."

He grinned as he left, listening to her groan.

21

"What's all this?" Opal walked out of the room, carrying Kye. She stared around at the food in amazement.

"This is Tanner restraining himself, apparently," Lilac replied dryly as she put away another bag of groceries.

"There's enough food here to feed an army for a month."

"Really?" Tanner said, eyeing the bags of food skeptically. "This is as much as Mia used to get when we were all living on the Ranch."

"How many brothers do you have?" Opal asked.

"A lot. I've lost track."

Whatever.

He was such a liar.

She reached down to put the milk in the bottom of the fridge. As she stood up, the room spun slightly.

"Lilac? You okay?" His arm went around her.

Okay? No, she didn't think she was at all. Ryleigh was sick and not with them. Lilac had gone over to see her before, but Linc had told her that she was sleeping.

He'd been kind of cold and standoffish, which had hurt. Because she'd been starting to think of him as a friend.

She'd likely been fired from her job at the diner. And she didn't know how she was going to earn the extra money they needed to fix Sugar.

Oh, and Tanner thought he was claiming her. God only knew what that meant exactly, but she had a feeling her life was about to change.

"I'm all right. Just stood up too quickly."

"Right. Sit down. I've got pizza." He ushered her over to the table.

"Pizza!" Opal put Kye down on his blanket on the floor, before digging into the pizza.

Lilac wished they could get him more things—stuff that other babies had. But they needed every cent at the moment.

However, she knew what the polite thing to do was. Even if she'd never have bought all these name brand items. What was Tanner thinking?

"How much do I owe you for the groceries?" she asked as Tanner grabbed a piece of pizza. "And for Ryleigh's visit to the doctor?"

He froze.

That was a strange reaction.

"What did I say?" she asked.

"You're not paying for the groceries," Tanner said in a low growl. "Or the medical bill."

"But . . . you can't just buy us all this stuff and pay for the doctor."

"I can. And we already had this conversation."

They had?

"I'm claiming you. You're mine. I take care of you. This is part of that."

"You can't just buy me stuff. The pizza is enough. All of this . . . it's not being restrained, Tanner."

"I'm a Malone." He shrugged. "We don't like restraints."

"That's a shame," Opal drawled, finishing up her fifth piece of pizza. Where she put all of that, Lilac had no idea. She was still picking apart her first piece.

Tanner gave the bits of pizza on her plate an annoyed look. Then he turned to wink at Opal. "Well, we like to use restraints on other people."

"Thank fuck. I wouldn't want to think that such a hunk of man candy was a dud in the sack."

"Opal," she groaned.

"What? Just looking out for you, my friend. She could use a good fucking," she told Tanner. "Help relax her."

"Opal!" she shouted.

Kye let out a cry and she immediately felt terrible. She grasped hold of her head. Why couldn't she get anything right?

"Lilac, hey. It's all right," Tanner said soothingly. He lifted her onto his lap.

"Shit, babe, I didn't mean to upset you."

Opening her eyes, she saw Opal watching her worriedly.

"I'm fine. Sorry."

"I'm going to take Kye for a walk," Opal said, getting up.

A walk? She glanced out the window.

"It's not that warm out," she said worriedly.

"Don't worry, babe. I won't be long."

Picking Kye up, Opal bundled him up in a warm blanket and stepped outside.

"She shouldn't walk around outside in the cold with him," she said. "I'm going to go get her."

Tanner wrapped his arms around her. "She's giving us a moment to ourselves."

She was? Oh. She should have realized that.

"Opal can be thoughtful."

"Yeah. She also doesn't have much of a filter, does she?" he said.

Lilac snorted. "No. Sorry about everything she said. I hope you're not embarrassed."

"I'm not embarrassed," he reassured her. "But I don't like seeing you upset."

"I'm fine. I just . . . I shouldn't have yelled like that. I upset Kye."

"Kye is fine. He knows that he's got three women wrapped around his little finger. Lucky kid." He winked at her.

She shook her head. "I really think I should pay you for the groceries."

"And I think you should shut up about that before I spank your ass."

Her mouth dropped open. "Tanner Malone!"

"Yes, baby?"

"You can't tell me to shut up or threaten to spank my ass for wanting to pay for groceries I'm going to use."

"Are you?" he asked seriously.

"Am I what?"

"Going to use them."

"Well, yeah." She frowned, not liking where this was going.

"Are you eating, baby?" He rubbed his hand up and down her back.

"Yes," she told him.

"Three meals a day? Snacks?"

She pressed her fingers together. "I'm doing the best I can."

Shit.

She hadn't meant to say that. Or in that tone. It was a mix of longing and sadness. Of regret.

God. She had so many regrets that she didn't even know what to do with them all.

"Shh, baby. I know you are. Shh." He pressed her face against his chest and rocked her back and forth.

The front door opened, and Opal stepped in. "Sorry, Kye needs a bottle. Everything okay?"

"Yeah. Everything is good." She climbed off Tanner's lap, surprised that he let her. She walked over to Opal and gave her a gentle hug, before taking hold of Kye. "I'll get the bottle for him." Then she glanced at the clock. "Shit! I've got to get to Dirty Delights. I'm going to be late."

How could she have forgotten about work?

Idiot.

She handed Kye back to Opal and rushed to her suitcase by the sofa.

"Whoa. Wait." Tanner reached for her, but she shook his hand off. "Lilac, I think you should call in sick."

"I can't call in sick. I'm not ill!"

"You don't look that great to me, babe," Opal said as she made Kye a bottle. He was really starting to fuss. She should help with Kye. But she had to go to work. She likely only had one job left and she had to keep it.

"Lilac, I don't want you going to work tonight." Tanner took hold of her shoulders, holding her still.

Panic started to eat at her insides. "I have to go. And you can't stop me."

He eyed her for a long moment. "Fine. You can go."

So gracious of him to allow her to go to her job.

"But I'm going as well. I'll be there all night, making sure you don't push yourself too hard."

She sighed but didn't argue, knowing this was the best compromise she would get.

22

Fuck.

He hated this. Hated that she was pushing herself so hard when she had nothing left in her tank.

"Tanner."

Glancing up, he saw Devon frowning down at him. He didn't know what his problem was.

Oh. Wait. It might have something to do with what happened last night. Actually, Tanner had his own beef with the owner of Dirty Delights.

"You didn't protect her."

Devon gaped at him, looking like Tanner had just socked him in the stomach.

"You're right."

Okay, now it was Tanner's turn to be surprised. He wasn't expecting Devon to admit that he'd been in the wrong.

"And I feel fucking awful about it. I need another bouncer on during busy nights like last night. But did you seriously have to wreck half my bar?"

"Looks okay to me." Tanner glanced around. Sure, there

were a few missing chairs and tables, but thankfully, it wasn't as busy tonight.

"Going to cost me money to buy new stuff. Not to mention having to deal with Jake last night."

"Yeah, he's a real buzzkill. Can you get me a beer?" he asked.

"Tanner!"

"What?"

"Fuck. I don't know whether to thank you or strangle you," Devon said.

"Strangely, I get that reaction a lot."

"Nothing strange about it," Devon muttered, pouring him a beer.

Thank God for that. Maybe he'd go away now.

"I don't want any trouble tonight," Devon warned.

"There's not going to be any trouble."

Devon shot him a skeptical look.

"As long as no one touches her, upsets her, or tries to claim what is mine." That last part had been aimed at Devon, and he wasn't even going to pretend that it wasn't.

"She's a beautiful girl. Hard-working. Kind. Loyal. But what she needs is someone to take care of her. To ensure she gets what she needs even when she protests. To do what's best for her. You think you can do that?"

"I know I can."

"You better."

"Hey, everything all right?"

Tanner turned to see Lilac standing there, watching them both worriedly. "I'm really sorry about last night, Devon. If you need to take any of the repairs out of my pay, you can."

"He won't be doing that, will you, Devon," Tanner warned.

"Of course I won't be," Devon replied. "If I'm going to charge anyone for the damage, it will be him." He pointed at Tanner.

"But that's not fair. He was just coming to my aid. It was that other guy who was the asshole. He should pay."

Was she... sticking up for him?

Damn. He was getting hard. Not exactly the time or place.

Devon sighed, nodding. "You're right. Those assholes aren't welcome back here. No one is in trouble or has to pay for the damages. Okay?"

Lilac gave Devon a relieved smile. Tanner hated that she'd been worrying about this.

"Baby, you need a break." He brushed some of her red hair behind her ear.

"I just got here. I can't take a break." She gave him an exasperated look and turned away.

Reaching out, he lifted her onto his lap. "I don't care how long you've been at work, if you need a rest, you take it. Understand me?"

He kissed the side of her neck, feeling a tremble run through her before he placed her on the floor again.

Devon gave him a nod of approval. Not that he needed it. But he was glad they were both on the same page when it came to her health.

The other man walked away.

"You got me all hot and bothered standing up for me like that."

"What? You're kidding."

"Nope. I'm not. Now I'm going to have to sit here with a hard-on for the rest of the night. Do you feel sorry for me?"

"No." She slapped his chest. "You're terrible."

But he noticed a smile on her face as she turned away to go back to work.

He resumed watching her and glowering at anyone who dared to even look at her for longer than a few seconds.

Nothing was happening to her on his watch.

Devon walked out, carrying a bowl of fries and chicken bites, which he placed on the bar beside him. He frowned. Who were those for? No one had been sitting there all night.

"Lilac!" he called out. She glanced over and he pointed to the food. "Break."

Tanner's eyebrows rose.

"I'm fine," she replied.

"Sit. Eat." Devon shot him a look, then disappeared down the other end of the bar.

Lilac turned away as though she was going to walk off. But Tanner grabbed her, lifting her onto the stool.

"Hey! I'm working. You can't come sit here if you're just going to manhandle me."

"Manhandle you? Hmm, I do like the sound of that." He leaned in close to her. "Eat your dinner, baby."

"I already had dinner."

"Um, if you're talking about that pizza, then no, you didn't. But if you don't want to eat this, I'd be happy to get you something else."

"W-what?" She turned to stare at him in shock.

"If you don't want to eat this, I'll go get you whatever you want," he repeated. "What would you rather have? A burger? Some fruit? Salad? I don't actually know your favorite food." He frowned. That wasn't really good enough, was it? He had to do better.

"I . . . I don't need anything else."

"Then you want this?"

She stared at the food as if she'd never seen anything like it before. "I . . . I . . ."

Fuck. He hated seeing her like this. She seemed so deflated. As though there was little of the old Lilac left.

He wanted to know how that had been beaten out of her . . . and how he could fix it all.

"I have trouble eating," she whispered.

This wasn't the place for this conversation, but he wasn't telling her that. If she needed to talk to him, then he was here for her. Always.

"Why, baby?" Was it a body dysmorphia thing? Did he need to get her a therapist?

"It . . . I . . . I was never allowed to eat whatever I wanted. There was a strict diet I had to follow when I was growing up. I didn't eat sweets or bad fats and few carbs. Everything was a bad or good food."

Fuck.

Even he knew that wasn't a good thing. And no way for a child to be raised.

"Your parents decided that?"

"Um. Not exactly. My mom died giving birth to me and my dad, well, he had a lot going on, so I was raised by a very strict woman. I called her Mrs. Jansen."

"You had to call someone who raised you by their last name?"

"Yes," she whispered. "She really was an awful woman. Well, to me. She loved my brother. She constantly praised him. He was handsome, smart, well-mannered. I was chubby, ill-kept, and ill-mannered."

"That bitch!"

She startled, then looked around her. "I need to get back to work."

"You're on a break, remember?"

"I can't . . . I don't think I can eat this."

"Would it help if we went out the back?" he asked.

She gave him a surprised look. "Um, yeah, it probably would."

"Hey, I can have good ideas sometimes," he told her.

Lilac's eyes grew wide as he picked up her food and then held out a hand to help her down.

"I didn't mean . . . I wasn't trying to imply . . ."

He couldn't stop himself from grinning as she stumbled over her words.

"You're a rat, Tanner Malone."

"A rat, huh? No, I think I'm more of a puma. Lying in wait, watching, ready to attack. All sleek, sexy, and beautiful."

Her mouth dropped open. "You need to be careful or you'll need a neck brace."

"For what?" he asked in confusion.

"To help carry around that huge head of yours," she commented.

"Ha-ha," he said. But he secretly loved that her sassy side was peeking out.

She finally slipped her hand into his, and he couldn't help but frown. "You're cold."

"Oh, I'm always cold. It's fine."

It wasn't, though. He was really concerned about her. They walked out into the staff room. "I don't know if you should be out here."

"Baby, I go where I want."

"See what I mean? Giant ego."

He just grinned and placed her food on the table. She sat and he picked up a chair, moving it around to sit next to her. Grabbing a piece of chicken, he brought it to his mouth, then blew on it.

"What are you doing?"

"Making sure this isn't gonna burn you."

She blinked at him. "Seriously?"

"Uh, yeah. Why is that hard to understand?" he asked.

"Well, no one has ever . . . I mean . . . I don't need you to do that."

"Didn't think that you did. I want to do it."

"You're a strange man, Tanner Malone. One minute you're easygoing and fun. The next you're all stern and bossy. One minute you like me, the next you don't, then you do again."

"That's just the mystery of Tanner Malone," he told her, holding piece of chicken to her mouth. "Open for me, baby."

A blush filled her cheeks.

"Ooh, what are you thinking about right now?" he teased.

"Nothing." She bit down on the chicken. Probably so she didn't have to answer him. But he didn't care. She was eating and that was a win.

"Hmm, I'm not sure. I think you were thinking about something else. Like, maybe you were thinking about opening your mouth so I could place my —"

"Tanner!"

"Finger into it." He fed her another fry. "Why, Lilac, what did you think I was going to say, you naughty girl?" He leaned into her. "Did you think I was going to say my cock?"

With a groan, she rested her forehead on the table. "Dead. I'm dead."

"I sure hope not. Would make it less fun to tease you."

"Can you please leave and maybe not ever come back so I don't have to remember how embarrassing this was."

Something about those words hit him hard. "That's one thing I won't do. I won't ever leave and not come back."

Ouch.

Double ouch.

Sitting up, she looked over at him. She let all the sorrow she felt fill her face. "I'm so sorry I did that to you, Tanner. I don't think there are enough sorries to make it up to you, but I want to try."

He eyed her for a long moment. "You can start by eating a bit more dinner."

She sighed. "You can't guilt someone into eating."

He clasped hold of her hand. "I don't know how to ask this in some sort of sensitive way, so I'm just going to ask it."

Uh-oh.

This could be anything . . . from wanting to perform some strange sex act to something far more intense and emotional.

"Are you so thin because you aren't eating? Because that bitch put all these ideas in your head about your weight? You've lost a lot of weight in six months, baby, and that cannot be good for you."

She sighed, rubbing her hand over her face. "I know it's not good for me. God, if I hadn't realized it by how tired and cold I am all the time, then I'd know it from the amount of hair I'm losing."

"Fuck. Listen, Jake's wife, Molly, is a psychologist. She's not so bad to talk to. I mean, she tried to cure us, but then she figured out there's nothing to cure."

"I don't think psychologists *cure* people."

"Well, whatever. Us Malones are perfect the way we are."

She snorted and he held up a piece of chicken. She stared at it with a sigh, rubbing her tummy.

"Eat, please, baby. You need your strength to get through the rest of your shift. And to go home and help look after Kye."

He wasn't wrong.

"If you need to talk to Molly . . . "

"I don't," she said quickly. Part of her was scared. Because once she started talking to someone . . . well, it might all come out and she might completely fall apart.

But also, she didn't think she had an eating disorder. It was just that eating had become difficult with her constant anxiety and fear. Plus, she didn't like to spend money on food for herself when she could use it on Kye.

Then there was the fact that she'd have to talk about Stefan. No conversation about her mental health could bypass him. And could she really trust Molly not to tell her husband, who was the freaking sheriff?

"All right, I'll drop that for the moment. But I need you to start eating. You can eat whatever you like, so long as you eat."

Was he serious right now?

"Do you listen to yourself speak?"

"Of course. I sound so good. How could I not?"

She groaned. "It's just..."

"Just what, baby?" he asked, taking her hand.

Lord, he was being unbearably sweet. She almost couldn't handle it.

"It's hard for me to eat. My stomach is always tied up in knots. It wasn't just Mrs. Jansen who restricted what I ate. After I left home, I felt so free. I ate what I wanted, wore what I wanted, said whatever came into my head without having to run it through a filter. And then I met this cute, sexy guy in a bar."

"Hey! Don't tell me about some asshole you met."

"Dummy, I'm talking about you." She nudged him.

"Me? That's all right, then. Wait a minute, no it's not! I'm not cute. I will accept sexy. Handsome is fine. Gorgeous. More attractive than all of my brothers combined and far, far smarter is preferable."

She rolled her eyes. "Neck brace."

He scoffed. "What's the point of being all this if I can't brag about it?" He waved his hand through the air over himself.

Lord. He was too much. But she couldn't help but smile. What would it be like to be that confident in yourself?

She'd never had that.

"So, what happened after you met me?" he asked.

He fed her another bit of chicken. She was nearly full, but for some reason, it was easier to eat like this, while she was focused on their conversation. Usually, she didn't like eating in front of other people, but Tanner was just so relaxing. It was hard to be stressed around him.

"I was just . . . I got stressed, I guess. All I could think after we left was that you'd turn up at the bar and I wouldn't be there. That you'd be so mad at me. I was worried and anxious, and I felt ill. Which just made it harder and harder to eat. We were on the move and things were so unsettled. I've always hated feeling unsettled. Having things changing all the time. I didn't want to leave that day. I really wish I'd been able to message you. But I couldn't and I . . . I . . ."

She was gasping for breath by now, so he drew her onto his lap

"Easy, baby. It's all right." He rubbed her back with his hand.

Tears filled her eyes. "It's not. It's really not, though. I hurt you. You were so angry with me. You . . . you looked at me like you . . . like you hated me."

"Shh. There's no way I could ever hate you," he reassured her.

"Are you sure?"

"I'm sure." He cupped her chin, tilting her face back. He wiped away her tears with his sleeve. "It would be impossible."

"You don't know everything, though. What if . . . what if you hate me after hearing it all?"

"Are you some secret assassin come to murder me and my family?"

"No!" Sheesh. Some days she could barely walk without tripping over.

"Then I think we're good."

"That's it? That's the one rule you've got? I can't murder you or your family."

"Well, I mean, we probably wouldn't object if you took out West—"

"Tanner! Be serious."

He gave her a puzzled look. "Huh? I was being serious."

She rolled her eyes at him. "You can't tell me that I'm allowed to take out one of your brothers."

"But he's the one that no one likes."

"Isn't he married?"

"Well, yeah. I guess I see where you're going. Flick might care."

Might care? He was crazy.

"I'm not here to kill anyone. But I do have secrets."

"We all do."

Not like hers.

"Eventually, I'm going to want to know all these secrets of yours. But for now, all I want from you is your promise that you won't run again."

Shit. She bit her lip.

"Promise me, Lilac," he said in a low voice.

"And if I can't?"

"Then I guess you just found yourself a 24/7 guard dog."

She closed her eyes. "You can't be with me all the time."

"Wanna bet?"

Lilac blew out her breath. It was a terrible promise to make. Because could she keep it?

Then again, it wasn't like they could run at the moment. And maybe . . . maybe this time they'd be safe.

"What's going on, baby?" he asked.

Crap. How to answer him?

There was a knock on the door, and she glanced up to see Lemon standing there. "Sorry to interrupt, but we need you out there."

"Of course, I'm so sorry." She got to her feet. "I have to go back to work."

"If you're in trouble, I need to know. I get you don't want to tell me yet. But you have my number on your phone now, so if something happens, the first person you call is me. Got it?"

Jeepers.

"Yes. Got it."

"Good girl. Now, get back to work." He slapped her ass as she turned.

Lord. He was too much.

But also . . . he was just enough.

23

Lilac stumbled along the footpath.

She was completely wrecked. To her surprise, Peggy had called her this morning and demanded to know why she hadn't turned up to work at the diner on time.

So . . . that had been fun, trying to explain that she'd been late because she thought she didn't have a job anymore.

Peggy had told her that she was an idiot and put her to work.

Which was both horrible and a relief.

She needed the money for Sugar. But she wasn't sure how long she could work night shifts at Dirty Delights, then morning shifts at the diner.

At least she only had two morning shifts a week. That wasn't so bad. In fact, she could sleep in tomorrow since it was Monday, and she didn't have to work at the bar tonight or tomorrow night.

After he'd driven her home last night, she hadn't heard from Tanner again.

Not that she needed him to be in constant contact, of course.

But she guessed a part of her had thought he might have at least texted her this morning.

Demand that she give him the explanation he wanted.

She was dreading it, if she was honest with herself, but she also wanted to get it off her chest.

It was silly to be sad that he wasn't sticking to her like Velcro. He had a life to live and so did she. He couldn't be with her all the time.

She'd given him her new number, but that didn't automatically mean that he would start messaging her.

Still, she kind of felt down. She stepped into the guesthouse. She was starting to feel weird about staying here when Linc didn't seem to like her all that much.

As soon as she opened the door, she heard Opal singing to Kye as she rocked him back and forth.

Opal had the best voice she'd ever heard. Lilac could sit and listen to her forever. She should have been a country-western star, not on the run with her and Ryleigh.

"Hey, I just got him to sleep," Opal told her. "Let me put him down. We need to talk."

Shit. That sounded ominous. Sitting on the sofa, she toed off her shoes and sighed in relief. God, her feet hurt.

"I'm sorry you've had to look after Kye so much," she said as soon as Opal reappeared. "I'll look after him when he wakes up."

If only she could get off the sofa by then. Well, she'd figure it out.

"Kye is fine. He's easy to look after."

"I need to go check on Ryleigh too." Lilac was super worried about her friend. She'd never been apart from Kye this long.

"Right. We definitely need to talk." Opal sat on the coffee table, giving her a serious look. "You're being a shithead."

Lilac's mouth opened in shock. "What?"

"You're being a shithead."

"How? Why? Because I left you alone with Kye for so long? I'm so sorry, but I'm not working again until Tuesday evening so I can look after him the entire time. It's just that we need the money—"

"Shut up, Shithead."

"Opal," she groaned. "Stop calling me that."

"I call it as I see it. You want to know why you're being a shithead? Well, it's got nothing to do with Kye and everything to do with you. Damn it, Lilac. Why won't you let me help you?"

"What do you mean?"

"You won't let me help. You never do. I get why you shelter Ryleigh. She's more fragile. She has a young baby. And we both know that she's far too trusting and positive to deal with everything. But, Shithead, I'm not like that. Out of all of us, I grew up on the streets, fighting for my fucking life. I'm the one who knows how shitty life can get and how to survive it. So why won't you let me help?"

"There's nothing you can do."

"Of course, there fucking is, but you won't let me."

"What do you want to do, then?" she asked, bewildered.

"I want to help contribute to the finances."

"Oh."

"Oh, she said." Opal threw up her hands. "Like she doesn't think I can get a job? No, she's got to work two jobs, wear herself into the ground taking care of everyone else, and then look at me like I've grown two heads just for suggesting that I could get a job so she could maybe get some rest. Perhaps even have some fun."

"How can I have any fun when I've got to . . ."

"What? Protect us? Take care of us? Do everything?" Leaning forward, Opal flicked her forehead.

"Oww. That was mean."

Opal shrugged. "That's what shitheads get."

"Stop calling me that! I'm not a shithead for trying to look after you."

"You're gonna run yourself into the ground, and then what will we do without you? Lilac, I know that asshole taught you that everything is your fault. Because that's what a dickhead does."

"Not a shithead?" she asked dryly, feeling herself tear up.

"Nope. Dickheads and shitheads are very different things. You are not responsible for us, babe. We're all in this together. You have to let me help."

Lilac wiped at her cheeks. Stupid tears. "Right."

"But first, you have to tell me how bad things are. What's the repair bill for Sugar?"

Lilac found the bill in her suitcase and handed it over. Opal blanched. "Jesus, that's almost as much as we paid for the old girl."

"I know, but I don't know what else to do. We can't stay here forever. That's not what Linc agreed to, and I get the feeling he doesn't like me much."

"He was being a total asshole yesterday and you shouldn't pay any attention to him. You know it's not your fault that Ryleigh got ill. Don't be a shithead."

"I thought I already was?" she asked with a smile.

"You've move up to being just a little shit."

"Ahh, there's a scale. Good to know."

"You already knew that. Right, well, I've got good news. I got a job at the local clothing store here."

"Really? Opal, that's amazing! Wait, are they all right with paying you cash?" she asked.

"Surprisingly, yes. The owner, Laken, just gave me this odd look but said that was fine. People in this town are weird."

They kind of were.

"This will mean we can get Sugar fixed quicker," Lilac said.

"Or it could mean you just work one job."

She shook her head. "Once Sugar is fixed and we can get out of here, then I'll think about it. But not yet."

Opal sighed. "What if you get sick? Then what will we do?"

She wanted to brush off that concern as preposterous, but she had to admit feeling dizzy and weak lately.

"I'll just see how I go. I guess we'll have to be careful with our schedules so one of us is always with Kye while Ryleigh is still ill."

"You know that's going to be tough," Opal said.

"I know."

"There is another solution . . ."

"We can't. Not yet."

"I don't fucking see why not."

"Because Ryleigh has to make that decision, Opal," she told her friend gently.

Opal could be a bulldozer when she thought she knew what was best for someone.

The sound of someone yelling had them both standing up. Suddenly, the glass door to the guest house opened and Ryleigh walked in. She was dressed in a long T-shirt that definitely wasn't hers. Her hair was a mess, and she looked a bit pale and tired.

But she also looked a lot better than the last time she'd seen her. Relief flooded her. God, she'd been worried about her.

Linc walked in behind her, his face like thunder.

Lilac shied back. She'd had enough anger aimed at her in her life. She didn't think she would ever cope well with someone being upset with her.

Opal moved partially in front of her while Ryleigh stared at her. "What's wrong? Why do you look scared?"

Okay, she was a lot better if she could pick up on Lilac's feelings.

"I . . . um . . . just worried about you."

"Deputy Dickhead was a prick to her, so now she's concerned he's going to go off at her again," Opal said.

Ryleigh's mouth dropped open while Linc actually took a step back, looking like someone had hit him.

Why did he look like that?

"He's not a dickhead," she managed to say. Lilac wasn't defending him. But they couldn't put him on the same level as Stefan. That wouldn't be fair to Linc.

"Hmm. Somewhere between dickhead and shithead, I guess," Opal conceded. "Still, I like the alliteration of Deputy Dickhead."

Ryleigh turned to Linc, her hands on her hips. "You were mean to my friend?"

"Ryleigh," he said in a gentle voice. "You were very ill. They weren't taking care of you properly. They should have gotten you to a doctor earlier. You nearly ended up in hospital."

Ouch. The blows kept coming.

"Stop it!" Ryleigh said loudly before she started to cough. She bent over, gasping for air.

Linc stepped forward and rubbed her back, talking to her quietly. Lilac rushed over and got her a glass of water. Linc nodded his thanks as she reached them. Picking Ryleigh up, he carried her to the sofa, frowning down at it for some reason.

Oh, shoot! Lilac hadn't cleared off her blankets. She should have tidied up, but she'd been so tired this morning when she'd gotten up. And in a rush.

Linc set her down, sitting next to her so he could rub her back while giving her small sips of water.

"S-sorry," Ryleigh said, tears streaming down her face.

"Nothing to be sorry for," Opal told her.

"Where's Kye?" Ryleigh asked.

"Sleeping," Lilac said. "Lucky he can sleep through anything, huh?"

Ryleigh gave her a small smile.

"Sorry. I didn't have a chance to tidy up before I left for work this morning. I didn't think I still had a job and had to rush out when Peggy called me." Lilac grabbed her pillow and one of the blankets, putting them behind an armchair.

Linc frowned at her. Why was he always staring at her like that? "I thought you were working at Dirty Delights? Now you're at the diner?"

"She's working at both in order to save money up for the repairs," Opal said.

"Oh, Lilac, you look exhausted," Ryleigh said worriedly.

"I'm fine." Lilac smiled at her. "What's important is that you're all right. Are you feeling better? Is there anything you need?"

Ryleigh turned to frown at Linc. "Yeah, I need my friends and, most importantly, my baby."

Linc's face fell. "I wasn't trying to keep you from him. I was just trying to make sure that you were getting better."

"And you thought it was okay to make Lilac feel bad?"

"I'm sorry. I just thought she should have gotten you to a doctor earlier."

"Because I'm not an adult who can make her own decisions?"

Whoa. She'd never seen Ryleigh like this. She rarely got upset with people or told them off.

"You were sick."

"I still have a brain. And even if I didn't, you still shouldn't blame Lilac. You have no idea how saying things like that to her could upset her."

Great. Now everyone was staring at her. She squirmed, feeling awkward. "I need to check on Kye."

"You need to apologize to Lilac, Linc," Ryleigh ordered.

"It's okay," Lilac said hastily. "He doesn't have to do that. He's already doing so much for us. It doesn't matter, he can say whatever he wants to me. It's fine."

She just didn't want him to kick them out. They had nowhere to go. They needed to stay here a bit longer.

"Fucking hell," Linc muttered.

"It does fucking matter," Tanner said from behind her, making her jump.

Lilac turned to see him walk into the guesthouse, his gaze zeroing in on Linc. "Been meaning to have a chat with you, Linc."

Uh-oh.

She didn't like the sound of that.

"What do you mean, a chat?" she asked nervously.

Linc stood and placed a hand on Ryleigh's shoulder. "I want you to wait here. Rest. You need a blanket, or you'll get cold."

Lilac grabbed the blanket she'd set aside and handed it to him.

Linc grimaced.

What was it? What had she done now?

"It's clean. I mean, I know I slept with it. But it's not . . . dirty." God, she hated feeling like this. As though she was messing everything up, yet had no idea how to fix it. Was he going to lash out at her again?

But with his fists rather than his words?

She wasn't sure which one was worse. As Linc reached out to take it, she stumbled back.

Linc's eyes widened. "Lilac, did you think . . . what are you . . . fuck, I wasn't going to hit you. I'd never."

"I know that," she said quickly, forcing a smile on her face. "I'm not . . . I need to get a drink of water." She tried to rush into the kitchen, but Tanner reached out an arm to stop her.

Generally, she wouldn't be able to stand someone grabbing her like that. Especially when she was on edge. But it was like her body knew Tanner. Knew he wouldn't harm her.

"I'll deal with you in a minute, Linc," he warned before smiling down at her. "But first, good afternoon, baby."

"Hi," she said shyly. "I wasn't sure I was going to see you today."

"I thought I'd let you sleep in. You don't look very rested, though." Great, so she looked like shit. Good to know. He frowned and reached up with his other hand to touch her face. She had to hold in a flinch.

Okay, so she was still on edge.

He ran his finger under her eye.

"That's because she got up early and went to the diner," Opal told him. "She's barely slept."

That frown turned into a scowl.

She shot Opal an exasperated look. The other woman just gave Lilac an innocent look back.

Yeah, right. Innocent, my ass.

Opal knew what she was doing.

The shithead.

24

"What? Lilac," Tanner said warningly. "How much sleep did you get?"

"A few hours, I'm fine."

"A few hours on the couch?" Linc asked, staring down at the sofa. "Why are you sleeping on the sofa?"

"Oh, well, I'm fine. I'm used to it now. I sleep on the sofa in Sugar too. And I like to be by the door in case . . ."

"In case what?" Tanner asked. "In case someone breaks in? So you can be the first line of defense?"

Why was he getting angry? "You say that like it's dumb."

"Because it is!" he snapped.

"Shh, you're going to wake Kye," she scolded. "He's a good sleeper, but you're being way too loud."

As if on cue, they heard a baby cry.

"I'll get him," Ryleigh said.

But Linc turned to her with a frown. "No, you won't."

"He's my baby," she protested, trying to stand.

"You're still not well enough, Ryleigh," Linc told her gently as he pressed her back onto the sofa. "Let someone bring him to you."

"I'll just . . ." Lilac tried to move away, but Tanner refused to let her go.

"Tanner," she said firmly.

"You need to quit the job at the diner."

Right. So Mr. Bossy was here today.

"I'm beginning to think you have a split personality," she told him. "Mr. Bossy and Mr. Easygoing."

"How about I get Kye?" Opal said, clearly fighting a smile. "You two are busy with your men."

"He's not my man," both Lilac and Ryleigh said together.

"Split personality, huh?" Tanner said, cupping the side of her face. "Perhaps it's just that you bring out the bossy, protective side in me. Did you ever think of that?"

"I've personally never seen him act like this," Linc said.

Tanner shot a glare at Linc. "If you're trying to calm my anger toward you, it's not fucking working. We're still having a reckoning."

"I figured." Linc gave her a remorseful look. "It's not like I don't deserve it."

She opened her mouth and Linc shook his head. "Don't say anything. Just . . . I'm really sorry I spoke to you like that, Lilac. I was worried about Ryleigh."

"I know. But I love her. I'd never do anything to harm her."

"I get that. You also need to know that you are welcome to stay here for a long as you want. All of you. I'm not kicking you out, no matter what happens." He frowned. "I'd also never hit you, understand? My life is dedicated to protecting people, especially women. Got me?"

"Um. Yes." It should have reassured her, but she'd met too many dirty cops to simply believe what he was saying. And as Opal stepped into the room, she gave her a knowing look.

They'd both met their share of shitty humans pretending that they were upstanding and good.

But Ryleigh gave Linc a soft look, buying every word.

"Sorry, he was pooh-stinky, weren't you, little boy?" Opal said, walking over to show Ryleigh her baby. "Don't know how he can produce such a stink when he only has milk."

Ryleigh sighed. "I wish I could hold him, but I don't want to pass any of my germs on. I'm so glad he's all right."

"Of course he is," Lilac told her with a smile. "We've got him."

"I know you do." Ryleigh slumped back, looking exhausted.

"You need to go back to bed," Linc told her.

"I will," Ryleigh said with a frown. "In here."

"No. Not in here." Linc shook his head.

Ryleigh glared up at him. "I'm not going back with you when you're mean to my friends."

"Ryleigh, I apologized."

Ryleigh huffed, then coughed.

She was doing so much better. It seemed Linc was good at taking care of her. Better than they would've managed. Plus, it meant there was less chance of Kye catching anything from her.

"Still don't forgive you," Ryleigh told him.

Linc grimaced. She kind of felt sorry for him. She also hoped he didn't get mad and kick them out. That he'd meant what he'd said.

"What if I make him pay?" Tanner said.

She gave Tanner a surprised look. "What are you going to do?"

Tanner just winked at her.

Ryleigh stared at Tanner as Opal watched on gleefully.

"I don't know," Ryleigh said hesitantly.

Linc sighed. "I need to talk to Tanner, then I'll be back to take you to bed, Ryleigh."

"Ooh, lucky girl. I love it when a man says he's going to take me to bed. It's been so long."

They all gaped at Opal.

"What?" she asked. "Just because you all are in denial about your sexual needs doesn't mean I am."

"Don't say sexual needs in front of the baby," Linc ordered.

"Don't boss her around," Ryleigh said. "Opal, don't say sex in front of Kye."

Opal just shrugged. "I'm sure he's going to hear worse. Does anyone know if they have scholarships or something for the kink club in town?"

"Scholarships?" Linc stared at her in bewilderment.

"Yeah, you know, for people who need some attention but can't afford the fees. It should be a thing, right? Kink scholarships."

"If you really need to go, I can—"

"No!" Everyone cut Lilac off, and she stared at them in shock.

"You are not running yourself into the ground to pay for fees to Saxon's," Tanner told her. "If Opal needs to go, I'll pay for her membership."

"Done! Thanks, Cowboy." Opal smiled at him, before walking into the bedroom again with a sleeping Kye.

Lilac frowned at Tanner. "I can't let you do that."

Tanner just gave her a stern look back. "It's time you learned to let people help you, Lilac. Which means me. You need to let me help you. Linc, come on."

Tanner stomped out of the guesthouse, Linc following him, after giving Ryleigh another admonishment to stay on the sofa.

"I didn't mean to upset Tanner." Lilac worried at her lip with her teeth.

"You look so tired, Lilac. And he seems really protective of you. He's a good man, isn't he?" Ryleigh said.

"Yeah," Opal said, walking back into the room. "From all

accounts, the Malone men are all good. A bit crazy, but decent men."

Lilac gave Opal a surprised look. How did she know that?

"What? I've been talking to people." Opal sat on the armchair while Lilac sat next to Ryleigh.

"Sorry I got sick," Ryleigh said.

"Hey, you don't need to apologize," Lilac told her.

"I feel awful that you've had to look after Kye though. That I haven't been able to. He hasn't shown any sign of illness?" Ryleigh asked worriedly.

"No," Opal said. "And he's been such a good baby."

"I just feel useless. Linc's been great. But urgh, I'm tired of getting sick like this."

"We need to settle in one place," Opal said. "Get jobs and a place to live."

"How can we do that?" Lilac asked. "Our fake IDs aren't good enough to get a rental place. And we won't be able to work for cash forever. What about healthcare?" Lilac fought for breath. Everything seemed so hard, and she wasn't sure how to make it all work.

"Easy, Lilac. It's going to work out," Ryleigh told her.

Would it? How could she be so sure?

Ryleigh always thought everything would work out.

But Lilac couldn't have that same sort of hope. She couldn't afford to.

Tanner walked back into the room, looking satisfied with himself. Linc followed, holding a bag of frozen vegetables held to his eye.

She froze.

Holy. Crap.

"Wow. You hit a cop, Cowboy?" Opal asked. "That takes balls. How'd you know he wasn't going to arrest you?"

Tanner shrugged. "Linc knew he was in the wrong. That he deserved what he got."

"Linc!" Ryleigh looked worried as she got to her feet.

"Don't get up," Linc commanded, walking over to her. "I'm fine."

Ryleigh tugged the bag of frozen veggies away from his face, wincing. "Tanner, did you have to do that?"

"Yep."

Lilac shot Tanner a look. "Really? Violence isn't always the answer, you know."

Tanner stared at her in surprise. "Lilac —"

"I need to go have a shower." There was a strange feeling in her stomach. It felt like anger and disappointment. How could he do that? First, he'd started a brawl, and now this? She could forgive the brawl, because those assholes were to blame.

But this . . . this was different.

"And I don't think you should be here when I get out."

It hurt to say it. It hurt so bad. But Lilac knew that she had to protect herself. No one else would.

Sure, it had seemed like Tanner might have.

But now . . . she wasn't so sure.

The last thing she wanted was to go from one violent man's hold to another. She knew it was unfair to compare Tanner to Stefan. Stefan was a monster. Tanner wasn't like him.

However, she worried about Tanner's impulsiveness. Another woman, one who hadn't been around violence so much, might not have an issue with any of this. And she did like him sticking up for her.

But could she really do this with him?

It had been a pipe dream to think that something might happen between them. Foolishness. She should have known that. She had enough stress going on in her life without adding to it.

25

Fuck.

What had just happened? Tanner stared after Lilac. Didn't she understand that Linc had deserved the punch? That those men the other night at Dirty Delights had deserved it too?

That all he was doing was protecting her?

Why had she looked at him like she thought . . . like she'd thought that he might harm her?

He'd never do that. Everything he did was for her. All he wanted was to care for and protect her.

Linc picked Ryleigh up and carried her out of the guesthouse. Both of them had given him strange looks. He glanced to Opal who was staring worriedly after Lilac.

Yeah. Nope. He wasn't leaving things like this. He took a step toward the bathroom, but Opal moved in front of him.

"I need to go talk to her," he said.

"No, big boy, I think it's best that you don't." Opal's voice was firm but kind.

"I need to! I can't leave things like this. I can't have her thinking that . . . that I might hurt her. That's what she thinks, right?"

"I don't know if she thinks that, exactly. Listen, she just needs a bit of time and some rest. She's exhausted and stressed."

"I need to tell her that I'd never harm her. Ever." He ran a shaking hand over his face. "I can't believe she'd be worried that I would do that."

"Lilac hasn't had an easy life. She lived with a narcissist who blamed her for everything that went wrong in his life and . . . shit, I shouldn't have said that. Fucking big mouth."

A narcissist? Who was that? Opal said 'he,' so it wasn't the nanny. Her dad or brother?

"I know a bit about her childhood. She told me about being raised by her nanny and how that bitch cherished her brother yet hated Lilac. How she'd restrict what Lilac ate."

Opal nodded. "Honestly, if she's opened up even that much, then deep down, part of her already trusts you. It's just . . . you can't keep using your fists to solve shit. I fucking get it. I'm always tempted to smack the stupidity out of someone. But Lilac needs to know that you'll keep your cool."

"Linc fucking deserved it, and he knows it. That's why he didn't hit back. And those assholes at Dirty Delight definitely did." He started pacing. "She can't expect me to sit by and do nothing while people touch her, upset her."

"Hmm, she probably wasn't all that upset by those assholes in the bar. But Linc is supposed to be your friend. And my guess is she feels so guilty over Ryleigh being sick that she felt like she deserved his ire."

"That's fucking bullshit! He had no right to talk to her like that."

Opal held up her hands. "Hey, I fucking agree. He was a fuckhead. Hmm. Yeah, I'm putting that between dickhead and shithead. But the thing is, Lilac doesn't necessarily agree. And all she sees is you using your fists to hurt people. Which is what her brother does. Well, not usually his own fists. Maybe she even blames herself for the fact that Linc is now sporting a black eye. You see where I'm going with this?"

Tanner stilled with a groan. "I really fucked this up is what you're saying."

Her brother was violent? Did he ever hit Lilac?

Fuck. He was realizing how little he really knew about her past.

She shrugged. "Yeah. Kind of. It's not your fault. Lilac is . . . she's used to violence in some ways yet abhors it at the same time. It's a difficult mix. My advice?"

He sighed. "Yeah?"

"Give her some time to calm down, but not too much time. She'll stew and convince herself of all sorts of shit if you leave her too long. Then you show her that you're not going anywhere. The one thing she needs is consistency. Someone who is there for her and who puts her first. Oh, and also? If you need to punch any more of your friends, don't let her know." Opal winked at him before disappearing into the other bedroom.

Fuck!

With a sigh, he moved to the closed door where his girl had disappeared through. He didn't like that there was a door between them. That she'd closed him out.

"Baby, I'm leaving. But not for good. I'll be back and we can talk."

With no other choice, his stomach in knots and filled with regrets, he left.

∽

Lilac couldn't sleep.

She tossed and turned. She needed to sleep. Desperately. But her mind wouldn't shut up.

Had she made a mistake sending Tanner away? Why had she done that? Because he'd hit some guys?

While defending you.

Urgh, she was an idiot. She already knew he wasn't like Stefan. Her brother would never have stuck up for her. Oh no, he'd have turned things around and blamed her for everything. He'd have told her it was her fault that guy had grabbed her at Dirty Delights.

With a sigh, she rolled onto her other side, wincing as pain shot through her ribs.

Ouch.

Moving onto her back, she pressed her hands to her eyes. Had she just been looking for a reason to push Tanner away?

Was she playing games without even knowing she was doing it?

Sitting up, she tried to take some even breaths. It felt like there was a huge weight pressing down on her chest.

Maybe she should call him and apologize.

He said he'd be back . . . but what if he'd decided that she was too much work? That she was a bitch who ran hot and cold?

You could have had it all. And instead, like usual, you self-sabotage.

Why can't you do anything right, Lilac?

First, she couldn't fix Sugar. Then, she didn't notice how sick Ryleigh was. And now she'd ruined things with Tanner.

Out. She needed to get out. She couldn't breathe.

She was lying on Ryleigh's bed, having locked herself in here to avoid talking to Opal.

Which was something else to feel ashamed of. Opal had to work tomorrow and she'd left her to take care of Kye.

After quickly pulling on some clothes, she tiptoed into the

next room to check on Kye and Opal. Both of them were sleeping.

She'd just go for a quick run, then come back and listen out for Kye, so Opal could sleep. Checking the time on the oven, she saw it was just after three in the morning.

Yeah, no way was she sleeping now.

Slipping out the door, she walked toward the road. Sure, she knew it was probably a stupid idea to go running at this time of night. However, Haven was a safe place.

Well, safe-ish.

Still, she was sure that no one else would be up now. She started off at a slow jog, but it wasn't long until her lungs were heaving for air, her side protesting that it didn't like moving this much.

Shit. She was so unfit.

It probably didn't help that she had bruised ribs.

Slowing down, she tried to catch her breath, but couldn't. The world spun dangerously.

Oh great.

Just wonderful.

This was the icing on the cake, she thought as the world went black.

26

Fuck. What asshole would be calling him at this time of the night? With a groan, Tanner reached over and grabbed his phone. Seeing Linc's name, he answered.

"Why the fuck are you calling me at fucking four-thirty in the morning? If you've arrested one of my brothers, I don't fucking care. Call Alec. Bye."

"Wait! Tanner, don't you fucking hang up!"

There was an urgency in Linc's voice that made him pause. Fuck. What if something had happened to Lilac or Kye?

"What is it? What's going on?" he asked, sitting up.

"It's Lilac."

He got up and put the phone on speaker as he reached for his jeans. "What about Lilac?"

"Tanner, she passed out. I brought her to the hospital and the doctor is checking her over now. I know things weren't great between you yesterday, but I thought you'd want to know."

"You're fucking right, I do. I'll be right there."

He hastily finished dressing before sending Alec a quick text to explain why he wouldn't be around today.

Then he raced to the hospital, not giving a single fuck about the speed limit.

∼

Running into the hospital, he saw Linc waiting for him. "Come on back with me."

"What happened? Why did she collapse?" He'd parked his truck in the first place he found, not caring if he got ticketed.

All he'd cared about was getting to his girl.

Linc sighed. "I don't know why she fainted. All I know is that Opal woke up to Kye and discovered that Lilac was gone. She woke me and I went searching for Lilac. I found her unconscious several blocks from the house, and I drove her straight here."

Fuck. Fuck!

"Listen, I've got to get back to Ryleigh, Opal, and the baby," Linc said. "Can you stay here? I've told the nurse you were coming and to update you on her condition."

Tanner raised his eyebrows. "They'll update me."

Linc grunted. "I might have lied a bit and told them that she belonged to you."

Okay. He was glad that Linc had the foresight to do that.

"I know Lilac won't be pleased, she doesn't seem to put much into this 'guardian thing'. Jake was giving her time to come around. But I called him, and we both agreed that the three of them are out of time. I'm going back to talk to Opal and Ryleigh, but I'm going to act as guardian for them both. I'll be moving all of them into my house. If you don't want to be Lilac's guardian, or she'd prefer me or Jake, let me know. She can move in with me too."

Tanner just stared at him in shock. He wasn't even mad at

the assumption that she might not want him as her guardian. Because he understood it.

That didn't mean that she was choosing anyone else.

Nope. It was becoming abundantly clear that Lilac was so busy looking after everyone else that she was failing to take care of herself.

That would stop.

Someone needed to put her safety and health first.

That person was going to be him.

And he'd be telling her that.

Just, please, let her be all right.

"That won't be necessary. Where would she be going so early in the morning?" he asked.

Linc shook his head grimly. "I don't know. Jake isn't happy about any of this, so he'll want you to tell him once you find out. Keep me updated too."

Tanner nodded and started pacing after Linc left. He couldn't settle enough to sit.

His phone buzzed.

Alec.

"Hey," he said into the phone. "Sorry I had to bail today."

"You know I don't care about that," Alec replied gruffly. "Are you all right?"

Their father had never really been in their lives. He'd been around but not involved, happy to leave them with a parade of nannies. But Tanner had never really felt his loss that badly.

Because he'd always had Alec. Even when he was young, Alec had watched out for him, taken care of him. So yeah, he might have had a useless father, but he'd had the best big brother he could ask for.

"Yeah, I'm all right."

"Tanner." That was all he said.

Letting out a deep breath, Tanner told Alec everything.

About meeting Lilac. About her showing up in Haven. To their argument yesterday and the call this morning from Linc.

"Right," Alec said after a few seconds of silence. "And you don't know why she came to Haven with her friends?"

"We haven't talked about that yet. She's so closed-off. So . . . scared at times. I don't know everything that's happened to her, but I can tell it's bad. But I'm not sure she trusts me enough to tell me."

"I think she trusts you more than you realize," Alec replied. "If she came here because of what you told her about Haven, I think that's a good sign."

"Yeah?" he asked.

"It might be that they were searching for safety and thought Haven might give them that."

"I hate the thought of her in trouble, and not knowing what it is."

"I'm going to call Jake, see what he knows," Alec told him. "Then I'm coming to the hospital."

"Alec, there's no need for you to come here."

"Are you going anywhere without her?" Alec asked.

"Of course not!" Fuck, no. He didn't plan on leaving her again.

"When she's allowed to leave the hospital, are you taking her back to Linc's?" he asked.

"No fucking way. She's terrible at taking care of herself and Linc has his hands full. Plus, he can't handle her."

"Obviously," Alec agreed. "Then you'll need support too. And she needs to know that if she is with one of us, the rest come as a package. And that we defend our own. From any threats."

"No one fucks with the Malones," Tanner repeated the family motto.

"Exactly."

"She's so thin, Alec. She wasn't this thin before. To lose that much weight in six months ... what if something is really wrong with her?"

"Then we'll deal with that like a family too. We're all here for you, Tanner. And for her. The biggest challenge will likely be convincing her to let you in. To allow you to take care of her. And find out what is going on with her."

Yeah. He knew that.

That's why he wasn't going to give her a choice.

27

Why were people talking? And what was that smell?

"Opal, turn the TV down. And I think you used too much hairspray again. Think of the ozone layer."

A low chuckle greeted her, and she stiffened.

"That isn't Opal," she muttered.

"No, it isn't. Also, I'm afraid I don't use hairspray and it's not the TV making that noise."

Lilac opened her eyes, looking around in fright. This wasn't Linc's guesthouse. She was lying on a bed in the middle of a stark white room. "Where am I? What's going on?"

As she attempted to sit up, Tanner moved into her line of sight, his face filled with concern and affection.

What the heck?

"It's all right," he said soothingly. "You just need to stay in bed."

"In bed?" she asked.

Panic started to take hold. This was...

"Am I in the hospital?"

Oh God. She couldn't be here. What if they'd used her real name? How much was this going to cost?

"I can't be here. I don't have insurance."

Fuck.

"They can't enter my name into any databases." Her breathing grew rapid.

"Shh." Tanner stood, leaning over her. "Okay, baby, you really need to calm down, or I'm going to get a nurse in to sedate you."

"You wouldn't!" she cried.

He just shot her a stern look.

Damn. Seemed like he would do just that.

"That's mean," she muttered.

"That me, Meanie Malone."

She snorted. That was actually a pretty funny nickname. She might have to use that when he was being Mr. Bossy. Not Mr. Fun.

"Don't get any ideas." He waggled a finger at her. "You're not allowed to call me that."

Yeah... too late.

Tanner sighed. "You're totally going to call me that, aren't you?"

She nodded, her head spinning slightly. She took a deep breath.

"Okay, baby?" he asked quietly.

"Just a bit dizzy. I really can't afford this."

"You don't have to worry about medical insurance or your name going into the system."

She raised her eyebrows.

"I told them you were my wife."

"Tanner! You can't do that! That's fraud."

"Eh, what are they gonna do about it?"

"Arrest you!"

"Don't worry about that. Alec will bail me out."

"Tanner." She started pulling at the monitors attached to her. That's when she noticed a needle in the top of her hand. She had a drip? Why?

"Stop moving," he said firmly. "You going to injure yourself."

"Tanner... there's a drip."

"Yes, it's giving you fluids. You were severely dehydrated." He gave her another stern look. "That won't be happening again."

"M.M," she muttered. Old Meanie Malone strikes again.

"Lilac, you're in big trouble."

Her mouth dropped open. "How am I in big trouble? It's not my fault I'm sick. Although I don't really feel sick, just kind of dizzy and weak."

Tanner sighed, looking at her worriedly. "I should get the doctor."

"No, please. Wait." She rubbed at her forehead. "I want to know what's going on first. How did I get here? Why are you here? And did you really think the best idea was to tell them I'm your wife? Don't people here know you?"

He hummed. "Yeah. Good point. Might be why I've had a few strange looks."

"Tanner!"

"Don't panic. I told the administrator that I would settle the bill but that you needed to use my last name as you're on the run from an abusive brother."

"You... what?" she whispered.

"Figure that's close enough to the truth, am I right?" He sat down again.

"You know?" she asked. She hadn't told him that exactly.

"Not everything, baby. You'll have to tell me the rest. But we've pieced together enough details to come to that conclusion. I'm still not sure where Opal and Ryleigh come into it, though."

"We?" she asked, focusing on that part.

"Me, Jake, Alec, and Linc."

"You've been asking questions about me?" This just kept getting worse and worse. "What if he finds me? He's going to find me."

She couldn't breathe. What if Stefan discovered them?

"Listen to me." He grabbed her chin, turning her to face him. "Listen. No one is going to hurt you."

"You don't understand."

She felt so helpless. So weak. She couldn't afford to be weak. She had so much she had to do.

"I don't. But I will soon because you're going to tell me."

"You can't . . . you can't bully me into it."

She'd already decided to tell him. Heck, six months ago, she'd been going to tell him some of what was going on. Now . . . she'd tell him it all. He deserved to know.

However, he couldn't just demand it. That was rude.

"I won't have to. You'll tell me because you want to. Because me and my family will take care of you."

She gaped up at him. That wasn't exactly what she'd expected him to say. "Your family?"

"Yep. No one fucks with the Malones."

"But I'm not a Malone." Her heart raced for an entirely different reason. She didn't even know his family. She'd only met Raid.

"Didn't we just have this conversation, baby? You're a Malone now. And we look after our own."

"You do?" she whispered.

He gave her a strange look. "Yeah, Lilac. Of course we do."

"Family is important?"

Understanding filled his face. "Yeah, family is important. Not everyone treats their family like your brother treated you."

Oh. That's why he looked like that. He thought she was thinking about Stefan.

"You and your family don't owe me anything. I can take care of myself," she said firmly.

He snorted. "Right. Clearly, you can't, or you wouldn't have collapsed on the side of the road early in the morning."

Oh God.

So that's what had happened? That's how she ended up here? A vague memory came back to her.

"Who found me? When? What time is it now?" she asked.

"It's ten. Opal woke up and discovered you were gone and alerted Linc. He went searching for you. He found you on the fucking pavement, passed out. Do you know what could have happened to you? What were you thinking?"

She flinched as his sharp tone and words hit her. Fuck, what had she been thinking?

Obviously, she hadn't.

What sort of idiot went for a run on their own at that time of night? And then she'd collapsed . . . what if she'd passed out in the middle of the road and someone had run her over?

What would happen to Ryleigh, Kye, and Opal then?

She was supposed to look after them, but apparently, she couldn't even look after herself.

Shit. What an idiot!

Lilac rubbed at her chest as her heartbeat raced.

"Tanner." A low, commanding voice spoke from the doorway. She glanced over to see a large, intimidating-looking man standing there. He wore a faded checked shirt and jeans. And there was a scowl on his face.

Shit.

Who was he?

He was frowning at Tanner with disapproval. "Don't speak to her like that. Not while she's lying in a hospital bed. She's fragile. She needs care and understanding. Not a scolding."

Her mouth dropped open as she stared at the large man. Her heartrate slowed. "You're my new favorite person."

"Hey!" Tanner cried. "I should be your favorite person."

A look of surprise entered the big man's face. Then he grinned. Wow, he was even more gorgeous when he smiled. "I wouldn't say that too loud. It doesn't mean I don't believe you deserve to be scolded and punished. Just once you're feeling better."

She frowned. "That's not very nice. And no one said anything about punishment."

"Oh, there's gonna be punishment," Tanner said darkly.

The other man stepped into the room and slapped his hand around Tanner's head. "Don't upset her."

"What . . . who . . . why . . ." Tanner stared up at the man, flabbergasted.

"You forgot when and how," she teased.

Surprise filled her as she realized she was actually having fun teasing Tanner. With this stranger.

Although she had a pretty goo idea of who he was.

"Alec, you're the one that mentioned punishment," Tanner grumbled.

So, she was right. This was Alec Malone.

"Yes, but she wasn't upset when I said it. She knows I'm not the one who will be delivering it." Alec winked at her.

"No one needs to deliver it."

This man was the head of the Malone family. The person she really needed to find out more about because he made the decisions for the family.

Not all families work like yours.

Alec moved to stand at the end of the bed and stared down at her with a serious look on his face. His arms were crossed over his broad chest.

"You worried us."

"Um. Sorry?" she said.

Shoot. Why was she apologizing? She didn't even know this guy.

He nodded solemnly. "That will do. For a start."

Yikes. For a start?

She gave Tanner a wide-eyed look, but he was glaring up at Alec while rubbing the back of his head. "You've got a hell of a slap on you."

"You're fine," Alec said dismissively. "I can slap the other side, even it out."

"And Lilac doesn't like violence," Tanner added. "You'll upset her."

Alec raised his eyebrows. "I don't think she's upset that I slapped your head. She's worried about getting her butt slapped. Don't worry, you'll have a safeword, Lilac. And Tanner will discuss your limits first. I raised him to know better than to just shove you over his lap and smack your butt."

"Did you teach him not to hit his friends?" she said.

Alec turned to look at Tanner, who sighed. "I punched Linc."

"Oh, is that all?" Alec shrugged.

"Is that all?" she repeated dumbfounded.

"He was probably being a dick. Was he?" Alec asked Tanner.

"Yep." Tanner was smiling now.

"You still shouldn't have hit him." She glared at Tanner. "He's your friend."

"Not really." Tanner shrugged. "We're friendly, but he's a still a cop. Malones and cops don't mix."

Alarm filled her. "Why?"

"Malones don't like to follow rules other than their own," Alec told her. "And some of my brothers, well, let's just say that they have impulse control issues."

She snorted. "That's one way to put it."

Alec's gaze moved over her. "You're still too pale. Dehydrated?"

"Yep," Tanner replied before she could. "They want to monitor her heart rate too. Apparently, it was too low."

It was? Worry filled her.

Alec grunted. "Doctor been in?"

"No, I need to go tell them she's awake."

"I'll do it in a moment." Alec's gaze landed on hers. "We're going to take care of you, Lilac."

She sucked in a breath. For some reason, she felt like crying.

"I don't want to have my butt smacked."

Holy. Crap.

Why had she said that?

Alec's lips twitched. "Can't help you with that one, sweetheart."

"You could tell Tanner that he's not allowed to do that. He'll listen to you."

"But he's your guardian now. It's in the job description. And if he didn't smack your butt, then he'd have me to answer to."

Yikes.

So, she was going to find no reprieve from him.

"Why'd you go running so early in the morning, sweetheart?" Alec asked.

"I . . . I couldn't sleep," she muttered. That was the simplest explanation, though not precisely the full one.

Alec just nodded. "Right. Well, you won't be doing that again. Getting your butt spanked will help you remember. I'll go find the doctor."

28

A beat of silence followed after Alec left the room. Lilac peeked over at Tanner, whose jaw was clenched as he stared down at his hands.

"I'm sorry, Tanner."

"What?" His gaze shot up to her. "Why are you apologizing?"

"I shouldn't have reacted the way I did yesterday. It's part of the reason I couldn't sleep. I kept thinking about how I pushed you away for defending me. By rights, you should still hate me, yet you keep looking out for me. All my life, I wanted someone to defend me, and you did that. And how do I reward you? By telling you to go. I . . . I didn't mean it. I don't w-want you to g-go. I think I k-keep thinking that you'll w-work out I'm not w-worth it. I mean, we hardly know each other. Why would you want this?" She waved her hand through the air over her body.

He leaned forward, his face intent as he took hold of her hand. "First of all, do not speak about yourself like that. Why wouldn't I want you? You are smart and funny. Loyal and beautiful. The way you take care of your friends . . . fuck, Lilac, I would be damn lucky to have you as mine."

A sob escaped her, tears dripping down her cheeks. "I'm messed up, Tanner. I've got s-so many problems. I never should have come here, never should have brought those problems with me."

"Hey, if you hadn't come here, I would be even more upset with you, understand?"

"You wouldn't have known, though. You could have m-moved on with your life."

He shook his head. "I've had this gaping hole inside of me ever since you took off, Lilac. I've been a grumpy asshole. Ask any of my brothers. Out of all of them, I'm the most easygoing and fun, but I haven't felt like myself since I lost you."

"How can you ever forgive me?" she asked.

"Because I know you have your reasons for what you did. And you're going to tell me them so I can handle them for you."

She let out a small, watery laugh. "Do you realize how arrogant you sound?"

"I do?" He gave her a pleased look. "Good. That's what I was going for."

Lilac groaned. What was she going to do with him? He was terrible.

Before she could say anything else, the door to her room opened and a doctor and nurse stepped in.

Nerves filled her as she remembered what had happened.

She'd collapsed.

God. What if something was really wrong? What was she going to do? And what about the cost of this room and all of her care? There was no way she was letting Tanner pay for it.

But she was grateful that he'd thought to give her his last name to use. Sure, a hospital database should be private. There was no way that Stefan should have access to it. But she knew what sort of resources her brother had. He'd found them before. She just hoped to God, he wouldn't find them this time.

The doctor was an attractive woman with dark hair. She smiled at Lilac. "Hello, Mrs. Malone."

Jeez. She liked the sound of that a little too much.

Focus, Lilac.

"I'm Doctor Ann Martin and this is Abby." She gestured at the friendly-looking, blonde nurse.

Abby gave her a small wave.

"I'm glad to see you're awake and looking better."

"Um, yeah. Do you know why I fainted?" she asked.

Doctor Martin glanced over at Tanner. "Would you like to have this conversation in private?"

"I'm her husband!" Tanner protested.

Abby snorted, then put her hand over her mouth. "Sorry."

"Yes. Her husband," Doctor Martin said, looking doubtful. "Mrs. Malone? What would you prefer?"

"Please call me Lilac. And . . ." She should kick him out, but he'd done so much for her. And the truth was that she was tired of pushing him away. She wanted him close. "I want Tanner to stay please."

"Very well. When you were brought into the hospital, your heartrate and blood pressure were very low. We took some blood and ran some tests. We're still waiting on the full results, but it wouldn't surprise me if you were low in iron as well as some other vitamins. You were also very dehydrated which is why we put the drip in."

"Okay." None of that sounded terrible, right? "Was it due to low blood pressure that I fainted?"

"That's the most likely scenario. However, we want to run a few more tests. We also checked your blood sugar, and it was low."

"Oh."

The doctor's face softened. "Lilac, when was the last time you ate?"

She swallowed heavily. "Um. Well, I . . . I had some dinner last night at Dirty Delights. Wait, no, that was the night before. Yesterday . . ."

Shit. Did she eat anything? "It was an eventful day."

"Do you often skip meals?" the doctor asked.

"It's not . . . I'm not . . . I just forget. When I get stressed, my stomach ties up in knots and I can't eat. I don't know. I just haven't had an appetite."

It sounded so lame, but she didn't know how else to explain it.

Did they think she'd deliberately not eaten?

Her gaze went to Tanner, and he gave her a small smile, squeezing her hand.

"It's all right, Lilac," the doctor said in a kind voice. "I understand. I get the same way. My emotions are definitely tied to my stomach. When I'm stressed or working too much, I forget to eat as well. I keep some protein drinks in the staff fridge to keep me going. And keeping hydrated is really important."

"Yes. You're right." She didn't know if the doctor was telling her the truth or just making that all up, but it made her feel better. As though she wasn't the only one struggling with eating and anxiety.

"Talking to someone can help too."

Lilac tensed again.

"It's just something to think about, okay? We all need someone to talk to at times."

"I've been seeing a psychologist," Abby offered. "I had something bad happen to me as a teenager and I repressed it. It . . . it came out recently, so I've been seeing this really nice lady in Haven."

"Molly?" Tanner asked.

"Yep. She's awesome. Not judgy or bossy or anything like that."

"I'm not sure I can talk about my past with a stranger," Lilac said, feeling ill at the thought.

"Sometimes, it doesn't need to be a stranger." The doctor patted her leg. "Now, we want to keep you here while we do some more tests and wait for the full blood results. We also need to continue to monitor your heart rate and get you rehydrated."

"Will . . . can I go home by tomorrow morning? I have work tomorrow night," she said.

"I think it would be best if you took some time off. At least a few days but a week would be ideal," the doctor told her.

"I can't miss work." That just wasn't a possibility.

"We'll work that out," Tanner said.

What was to work out? But she didn't say anything else as she knew the doctor had to be busy.

"Thanks, Doctor," she said.

"I'd also like you to talk to our nutritionist. She might have some ideas about things you could eat that won't hurt your stomach. And we'll do an ultrasound to ensure nothing else is going on."

"All right."

More money. Perfect.

Abby fussed over her for a bit, then told her she'd arrange some lunch for her.

They were already trying to feed her. But then again, she had to start eating, or she was going to get into a worse state.

Fuck. What a mess.

Tanner squeezed her hand once they were gone.

"You don't have to stay, you know," she said.

Urgh. Why did she say that? She didn't want to be here alone.

"I'm not going anywhere until you do," Tanner told her firmly.

"Um, I don't think they'll let you stay here overnight."

"You'll be surprised what they'll let me do." He winked at her.

"Your charm doesn't work on everyone," she informed him.

He gasped, placing his hand on his chest as he sat back in his chair. "Lilac, you wound me."

"Your ego will protect you, I'm sure," she replied dryly.

"This is true." He grinned. "But I'm staying the night. No arguments."

Abby knocked before walking into the room carrying a tray. "Doctor Martin said to bring you one of her protein drinks to see if you liked them."

Okay, maybe the doctor had been telling the truth after all. That helped settle her nerves even further.

"Someone will collect that tray later," Abby told her. "You hit the buzzer if you need me, okay?"

"All right. Thank you." She smiled at the other woman.

"Welcome, Lilac. Oh, don't try going to the bathroom by yourself just yet. Doctor Martin is worried you might get dizzy and collapse. So, call for me, okay?"

Great. Just what she needed. Someone to escort her to the bathroom. How had things gotten to this?

"I'll help her," Tanner assured Abby.

Abby eyed him. "All right. I guess you won't let her fall over and hit her head."

"Of course not!" Tanner looked offended.

Before Lilac could offer her opinion, Abby left.

"What if I don't want you to take me to the bathroom?" she asked him huffily.

"Guess I could arrange a bed pan."

"Tanner!"

He just grinned at her. Urgh, he was terrible. His phone started beeping with messages. Pulling it out, he sighed before putting it face down on the nightstand.

"Um, shouldn't you read those? Answer them?"

"Eh, it's just my brothers. Some from my sisters-in-law. I'll answer them when you're napping."

"I just woke up."

"They'll wait."

"Tanner," she chided.

"What? They're just being nosy. Wanting to come to the hospital to meet the new Mrs. Tanner Malone."

"Tanner! You didn't tell them that we got married!"

He grinned. "Nah, but I could."

She rubbed her hand over her face. "I can't believe this is happening. I was so stupid!"

"Okay, you need to stop doing that." He drew her hand away from her face. "You were not stupid."

"I was, Tanner! I pushed you away when I really didn't want you to go. I regretted it so much, and I was worried that you wouldn't want anything to do with me anymore. My brain wouldn't shut up. I . . . I couldn't sleep, so I thought it was a good idea to go running at three in the morning to clear my head. What if I'd died? What then?"

"Do not say things like that," he told her darkly. "You are not going to die."

"I was such an idiot."

"One more time," he said in a low stern voice.

"What?" She gave him a startled look. What was he talking about?

"You call yourself an idiot or stupid one more time and we're gonna have problems."

She reared back. "You'll leave me?"

Tanner's eyes widened. "No, baby. Christ, no. I'm not leaving you."

"You should," she said bitterly. "I bring nothing but problems wherever I go."

"That was your third strike."

Um. What? "I didn't say stupid or idiot."

"No, but you basically called yourself a problem and that's the same thing."

"Is not."

"You really want to argue over this?" he asked.

"Well, that depends on what strike three gets me."

"Nothing at the moment. But eventually, it's going to get you a hot ass. We'll add it to the punishment you've got coming for endangering yourself."

29

"I don't need a spanking!"

"Uh, yeah, you do."

She huffed out a breath. He was terrible.

"But, like I said, it will wait until you're feeling better."

"There's nothing really wrong with me. And I don't want you to feel like . . . like you're obliged to look after me."

His eyes looked sad as he stared at her. "Baby, you fainted. You aren't eating or getting enough sleep or rest. I want to take care of you. The last thing I feel is obligation or like you're a burden. Taking care of you . . . it feels like something I was born to do."

She sucked in a breath. Had anyone ever said something that nice to her? If they had, then she couldn't remember.

"I've heard a lot of women in Haven get spanked if they break the rules. It seems to go against the whole ethos of protecting them."

To her shock, he laughed. "It does, doesn't it? But all the women agree to the rules they're given. As well as the consequences."

"They do? Why?"

"Hmm, well, I have my suspicions some of them like the punishments."

They did? Huh. Actually, she could see Opal loving a spanking. Ryleigh, on the other hand, probably wouldn't.

And you?

Well, she liked the idea of a fun spanking. But a punishment spanking? Hmm.

Her nanny had spanked her a few times when she was a kid and she'd hated it. After she'd told her dad, he'd put a stop to that. Of course, she'd just come up with other forms of punishments.

"And the others . . . well, I guess they know that those rules are there for them. And that the men in this town would lay down their lives to keep them safe. Have you seen anyone who looked unhappy? Downtrodden?"

"No, everyone is sickeningly happy and nice."

"Thank you!" He clapped, startling her. "It is a bit sickening, isn't it? That's why we have to shake things up every now and then. If it wasn't for a few bar brawls and some pranks, no one around here would have anything to moan about."

Lord.

"You're trouble."

"I try my hardest. But, seriously, baby. You know I won't spank you if you tell me no. Although as your guardian, I'll have to come up with some other punishments."

"So you've just declared yourself my guardian? Without my consent?"

"Would you rather have someone else be your guardian? Linc is going to act as guardian for Ryleigh and Opal."

She wrinkled her nose at that idea. Linc might have apologized but she didn't think that meant he liked her.

"Jake would do it."

Still not ideal. She didn't know him, and he was the sheriff. Lilac wasn't sure she could entirely trust him.

"No. Not them."

"I'm sure Alec would."

She licked her lips. "Alec?"

"Yep."

"He's a very nice, scary man," she said carefully.

Tanner grinned. "He is. I'm not sure he'd appreciate the nice part, he has mellowed over the years. Especially since meeting Mia. Although, threaten his family and there is nothing he wouldn't do to protect them."

Would he consider her a threat to them? When he found out who she was?

"I don't think I want Alec as my guardian."

"Sure? The women in this family sure have him wrapped around their little fingers. Even though he thinks he's in charge, he's really not."

That was . . . sweet. It was hard to believe that such a big, dominant man might be wrapped around the finger of a woman. But she knew that not every man was like Stefan.

Not every man hurt the people he was supposed to care for and protect.

But she didn't know Alec, couldn't trust him. And what would that say to Tanner? That she trusted his brother, a stranger, more than him?

Nope. She wouldn't do that. Not to her Tanner. Not after everything he'd done for her. Not after what he meant to her.

"I'm sure. If I wanted anyone, it would be you."

The smile that took over his face could only be described as boyish and charming. As though he couldn't quite believe she'd chosen him.

God, who wouldn't choose him?

"There're other benefits of being punished if you break a rule," he said.

She eyed him sceptically.

Like what?

"A punishment wipes the slate clean. No more guilt for breaking a rule. No bringing it up over and over and hashing it out. Both parties move on."

Oh. Now, that was something she did like the idea of. Lilac tended to overthink everything. To punish herself over and over.

"You really think that would work?" she asked.

"From what I've heard, yes."

"All right. Do it now." She pushed the blankets back. But he grabbed them and laid them back over her.

"What? What are you doing?" he asked.

"I want the spanking. I want to get rid of all this guilt." She shoved the blankets back off herself.

"Baby, no." He drew the blankets back over her. "Stay put."

"Tanner, I want to get rid of this guilt."

"I hate that you're feeling guilty, pretty girl. But I won't do anything to risk your health. And I think you still need some time to think. No rash decisions."

"I'm not being rash."

"You are. No more arguing. Your guardian has spoken."

Dear Lord help her. He was out of control.

Although he did have a point about not making a rash decision.

"Maybe you should take some time to think about being my guardian."

"Nope."

"But there's still so much we haven't talked about . . . you might change your mind once you hear it all."

"I won't be changing my mind. I've wanted you since the first night that I met you, pretty girl. Even though you were crap at darts."

"I wasn't crap," she muttered.

"Lilac." He waited until she was looking at him to continue speaking. "Did your brother hit you? That bitch of a nanny? Your dad?"

"My dad? No, he would never. My dad loved me. He was just . . . busy most of the time."

Doing things she didn't want to think about.

"My nanny spanked me a few times, but I tattled on her to my dad, and he put a stop to that."

"But he didn't fire her?" He sounded outraged.

"My brother loved her. And he always got what he wanted." Even she could her the bitterness in her voice.

"Asshole. What about your brother? Was he abusive, wasn't he?" Anger filled his face, and she sucked in a deep breath to keep herself calm.

How did she describe the hold her brother had over her? About all the things that he'd done? It was hard to explain that he was a psychopath who could be charming and loving, then turn around and smack you in the face for disagreeing with him.

"Yes," she whispered.

"Did he hit you? Hurt you?"

"Sometimes," she admitted. "But that wasn't really the worst of it. I could handle the bruises. The pain. Those were things I was used to. But Stefan was a pure genius when it came to emotional abuse and torture. He could be so loving, you know. Once, I fell out of a tree and skinned my knee. Mrs. Jansen told me to stop crying and shut up. But Stefan carried me inside and cleaned it up, bandaged it. Hell, he even kissed it better."

She shook her head, holding back tears. "But then a few weeks later, I annoyed him. I can't even remember what I did. And he took my favorite stuffed toy and burned it."

"Fuck. Did you tell your dad?"

"Oh no, I never told my dad on Stefan." She shuddered at the thought. "Stefan was his heir. My dad loved me, but Stefan was the future. I was just a girl."

"Fuck your father," he said.

She gave him a startled look. None of this was her father's fault.

"Just because you are a girl, he let your brother and nanny abuse you? No. That's not the way things work. He's supposed to protect and take care of all of his children, understand me? If we'd had a sister, she'd have been the most protected out of all of us. The most cherished."

"Really?"

"Hell, yeah. You think she would have been allowed to date? Nope. She'd have had to wait until we were all dead and buried. She'd have been lucky to have been let out of the house."

Swallowing heavily, she drunk in all of his words.

"Poor girl would have been completely smothered. If any boy interested in my sister had come on our property, I'd have shot the tires out on his car."

"Tanner! You would not!"

"Why not? I've done it before. Mostly to Jardin. He's a pretentious ass."

"Who is Jardin?" she asked.

"Didn't you hear me? He's a dick."

"No. I mean . . . who is he?"

"Oh, just one of our cousins. The New Orleans Malones. All of them are assholes. Well, except Lottie. She's a sweetheart. Where was I? Oh yeah, your asshole of a father. Fuck, what sort of family did you grow up in? Sounds like the fucking mafia."

Oh hell.

She'd said too much. She'd known that as she was talking.

His eyes widened. "Oh, fuck."

Tanner started to pace.

"Please don't go looking into him, Tanner. That will just alert him to where we are. He's clever and he has people searching for us. Please." There was a reason she'd always been careful not to say his name. Even though Tanner didn't know her real last name it might not take much to find Stefan.

"Hey." He walked over to her, sitting on the bed and facing her. "I'm not going to do anything rash."

She eyed him doubtfully.

"Sheesh, you do a few impulsive things in your life, and you get labelled as a hothead," he teased.

She laughed, then snorted before putting her hand over her mouth. "Oops. Sorry."

"I've missed your snort-laugh, pretty girl."

"Tanner," she moaned.

"I won't go looking for him. I promise."

She breathed out a sigh of relief. "Thank you."

"But I can tell you right now that when I find this fucker, he's a dead man for touching you. For hurting you."

"No! No, you won't. You'll go nowhere near him. He's dangerous. If he knew how I felt about you, he'd . . . he'd hurt you. That's what he does to keep me in line. After my dad died, he moved away from punishing me by destroying my stuff and moved onto destroying people. I couldn't make friends with any of the staff because he'd use them to punish me. He finally figured he could get me to do what he wanted by threatening people I cared about."

"That motherfucker. He needs to die, Lilac."

"I know." It was the only way they were ever going to be free of him. That *she* would ever be free.

"I take it that's why you disappeared on me six months ago?" he asked.

"Yes. I was going to tell you some of it when I saw you that night. But as I was heading toward the bar to meet you, I spotted one of his men stepping out of a car. I knew I had to lose my phone and get out of there. I rang Opal and Ryleigh before I turned it off and shoved it in a bin. They picked me up and we fled. I'm so sorry, it wasn't until we were on the outskirts of town that I realized I should have texted you too. But if they were tracking us through our phones . . . I don't know. My brother has his ways, and I couldn't have you involved with me. So, I took off and I . . . I've regretted it ever since. I hated hurting you. Lying to you. God, so much that it felt like it was a cancer growing inside me." Her voice cracked as she finished her explanation.

"Baby, fuck." He cupped the side of her face. "You don't know how much it kills me that you didn't know you should run to me."

"I had to protect you—"

"No, Lilac," he said firmly. "No. That ends right now. You don't protect me. Understand? You. Do. Not. Protect. Me. I look after you. That is the way it works from now on. And if you take away my opportunity to protect you, I will not be happy."

Looking up into his face, she knew he meant every word. Her mouth was dry as she tried to get out the words to explain why she had to protect him. "I don't want you to get hurt because of me."

"Then why come here?"

She sniffled. She couldn't tell him that part. It wasn't her secret to tell. "I know it makes no sense."

"Why? Why come here? Was it for me?"

"Yes, it was for you." It wasn't a lie. It just wasn't the whole story.

"Because you knew I'd protect you and your friends. That the entire town would."

"We did some research into Haven, although I wasn't sure I really believed that a town like this could truly exist. I know it was wrong and selfish to come here. I've probably put you all in danger."

FUCK.

He couldn't stand this. Tanner knew he had to get her to calm down. To eat some food. He was doing a terrible job of looking after her.

But this was the most he'd gotten out of her, and he was loathe to stop her from talking.

"You don't need to worry about us. We can take care of ourselves. And protect you guys."

She wiped at her cheeks. Fuck. He hated that she was crying.

"I don't want anything to happen to you."

Her brother had so much to answer for. Tanner was going to find that fucker, and then he would make him pay for all the pain and sorrow he'd caused Tanner's girl.

Fucker would pay in blood.

And he knew his brothers would help. They might be ranchers now, but they'd come from the same world it sounded like her brother was in. And they knew how to fight hard and dirty.

"It's time to take a break, baby. To let someone else take over for a while. You've worn yourself out. However, lucky for you, you've got someone willing and able to take the reins for a while."

"A cowboy metaphor?" she asked dryly as he wiped her tears away.

"Hey! There's nothing wrong with that."

"You don't think it's cliched?"

"I think it's inspired. Like most things I say."

She rolled her eyes at him.

"What do you say? Stop worrying about me, about everyone

else and just concentrate on you for a while. On letting me help you."

He could see her thinking and then, to his surprise, she nodded. "All right. I'll try. For a short while."

He figured it was as good as he was going to get.

"Good girl."

Her eyes lit up at his words.

"Right, you need to eat something and then have a nap. How about I tell you about some stories from when I was a kid? That will cheer you up."

Tanner lifted the cover off the plate of food that Abby had brought her. He grabbed the fork and picked up a piece of strawberry. To his relief, she opened her mouth and took it.

"All of my brothers are idiots, who got themselves into some real scrapes. Well, not Alec or West. Alec, because he's the head of the family. And West, well, because he's a dick. And boring."

"You're so mean to him," she scolded.

"It's not mean when it's the truth," he protested. "He's always been an asshole."

"Is he mean to you?" she asked.

He shot his gaze to her, reading her expertly. "Nothing like what you're thinking. West is West. And he'd never harm you. None of us would. Here, have a bit of melon. That's it. You're doing so well, pretty girl."

Oh yeah.

She definitely liked hearing him praise her.

Such a good girl.

30

"Hello? Who is this?" Opal asked.

"Opal," she answered. "It's me. Lilac. I'm on Tanner's phone." Her phone battery was dead.

"Fuck. Lilac, are you all right? What happened? Linc said you were okay, and that Tanner was with you, but Ryleigh nearly took his balls off for leaving you at the hospital."

"She did? She shouldn't do that." What if he got upset and kicked them out? They could end up on the streets.

Shit. Fuck.

Anxiety filled her.

She glanced over at the closed bathroom door. Tanner had given up trying to feed her anymore lunch. She'd managed to eat some fruit and drink some of the protein drink the doctor had sent for her to try.

It was actually not too bad.

He'd agreed to let her use his phone if she promised to take a nap after he finished showering. Alec had brought him a bag with some clothes.

Lilac still couldn't believe he was insisting on staying the night.

"Lilac, chill. He's not going to kick us out. Not with the way he looks at Ryleigh. It's like she's a triple layer chocolate cake with whipped cream. Yum. I could do with some of that right now." Opal sighed.

"Opal, I'm sorry," she whispered.

"What do you have to be sorry about?" Opal asked. "You didn't ask to faint and end up in the hospital."

"No, but I shouldn't have been out running at that time of the morning. I can only imagine how worried you were when you woke up to find me gone. You were supposed to start your new job today. I ruined that."

"Oh, don't worry about that," Opal replied. "News around this place travels really fast, and before I could even contact Laken, she'd left me as message not to worry about working today. Also, Ryleigh reckons she's fine now to look after Kye. I'll start my new job tomorrow. That's no big deal. Your health is. Lilac, you have to start taking care of yourself. What would we do without you?"

"I know, I know," she said hastily. "I'll get back to work as soon as I can. We can't afford for me to be off—"

"I'm not talking about the money, Lilac!" Opal yelled.

Lilac paused, shocked.

"I'm talking about you running yourself into an early grave. I . . . I'm terrified that something is going to happen to you, Lilac. You scared me. I don't want to be without my best friend."

Shit.

Lilac sniffled. "Nothing is going to happen to me."

"Something already did," Opal replied quietly.

Ouch. Okay, she got it. She wasn't feeling the greatest and she'd done a dumb thing. Plus, she was struggling with anxiety and all of her worries. About not being able to take care of anyone.

But she found it so hard to look after herself. It felt selfish.

And what if something had happened to you?

"I'll try to do better," she whispered.

"You do that, I'm going to come see you."

"No! No, don't do that. I'm all right and I don't want you bringing Kye along or leaving Ryleigh behind. Honestly, I'm fine. And Tanner is here."

"That's a good thing? Because yesterday you wanted nothing more to do with him."

"A good thing? I'm not sure I'd say that. I . . . it's all so fucking complicated. But I . . . I just . . . "

"You need this," Opal said. "It's okay to be selfish sometimes, Lilac."

"Is it?"

"Yes. Don't be such a pessimist."

"Um, Opal." That was rich coming from her. She was born a pessimist.

"I know, I know. I can hear myself. And I admit that I didn't think that this place was going to live up to its promise. But it's growing on me. We could be happy here, Lilac."

If they could get rid of her brother.

"Stefan isn't going to win," Opal said fiercely. "I won't let that happen. We're all going to live happily ever after. Hear me?"

She did.

Tanner stepped out of the bathroom.

Wearing just a towel.

Holy. Moly.

Her mouth went dry, her heart racing. She needed to calm down before she set off the monitor.

Sure, she'd seen him naked before, but the memory of what he looked like was nothing compared to the reality.

He hadn't dried himself properly, so there were drips of water running down his chest.

Damn, she'd love nothing more than to lap up every one of those drips with her tongue.

Then she'd follow them down his abs to where that towel was very loosely secured. And she'd undo that knot so it fell to the floor so she could follow the drops of water over his cock...

"Lilac? You okay?" Opal asked through the phone.

Her gaze shot away from his crotch, up to his smirking face.

Oh Lord help her. He knew exactly what she'd been thinking.

"I've got to go. Tanner is out of the shower."

"Hmm, and I bet he looks delicious. You can tell he's got a fucking hot body under those jeans and flannel."

"Opal," she groaned. "I'm ending this call now."

Tanner leaned against the doorway to the private bathroom. She didn't know how she'd gotten such a nice room and honestly, she was scared to ask.

Well, scared to ask how much it cost.

"Talking to Opal?" he asked as she set his phone down on the rolling tray.

"She sends her regards," she replied stiffly.

He snorted. "Somehow, I can't see Opal saying something like that."

No, she'd commented on his hot body. And it was smoking.

"You're looking hungry. Want one of your snacks?" He moved closer to her.

No. Nope. He could not come near her. It wasn't safe. Oh, holy heck. He was here. Right in front of her. That bare, muscular chest was so close that she just wanted to reach out and touch him.

Before she could stop herself, she was running her finger along his abs.

"Want me to lose the towel, baby?" he murmured. "You look like you do. You're looking at me like you think *I'm* the snack."

She snatched her hand back, feeling her cheeks growing red. "That's not . . . I wasn't . . . sorry."

"No reason to be sorry. I'm hungry myself."

"Oh, do you want one of the snacks that Abby bought in?" she asked. Abby had brought in several snacks to try and tempt Lilac.

She hated that she was being such a hassle for people. But at the same time, she was kind of enjoying being fussed over.

He smiled. "No, baby. Those are yours. And I had my heart set on a different sort of snack."

His gaze ran over her body.

Shock filled her as she realized what he was talking about. She could feel herself grow red. "You cannot find me attractive."

He frowned. "What do you mean? Of course I do."

"I'm lying in a hospital bed. My hair is a mess. I haven't had a shower yet. I'm . . . I'm gross."

"That's two."

She gaped up at him. "Tanner!" Two?

"What? You were warned about speaking badly about yourself. And you look fucking beautiful, in a hospital bed or not. If you're not careful, I'm going to forget the fact that anyone could walk in here at any time and I'm going to go under those covers, spread your legs, and lick your pretty pussy until you scream."

"You wouldn't!" She gaped at him even as her body heated as an image of him doing just that filled her mind.

Damn him.

She couldn't get aroused while she was lying in a hospital filled with probably hundreds of people!

"I haven't shaved my legs!" she cried.

Really? That's what she was going to focus on? That's what she the best thing you could come up with?

She groaned.

Idiot.

His lips twitched. "And that's your only objection, is it? I'd be happy to help take care of that for you."

"Tanner Malone!" she said primly. "You are not shaving my legs."

"Why not?"

"B-because . . . because . . . that's not . . . it's not sexy." She wanted him to see her as beautiful. Gorgeous.

She wanted to be irresistible. Not a burden with hairy legs.

Right. Because you're so sexy right now, lying in this hospital bed in the clothes you put on to go running in. Hair a mess. Looking pale and gaunt.

And he still seems to want you. Huh.

She had no clue why.

"You don't think so? You don't think I'd enjoy giving you whatever you needed, having you depend on me? Because I think that's sexy as fuck. Plus, you know, I'd have you naked in the shower . . ."

She swallowed heavily. "Yeah, I'm not sure that's a good idea."

"Maybe once I get you home," he said casually as though it was a done deal.

She swallowed heavily. "I can't go home with you."

"You can and you will," he replied as he turned away. "You're going to need someone to look after you. And I happen to be that someone. As your guardian, it's my job. But as your man, it's my privilege."

"Tanner," she whispered. He kept saying the sweetest things to her.

Suddenly, he leaned down and kissed her. Oh man, she'd missed his touch. It felt like she had this empty well inside her that was slowly filling it up.

Drip by drip.

"Hush. No arguing. When you're feeling better, you can argue. But today we're just relaxing and concentrating on you eating and resting. All right?"

"All right." She was too tired to argue.

"That's my good girl. Now, I forgot to take my clothes into the shower with me. I'll go get dressed and be back in a moment." He grabbed his bag.

Yeah, right.

Left them behind, huh?

As he walked back into the bathroom, he also failed to shut the door properly.

And she totally watched as he dropped the towel to reveal the most perfect butt on the planet.

Sigh.

There was a God.

How could she not believe with that butt on display?

31

Lilac tried to stifle a yawn, but Tanner immediately spotted the movement.

"Time for you to nap."

"I don't need a nap. What I need is to get up and move around."

Actually, what she really needed was to pee. Between the IV and Tanner reminding her to keep having some of the protein drink, she was busting.

He eyed her. "No."

She raised her eyebrows. "No?"

"No."

She frowned. "Bossy Tanner."

"You bet. When it comes to your health, I'm all about bossing you around. Now, do you need to pee before you sleep?"

"Are you a mind reader?" How did he know? She didn't think she'd done anything to give herself away.

"Nope. I just figured you were beyond the time that you should need to pee, and that you weren't going to ask me. Am I right?"

Well, he wasn't wrong. But she still wasn't going to admit that he was right.

That seemed like the wrong avenue to take with a man who always seemed to think he was right. No way was she validating that belief.

"Come on, baby." He stood and drew her covers back.

"What are you doing?" she asked in alarm.

"Taking you to the bathroom."

"I don't need anyone to take me," she complained as he lifted her in his arms. Thankfully, she'd been disconnected from the drip although the line was still in her hand.

This wasn't a good idea.

Because she liked this way too much.

He shifted her so she was lying against his chest with his arm under her bottom as he walked into the bathroom. Her bladder protested the movement.

Shoot. She might have left it too long to pee.

"You're certainly not doing it alone. You could get dizzy, fall, and hit your head."

"It's like five steps," she told him dryly as he set her on her feet in front of the toilet.

"Five steps too many. Put your hands on my shoulders."

His tone was so dominant that she immediately obeyed him without thought. Then he crouched down to pull down her pants and panties.

"Tanner!" she cried.

"What?"

"You can't do that!" She knew she had to be bright red.

"Why not? Nothing I haven't seen before. I think we should take these shorts off and get you changed into one of my T-shirts. It will be so big on you that it will cover everything."

"Shoot. I didn't think about what I was going to sleep in." She really needed some fresh clothes.

"It's either my T-shirt or a hospital gown." He nodded at the shelf filled with hospital gowns.

Yeah. No thanks.

"Do you have a spare one? Are you sure it will cover me?"

"Yep, and you're tiny. Of course it will cover you. I'll go get it while you use the toilet. Don't get up off the toilet without my help. Call me if you need me."

Um. Yeah. That wasn't happening.

He stood there. What was he waiting for? She really had to pee.

"Sit down," he commanded.

"Good Lord," she muttered. But she sat, still blushing.

He disappeared, leaving the door open. Um, no. She didn't think so. Leaning over, she managed to nudge the door closed.

"Lilac," he said warningly through the closed door.

"I cannot pee with you listening," she told him.

That was a step too far.

She ignored the sound of his sigh.

After she was finished, she slowly stood. Then she flushed the toilet before moving to the sink to wash her hands.

The door immediately opened like she figured it might.

"That's three, baby," Tanner said from behind her.

She turned with a gasp, the room spinning slightly.

"Damn it, Lilac." Stepping forward, he lifted her into his arms. "What were you thinking?"

"I was thinking that I can pull my own panties up and wash my own hands."

"All right, then how about this? Stop thinking and start letting me do the thinking for you."

That really shouldn't be so appealing. But it was. It really was.

"I need clean clothes for tomorrow," she mumbled as he

carried her into the bedroom and laid her on the bed. Turning, he grabbed a large T-shirt out of his duffel bag.

What did it say about her that she really wanted to wear his clothes?

She wasn't really sure.

As he reached for her T-shirt, she suddenly changed her mind. She really did feel gross and dirty.

"I really need a shower."

"And you can have a shower, but I'll need to help you."

"You'll get all wet."

"Hmm. I won't be the only one." He winked at her.

Lilac groaned. "That was awful."

"Really? Huh. I thought it was some of my best work."

She sighed. "B minus at best."

His eyes widened. "B minus? I'll take it. I was always a C student."

"You're terrible."

"Terribly good?"

"I think you know the answer to that. And I'm pretty sure I'll be okay to shower by myself." She was being honest about her hairy legs.

"Baby, I don't care about your hairy legs. Besides, I just had my face right next to them when I helped you go to the toilet."

She gasped in realization. "Damn it."

Tanner gave her a wicked grin. "Come on, you'll sleep better if you're clean. Stay there and I'll turn the shower on."

As he turned the shower on, she carefully sat up and reached behind her to undo her bra, pulling it off while keeping her T-shirt on.

A sigh of relief left her, and she heard him chuckle.

"That was a big sigh."

"Men have no idea how good it feels to take a bra off. I mean,

I know I don't really have anything there anymore, but . . ." she trailed off as his smile turned into a frown.

Yikes.

Okay, she shouldn't have reminded him of that.

She basically had a whole new body now. Would he like it better? Or not?

"I think I might call Abby and get her to help me," she told him, feeling even more self-conscious.

Tanner eyed her for a moment. Then he walked closer. Stopping in front of her, he placed his hands on the bed on either side of her.

"Let's get one thing straight, shall we? No matter what you look like, I am still going to want you. Did I think you looked sexy before? Fuck, yes. I thought I was going to come as soon as I got inside you. Very nearly did."

She snorted. Urgh. She had to stop making that sound.

"Am I hard at the thought of getting you naked now? Hell. Yes. Do you want to see the evidence?"

Yes.

"No!" she cried.

His lips twitched. "Liars get their bottoms spanked."

Lilac scowled at him. "That is not three."

"Nope, it's four." Reaching up, he ran his finger over her lip. "I'm hard as fuck over the idea of seeing you naked, touching. I still want to eat that pussy until my appetite is sated, knowing it will never be. All I want, baby, is for you to be healthy and happy. Okay? And I think we can agree it's not ideal to skip meals."

There was no condemnation in his voice. He didn't look at her like he blamed her in any way.

"I guess so," she said, letting out a sigh.

"Come on, let's get you clean. It's well past your nap time." Picking her up once again, he carried her, along with his T-shirt, into the bathroom.

Setting her on the counter, he stripped off the T-shirt she was wearing. Bending down, he cupped one breast. She hadn't been lying, there really wasn't anything there anymore.

But the look on his face was one of wonder, of reverence. Dropping his mouth to her nipple, he took it into his mouth, sucking.

A whimper escaped her. She wasn't ready nor had the energy for sex. She still didn't feel that desirable . . . although with the way he was staring at her, touching her, perhaps that was all in her head.

His mouth slid to her other nipple, sucking on it.

"Tanner, we can't . . . we can't do this," she said, breathlessly. She didn't want him to stop, but she wasn't prepared for anything more.

He drew back, regret on his face. "Sorry, baby. I got carried away."

She nodded. She understood that. He lifted her onto her feet.

"Hands on my shoulders."

"I *can* balance, you know," she told him as she did as ordered. He crouched in front of her and drew her panties down.

She gasped.

Crap. She just remembered what other part she hadn't had time to take care of. It used to be that she had a standing appointment to get waxed. Stefan had even made noises about having her hair lasered off.

Was it weird that her brother cared about her appearance? That he insisted that she keep her pussy and legs waxed?

Oh yeah. Uber weird.

But that had been her life.

"Baby, you okay?"

"What?" She stared down at him. Lord, his face was so close

to her pussy. All he had to do was lean in and he'd be touching her.

"You're trembling." He had her lift one foot, then the other, before he had her panties completely off. "This is too much for you."

"No, it's not that. I was just thinking about my brother."

He stood and grasped hold of her hips. "What?"

All right, she could understand how that sounded weird.

"It's nothing," she said hastily. "Can we get in the shower?"

"I'll shelve the conversation because I want you back in bed, napping. But we will circle back to this, make no mistake."

Something to look forward to.

He checked the temperature of the water before helping her into the shower. She sat on the bench seat as he stripped off his own T-shirt.

Lilac sucked in a breath, watching him hungrily. But all he did was pump some shower gel onto his hand.

She didn't even bother to protest as he started to wash her. Truthfully, she was already tired and feeling a bit woozy. And his touch felt so nice.

"You're so tense. You need a massage."

Lord, yes.

"Want me to wash your hair?" he asked.

"No. It will be all right."

He moved his hands over her breasts and stomach. Then he had her sit forward so he could do her back.

Finally, he moved down to her legs. "Part your legs, baby."

With a whimper she did as directed. But he kept his movements soft and brief as he cleaned between her legs. Finally, he turned the water off and grabbed the towel.

"I don't want to put those panties back on," she grumbled after he'd dried her off.

"Then don't."

"I can't get back into bed without panties on."

He huffed out a laugh as he carried her back to the bed. He drew the curtain around the bed for privacy in case someone came in before stripping off the towel.

Then he put his T-shirt on over her head. By this time, she was completely exhausted. He tucked her into bed, even fluffing her pillows up for her.

"Tanner, I need panties."

"You're fine, baby. No one will know. I can get one of my brothers to stop at your place, though, and pick up a bag for you."

"I can't ask them to do that, they'll be busy. Especially as I'm sure I will be going home tomorrow." She yawned. Lord, she was so tired.

He snorted. "Busy. Good one. They're not busy. Lazy slackers. You'll need stuff to wear tomorrow. And in case you have to stay longer."

No way was she staying in the hospital any longer. There was too much she had to do. Plus, she hated to think of the cost of staying here.

"I can get Raid to pick up a bag of your stuff. But I'll text Opal and ask her to get everything ready. I don't want him touching your panties."

She was sure that Raid had no interest in her panties.

"You have Opal's number?" she asked with surprise.

He shot her a look. "Baby, you called her from my phone."

"Oh, right. Sorry, I'm tired," she said.

"Then go to sleep."

"I don't think I can," she grumbled. Sleep was so hard when your brain just wouldn't shut up.

"Roll over and face the other way," he ordered.

Confused, she did as he said. He drew the blanket down to

her waist and started massaging her back. The massage was gentle, but it started to relax her.

"That's it," he said in a low, soothing voice. "Off to sleep you go, good girl."

She really didn't deserve him. But perhaps she could find a way to keep him.

32

Lilac gasped as a hand was pressed over her mouth.

Opening her eyes, she stared up into Stefan's face. Horror flooded her.

What was he doing here?

How had he found her?

She glanced around, but she couldn't see Tanner. Where was he? Had he left her?

He'd abandoned her and now Stefan had found her.

This is a good thing. You don't want Stefan to see Tanner.

It didn't feel like a good thing right then, though. It felt utterly terrifying. Her heart raced as she tried to breathe.

"Did you really think you could run from me? That I wouldn't find you? You always were a stupid bitch, Lilac. Always one step behind. Thick as a brick. Fat. Ugly. Although I see you took care of the fat part. I knew the fucking staff were feeding you behind my back. No way could you eat what I told them to feed you and still look like you did."

She whimpered. Why was no one coming to save her?

Where was the nurse? Tanner? Someone?

She wriggled around, trying to push his hand off her mouth.

"Uh-uh, no fighting back, Lilac. you know that will make it worse and I'd hate to have to punish you by hurting your friend."

Her eyes widened as she continued to fight to breathe.

Did he mean? Surely, he didn't know about Tanner, right?

"That's right. I know all about your friend and I'm coming for him. I'm going to hurt him to hurt you. And you know I'll do it, don't you?"

No! No, no, no! She wouldn't let Stefan hurt him.

"I'm coming, Lilac."

"Lilac! Lilac, wake up!"

Lilac opened her eyes, staring around wildly. Sitting up, she grabbed at her throat. She couldn't breathe! He was choking her!

"Baby. Fuck, Lilac, you're all right. It was just a nightmare. You're okay, baby."

She clawed at her neck. The pain of her fingernails slicing into her skin didn't even register through her panic.

"Lilac." Tanner's firm voice finally managed to penetrate her panic and she gaped at him.

"Breathe."

She couldn't!

"You. Will. Breathe. I want you to match my breathing." He grabbed her hands, tugging them away from her neck. He placed both of them on his chest. "Breathe. Right. Fucking. Now."

There was no ignoring that command. Her throat relaxed slightly, and she gasped in some air.

"Good girl. And another."

She took another breath. Then one more. Gradually, she

became aware that she was trembling. She glanced around frantically. Was he here? Had he come for her?

"Lilac, listen to me, baby. It was just a nightmare."

She shook her head. No, no, it wasn't. It had been real. *He'd been here.*

"Tell me what it was about." Tanner cupped her face between his hands.

She tried to shake her head again, but he held her face still.

"Tell me."

"He was here," she said in a raspy voice.

"Your brother." It wasn't a question.

A sob escaped her. "Y-yes."

"He wasn't, Lilac."

"He was!" The door to her room opened and she shied back with a cry.

"Is everything all right in here?" A harried-looking nurse walked in. "We heard a scream, but we had an emergency down the other end of the ward. Lilac? I'm Grace. Are you okay?"

An emergency? Or a diversion so he could get to her? She wouldn't put it past Stefan.

He was sneaky like that.

"Lilac had a nightmare," Tanner explained. "But I'm here. I'll take care of her."

"All right. If you're sure, Lilac?" Grace asked.

"Y-yes." She didn't want the nurse here to witness her losing her mind. Abby must have gone home sometime during the night.

After her nap, she'd woken up to find that Raid had dropped off a bag of her clothes. Tanner had helped her put some panties on. Which was just as well, since she'd been wheeled away for an ultrasound soon after.

By the time she'd returned to the room, it had been dinner

time. Then she'd fallen asleep watching some reality show on TV.

"Tanner, he was here," she whispered after the nurse left.

"Baby, he wasn't here, I promise. It was a dream. I've been here with you the entire time."

"Are you . . . are you certain?" she asked. It wasn't that she didn't believe him. But Stefan could be tricky.

Tanner drew back the blankets and then lifted her onto his lap. Taking hold of the top blanket, he wrapped it around her as he held her tight.

Ooh, okay. This was nice.

She felt so much more secure.

"I'm certain, baby. I wouldn't leave you. I promise. I've been right here. I haven't gone anywhere." He rocked her gently back and forth. "It was just a nightmare."

"It felt so real." She sobbed. It was hard to believe that he really wasn't here.

"Please stop crying, baby," he murmured. "I hate listening to you cry. I don't like that he infiltrated your dreams. You should only have happy dreams."

Yeah. She wished.

The only time she had happy dreams was when they were about him. Reaching over her, he grabbed a tissue and wiped her face clean. Heck, he even wiped her nose!

Yikes.

But she simply lay there and let him take care of her. Maybe he was right. Perhaps she would benefit from giving him control. At least for a short time; she wasn't sure she could do it as a lifestyle. But to not make decisions, even simple ones like what to wear or eat, could be freeing.

"I hate seeing you like this, baby. Will you talk to me about it?"

She swallowed heavily. "I, uh . . ." Shoot, her throat was dry and scratchy. How much screaming had she done?

Hopefully, she hadn't woken up anyone else.

"Wait a second." After shuffling her so she was sitting up straighter, he reached over and poured her a glass of water. Then he lay her back against his arm and held the glass to her lips.

Her cheeks went hot. He was treating her like she was helpless. Fragile.

God, it was nice.

"Tell me, baby," he urged after drawing the glass of water away from her mouth.

"It felt so real. Like he was here. I woke up to his hand over my mouth. I couldn't . . . I couldn't breathe."

"Shit. That's why you woke up scratching at your throat and not breathing."

"Yes."

"Fuck. I need to look at your neck." He set her on the bed and turned on the light by the bed. It wasn't that bright, but she still winced.

"Sorry, baby. I just need to see. I'm going to find something to clean these scratches."

"They're fine," she said dismissively. It was just a couple of scratches. She'd had far worse.

"No, they're not fine. They need cleaning in case they get infected. There might be something in the bathroom I can use." He disappeared into the bathroom, and she started shivering again.

Strange, his touch seemed to hold her fear at bay. And now that he wasn't touching her, all of that fear came rushing back.

Just hold on.

"Baby? Fuck. Are you all right?" Tanner rushed over to her, cupping her face in his hands.

"I'm j-just . . . I c-can't stop t-trembling." She stared up at him.

"Shh. Shh. It's all right. You're okay. I'm sorry I left you." He bundled her against his chest and rocked her back and forth.

"I'm b-being silly," she said.

"Hush. No, you're not."

"It was just a d-dream."

It wasn't real. He wasn't here.

The trouble was that the nightmare didn't really stop once she was awake. Because Stefan was still out there. Still searching for them.

Was that nightmare her brain's way of warning her to stay away from Tanner? To protect him from Stefan?

"It was a nightmare about someone who has been traumatizing you for a long time."

"I could n-never see a way free. Not u-until the opportunity c-came to run. Sorry for being s-silly."

"You don't have to apologize. And you are not being silly. Understand?"

"Yes," she whispered, snuggling into him.

"I need to get some antiseptic from the nurse since I couldn't find any. Then I'll bandage your neck."

"I don't need any."

"Yeah, you do. I'm not risking your health." He hit the buzzer and sat back down in the chair with her on his lap.

"You can put me on the bed." She didn't want him to do that, but thought she better offer.

"I don't want you to start shaking again."

Fair enough.

"What else happened in the nightmare?" he asked.

"I don't know. Just a lot of threats, calling me names. The usual."

He started swearing right as Grace walked into the room.

"Everything all right?" she asked as she came and switched off the buzzer.

"We need some antiseptic for her neck," Tanner said.

"I'll get some now," she promised after checking Lilac's neck.

Damn. This was so embarrassing.

Lilac buried her face in Tanner's neck. "You smell so good." And from memory, he tasted even better.

His chest moved as he laughed. "Do I? Even after sleeping in these clothes?"

"Uh-huh."

The nurse returned and Tanner took the antiseptic from her with thanks, turning down her offer to help.

Then he set Lilac on the bed and cleaned up her cuts, putting a light bandage on them.

"There, all better."

Surprisingly, she did feel a lot better.

"Let's get you back into bed."

As he tucked her in, she let out a small whimper. Damn it. Where did that noise come from?

"Hey, you okay?"

"I just . . . I feel . . . scared." It was hard to admit it. But it was the truth. She was so scared.

He leaned over her, his face close to hers. "I won't let him touch you, Lilac."

Yeah, that's not why she was so terrified. She was concerned about Tanner, about what Stefan might do to him if he ever discovered his connection to her.

"Is it crazy to want you so much when I barely know you?" she asked instead of telling him what was actually going on in her head.

"You know me. I'm the guy you met in that bar six months ago." He grinned at her.

She rolled her eyes.

"And I don't think it's crazy to know when you've found someone special. Someone you want to spend your life with."

Closing her eyes, she nodded wearily.

God, she wanted that.

"Would you . . . is it wrong to ask for . . . never mind."

"Look at me."

She opened her eyes, moving her gaze to his.

He stared down at her. "You can ask me anything. It would never be wrong. Unless you ask me to harm you. I won't do that."

"Lie with me," she said quickly before she could chicken out. "I don't feel safe unless you're touching me."

"Of course I will."

He slid into bed next to her, lying on his back. She curled around him, putting her arm and leg over him.

It felt so nice to have someone hug her, touch her. She got the feeling that if Tanner was ever hers for good, she might become a bit addicted to touching him.

"What are you thinking?" he asked as he kissed the top of her head.

"Just that I could become addicted to touching you."

He snorted. "Suits me."

"You say that now. But I'd be a grade A clinger, hanging off you wherever you went, sitting on your lap, hugging you, holding your hand, the whole deal."

"And I'd like that," he told her firmly. "I get the feeling you haven't been touched a lot by someone who cares about you."

"Ryleigh is a hugger," she said.

"I can see that. But that's not quite the same, is it?"

No. It wasn't.

"Go to sleep, baby. I'll keep your nightmares at bay."

33

"Where is the doctor? I need to get out of here. I can just discharge myself, right?" She felt antsy. Worried about getting home and then to her shift at the bar.

What if Ryleigh needed help with Kye? Had Opal gotten to her job on time?

"You won't be doing that," Tanner told her firmly. "Have some more of your protein shake."

Lilac shook her head. She didn't want the shake. She just wanted to get out of here. Tanner had helped her take a shower and get dressed. It was now getting close to lunchtime, and she had a shift starting in six hours.

Thankfully, Opal had thought to pack her phone charger, so Lilac now had access to her phone. It had been a bit of a shock to plug it in and have so many messages pop up. Most were Opal and Ryleigh, but there were also messages from Devon, Cherie, and Peggy. Those had nearly had her tearing up.

"But I need to get out of here."

"Lilac, everything will be fine. Just relax."

There was a knock at the door and the doctor walked in with Abby.

Thank God.

She smiled at them both even though she wanted to ask what had taken so long.

Be polite, Lilac.

"Good morning, Lilac. How are you feeling today?" Doctor Martin asked.

"I'm feeling really good. Ready to get out of here."

The doctor smiled. "That's good. Any dizziness? Feeling of weakness? Headaches?"

"Nope. I've been all good."

"I've been keeping a close eye on her when she gets out of bed," Tanner offered.

"I've heard you've been a big help," the doctor smiled at Tanner.

For some reason, that made her want to frown. Was she feeling jealous? Of the doctor who had to be at least fifteen years older than Tanner?

Don't be an idiot.

Besides, Tanner doesn't belong to you.

Still, she felt like she needed to lay some sort of claim on him. It was an itch beneath her skin.

To her surprise, he placed his hand on hers. Immediately, she felt calmer.

It was so strange, sometimes his touch was calming. Other times, it excited her.

"The ultrasound came back clear. But your bloodwork showed that you are anemic and low in several vitamins. So, I'm going to prescribe iron tablets. And you will need another blood test in three months."

Great. She had no idea where she would be in three months.

"I'd like you to consider talking to someone as well," she

went on in a kind voice. But it still made Lilac squirm on the inside.

Tell a stranger everything?

How could she possibly do that without endangering them? Without stripping herself raw?

Would there be anything left if she did that?

"How did the protein drinks go?" the doctor asked.

"They're nice," Lilac said in a cheerful voice.

Yep, she was gonna fake it until she made it out of there.

"It's hard to get her to drink a whole one," Tanner said. "Or to eat much more than a few bites."

Shoot. What a tattletale. She glared at him.

"All right, the dietitian at the hospital is coming to see you soon so she can talk through some food plans."

Crap.

"But I need to leave. I have to get home."

The doctor studied her. "Your color is better. You seem more alert today, but I am worried about you. However, I'd be willing to discharge you if you promise to take it easy for at least a few days. No running. No work. Try to eat regularly, drink lots of water, and attempt to get rid of some stress."

Right.

The only way to get rid of most of her stress was to kill Stefan.

Sure, she'd get onto that.

"Okay, I can do that," she lied.

"Very well. After you've seen the dietitian, we'll put through the discharge papers."

Urgh. She nearly groaned. But she could still make her shift. Hopefully.

"All right."

"And I'd prefer that you had someone take care of you while

you're resting. I don't want you moving around too quickly and getting dizzy."

"That's covered," Tanner said.

"I thought it might be." The doctor smiled at him again.

The doctor was really nice, but Lilac didn't like the way she kept smiling at Tanner.

You're being irrational.

The doctor and Abby left, and Lilac turned to Tanner. But a knock interrupted her before she could ask him anything.

In walked another woman who introduced herself as the dietitian.

Damn it.

Keep on faking it, Lilac.

~

Twenty minutes later, the dietitian left, and Lilac's mind felt like mush.

Tanner had done most of the talking and he now held several pages filled with menu plans and food suggestions.

"You took that very seriously," she commented. He'd listened to everything the enthusiastic woman had to say.

"Of course I did. I need to know what to feed you. Apparently, lots of liver and spinach. Yum-yum."

"Tanner! That's not what she said!"

"Joking." He grinned.

"And you don't need to feed me. I can feed myself."

He shot her a look. Okay, so they both knew that was a lie. Still, what was he planning on doing? Coming into town each night to feed her dinner? That would be crazy.

"The bunkhouse isn't the nicest place in the world, but all of my brothers have moved out so it's private. I can't really cook.

Mia is a great cook, though. I'm sure she can cook liver and make it kind of palatable."

She sighed. "I can't go home with you, Tanner. I've got responsibilities."

He raised his eyebrows. "Your friends and Kye are welcome to come too."

"It's not that . . . how would I make my shifts at the bar and diner if I'm staying on your Ranch?" she told him, reasonably.

"Baby, you're not working for at least a week. You heard the doctor. You need to rest."

"First of all, she said a couple of days."

"A week would be better," he told her. "And I don't think we should give it a time limit. You need rest."

"But I can't rest. I only just got those jobs. How will I pay to fix Sugar if I can't work for the next week?"

Frankly, the idea terrified her.

"No, baby. You're not hearing me. You don't have to take care of anyone. Not even yourself. Because I'm doing it all now. Remember? You're giving the decisions to me to handle."

But that was just a pipe dream. It wouldn't work in reality.

"I appreciate you wanting to help me. To take care of me. But that just won't work."

His eyebrows rose. "You're talking like you have a choice."

"Tanner, be serious."

"Lilac, I know that a lot of the time, it might seem like I'm not taking things seriously. But I can assure you that when it comes to someone I care about, I am very serious about their health and safety. You are coming home with me so I can look after you."

FUCK.

Tanner hated how lost and vulnerable she looked. She was

staring at him with a mix of confusion and longing. As though she couldn't imagine someone wanting to take care of her.

Her brother had a lot to answer for.

Fucking asshole.

Tanner knew he was going to have to undo years of damage that asshole had done. Along with that bitch nanny who was meant to take care of her. Who should have protected her.

Then there was her father, who had put his son before his vulnerable daughter.

Fuck. Had no one ever put this girl first?

But that was all right. He wasn't entering into this relationship with anything but forever in mind. So, he had time to undo all of her beliefs. That she had to do it all on her own and take care of everyone else. Put herself last.

Yep. He wanted forever.

And a Malone always got what he wanted.

"You know, I think I started falling for you the minute I met you. Definitely when I saw you try to throw that first dart."

A sob escaped her, and he stared at her in confusion. He didn't think that would upset her.

"You won't feel that way once you know the full truth," she told him.

He frowned at the despair on her face. The fear in her eyes. He was trying to reassure her. "What do you mean? Is this about your brother? Baby, I don't know how you came to be on the run from him or how Opal and Ryleigh come into it. But I am going to protect you from him. You are never going back to him."

"No, you don't understand, Tanner," she said. "I'm not talking about Stefan and why I left. I'm talking about meeting you. It wasn't an accident. It wasn't a chance encounter."

He froze. "What does that mean?"

"I've always known who you were. I searched you out. I went there to get to know you."

"Why . . . why would you do that?" he asked.

He was vaguely aware of the door opening slightly. But he couldn't look away from Lilac.

He had a feeling that whatever she was about to say was going to blow his world apart.

Another sob. God, she was so sad that he couldn't stand it.

"Just tell me, Lilac."

"I c-can't."

"Lilac," he said sternly. "I'm your guardian. More than that, I'm the guy who fucking loves you. So, you need to be honest with me."

"You l-love me?" Her eyes were wide, her breathing fast. Abby had disconnected her from all of the monitors already.

He took her hand in his, holding it. Fuck, she was so cold.

"I love you," he stated.

"You shouldn't. I'm a fucking cancer."

"Stop that," he said fiercely. "I've told you about talking about yourself like that."

Standing, he grabbed the blanket from the end of the bed. That's when he spotted Alec standing in the doorway, hidden from Lilac. Tanner shot him a look. What was he doing? Eavesdropping? Alec had always gotten angry when they used to do that to him.

Alec was frowning fiercely. Tanner didn't like the look on his face. This was between him and Lilac.

He didn't need his big brother riding to his rescue. Or interfering.

Fuck. Who was he kidding? All of his brothers were interfering bastards. He should be grateful that only Alec was here.

Tanner covered Lilac with the blanket. She stared up at him listlessly. As though she'd retreated into herself to protect herself.

"Now, tell me why you searched me out. Did you hear how

sexy and smart I am, and you had to find out for yourself?" he teased, but that knot in his stomach was growing.

What reason would she have to seek him out?

"I really can't. It's not my secret. I just . . . I didn't want you to find out later. I didn't want to fall into the fantasy of being yours, only for you to reject me."

He frowned. "Lilac, that wouldn't happen. I'd never reject you."

She smiled sadly.

"Just tell me," he urged. "We'll work through it. Tell me why you sought me out. Why me in particular?"

"That's just it. It wasn't you in particular. I just found you before I found Raid."

His frowned. "So, you were after one of us because . . ."

"You were a Malone. I went to that bar to find a Malone."

"Why, Lilac?" Alec chose that moment to step into the room. Bastard. "Why were you searching us out? I thought it was odd that you ran out on Tanner and then turned up here six months later. But I figured maybe you were here because you were tired of running. Because you liked the sound of Haven. Or perhaps you realized what a mistake you'd made, leaving Tanner. Seems I might have been too generous in giving you the benefit of the doubt."

Lilac flinched, going pale. Tanner turned to glare at his brother. "Alec, that's enough!"

"She has an ulterior motive in coming here, Tanner," Alec warned.

"She's scared. She's on the run from her asshole brother and needs protection."

Alec nodded. "I can believe all that. But if she was sent to spy on us, to gather information that might hurt us . . . then that becomes a different story. So, what is it, Lilac? Were you sent to destroy us? Or is there something else going on?"

"You can tell us, baby," Tanner told her. "I don't care if you were sent to find us for someone. Is it your brother? Do we know him? Did he send you to spy on us?"

"What? No. No, that's not it. I'm trying to hide from him. I shouldn't have said anything . . . I just wanted you to hear the truth from me. Because I couldn't stand to have it all, then have it ripped away from me."

"Lilac," Tanner whispered. "Just tell us. Whatever it is, we can fix it."

"Are you a threat to my family, Lilac?" Alec asked in a low voice.

"No! No, I promise I'm no threat. I wasn't sent to gather information for anyone. Especially not my brother. I don't want to harm any of you."

Alec nodded, some of the tension leaving his body.

Tanner knew there was nothing that Alec wouldn't do to protect his family. He wouldn't physically hurt Lilac, but he wouldn't hesitate to ensure that she never came near them again.

"Then you shouldn't mind telling us," Alec said.

He wasn't getting angry or being overtly intimidating. But she still stared at Alec with wide eyes.

"Alec isn't going to harm you, Lilac," Tanner reassured her. "We just need the truth."

"And I keep telling you. I can't tell you. It's not my secret."

Alec grunted. "Then I'm sure you'll understand why I can't have you around my family until I know."

"Alec!" Tanner protested.

The door to her room opened and Abby stepped in. She stared around them, frowning. "Is everything all right in here?"

She managed to force a smile even though she felt like crying. It was fine. Everything was fine.

"Fine," she said tightly. "Am I good to go?"

"Uh, yes. Discharge papers with the doctor's instructions. A script for iron tablets. You'll need another blood test in three months. You can go to the clinic in Haven for that."

Right. Except she wouldn't be here.

"Doctor Martin would like you to follow up with one of the doctors in Haven in a weeks' time to check on you. If you feel faint, dizzy, or have any chest pains, then come back here. Tanner, you're taking her home?"

"No, he's not," she managed to say.

Abby gave her a worried look.

"I'm here to pick them both up," Alec said. "Tanner's truck got towed."

It had? He'd never said anything.

Abby grimaced, nodding. "They're really strict. I wish it was a business from Haven, but it's that one in Freestown. You'll have to go there and pay the fine."

"I will," Tanner said gruffly. "Thanks for all of this, Abby."

"No problem. I'll get a wheelchair."

She thought about asking Abby to order a rideshare for her. But she could do that herself. Abby left and she grabbed her phone, bringing up the app.

"What are you doing?" Tanner asked, frowning. He peered down at her phone.

"Have you ever heard of privacy?" she snapped.

"You're trying to order a ride?" he asked.

"You're not taking a taxi," Alec replied. "We're taking you home."

"I don't think that's a good idea." She was trying to keep herself from losing it, but she was on the verge of tears.

She just wanted to get away from them.

Away from Tanner...

Don't lose it. Don't lose it.

Before Alec could reply, Abby returned. Tanner pulled the blanket off her before lifting her into the wheelchair.

"I've got this, Abby," he told her.

"All right. You're in good hands." Abby patted her shoulders. "Don't take this the wrong way, but I hope I don't see you back here, Lilac."

She smiled up at the kind woman. "Same."

"But if you ever want to catch up some other time, that would be fun. Don't let these guys bulldoze you."

Abby left and she was left alone with the two Malone men.

So. This was going to be fun.

34

They wheeled her down to Alec's truck, where Tanner lifted her into the backseat while Alec took the wheelchair back.

Lilac reached for her seatbelt at the same time as him, their hands knocking together.

"I've got it," she said.

Tanner clenched his jaw tight, a muscle ticking in his cheek, but he stepped back and closed the door.

She blinked rapidly.

Do not lose it. Do not lose it.

Fuck. She'd tried twice to buckle her belt until finally, on the third time she got it. By that time, Alec had returned. The drive to Linc's place was silent.

Only a few more minutes.

Then you can cry.

Why weren't they saying anything? She'd been expecting more questions. Not this silence.

"After we drop Lilac off, I'll take you to get your truck," Alec finally said to Tanner as they pulled onto the street that Linc lived on.

A rogue tear dripped down her cheek.

"That won't be necessary," Tanner replied as they pulled up at Linc's house. Tanner climbed out of the truck as soon as it came to a stop.

He opened her door and reached over to unbuckle her belt. She sucked in a sharp breath.

God. She was going to miss his touch. His smile. His teasing. She'd even miss Meanie Malone.

Then he lifted her into his arms.

"You don't need to carry me," she protested.

But he ignored her. When she glanced up, he was still looking mad. Her stomach was knotted.

She'd known he would be upset. It wasn't a surprise. But that didn't mean it didn't hurt.

Because she loved him.

She closed her eyes, wishing she had told him.

"Tanner," Alec said warningly.

"Will you get our stuff?" Tanner asked gruffly, before turning away from the truck and heading to the guesthouse. It took a moment for his words to penetrate.

Our stuff?

"Tanner!" Alec yelled out.

"Don't yell, the baby might be asleep."

They reached the guesthouse and Tanner opened the door, carrying her in. It was quiet. Empty. She guessed everyone had moved to Linc's house.

A strange feeling crept over her.

They didn't need her now. They had Linc to take care of them. She was surplus. Unnecessary.

Panic started to take hold of her, muffling her hearing. She was aware that Tanner and Alec were talking, but she couldn't seem to focus on their words.

This is what you wanted.

Only trouble was, she didn't know what to do with herself now. Who was she if she wasn't needed by anyone? If she wasn't holding everything together?

Would she shatter?

"Fuck, Alec, shut up. You're stressing her out."

"What?" Alec asked.

Tanner sat her on the sofa. Then he crouched down in front of her, placing his large hands on her thighs. "Baby, you need to calm down. Everything is fine. I'm not going anywhere. I'm going to stay here with you."

What?

She gaped at him.

"But I need you to start breathing. Come on, you know the deal. Follow my voice. Listen to me. Breathe in. One. Two. Hold. One. Two. Now, out. Good girl. You are doing so well. In. One. Two. Hold. One. Two. Let it out, baby."

"Fuck. I didn't mean to upset her."

She glanced up at Alec. She should tell him this wasn't his fault. That he was right to protect his family. To be suspicious. She came with a whole lot of dangerous baggage.

"That's it. Don't worry," Tanner told her. "I'm not going anywhere. Alec will just have to grab more of my stuff. I'm staying right here to take care of you."

Her mouth dropped open.

"Tanner, you don't know anything about why she searched you out. What if her brother is looking for us?"

"Why would he be looking for us?" Tanner replied. "And if he is, then Lilac would tell us."

"Clearly not, seeing as she is refusing to tell us why she

searched you out in Hopesville. Until we know what is going on, you should stay away from her."

"I'm not staying away from her." Tanner glared over his shoulder at his brother.

What was happening right now?

She'd thought that Tanner was upset with her. But was he angry at Alec?

"Whatever she is keeping from me, she has her reasons. I love her. She's my girl, my responsibility. I'm going to stay here with her and look after her."

Lilac gaped at him.

Turning back to her, he squeezed her thighs. "I don't like that you're keeping things from me. But I know you. You think you have to look after everyone else, but like I told you before ... I'm going to look after you, Lilac. I'm not running off at the first hurdle."

This man.

She definitely didn't deserve him. But she was never going to let him go.

Tanner turned back to Alec. "You were the one who always told us that when we found someone special that we needed to do everything we could to keep her. To protect her. That I should take my responsibilities seriously."

"That does sound like me," Alec grumbled.

She might have smiled over his disgruntlement under different circumstances.

"But until you know the truth how can you trust her?" Alec asked.

That made her tense. It was true. Tanner would never trust her without knowing everything. He couldn't.

But Tanner stared at her, his face serious. "I trust her. She has her reasons for keeping this to herself. And as long as she isn't in any danger, then I will trust her to tell me when she can."

"It's because of me," a voice said from the doorway.

Alec must have left the sliding door open, or they just hadn't heard it open. Ryleigh stepped into the guesthouse. She looked slightly pale, but otherwise healthy.

Lilac breathed out a sigh of relief. "Ryleigh! You're feeling okay?" She attempted to stand, but Tanner placed pressure on her legs, keeping her in place.

"I'm good. Are you all right? We've been so worried about you!" Ryleigh moved forward, giving Alec a wary look before she reached Lilac. Sitting beside her, she hugged her tight.

Lilac let out a tense breath, trying to relax in her best friend's arms.

"I'm fine. Really. A lot of fuss over nothing."

"Not nothing."

To her shock, it was Alec who spoke. His voice was strained, and she glanced up to find him giving her a stern look.

"Alec is right," Tanner said. "It wasn't nothing. You fainted. That's not nothing."

"What did the doctor say? What do you need?" Ryleigh asked.

"Just some iron tablets."

"And to take it easy for a week. No work. No stress. Lots of fluids and good nutrition," Tanner added sternly. "I'll be staying here to look after her. You're all in the main house?"

"Yes," Ryleigh replied. "But we can move back over here to take care of her. We don't want to put you guys out." She gave Alec a strange look.

Alec crossed his arms over his chest, staring down at her friend. She tightened her hold on Ryleigh, as though she was trying to protect her. "You should go back to the house, Ryleigh."

"No." Ryleigh shook her head. "It's time. I overheard part of your conversation. Lilac told you that she sought you out when you were in Hopesville." She directed this to Tanner, who nodded.

"She did," Tanner said.

"She wouldn't tell us why she was interested in my family though," Alec added. "You said it was because of you. But who are you?"

Ryleigh stood up and held out her hand to Alec. "Hi, I'm Ryleigh Malone. I'm your sister."

35

Fuck.

That was a twist he hadn't seen coming.

Tanner stood, studying Ryleigh. She didn't really look like them. Then again, most of them had different mothers, so they all looked slightly different from each other. Only Alec, West, and Jaret shared the same mom.

Still . . . this was insane.

"There are no Malone girls other than Lottie," he said. "There haven't been any born for generations."

"I don't know what to tell you," Ryleigh replied in a shaky voice. "I'm a Malone. You don't have to believe me. I mean, we can just do a DNA test or something. I don't know. I don't care. All I know is that I'm a Malone and I'm your sister."

"And how do you know that?" Alec asked in a low, soft voice.

Ryleigh bit her lip and Lilac got to her feet, wrapping an arm around her friend.

Okay, nope. That wouldn't do.

"Lilac, sit down." He reached for her.

She shook her head.

"Lilac," he said warningly. "I don't care what family drama is about to happen, you need to rest. Sit down."

"I'm fine. Ryleigh, I'm so sorry. You don't have to say anything more."

"I do. I've got this. It had to come out at some stage. And I don't want them to be mad at you for keeping my secret. That's not fair. Lilac went to meet you guys for me. I . . . I was too nervous. I thought if I saw one of you it might just all come out. I've never been good with secrets or lies."

"Yo, Ryleigh, if you've come out here for some alone time, you might want to put your pants back on because Linc is . . . " Opal trailed off as she walked into the guesthouse, staring at them. "Hey! You're all having a party without me. Lilac! Babe! Thank God they let you break out of the hospital."

Opal rushed toward her, but Tanner held a hand out to stop her. "Easy, Opal. She's fragile at the moment."

"I am not!" she said as Opal snorted.

"Lilac? Fragile?" Opal stared down at Lilac, concern filling her face. "Hmm. Okay, I get your point. I'll go easy."

Lilac ignored the look Tanner shot her, wrapping her arms around Opal.

"What's going on?" Opal whispered.

"Ryleigh's about to tell them."

"Oh, fuck." Opal drew back and turned toward the door. "Linc! There you are!"

Linc stepped inside, staring around in surprise. Kye was cradled in his arm. He looked tiny in the big man's arms. "Uh, what the heck is going on here?"

Alec stared down at Kye, looking a bit ill. As though he'd seen something unexpected. Then he glanced over at Tanner.

"What? What is it?" Tanner asked.

"Nothing . . . he just . . . it's nothing."

"What?" Ryleigh asked, moving quickly to take Kye from

Linc. She held him against her chest as though she thought that Alec might harm him.

"I just forgot you had a baby. Fuck." Alec blinked, staring at Ryleigh. "Are you really our sister?"

"What?" Linc asked. "Sister?"

Ryleigh stepped away from Linc, moving toward Opal and Lilac. They flanked her, giving her strength.

"Yes, I am," Ryleigh replied. "I'm really your sister."

"How did you know about us?" Alec said.

"My dad told me," Ryleigh replied proudly.

"Lilac, I want you to sit," Tanner demanded.

"Who is your dad?" Alec asked.

"Thomas Sanders was how I knew him, but he told me that his last name was really Malone."

"Wait. I'm still trying to catch up here," Linc said. "You knew you were their sister before you came here?"

Poor Linc. He really was struggling to keep up.

"Everyone needs to sit the fuck down!" Tanner said.

Kye let out a shocked cry.

Linc shot Tanner a dirty look, stepping forward to take Kye out of Ryleigh's arms. Then he started lightly bouncing him, patting his back.

"What's going on?" Lilac whispered across Ryleigh to Opal.

"Linc has turned into Mr. Mom. It's pretty funny. This morning when I got up, I found him vacuuming in a flowery apron."

"Why aren't you at work?" she asked.

"I don't go in until later this afternoon for training. Then I start for real tomorrow. The apron was pure gold."

"Are the two of you finished?" Linc grumbled. "And it was not a flowery apron. Those were birds."

"The birds were sitting on flowers," Opal muttered.

"I think the fact you were wearing an apron says it all," Lilac added. "Flowers or birds, doesn't really matter."

Poor Linc. He looked rather red in the face. Tanner would be amused if he wasn't so worried about Lilac.

"Lilac. Sit. Down."

WHOA.

Lilac found herself sitting before she even had time to process Tanner's words. To her surprise, Ryleigh was seated beside her.

"Whoa. Didn't know you had that in you, Cowboy," Opal drawled as she sat slowly. She crossed one leg over the other. "Are you sure you're not a Dom?"

Tanner shot her a quelling look.

"Right. Enough talking. Except for you." He pointed at Ryleigh. "You need to keep talking."

"Don't point at her," Linc growled, stepping in front of Ryleigh. "And do not growl at her like that. Understand me?"

Lilac turned to Ryleigh, who was staring at Linc's back, her mouth open in shock.

"If Ryleigh is our sister, then she's under our care," Alec snapped back. "And you have no say in this."

"I have every say since I'm her guardian. And I don't care if you are her brothers or not. Ryleigh is mine."

"Holy moly," Ryleigh whispered.

"Okay, maybe everyone should calm down a bit," Opal said as she stared down at her nails. "I really need to get a manicure. Where was I? Oh, yeah. You do remember that we're all in the room, right? All of this male posturing is cute and stuff. But we've all got shit to do and Ryleigh has a story to tell. So why don't you all sit your butts down so she can tell it."

Linc turned, staring down at them. His jaw was clenched.

"Please," Ryleigh whispered. She had taken hold of both Lilac and Opal's hands. "I need to get this all out and I can't do that if you're all at each other's throats."

Linc nodded and stepped away to sit in an armchair. Tanner squeezed in next to her even though they all had to shuffle over. Then he lifted her up onto his lap.

"Tanner!" she protested.

"Hush. I need this. And you're going to give it to me."

Damn it.

She was. Because she wanted to give him whatever he needed. And because he'd stuck by her, even when his brother was telling him not to. Even when he should have been angry at her, he'd decided to trust her.

So yeah. She'd give him whatever he wanted right now.

"When were you born?" Alec asked. He was the only one still standing. His face was stern, but he didn't appear angry. More thoughtful.

Ryleigh told him her date of birth.

"Right, so you're about four years younger than Tanner. Fuck, why did he never tell us about you! That fucking bastard."

"He wasn't a bastard!" Ryleigh jumped to her feet. "My dad was a good man. I loved him."

Lilac shot a look at Opal. They both knew the truth about Ryleigh's dad. And it wasn't pretty. But they'd agreed not to tell her since she still held him up on a pedestal.

Perhaps that had been a mistake.

"A good man?" Alec asked. "Would a good man leave his sons to the mercy of a dangerous Mafia boss so he could save himself?"

"What? My . . . my dad didn't do that."

"If we have the same father, then he did," Tanner said gently.

"Fuck. I'm not sure I should hear any of this," Linc said with a sigh.

"You can leave," Alec told him.

But Linc didn't move.

"No. Nope. My dad was a good man." Ryleigh shook her head.

"Was?" Alec asked. "He's dead, then?"

"Y-yes. He died about nine months ago. He had liver cancer."

She felt Tanner tense under her. No matter how they all felt about him, that was his dad. Was he upset to hear he was gone?

"Surprised the asshole lasted that long," Tanner muttered.

Okay. Maybe he wasn't upset at all.

"That's a terrible thing to say," Ryleigh said.

"Fuck." Tanner sighed. "Look, Ryleigh, from what you've just said, it seems you had a different relationship with the old bastard than we had. But I haven't seen him since I was around nine or ten. I don't even remember what he looks like. All I know is that he was never around. That he left us with a series of nannies. And that when shit went down and we were all in danger, Alec was the one who stepped up and saved us all. In fact, the old bastard probably did me a favor. Because no doubt that Alec is a hundred times the father he ever was."

"You . . . you never saw him after that?" she asked. "Really?"

"He never even knew I was alive most of the time," Tanner told her.

"He abandoned you all?" She looked to Alec. "I can't believe it."

"Obviously you had a different upbringing with him," Alec said.

"Well, sort of. He . . . he had to go away a lot. Sometimes I wouldn't see him for months. But he always came back. And he'd bring me a gift from wherever he'd been traveling. Or that's what he'd tell me. I loved it when he returned home. Mom would actually get out of bed. She'd make an effort. She . . . she suffered from depression and when dad was away, she'd just stay in bed a lot."

"Ryleigh," Linc said in a broken voice.

"But it was okay. Because Dad always came back."

"Fuck, maybe you're not our sister," Alec said. "Seeing as your father sounds different to ours."

"He told me about you all, though. When I was twelve and there were some bullies hassling me at school, I told him I wished I had some older brothers to help protect me. He said that I did. They just had other lives away from me. But if I ever needed them, I could go to them, and they'd help me." Ryleigh let out a sob.

"We would have been there for you, Ryleigh," Tanner told her. "I promise."

Ryleigh turned to him. "I just . . . I don't know why I didn't ask to see you. To see some photos. Why didn't I ask him for that?" She rubbed her forehead.

"It doesn't matter," Alec told her gently. "What's important is that you're here now. But why didn't you come straight to us yourself?"

"There were . . . are complications."

"My brother," Lilac said. "My brother is a complication."

"What does he have to do with Ryleigh?" Alec asked.

"He . . . he's my fiancée," Ryleigh said.

36

Linc stood up suddenly, making Lilac jolt.

"Fiancée? How can you have a fiancée?"

"Easy," Opal warned. "You don't want to snap at her."

"Ryleigh?" Linc asked.

Ryleigh raised her face, her eyes swimming with tears. "I thought Stefan was amazing. Dad had been diagnosed with stage four cancer, but he hadn't told me. I knew he wasn't feeling well, but I didn't know the extent. Mom died when I was nineteen. Dad said he wanted me to be taken care of and he introduced me to Stefan. Stefan swept me off my feet. Gave me everything I wanted. When he proposed, I said yes straight away. I had some misgivings, but Dad told me that he would feel so much better if I was with Stefan. He was so kind and caring, especially when dad died. He even moved me in with him. Said he didn't like where I was living, that it wasn't safe. I thought he was so caring."

"Fuck," Tanner muttered.

"Until I discovered one day that he wasn't." She took in a

deep breath. "Stefan said he wouldn't sleep with me until our wedding night. I thought he was being kind and understanding since I'd lost my father recently. What I didn't realize was . . . was . . ."

"That Stefan got his needs met elsewhere," Opal said. "That would be me."

"What?" Linc asked.

"Yeah. I was Stefan's mistress."

37

Tanner almost couldn't keep up with everything.
Lilac was Stefan's sister.
Ryleigh was his fiancée.
And Opal was his mistress?

"Lilac and I had gotten close," Ryleigh kept talking while they all struggled to keep up. "But I could sense there was stuff she was keeping from me. Anyway, one night, I couldn't sleep, and decided to go searching for Stefan. He wasn't in his bedroom or office, but I decided to keep searching. I hadn't gone into one wing of the house as he said it was for guests and that there was nothing there. I could hear . . . I could hear voices. Muffled sobs. And then I found Lilac and Opal."

"I was a bit of a mess that night," Opal said. "He'd been very . . . extra."

"Extra psycho," Lilac whispered.

"Yeah. Psycho is the word. I couldn't believe that Stefan would hit someone like that. A woman. Lilac told me that Stefan was the one who'd hurt Opal. That she was . . . she was . . . "

"His mistress," Opal said bitterly.

"You didn't have a choice," Lilac said fiercely.

"Wish I'd never met the bastard," Opal said. "But yeah, I didn't have a choice then. Earlier . . . fuck, maybe not then either."

"What did you do?" Linc asked Ryleigh.

"Something really stupid," she said. "I ran out of there. Through the house until I collided with someone."

"Stefan?" Alec said grimly.

"Yes. I asked him if it was true. If he'd hurt Opal? If she was his mistress? And he just . . . he smiled. Then he grabbed my throat and pushed me into the wall. He said . . . he said did I really expect that he didn't have needs? That he wouldn't get them met from someone else? But I didn't . . . I didn't even care that he'd been sleeping with Opal. He hurt her. For the first time, I was really scared. He cut off my air. I thought he was going to kill me."

"What stopped him?" Linc asked, looking ill and furious.

"Me," Lilac said.

Fuck. Fuck.

"When Stefan is in a mood, the only person who has a chance of breaking through to him is Lilac," Opal said.

Christ, he hated that. He wished she'd been able to run and hide, even knowing that she wouldn't do that.

Fuck. This conversation was the last thing she needed after coming out of the hospital.

His poor girl.

Lilac cleared her throat.

"Alec, can you get Lilac some water?" he asked.

"I'm all right," she protested.

But Alec was already moving to the kitchen. He returned with a glass of water, handing it to Tanner.

Tanner ignored the blush on her cheeks and the way she

tried to take hold of the glass. He held it to her mouth. "Small sips. Good, baby."

"Fuck. I want that," Opal moaned. "Without the being in the hospital part. They fucking suck."

"Back to what happened," Linc said.

"Lilac called out his name," Ryleigh said.

"I didn't know if I'd get through to him," Lilac said. "I never know how he's going to react. I told him that I needed his help picking a dress for my date with Don."

"Who the fuck is Don?" Tanner demanded.

"The guy who became our ticket out of there," Lilac explained. "He was one of my prospective grooms. Stefan had plans to marry me off to help build his empire, and there were several men vying for my attention. Not because they wanted me. They wanted a connection to Stefan. Don was the best of them. The others were creepy. The way they looked at me, touched me. Once, one of them . . . he tried to, uh . . . he tried to rape me in the backseat of his limo. I managed to fight him off and I jumped from the car. Thankfully, it had slowed for a stop light. There was a car coming the next way. They nearly ran me over. But they stopped in time and took me to the hospital. God, Stefan was so angry."

"At that asshole for trying to rape you?" Tanner would have fucking murdered him.

"No, at me. For jumping out of the car and attracting so much attention."

"What the fuck?" Tanner was going to kill him. Extra slowly.

"It must have been my fault," she said. "It was always my fault if I attracted a man's attention. And he was always upset at me."

"Because he wanted you for himself but couldn't have you," Opal said.

Lilac shuddered. "Gross."

"He was fucked in the head," Opal said. "You were his toy. He wanted to give you out to others to play with, but at the same time was jealous that you gave them your attention."

Lilac took in a sharp breath. He wrapped his arms tight around her.

"Yeah. I guess you're right. Stefan was an expert at reading people. Early on, he figured out that the way to punish me was to hurt people I cared about. Sometimes, he'd hit me. Usually when he couldn't hold back his temper. But often, he'd find some way to strike deeper. So, I knew it was a really dumb idea to let him know how much I cared for Opal. For Ryleigh. Interrupting him, strangling Ryleigh could have backfired, yet there was nothing else I could do. Mentioning Don's name was also a dumb move. I knew it would upset him if I seemed to favor one of them. And like I said, Don was the best of the lot. I didn't want Stefan to hurt him. So I told Stefan I needed help choosing a dress that didn't show too much skin because the way Don looked at me grossed me out. He liked that."

"He laughed," Ryleigh said.

"Yeah. He did. Then he let Ryleigh go and took me upstairs to choose a dress. But I knew . . . I knew I had to somehow get Ryleigh and Opal out of there. He'd pulled the rose-colored glasses off Ryleigh's eyes. And he wouldn't play nice anymore. Plus, he was becoming increasingly violent toward Opal. I was worried that he'd . . . that he'd kill her one day and I wouldn't be there to save her."

"Wasn't your job, Lilac," Opal told her. "You think you had to save both of us, but you needed saving just as much."

"I came up with a plan," Lilac said. "I just needed Don's help. God, I was so scared to ask him. He might have told Stefan. But for some reason, he agreed to help. He got us some false identities and a pile of cash. Then I just needed a distraction for the guards. But Don had that under control too. Stefan had gone out to his club that night, and Don decided to join him to provide himself with an alibi. Not that Stefan would likely guess he'd helped us, but better safe than sorry. Don paid some young guys to ram the front gate, then take off. As security responded, I grabbed Ryleigh and Opal and our stuff that I'd had the cook keep safe for me. She always liked me."

"All the staff did," Ryleigh added.

"Yeah. And then we ran. And I foolishly thought we were free," Lilac added. "But we weren't."

"He came after us," Opal said.

"It didn't take his goons long to find us the first time," Lilac said. "We only managed to get away that time because we spotted them outside the motel we'd been staying at. We were on our way back from dinner. We got in the car and left without our stuff. I had all of our money and identities, but none of our clothes. We had to start over with new phones and new IDs. We sold our car and bought Sugar. But we managed to pick up jobs here and there. I thought we were going to be okay."

"Until I did something really stupid," Ryleigh said.

"It wasn't stupid," Lilac insisted. "Not when it brought us Kye."

"No, you're right, I could never regret him." Ryleigh gazed at Kye with love. "I decided I needed to lose my virginity. It was something Stefan prized. The fact that I was untouched. So, I went out one night and I found a guy to fuck. I know that sounds terrible. But I was just . . . I was so angry. Then, six weeks later I took a pregnancy test and found out I was pregnant with Kye."

"The dad?" Linc asked.

Ryleigh winced. "I wouldn't even know how to find him if I wanted to."

Linc just nodded, not showing any emotion either way.

"We knew that we couldn't run forever," Lilac said. "Not with Ryleigh pregnant. And that's when she told us about her brothers. We weren't even entirely sure that her dad had been telling the truth about you guys or whether he made everything up just to make her feel better when she was younger. We had to do some research first. Luckily, he told Ryleigh their names and it wasn't hard to find out that Tanner and Raid would be in a rodeo in about six weeks' time. We drove to Hopesville, and debated what to do."

"I knew it should've been me that came to see you," Ryleigh said, looking over at Tanner. "I shouldn't have let Lilac do that. But I just . . . I didn't know what to say. What if you weren't great guys? What if my dad had made it all up? I didn't think he had. I knew he wouldn't lie to me, but I was still too scared. What if you were like Stefan? So, instead, Lilac said she would go and try to figure out what sort of men you were."

"And what happened then?" Alec asked. "Instead of telling Tanner the truth, why did you run off like that?"

Lilac tensed and Tanner shot Alec a look, not liking the accusatory tone to his voice. None of this was Lilac's fault.

"Stefan's men found us again," Lilac said. "I already told Tanner this part. But I was on the way to the bar to meet him when I saw Stefan's guys. I ditched my phone, and we ran. We couldn't risk them finding us. They would've killed both of you." She turned to Tanner as she said that.

"I would have protected you all."

"No. No, that just wasn't an option. He would have sliced you up into pieces and made me watch as punishment. And he would have enjoyed it." Lilac felt ill at the thought. The memory of her nightmare was still fresh in her mind.

Nothing could happen to Tanner.

"Stefan isn't going to harm me. And he's definitely not going to harm you," Tanner told her firmly.

Lord. She wished she could have that sort of faith.

"And then you decided to come here?" Alec asked. "Why wait six months?"

"Because we were worried that his guys might find our trail again. So, we knew we had to go to ground. We couldn't pop up in any town. Certainly not one close to Hopesville," Lilac told them.

"And I was scared," Ryleigh said. "I couldn't take my baby into another bad situation. We traveled north to Montana. We kept out of the big towns. It was only as I became more pregnant that we knew we had to get close to a hospital. Kye was born a bit early, and he needed some help. We were so terrified that Stefan would find us, even though Lilac got us some new identities."

"I knew we needed money quick," Lilac explained. "Luckily, I still had two of my mom's rings. I pawned them to pay for our new identities and the medical bills. And as soon as we were able to, we ran again. We decided that we had to come here. You guys were kind of our last chance. We were out of money and options. Plus, with Kye, well . . . we needed someone to help us protect him. Stefan wouldn't be above using a baby to keep us in line."

She took a deep breath. "So, we came here to find you guys. Well, we did some asking around first about Haven. The things we heard seemed crazy. But we were out of options. I knew . . . I knew that Tanner would likely hate me. I was just hoping that his brothers were good men like him. And that you would all be able to look after Kye, and Ryleigh and Opal."

Tanner turned her to face him. Grabbing her chin, he tilted her head back. "And what about you, baby? Sounds like you need the most protection from this asshole."

She shook her head, smiling sadly. "That's just it. I can't stay here."

"What do you mean, you can't stay here?" Ryleigh asked.

"Lilac, don't say it," Opal warned.

"I'm not staying, because I'm going back. The only way to ensure we're all truly safe is to take out Stefan. And I'm the only one who can manage that. I'm the one that he really wants. That he won't kill. So, I'm going to go back. And I'm going to make sure that he can't hurt any of you ever again."

38

To her shock, Tanner just started laughing.

Okay, that wasn't the reaction she'd been expecting.

She'd thought he'd immediately tell her that she couldn't go. That Mr. Bossy or Meanie Malone would make an appearance.

This was . . . unexpected.

Standing, she put her hands on her hips as she stared down at him. "Why are you laughing?"

"Because you're funny."

"I'm not funny. How is that funny?"

"Because it's a joke." The smile wiped off his face as he stood. Okay, this was more like what she'd been expecting. Only, he was very intense. A bit scary. She didn't think she'd ever seen him look like this before.

Lilac swallowed and stepped back.

Bad move.

Because all he did was take another step forward. And another and another. Until she was backed up into a wall. He placed his arm against the wall above her head, leaning into her.

"Uh-oh."

"Yes, pretty girl. Uh-oh is right," he rumbled.

"Tanner, I think you should back away from my friend, you're intimidating her," Ryleigh said.

"Pretty sure that's the point," Opal said dryly. "Lilac, say your safeword if you want him to back off. Or you want me to make him back off."

Tanner seemed to ignore all the banter behind him, staring down at her from those deep brown eyes. "You were joking, weren't you, Lilac?"

"Um." Okay, so he seemed like he really wanted her to say she was joking.

There was just one teeny-tiny problem . . .

"Linc, get him to back off her," Ryleigh demanded.

"Nope," Linc replied.

"Why not?" Ryleigh asked in frustration.

"Because she needs to learn the truth," Alec said firmly.

What was that?

"Baby, I'm a Malone. And Malones don't allow their women to head into danger. They protect them from the danger. So get any thoughts of going to Stefan out of your head right now. It's not happening."

She closed her eyes, leaning against the wall. God, she was so tired. And it wasn't just the fact that she was worn thin physically. Or that her emotions that were near breaking point.

It was . . . every. Fucking. Thing.

She really wanted to just fall into his words. To wrap that protection around her.

But she couldn't.

"You don't understand." She opened her eyes and looked up at him imploringly.

He ran a finger down her cheek. "No, baby. You're the one

who doesn't understand. I will protect you. My family will protect you. All four of you."

"And I want your protection. For them. But I have to go. There's no way that he'll ever stop looking for me. And if you try to stand between me and him, then you'll die. Don't you understand?"

Please let him get it.

She couldn't handle anything happening to him.

Tanner cupped her face between his hands. "I know that you've been making all the decisions, doing everything you can to protect your friends and yourself. You've been on the run for so long that you've run yourself into the ground. You've stopped eating and sleeping, you don't know how to relax, and you're in a constant state of stress. It has to stop."

"And it will as soon as I kill Stefan. Um, you didn't hear that Linc."

Linc just snorted.

"Don't worry about Linc," Tanner told her. "He might have a stick up his ass, but he doesn't like abusers any more than the rest of us."

"I do not have a fucking stick up my ass. I'm an officer of the law."

Tanner widened his eyes at her. She wished she could laugh, she really did. But there wasn't anything funny about any of this.

"Tanner . . ." she said in a low voice. But she didn't know what else to say. Her mind was a mess. It went from one thought to another, chasing them around and around.

And she wasn't being fair to Ryleigh. This was her moment and Lilac was stealing the attention.

Suddenly, Tanner slipped his arm around her, the other went under her ass. He lifted her up to cradle her against his chest. "Lilac is getting tired. She should be in bed. She needs rest and care."

"We need to pack up her things and bring her out to the Ranch," Alec said.

She stiffened in Tanner's arms. She thought Alec didn't want her there if she was a risk to his family? Moving her there would be a definite risk.

"All four of you will be coming with us," Alec declared. "If you could pack up everything, I'll call West and get him to bring another vehicle to transport everything."

She shook her head. "I don't think I should move out to the Ranch."

"Too bad you don't get a choice," Tanner told her cheerfully "You're coming."

"Tanner, the only way he'll stop hunting me is if he's dead."

"Then we'll kill him."

39

Why couldn't she catch her breath?

It was trapped in her lungs. Strangling her.

"It . . . it's not that s-simple. You don't know who he is."

"Then you will just have to tell us."

It was Alec who spoke, but when she turned her head to see him, he was staring down at Ryleigh with a frown on his face.

Right. Because he'd just learned that he had a younger sister. That his father was dead. All of that had to be messing with him. With Tanner.

Ryleigh stared up at her worriedly, then over to Alec.

"I think everyone should stay here. With me," Linc said.

She attempted to wriggle down from Tanner's hold, but he tightened his hold on her.

"Tanner, let me down."

"No."

No?

"They're not staying here," Alec replied. "They need protection."

"I'm a cop," Linc said.

"And you barely have any security," Alec said. "Your guns are probably locked up and inaccessible to anyone else on the property. Plus, you have to operate within the law."

"For fuck's sake," Linc muttered. "Of course, they're locked up when I don't have them on me. And we all have to operate within the law."

Alec and Tanner just stared at him.

She understood where they were coming from. She didn't plan to follow the law when she killed Stefan.

"Ryleigh is my sister," Alec said. "Kye is my nephew. Lilac is my brother's woman, and he is her guardian. That leaves Opal. You want to come with us, Opal? We'll take care of you."

"Not really sure that a ranch is my scene, but I go where my girls go."

"Fine, then. It's settled. All of you start packing except Lilac. She needs to rest."

Wow. He'd done a complete one-eighty, huh?

"I'm their guardian, Alec," Linc said.

"Not anymore. And if you stand in the way of me protecting my sister and nephew, then we are going to have trouble," Alec said in a low voice.

"You . . . you really believe me?" Ryleigh asked.

She was staring up at Alec in wonder, tears dripping down her face. Alec watched, his face softening.

Walking toward her, he crouched in front of her. He didn't touch her. He just sat there as Ryleigh wiped her cheeks.

"I do. I don't know why our father kept you from us. Why he never said anything. Maybe it was because of your mom. It sounds like he was a much better father to you than us, but I do believe you. Kye looks like Tanner when he was a baby. And you have Jaret's eyes. Maybe Beau's chin. There are bits of us in you."

"You . . . you don't have to take us in, though," Ryleigh said. "I know we don't know each other. We can stay here and maybe . . . maybe get to know each other."

God. Please don't reject her.

There was such hope in Ryleigh's voice that it hurt Lilac. If Alec pushed her away . . . she didn't know what it would do to her best friend.

She didn't need to worry though.

"All of my life, I hoped that one day my father might bring me home a little sister. Someone to take care of and protect and cherish."

Holy. Shit.

How had he known exactly what to say to her?

"Instead, he kept breeding these rough, troublemaking, ungrateful boys. And then he left me to take care of them. Can you imagine how hard that's been? Imagine if they'd all had a little sister to look after?"

"I'm guessing she might have been smothered to death," Opal said dryly.

"Most likely," Alec said. "She'd also have been loved. And now, it seems, I've been given that thing I always wanted. I'm just hoping it's not too late to show her how much the Malones will cherish a little sister."

Ryleigh let out a sob and threw her arms around Alec.

"For all his fucking faults, at least our old man did this for us," Tanner muttered. "At least he told her about us, so she knew to come to us."

She sucked in a breath. "Thomas sold her to Stefan."

Tanner stiffened. "What the fuck?"

She knew Ryleigh and Alec couldn't hear them, but Linc had turned their way, his face filled with horror.

"I never wanted to tell her. But I was there when they . . . when they made the negotiations. It was sickening. She has no idea that her father basically gave her to Stefan to wipe his debts. I like to think that maybe there was a part of him trying to look out for her. That he'd known that when he died all the people he owed money to would come looking for their payment. I don't know, though."

"It's entirely likely that prick just wanted the money he got for selling her," Tanner told her bitterly. "Fucking asshole."

"It was practically a point of pride that she was a virgin. Thankfully, in Stefan's twisted mind that was something to be celebrated. He decided to wait until their wedding night. I think he got a kick out of the fact that she thought he was a good guy. That he loved her. I just couldn't tell her about what her dad did."

"It's all right, baby," Tanner soothed. "The old man is gone now. There's no point in her knowing."

"When she found out about Stefan . . . I knew that I had to get her away from him. Before he hurt her."

He hated the dead tone of her voice. He was determined to bring back life into her voice. All he wanted was her happiness and safety.

Like hell would he ever let her go back to Stefan and put herself at risk again.

Tanner couldn't believe she thought that was an actual possibility. Obviously, she still didn't know him at all.

"Right, let's get moving," Alec said. "I'll feel better once you're all under lock and key at the Ranch. We can keep you safe there. Unlike here."

"I've been keeping them safe," Linc said between clenched teeth. He was still holding onto Kye as he stood. "Why would Ryleigh want to go with you when she hardly knows you?"

"Because we're her brothers," Alec said. "And Malones look after their own."

"No one fucks with the Malones," Tanner added.

Linc held his hand over the baby's ears. "Don't swear in front of the baby."

The funny thing was that Alec had said it at the same time.

Both men glared at each other.

Tanner glanced down at Ryleigh, who was starting to look increasingly worried as she gazed from one to the other.

"I mean, maybe we could spend time at both," Ryleigh offered.

Both men frowned.

"They're being jerks," Lilac whispered to Tanner.

"The main thing is that I'm not being a jerk," he replied.

"You can be," she informed him.

"Ouch."

"You know what," Linc said with a strange look on his face. "You're right."

"I am?" Alec asked.

"You shouldn't stay here, Ryleigh."

"Oh?" she said.

"No, I should come stay with you," Linc said. "I'm moving out to the Ranch."

"Oh, fuck no!" Tanner said.

"Stop swearing in front of the baby," everyone but Opal told him.

Tanner rolled his eyes. "He is not coming with us, Alec."

Alec was quiet.

"He's a cop!" Tanner said.

"With a gun," Alec said. "Trouble is coming."

"Yeah, and he'll make us stick to the rules."

"If I need to, I'll look the other way," Linc said with obvious reluctance. "Only in this instance and only to protect the girls and Kye."

Alec nodded. "Fine, you can come too. But you're not staying in the house with my sister. And if I catch you looking at her, touching her, or making fucking eyes at her, you're out!" Turning, he walked out.

Silence filled the room.

"Huh," Opal said. "I'm glad I don't have any long-lost brothers coming out of the woodwork, it seems like they'd be a real downer on my love life."

40

"I really don't need a nap."

Tanner just gave her a firm look. "Yeah, baby. You do. You're only just out of the hospital and you've already had an eventful day."

"You wouldn't even let me do anything. I was only allowed to sit and supervise." She hadn't even been allowed to pack her own underwear, for goodness' sake.

And now they were at Tanner's family Ranch. Apparently, Tanner usually lived in the bunkhouse on his own. All the rest of the brothers had their own places. West and Flick had built a house on the property. Butch and Lara had moved into a house they'd had transported onto the Ranch. Jaret, Beau, and Maddox lived on other properties close by, while Raid lived in Haven.

But Alec wanted them all in the main house. Ryleigh and Kye were in a room across the hall while Opal was next to them.

Linc was in the bunkhouse. Alec wasn't letting him stay in the house. In fact, he'd even told him that he wasn't allowed upstairs.

Lilac was beginning to agree with Opal. Alec was over-the-top protective.

A different breed of brother than she was used to.

Crap. How was she going to convince Tanner to let her deal with Stefan? It would be so much easier for everyone. Right now, Alec was calling all of his brothers in to explain the situation.

And to tell them about Ryleigh.

She wondered how the heck that would go.

"Shouldn't you be downstairs with your brothers?" she asked.

"Why?" he asked as he tucked the blankets around her. "I see their ugly faces all the time."

"But . . . don't you want to talk about everything. About Ryleigh?"

"What is there to talk about? She's our sister and we're gonna take care of her. She'll move in here and she's never allowed to date until she's fifty. Done."

She rolled her eyes at him. Only . . . he looked kind of serious.

"You do remember that she has a son, right?"

"Immaculate conception."

"Tanner!"

"I won't believe anything else."

"Oh my God. You're utterly insane. What about Linc? He seems interested in her."

Tanner placed his hand over her mouth. "No. Nope. Not happening. No sister of mine will be involved with a cop."

"The two of you were friends."

"More like acquaintances." He sat on the bed, facing her. Reaching out, he cupped her chin with his hand. "You're so beautiful."

Blushing, she lowered her gaze from his. "I'm not."

"You are. You're beautiful and precious and mine. I hold on

to the things that are mine, pretty girl. I lost you once. I won't risk losing you again. I can't."

She sniffled, her eyes rising to his. "And I don't want anything to happen to you. It's the most selfish thing I've ever done in my life, falling in love with you."

Tanner's face softened as he leaned in to kiss her. This kiss was gentle, soft. Then, it deepened into something more. Something more hotter. Harder. Arousing

A whimper escaped her. She wanted to be closer to him. To have him wrapped around her.

But he drew back, brushing her hair away from her face.

"Tanner," she whispered. "Come to bed with me."

A groan escaped him. "God, baby. I want that more than anything. But you're just out of the hospital."

"I feel fine."

He shot her a look.

She bit her lip, looking away. "I don't like being weak."

"Look at me." He waited until she turned back. "Your body might feel weak right now, but there is nothing weak about you. You're the strongest person I know. However, even strong people know that they need to lean on others now and then. Just let me take care of you. Please."

There was such longing on his face. Such need in his eyes.

But could she do it?

This was scary. Stefan was terrifying. And she was the one who understood him the best.

"How about this? Let me look after you until you're feeling stronger physically. Then I'll let you help us take him down. I'm not stupid, I know we'll need you."

"But?" she asked, sensing one.

"But you need to know you'll never be allowed to put yourself in danger. You're not going near him. You can help. Give us advice, intel, but that's it. No leaving the Ranch without me. No trying to go to him."

It wouldn't work. She knew it wouldn't. But what could she say?

"I promise that I won't do anything rash."

Tanner sighed, looking a bit sad. Shit. She hated that she'd done that. But she couldn't promise anything more.

"Lie down, I'm going to get you a bottle of water and a snack." He stood and she reached out to grab his hand.

"It's not . . . it's not that I don't trust you. That I want to go near him. I don't. I just think I'm the best option to take him down."

"Even if that means that you never come back to me? How is the two of us never being happy the best option?" Turning, he walked away.

Fuck. Ouch.

She lay back, closing her eyes.

Sacrificing herself hadn't seemed that hard before. When she had nothing to lose.

Now, that she had the promise of everything could she do it?

41

Tanner walked into Alec's office. Nearly everyone was there. All of his brothers and their wives.

And Linc.

"Everything okay?" Alec asked, glancing over at him. Mia sat on his lap, and he was holding her tight, his hand held protectively over her stomach.

Hmm.

"She's asleep," Tanner said, leaning against the wall to glare down at Linc.

What was he doing here?

"She still thinks the best idea is for her to sacrifice herself?" Alec asked.

Around him, everyone was quiet, listening. Jaret was leaning against the wall on the other side of the room. Clem was next to him. She had something in her arms. Was that a damn bunny?

Flick, Lara, and Hannah were on the sofa. Raid, Butch, and West were behind them. Mitch was being held against West's chest as he stood behind Flick. Usually, he liked to stand behind Alec.

But Tanner got it.

He'd always choose Lilac first.

Maddox was on an armchair with Scarlett in his lap while Beau sat in the armchair next to them. He wondered where the twins and Seb were.

Linc was leaning against the wall along from Jaret and Clem.

"I think I'm slowly getting through to her." He hoped he was. Not that he intended to let her leave the Ranch until Stefan was taken care of. "She seems to think it's the only way to take Stefan down."

"She wants to Trojan horse him?" Clem asked.

Tanner grinned at her. "Is Trojan horse a term now?"

"Sure. Only thing is . . . is he smart enough to see that play coming?"

She had a point. Tanner looked over at Alec. He had the best mind for this sort of thing.

Alec looked thoughtful. "Perhaps. Or he might be arrogant enough to believe that no one can take him down, including his sister."

Tanner straightened. "I will not allow her to go near him."

Alec waved his hand in the air. "Of course not. She's yours, therefore she's under all of our protection. We don't send our women into danger. I took the liberty of calling Devon and Peggy to let them know she wouldn't be working for them anymore," Alec told him.

"And I've informed Jake about everything," Linc stated.

"Okay . . . okay," Beau said, clapping his hands. "Can we talk about the elephant in the room?"

They all stared at him.

He pointed at Linc. "What the hell is he doing here? And talking to Jake? Since when do we involve the cops in family business?"

"Since this cop wants to feel up our baby sister, apparently," Tanner said dryly.

Everyone in the room stilled.

Oh. Fuck.

He met Alec's resigned look with one of surprise. "Uh, I take it you hadn't told them yet?"

"You guessed correctly. I told them that there was a threat to your woman. That her brother was going to come for her. And that he's an abusive asshole. That's why she ran from you six months ago and why she came here now. But I haven't had a chance to tell them the rest."

"Then, surprise! We have a sister." He held his arms up in the air.

Everyone started talking at once. Well, everyone except West and Alec.

"Everyone, quiet!" Alec ordered. He didn't yell, but he didn't need to.

Beau was up and pacing.

"A sister?" Jaret asked. "How?"

"Apparently, the old man wasn't finished after me," Tanner said. "Hey, there could be dozens more Malones and we wouldn't know."

"Shit. That's a thought," Clem said.

Not entirely pleasant one. Especially for Alec who was hugely protective of his family.

"Who?" West asked.

"Ryleigh, Lilac's friend," Alec explained. "Apparently, she grew up with her mother and our old man used to visit them regularly."

"She seems to have had a different experience than us with him," Tanner said. "He was semi-decent to her. At least up until he sold her."

"He fucking what?" Beau snapped.

"Language," West snarled.

Beau winced. "Sorry. But, come on, West. He sold our sister?"

"What the hell?" Alec asked in a low voice.

"Yeah, Ryleigh doesn't know this, but he sold her to Stefan. That's Lilac's brother. The old man died of cancer not long after and Stefan moved her in with him. It wasn't until Ryleigh saw what he'd done to Opal, his mistress, that her rose-colored glasses came off when it came to Stefan."

"You're sure she's our sister?" Maddox asked, rubbing his hand up and down Scarlett's back.

Alec sighed. "There's a chance she's not. But she said the old man told her about us. Also, her son, Kye, looks like Tanner when he was a baby. We can do some tests . . . but yeah, I think she belongs to us."

"Wow. A sister," Butch said. "Fuck. Is that asshole the father of her son?"

"I'll fucking kill him if he raped her," Raid snapped.

"No. He didn't touch her," Tanner said. "Lilac got them all out of there before he could. But they've been running a long time from him, and Lilac is worn through."

"She's protected them this long. It's time for her to let someone else take over," Alec said.

"We're going to slaughter the bastard," Maddox said.

"I'm still in the room," Linc said.

"Then leave." Beau shot him a grin.

"I'm not the enemy," Linc said. "You guys have known me a while. I consider some of you friends."

"That was before you started putting your filthy hands on our sister," Maddox said darkly.

Linc put his hands in the air. "I didn't know she was your sister! You didn't know she was your sister. And I haven't put my hands on her."

"Good. Keep it that way if you want to keep your hands," West told him.

Linc was fucked. He actually found himself feeling sorry for the big guy.

"Back to Stefan," Jaret said. "Do we have a last name? Details? Who are we up against?"

"I managed to get some details from Lilac," Alec said. "Her brother's name is Stefan Weber. His father was Anselm Weber. Anselm owned an import business in San Diego. Stefan took over from his father when he died. That's as far as I've got."

"What are they importing?" Tanner asked.

"I've heard of them," Linc said with a frown. "No one has found anything dirty on them, but it's widely believed to be guns and women."

"And our father sold our sister to this guy?" Butch asked. "Fuck."

"Lilac has lived with him her entire life," Tanner said. "She's been emotionally and physically abused by him, and it got worse after her father died."

"Opal was his mistress," Alec added. "Seems it wasn't by choice."

"I have a question," Lara said.

"Go for it." Alec nodded to her.

"Wouldn't Stefan know that Ryleigh might come here? Didn't she have your last name? Would your dad have told him about all of you?"

There was silence.

"Fuck," Linc said, ignoring West's glare at his language. "But that would mean he could know where they are. If he did . . . wouldn't he have grabbed them already?"

"It's possible that he knows our last name," Alec said. "But Ryleigh said the old man used the last name, Sanders. And even if Stefan did think that they'd come here, he'd have to have some way of knowing when they arrived here. We would have noticed a stranger hanging around."

Linc nodded. "That's true, and it's been what . . . ten months since they ran? Even if he'd had someone here to begin with, he probably had to pull them back."

Alec rubbed at his head. "If he comes for them, then we need to be prepared. We have to protect them."

They all nodded.

"We need to talk to Ryleigh," Alec said.

Linc tensed. "I won't have you all intimidating her."

"You think we'd scare our own sister?" Butch snarled.

"Calm down," Alec ordered. "Tanner, would you go find Ryleigh?"

"This might be too much for her," Mia said, climbing off Alec's lap. "I need to check on the kids anyway. I don't know how much experience Opal has with kids."

Oh, so that's who had the boys.

"And I'm in the mood to bake cookies," she added. "Everyone needs cookies."

"I'm coming too," Flick said. West rushed around to hold his hand out to her and help her up. The guy acted like she was still pregnant. She smiled up at him in thanks. He handed her Mitch, and she followed Mia out. Hannah and Lara followed.

Scarlett stood and turned to Clem. "Want to come?"

"I guess so. Carrots likes the idea of cookies, don't you, Carrot?"

"Do not feed that rabbit any cookies," Jaret ordered.

"So bossy," Clem whispered.

Tanner left to go find Ryleigh, discovering her outside on the back porch. "Hey, you all right?"

She glanced over at him. "Kind of overwhelmed. I . . . I always wondered how this moment would go, and now that it's here . . . it's a lot."

"I get it. My brothers can be overwhelming. They're a lot. But they're also the best people you'll ever meet. We will protect you, Ryleigh."

She bit her lip. "And Kye? Opal? Lilac?"

"They'll be protected too. Nothing will happen to them."

Especially Lilac.

"Lilac's always sacrificing for us," Ryleigh said. "I always felt so bad. Like a burden."

"She never felt that way about you, I'm sure," he said.

"I know she didn't. I think she shows her love through sacrifice. Through doing. She isn't like me . . . she never had any happiness. Any normalcy. She only ever had terror and fear. I don't know much about her life with Stefan. But I imagine it's hard to learn how to stop living in fear, to go from always being stressed to being happy. I think she's probably scared to be happy, Tanner. For fear it will all get ripped away from her. Like it always has before."

"I know. I'm going to show her how to be happy. That she doesn't have to do anything to earn my love because she already has it."

"You're a good man. I'm glad you're my brother."

Tanner drew her against him, holding her close. "Ready to meet the rest of them? Just don't be shocked."

"By what?" she asked.

"Well, I am the most handsome and intelligent of the bunch. Just didn't want you to get a fright when you see their ugly mugs."

She started giggling.

Tanner knew that Stefan didn't have a chance in hell of hurting these girls again. Not with his family to protect them.

42

Lilac stared at herself in the mirror.

Urgh.

This wasn't her. This pale, haunted-looking woman with dark marks under her eyes.

Well, it wasn't who she wanted to be. She wanted to be vibrant and happy. Not chased around by a nightmare who wouldn't just stay in her dreams.

She sucked in a breath. She couldn't believe she'd fallen asleep yesterday, and then slept through the night.

This morning when she'd woken up, she'd been alone. She wasn't even sure when Tanner had come to bed.

Or if he had.

She didn't want him to be mad that she wouldn't just let him protect her.

As much as she'd love to just hand over all her stresses and worries, that wasn't how things worked for her.

So, this morning, she'd gotten up and dressed. It had nearly zapped all of her energy which was a worry. What day was it today?

Wednesday?

Shit. She had to get to the bar tonight. Would Tanner drive her in?

With a sigh, she headed out of the bathroom and through the bedroom. She'd made the bed and tidied the room. Not that there was much to do. She'd left her stuff in her bag. She didn't feel right unpacking it.

Heading out of the bedroom, she walked downstairs. There was the sound of laughter and women's voices coming from further down the passage.

But that wasn't where she headed. She had to find Alec.

Moving down the hall, she peeked in different rooms. Where would he be? Then, a door opened, and he stepped out. He looked tired, but he paused as he saw her.

"Lilac? Are you all right? What are you doing out of bed? Where's Tanner?"

She felt her cheeks growing warm. "I'm fine. I'm not ill, you know."

"You just got out of the hospital yesterday." He sent her a stern look.

"I just didn't eat enough, and my blood sugar got low. No big deal."

"I'll be sure to tell Tanner that."

"Um, we don't need to do that," she said hastily. She was already up to strike four. She didn't need anymore.

You don't think you're going to be on strike five for ignoring the note he left you?

Yeah. The note had said to text him when she woke up and stay in bed.

"Let me guess," he said. "Tanner doesn't know you're out of bed yet. Have you eaten breakfast?"

"I'll get some soon. I just needed to talk to you."

Alec sighed, shaking his head, and her stomach dropped. He wouldn't talk to her?

"You better come in, then. But just know that when Tanner comes looking for you, I won't stop him from whatever he feels he need to do."

Ominous warning.

She stepped into a room that was obviously his office. Another man was in there. Tall and imposing, even with a baby pressed against his chest. He frowned down at her.

"This is West."

"Right. I've heard about you."

West just snorted. "I can tell it was all good."

"Oh, it was," she said hastily.

"No, it wasn't. Sit." The word was barked, and she immediately sat on a chair facing Alec's desk.

Yikes. He was intimidating.

"West, go easy. She's been in the hospital."

West eyed her. "Tanner needs to take better care of her."

"Tanner takes care of me just fine," she protested, defending him.

Wait. That wasn't what she'd intended to say.

"I mean, I can look after myself."

"Clearly not," West said.

"Wow. I can see Tanner wasn't exaggerating about you."

West just raised an eyebrow. "Shouldn't you be in bed? If you were my woman you wouldn't be allowed out of bed for a week. And then you wouldn't be sitting for a week."

Lord help whoever his woman was.

"If I was your woman, you'd probably have been suffocated with a pillow by now."

To her shock, West grinned. "I like her."

Great. She could die happy.

Alec took a seat behind the desk. Sitting back, he studied her. "What can I do for you, Lilac?"

"I need to talk to you about your plans. For Stefan." She swallowed heavily against the nausea in her stomach.

"You didn't discuss this with Tanner?" Alec asked.

"I, uh, fell asleep yesterday afternoon and didn't wake up until about forty minutes ago."

She was embarrassed by how much she'd slept when they were about to enter into a fight for their lives.

"There's nothing wrong with resting, Lilac," Alec said. "With letting someone else be strong for a while."

She clenched her hands together.

"Surprised Tanner left you. Or at least didn't leave some instructions," West said.

"Instructions?" she asked. Even though that's precisely what he'd done.

"If it was me and I had to leave Flick while she was sleeping and I wanted her to rest and recuperate, if I was worried about her health, then I'd probably have left her a note telling her to call me when she woke. Or I'd put a camera on her," West added. "Yeah, probably that."

"Flick is a brave woman," she said without thinking.

"And patient," Alec added, his lips twitching.

"Look, I need to know what you plan to do about Stefan. I know him best. I can help."

"And by help, you mean you can sacrifice yourself," Alec said.

Damn it.

"Look, you didn't even want me here because you knew I was a risk to your family. Nothing's changed."

"Except for everything," West said. "You protected our sister and nephew when we couldn't."

"And by our reckoning that means we owe you," Alec said gently. "You aren't going back to that asshole. I never should have said what I did and for that I apologize. I should have had more faith in Tanner and his feelings. But I practically raised Tanner, and sometimes I seem to forget he's his own man. With his own mind."

"Since you raised him, you should know he's a good man," West said. "Even if he's an asshole sometimes."

She was trying to keep up with them. But all she was getting was that no one was going to support her plan.

"He'll come for me eventually. You have children. Women. I can't risk them."

"And we can't risk you," Alec said.

"I'm no one. I'm not important. Everyone else is."

West whistled and Alec looked over her head. "I can see the issues you're facing here."

Uh-oh.

Turning, she looked up . . . into the furious face of Tanner Malone.

Shit.

"I've been looking all over the house for you."

She gulped.

"I was starting to worry that you'd gone outside, wandered off, that you'd left."

As well as anger there was a stark worry in his voice. The last thing she wanted was to hurt him. To scare him.

"I'm sorry."

He narrowed his eyes at her. "Why didn't you text me?"

"Um, well, I guessed that you'd be busy, and I, um . . ."

"You might want to tell the truth, girl," West advised.

Great. Thanks for the advice, West.

Her shoulders slumped. "I just wanted some information. Tanner, I need it. I can't stop my brain until I know what's going on."

"And you didn't think you could ask me? That I wouldn't tell you?"

"No, I didn't think you would," she said. "You're trying to shelter me."

"Of course I'm trying to shelter you!" he yelled. "You're the woman I love, and you've been through hell! You've just come out of the hospital. I think I'm entitled to shelter you under those circumstances."

"And if I didn't have my maniac brother out there, probably getting ready to commit countless murders to get me back, I would let you."

Tanner stalked forward. He moved around so he faced her chair. She twisted just as he leaned in to place his hands on the arms of the chair. "You are going to let me pamper and protect you or so help me I'm going to spank your ass every day for a month."

Lilac stared up at him in shock. Did he just realize what he'd said? But as she stared at him, she saw a very real fear in his eyes. What was she doing? Was she really insisting on going back to Stefan when it was the last thing she wanted? When it seemed everyone was against the idea?

And when it was causing the man she loved such pain?

"I'm sorry."

He blinked. "What?"

"You . . . I've spent so long thinking of ways to keep everyone around me safe, it's just . . . it's taking a bit to change my mindset to where someone might want to keep me safe. I just . . . I've never felt that worthy of being protected."

"Fuck, baby. That hurts me more than you can know." He picked her up and then sat in the chair, cradling her in his arms.

She buried her face in his chest.

"Please don't keep trying to risk yourself, baby. Please. For my sake. Stop self-destructing. I need you."

"I'll try. I promise I'll try."

"Damn," West said. "I was going to make a comment about how it serves you right to meet someone as reckless with their safety as you always were as a teenager, but it doesn't seem right now."

"You can always celebrate the fact that she's stubborn and won't give in easily to him," Alec said. "She'll give him hell. I'm taking solace in that."

"Hmm. True."

"Will the two of you shut up," Tanner grumbled without any real ire in his voice.

"Lilac," Alec said in a soft voice.

With a sigh, she lifted her head from Tanner's neck and turned to look at Alec.

"We're not trying to keep you in the dark. In fact, we need your help. But we don't want to add to your stress. And we don't want you doing something stupid."

Okay. Way to just get straight to the point.

"I won't do anything stupid."

Alec stared at her while Tanner ran his hand up and down her back. Then his gaze rose to Tanner.

Tanner sighed and started to massage her neck. "I'd like to keep you out of this entirely. To tie you to the bed to ensure you don't go anywhere. Then you'd stay where I put you, at least."

"Tanner Malone!" she said, shocked. Sort of. She glared up at him. "I'm never going to stay where you put me."

The gall.

Tanner sighed. "Too bad."

"Welcome to our lives," West muttered. "Told Flick that I wanted her to stay in bed for a month after Mitch was born. She managed two days."

A month? He wasn't serious?

"Also told her not to go up and down the stairs on her own while pregnant. Did she listen to me? Nope."

"That reminds me," Tanner said in her ear. "I haven't forgotten that you got showered, dressed, and walked down the stairs without me."

"I can't do any of those things on my own?"

"Not when you're just out of the hospital because you fainted. What if you'd gotten dizzy in the shower or coming down the stairs? No, that's a rule until you're feeling better."

"I am feeling better," she said.

"No, you're not."

Sheesh. She couldn't believe him!

"I feel so proud," West said gruffly.

"Since when did you start talking so much," Tanner grumbled.

"Babies need words," West replied. "Helps with their development."

Damn. That was sweet. He didn't look like a man who cared about a baby's development, but he obviously adored his son and wife.

"I can get up and down the stairs and dressed and showered alone."

"Definitely stubborn," Alec said.

"I am not!" It suddenly occurred to her that she was basically arguing with these men without a single concern that they might get upset with her. That they might hurt her or, worse, someone close to her.

On some level, she trusted them. Or trusted Tanner enough to trust that he wouldn't let anyone hurt her.

She glanced up at him in wonder.

"What is it, pretty girl?" he asked, cupping the side of her face.

"You wouldn't let anyone hurt me, would you?"

Leaning in, he pressed a kiss to her forehead. "No, baby. Never."

"Right. Shall we talk about where we're at, then," Alec said.

"Please," she replied.

"We were worried that Stefan would know about us, that he might think that Ryleigh would come to us."

"It's why we didn't do that straight away," she said. "And also, we weren't sure that you were the type of men who'd want anything to do with us. No offense."

"You were right to be cautious, Lilac," Alec told her. "And I want to reiterate something before we keep going."

"Yes?" she asked cautiously.

"That we can never thank you enough for keeping our sister and nephew safe. And thank you for keeping yourself safe too."

Oh, dear Lord.

She was about to cry.

"I don't know if I did that good of a job, but I did the best I could."

"You did perfectly," Alec told her. "We might wish you'd taken better care of your health. But you have Tanner to do that now."

Yikes. Okay, yeah. She got it. She needed to let Tanner help her.

"Now, like I said, we figured that our father might have told Stefan about Ryleigh having brothers."

"It's possible," she said.

"Ryleigh said that she used her mother's last name, Reynolds. And that our father was going by the name Thomas Sanders, so we're hoping Stefan didn't know about us, or if he did, he doesn't know our names."

"I think that might be a stretch to hope for that," she said. "Stefan has a way of ferreting out secrets. I was so certain he was going to catch on to what I was doing. I knew I had to act normal, but it was nearly impossible. With Stefan, it's always best to prepare for the worst. Ryleigh told me I was being a pessimist. She wanted to come to you guys straight away. But I knew it was safer to keep our distance. For you and us. I wouldn't have come here if we weren't desperate. But keeping Kye safe . . . it was more than I thought I was capable of."

"You did the right thing," Tanner told her.

Alec nodded. "You're where you're meant to be."

"If he knew about us, wouldn't he be here by now?" West asked.

She licked her lips. "Maybe he sent someone to begin with, then drew them back . . . I don't know. Perhaps he sends someone here every so often. Or perhaps he doesn't know at all."

"You researched us," Alec said. "Do you know about our cousins? Who they are?"

"Regent Malone and his siblings," she whispered. "Yes. I've heard of him. Stefan actually mentioned him a few times."

"I've spoken to Regent about all of this. He's looking into him and he's sending us some of his men. I've spoken to Mateo Marceras as well."

"I don't know him," she said.

"Our old man got in deep with Mateo's father, then he bailed and left us to pick up the pieces. Mateo helped us extract ourselves from that situation," Alec explained. "He's got connections to the underworld as well. He doesn't know your brother, but he's making some discreet inquiries. He thinks he knows some people who know him."

"They need to be careful," she said.

"They will be. In the meantime, I'm pulling everyone in. We're all doubling up. Raid and Hannah are moving in with Clem and Jaret. Butch and Lara will stay with Beau, Maddox, and Scarlett. I want the same promise I extracted from Ryleigh and Opal, that you will not leave the Ranch."

"But my jobs?" she asked.

"Devon and Peggy understand the circumstances and are fine with it," Alec told her.

She narrowed her gaze at him. "Did you call my bosses and quit my jobs."

"I did."

Wow. This guy.

"And you thought I was bossy and arrogant," Tanner whispered. "Bet I'm looking like a good catch right now, aren't I?"

"You might have competition for the title of Meanie Malone," she agreed.

He laughed and she had to smile at the sound. Something inside her eased.

Alec sighed, proving he could hear them. "Well?"

It didn't feel right not to work and contribute. She glanced up at Tanner, biting her lip. "Are you okay with that? I don't have much in savings, but I can give it to you all for groceries and stuff."

"Dear Lord, are you going to shut her up?" West grumbled.

She gasped in horror before Tanner kissed her. Hard and fast. Then he gave her a stern look. "Shut up. No one wants your money."

"Rude." But she didn't take offense. She was finally coming to realize that these men were real men.

Protective. Possessive.

A bit gruff and arrogant, but with huge hearts.

They didn't calculate every move and make a decision based on what they thought they would get out of something. They genuinely wanted to do what was best for the people they cared about.

"So, you're just going to wait and see what your cousin can find out?" she asked. "What is he looking for?"

"He's going to see what your brother is up to," Alec told her.

"See if he can get to someone close to him. Meanwhile, we've let some key people in Haven know what is going on. Don't worry, they won't tell anyone else. But we have allies, and we need to use them. There will be people patrolling the grounds at all times. We have excellent security. This isn't the first time we've had to protect our own."

She sucked in a breath, leaning against Tanner tiredly. "Stefan wouldn't understand that."

"What, baby?" Tanner asked.

"Loyalty earned without terror. All of his men are scared of him; they follow him out of fear. Any colleagues he has either want to overthrow him or fear him doing that to them. He has no friends. I sometimes think that's why he's obsessed with me. I'm his. No one else's. He wants me but can't have me. He's never been denied anything. But me. I know it sounds disgusting and I'm not saying it's sexual. It's about..."

"Ownership," Alec said grimly.

"Yes. That's why I know he'll come for me. I understand him best."

Alec nodded.

She tried to stifle a yawn. Tanner immediately stood with her cradled in his arms. "Lilac needs to eat and rest. But keep us updated. I'll be with her."

Alec nodded. "I can send Mia up with some food."

"I don't want to be a hassle," she protested.

"No hassle, Lilac," Alec told her. "You're family now."

43

You're family now.

"He really meant that, didn't he?" she said to Tanner as he set her down on the bed.

"What?" he asked.

"Alec. He really meant that I'm family now, didn't he?" she asked.

"Yeah, baby. Of course he did." He drew the covers back and lifted her again, placing her in bed.

"I don't want to go back to bed, Tanner. I'm sick of bed."

He tucked her in, then sat facing her, cupping her chin. "I'll make a deal with you. Today, you rest and let me feed you. Tomorrow, I'll take you outside to see the horses."

"Really?" she asked.

"Really. Maybe a picnic?"

"Okay. I like the sound of that."

"Good girl. Now, how many strikes are you up to? Seven? Eight?"

"What? Why? I'm not up to that many." She pouted. Whoa. She didn't think she'd ever pouted in her life.

"Let's see. Getting up on your own. Showering on your own. Dressing on your own. Not following the instructions I left you. And walking down the stairs. On. Your. Own."

Gulp.

"And that's without even talking about you going to Alec to convince him to let you help with Stefan. I think we're far past eight. But I'm being generous, considering you haven't been well."

"This is you being generous?"

"It is. You can thank me later." He gave her an overexaggerated wink and wriggled his eyebrows. In case she couldn't decode the wink.

"I'll be sure to get onto that," she said dryly. "Can't wait."

That part was true. Lilac couldn't wait. In fact, she thought she could get into that right now.

"Did you just lick your lips?" he asked.

"What? No. I didn't do that."

He grinned. Placing his hands on either side of her hips, he leaned into her. "You did. You licked your lips. Baby, were you thinking about sucking my dick?"

Her eyes grew wide. "Well, so what if I was?"

"Then I would tell you that I spend most of my time thinking about eating you out. Wanting to taste you. To hear you scream as you coat my lips in your pleasure. I want to fuck you bare and possess you. To have everyone know that you're mine. I want to tattoo that onto your skin and slip a ring on your finger."

"Tanner," she said faintly.

"Too much?" he asked.

"No. It's really not."

He smiled. "Good. Because I meant every word. Once you're better, I'm going to fuck you until neither of us can walk."

"I'm feeling better already," she told him.

A knock on the door interrupted them before he could reply. "That will be Mia."

Great. What would Mia think of the fact that she was having to make her food? And bring it up to her?

She felt awful.

Tanner got up and opened the door and a kind looking woman with red-blonde hair stepped in. She didn't look much older than Lilac, which surprised her.

"Hi! I'm Mia."

"Hi, I'm Lilac. I'm so sorry you had to bring that up to me. I promise, I'm going to be moving around tomorrow. I can help with the cooking. Although I'm not very good at that. I am good at cleaning, though. I can do the cleaning around here."

"Um." Mia handed the tray over to Tanner, looking from her to Tanner.

"Baby, you're not here to fucking clean."

"I need to help out," Lilac said, almost desperately. "I promise I'll pull my weight. I know all these people descending on you must be an inconvenience."

"Whoa, baby—"

"Lilac," Mia said gently, interrupting Tanner. She walked over to her and took hold of her hand. "You're not an inconvenience. And you're not here to work. I understand wanting to pull your weight. But you've been in the hospital. You need to rest and get better. I came here needing a safe place, somewhere to hide, and these guys all took care of me. They'll look after you too. Okay? Just have some faith. We've got your back."

"T-thank you."

"What's your favorite sweet thing? What do you like that I could bake for you?"

"You want to bake me something?"

"Mia always bakes our favorites," Tanner told her. "Mine is

chocolate chip cookies so of course she makes that the most since I'm her favorite."

Mia rolled her eyes at Lilac and, to her surprise, Lilac giggled.

"He thinks he is. They all think they are. So, what do you like?"

"Do you know how to make red velvet cake?"

"I sure do." Mia patted her hand. "Don't you worry, we'll have you feeling better in no time."

"She's really nice," she told Tanner after Mia left.

"All of the women in this family are too good for their men. Including you. But that's the thing about Malone men. When we find something we want, we grab hold. And we don't let go."

44

The nightmare was the same.

Only this time he found her in the bedroom at the Ranch, not the hospital. He held his hand over her mouth until she couldn't breathe.

"Baby! Wake up! Lilac, wake up, pretty girl! It's just a dream. Wake up."

She opened her eyes, gasping for air. Tanner grabbed hold of her, pulling her into his chest.

She trembled with the aftereffects of the nightmare.

"I think he'll have a hold on me until he's dead. Won't he?" she whispered.

"Baby, if that's what has to happen to free you, then that is what will happen." He rolled her onto her back, leaning up on one elbow. "Will you be okay with that?"

Would she? He was her brother, but he also wasn't a good man. After everything he'd done . . . she knew he deserved to die.

"Yes."

Tanner leaned in and gave the softest, sweetest kiss she'd

ever been given. By the time he drew back, there were tears in her eyes.

He rolled her over, then spooned her, drawing her back into his body. But she was too on edge to sleep. It felt like there was something crawling over her skin. She shivered.

"You're tense, baby."

"I don't think I'm going to be able to go back to sleep. Maybe I should get up and let you sleep." She tried to move away, but he drew her back down against him.

"Not happening, baby. You need your rest."

"So do you."

"Hmm. Perhaps we just need to tire you out."

"How do you suggest we do that?" she asked as he ran his hand along her side.

Her body started to tremble for an entirely different reason as he slid his hand under her pajama top and over her stomach.

Shoot. What was he thinking? Was he thinking that she was too skinny now?

"Stop thinking," he bossed. "Or I'll make you."

"You'll make me?"

"Yeah, I think I'll do that anyway." He moved her onto her back and grabbed the bottom of her pajama top, sliding it up over her head.

"Tanner," she whispered.

"Choose a safeword, baby."

"I'm going to need one?" She didn't think she was up for anything too exciting tonight.

"Just in case," he said.

"Um. Scotch. It was Stefan's favorite drink." She could remember the stench.

"Okay, pretty girl. I'm going to make you feel so good that you forget about everything bad, all right? I just want you to lay there and relax."

"But what if I want to touch you?" she asked.

"Not happening. Just lie still for me. Be a good girl and you'll get a reward."

He started kissing down her neck and between her breasts. Then he moved to her right nipple, sucking on it.

Slowly, he bit down.

"Ooh, Tanner."

"You're so fucking responsive, so beautiful," he told her.

"Please," she begged.

Moving to the other nipple, he bit it. Harder, this time. A cry left her lips, and she placed her hands on his shoulders as he lapped at the abused bud.

"Uh-uh, hands above your head," he bossed. "Or I'll have to punish you."

Another shiver.

One of pleasure.

"Seems my baby likes that idea. Does she want me to spank her bottom for misbehaving? Or perhaps she'd like me to spank her pussy."

"Nooo," she groaned.

"Are you sure about that?" He moved down her stomach. There wasn't much for him to hold on to. Was he put off?

"I told you to stop thinking, naughty girl," he grumbled, moving so he could take off her bottoms, leaving her naked.

Grabbing her legs, he raised them up into the air. "What are you doing?"

"Punishing you."

His free hand landed on her ass, leaving a sharp flash of pain across the skin.

Holy. Heck.

That shouldn't have been a turn-on. But it was. Another smack landed. More heat. More pleasure.

"My baby likes that." He made a scolding noise. "It's meant to be punishment."

Was it, though?

Somehow, she didn't think so.

Another smack. This time, it really did hurt. But then he rubbed the pain in.

She moaned and he let her legs drop down. "Have you learned your lesson, baby?"

"Uh-huh."

"Are you going to move your hands again?" he asked.

Maybe.

"I could always move on to the next punishment," he mused.

What was that? Another spanking?

"Orgasm denial."

Um. What? No, that didn't sound pleasant at all.

"No, thanks."

"Well, then, you better do as you're told. Spread your legs. I want to see that pussy."

He reached over and switched on a lamp.

"Tanner." She froze, unsure about him seeing all of her in the light.

She still hadn't shaved her legs. She hadn't trusted herself to bend over in the shower. Thankfully, she'd managed to shave her pussy.

"Hey, what's all this?" he asked. "You feeling shy with me?"

"I didn't shave my legs yet," she cried.

Darn it. Why did she point that out to him?

"Fuck, baby. I thought something was wrong. I don't care about your hairy legs. Although since they seem to be such a problem, I'll help you take care of them tomorrow."

All right . . . she wasn't sure about that. But she pushed that concern to one side.

"And I . . . I'm different now."

"I know you're different. And you know I still think you're beautiful. So stop fishing for compliments."

Fishing for compliments? Was he for real right now? That was not what she was doing!

"Show me that pretty pussy," he murmured. "Part your legs, then reach down and spread your lips. Let me see."

Oh. Dear. Lord.

She was helpless to deny him as she reached down to part her lower lips with shaking fingers. He kneeled between her parted thighs.

The look on his face . . . it was as though all of his Christmases had come at once, and slowly, she relaxed. Maybe he really did think she was beautiful no matter what.

Tanner lay between her legs, his fingers replacing hers. She heard him take a deep breath. "God, you smell good."

Before she could get embarrassed over those words, he took a long lick of her pussy. "And you taste divine."

She whimpered. More, she wanted more.

His tongue flicked at her clit, driving her slowly higher and higher, but as she was about to reach that peak, he drew back, moving his tongue lower.

"Noo," she cried.

"Shh, baby. Patience. You're going to get to come. You just have to wait. I don't want any thoughts in your head but the pleasure you're feeling."

And then he proceeded to torture her. There were no other words for it. He drove her up higher and higher, toying with her, teasing her.

Sliding fingers inside her as his tongue flicked at her clit.

Plucking at her nipple as he kissed along the top of her mound.

His tongue fucking her as his thumb played with her clit.

He played with her until she was a mess. Heaving for breath.

Shaking. And there was nothing in her mind but the need to come.

"Please. Please. Please."

"Good girl," he murmured. "Such a good girl for me. I'm going to let you come now. But you can't scream. There are too many people in this house." He handed her a pillow. "Put this over your face when you come."

And that's exactly what she did as he drove her up and pushed her over that edge. It seemed to go over forever, never-ending. A pleasure that didn't stop until the pillow was ripped out of her hold.

She gasped for breath.

"Jesus, baby. You weren't supposed to suffocate yourself. Are you all right?" he asked worriedly.

She smiled up at him dreamily. "I feel so good."

Tanner let out a small chuckle. Reaching up, he turned off the light. "Good, huh?" He gathered her against him, pulling her into his side as he lay on his back.

"Stupendous. Amazing."

He didn't bother to put her clothes back on, but she didn't care. She slid her leg up over his thigh, her hand dropping lower to where his dick was hard as it pressed against his boxers. That was all he was wearing.

All of that warm, smooth skin was pressed against her naked body.

Lilac ran her hand up and down his dick, but he reached down and grabbed her hand. "Not tonight, baby. Soon, I promise. It's not that I don't want you. I know you can feel that I do. But tonight was about you. So, I just want you to rest now. Sleep. We've got the rest of our lives."

45

"It's so beautiful."

For the first time in a long time, she felt like she could breathe. Earlier, Tanner had taken her to see the horses. She'd spent time with them, patting them, and giving them treats. Every minute with them seemed to ease her stress.

She didn't think she'd ever felt so at peace.

And then he had put her in his truck, doing up her seatbelt even though they hadn't left the Ranch, then driven her up this hill to have a picnic lunch.

She turned to look at him. He grinned at her as he pulled containers of food out of the picnic basket. "You talking about me or the Ranch?"

"Can I not be talking about both?"

He laughed. "Flattery will get you everywhere. Here, what would you like to eat?" He held out an empty plate to her.

She was seized with indecision. She didn't know what to eat. What might upset her stomach.

Without saying a word, he filled her plate. He didn't put so much on that it would freak her out, but more than she likely would have.

She breathed out a sigh of relief as he took the decision from her hands. He'd been like that all day. Directing her around without being bossy about it. Picking her up to put her in the truck. Driving her here without asking her where she wanted to go.

It was definitely freeing. What surprised her was that she wasn't obsessing over Stefan. Having Tanner take over helped clear her mind. Not entirely. She didn't think she'd be fully stress-free until Stefan was dealt with.

But it helped a lot.

Instead of giving her the food, Tanner moved in behind her, so his legs were cradling hers.

"Tanner?" she asked, hesitantly.

"Shh. Just keep staring out at the scenery." He set the plate off to the side where she couldn't see it. Then he held something up to her mouth. She tried to stare down at it. A piece of strawberry.

"Open your mouth."

Okay. Why did that turn her on? Maybe it was the memory of the fantastic orgasm he'd given her last night.

Perhaps you should return the favor.

Hmm. That was a thought.

"Good girl," he told her as she swallowed the piece of strawberry.

Next up was a piece of cheese on a cracker.

"Open up again. I want you to eat this."

"What is this? Tanner's way of getting me to eat?"

"Yep. I think it's pure genius."

He would.

As she swallowed the cheese and cracker, he kissed down her neck.

"Are you going to reward me every time I eat?"

"That's a nice thought."

"Not sure it's very practical. You can't do it all the time."

"Can't I?"

Dear Lord.

"Don't you eat with your family sometimes?" she asked as he held up a sandwich. She wasn't sure how her tummy would react, but she was quite relaxed, so she took a small bite, chewing slowly.

"Yep."

"You can't do this in front of other people."

"I don't see why not," he teased as he ran his hand up her thigh. She was wearing a pair of loose-fitting jeans. At one time they'd been a bit on the tight side.

"Tanner," she whispered.

"Just relax and let me take care of you."

"And what if I want to take care of you?" she asked. Okay, her stomach handled that bite, so she took another one.

"You are being so good, so brave," he whispered to her.

She wasn't, but she had to admit to liking the praise.

"You want to take care of me?" He cupped her mound.

She could feel her body reacting to him, wanting him. His scent was potent, it almost felt like a drug. His touch made everything go slightly hazy until all she could think about was where she wanted him to touch her next.

"I do. Please." She squirmed.

"Hmm, I'm not sure you've eaten enough to be allowed to eat me."

"Tanner!" She meant to scold him, but it came out more like a plea.

"Gosh, you want me that badly, don't you? A few more bites of food, then I get to eat you. Then I might let you have my cock. Since you're so desperate."

"I am not desperate."

She totally was.

"Uh-huh. Sure, you're not, baby." He slowly fed her several more bites of food even as his hand and lips explored her body.

By the time she was full, he had her long-sleeved top off and her jeans unbuttoned. His hand was down her pants, toying with her clit.

"I can't eat anymore," she managed to get out as he slowly flicked her clit.

"Hmm, not even a piece of chocolate?"

"Noo!" she cried as he slid his fingers lower, pushing them inside her.

She needed more. Wanted him to move. To drive her over that edge.

"Guess it's for me, then. Turn your face around."

It was a slightly awkward angle, especially with his fingers in her pussy, his palm against her mound, holding her down. But as with anything, Tanner made it work. With his other hand, he grabbed her chin, holding her still as he kissed her.

It was filthy. Hungry.

She could taste the chocolate on his tongue as he fed it to her.

Maybe it should have been gross.

But it was hot . . . so freaking hot.

"Good girl," he murmured. "You've always got to eat your dessert. And now it's my turn." He slid his fingers free of her pussy and she watched as he held them up to his mouth, licking them clean.

Her breathing quickened, a small whimper escaping.

"Take off your jeans and panties, then spread your legs wide."

She rushed to comply. She was meant to be going down on him, but if he wanted to eat her out first . . .

Well, who was she to complain?

He took off his shirt, revealing his muscular chest. The lean cut of his hips. Those delicious creases cut into his hips.

And then he positioned himself between her legs.

Perhaps she should have been back at the house, plotting and worrying about Stefan.

But Tanner was right. She needed some time to relax. To remember how to have fun.

So, she lay back on the blanket on a hill on a ranch in Texas and let her man eat her out.

And it was fucking amazing. He started slow and soft. As though he had all the time in the world. His fingers pressed inside her, moving back and forth. Faster and faster as her cries filled the air. He sucked on her clit before running his tongue over it. Then with his tongue moving rhythmically against the swollen bud, he sent her flying.

But he didn't stop. He kept going, moving his tongue faster, his fingers curling to find that spot. And to her shock, she flew up into a second orgasm. Or was it just a continuation of the first one?

She didn't know and didn't much care. By the time he'd slid his fingers and tongue away from her pussy, she was a mess. She watched through half-lidded eyes as he licked his lips, then cleaned his fingers.

That was so damn hot. Then he lay on his back and drew her lifeless body onto his chest.

Dead. She was dead.

"Poor baby, are you tired, now?" he crooned, rubbing his hand up and down his back.

"Uh-huh."

Then she stiffened. Wait. Was this all part of some plan?

Drawing back, she looked down at him.

"Wanna have a nap?" he asked.

Ooh, it was. He just wanted her to sleep. Well, she'd teach him.

"Nope. I'm hungry."

"Yeah? Want some more food?" He sat up with her in his lap.

"Nope. It's your turn to lie still and let me play."

He eyed her for a long moment. "I don't know if you're feeling up to that, baby."

Oh, that was his plan? To tire her out because he thought she wasn't up to sucking him off?

She so didn't think so.

"I feel better than I have in ages, and I know what I want. Are you going to tell me no?"

Lilac would stop if he said no. And when he shook his head, her heart dropped.

It's not a rejection.

"There's no way I could tell you no," he told her.

Huh? Wait. That was a yes?

She smiled at him.

"But if you get tired or dizzy or feel sick, you stop at once."

"I promise." Her hands were trembling as she undid his jeans. He sat up and helped her strip him naked, then he drew her onto his lap, his hand wrapping around the back of her head as he kissed her.

Drawing back, she pouted. "I thought I was in charge here."

"My baby wants to be in charge?"

"Yes."

"All right, then."

She wasn't sure if she believed him, but she slid her hands down his chest, touching all of him, running her fingers over his nipples. Then she bent down to suck on them.

"Fuck, yes." He clasped the back of her head again, guiding her to his other nipple.

"Tanner," she scolded.

"Sorry. Couldn't help myself." He drew his hand away and leaned back on his hands.

Okay, she guessed that was as much surrender as she'd get.

"Suck my dick, pretty girl."

So bossy.

But that was what she wanted anyway, so she decided to oblige him.

Moving down between his legs, she licked the head of him, humming in pleasure. This wasn't something she had much experience with. She'd only slept with one guy while they were on the run. And she hadn't really enjoyed it. It had been more about defying Stefan than anything else. His precious sister was no longer untouched.

"You're thinking too much," he said. "I might be insulted if I didn't know that's how your brain works. However, if you can't stop thinking I will take over."

Crap.

Determined to do this how she wanted, she took more of him into her mouth, sucking strongly.

"Fuck, yes, baby."

He lay on his back, and she moved to his side, leaning over him as she grasped hold of the base of his cock. He was thick and firm. And she wanted more.

He felt silky smooth. So warm. She ran her hand up and down his shaft, her mouth taking more of him in.

His breathing grew faster. "Fuck, baby, that's it. Hold me tight. Good girl. Now, lick across the head of my dick."

Instead of being annoyed at him taking charge, she found herself glad for the direction. She wanted to know what he liked.

"Cup my balls. Fuck, yes. Baby, you have no idea how good your mouth feels."

Lilac didn't realize how much she'd like this. But giving him pleasure made her feel so light, so happy.

She sped up, remembering how he'd started slowly, then gradually grown faster. Taking her hand from his balls, she wrapped it around the base of him again, jacking him off until his breathing grew erratic.

"I'm close, baby. And I want you to be a good girl and swallow."

Swallow?

Okay, she guessed she could try that.

A groan erupted from him as he came in her mouth. She swallowed hastily.

The taste of him was different, but not unpleasant, and his moans of pleasure were all she needed to hear to convince her that she wanted to do this again.

And soon.

46

When he lifted her out of the truck, he didn't bother putting her on her feet. His baby was done in. He was going to carry her inside and put her down for a nap.

Shutting the door with his hip, he winced at the creaking noise it made. He really had to go get his truck back. This was one of the Ranch trucks, and he missed his baby.

"Tanner, I can walk."

"Perhaps. But you're not going to. Just relax. I have you."

To his satisfaction, she rested her head against his chest as he carried her up the stairs.

"Tanner, I was just about to call you." Alec stepped out of the house onto the porch. "I need you guys to come into my office. Regent just called."

∽

"He thinks we should negotiate with Stefan?" Lilac leaned forward, nearly toppling off Tanner's lap.

He grabbed hold of her, holding her steady. "Careful, baby."

Her mind was reeling too much from Alec's words to hear him, though.

When Tanner had carried her into Alec's office, West, Maddox, and Raid had already in the office, looking pensive.

Well, she kind of thought West always looked like that.

"Yes," Alec replied. "Regent managed to get to someone in his organisation and pay them off for information. How much we can rely on that information, I don't know. His contact said that Stefan has been slowly spiralling. The longer you've been gone, the more obsessed he's become with you. Mateo's contact confirmed that last past."

It was sick and weird. She understood that. She just didn't know how to make it stop.

Beyond killing him.

"Then a few days ago, Stefan packed up and left with several of his men."

"What?" Her gaze shot up. "Where did he go?"

"Darlin', he's headed here. It's likely that he's here already. Somewhere around Haven. I don't think he'd show his face here yet. Although I could be wrong."

Would he do that? Just appear in Haven?

"He might," she said. "Stefan thinks he's more powerful than everyone else. He might be that bold."

"That's what Regent said, too," Alec replied.

"How did he find her, though?" Raid asked.

"A few days ago?" she whispered. So, it didn't sound like he'd had someone here all this time. Maybe he sent someone periodically or had paid someone off to inform for him. Or perhaps...

"It could have been the hospital," she said. "It was why I didn't want my name in the system. Lilac isn't a common name. And if he knew about Ryleigh's connection to you . . . he might have had someone scanning for Lilac Malone. I don't know.

Maybe that's a stretch. But he's powerful and rich and has some clever people working for him."

"That's a possibility," Alec said.

"So, by giving you my last name, I could have put you on his radar?" Tanner asked, sounding pained.

"Hey, no." She turned to cup his face. "The fact that someone called Lilac turned up in a hospital around my age was possibly enough for him to investigate. This isn't on you."

He didn't look convinced.

"How does any of this lead to Regent suggesting we negotiate with him?" Tanner asked. "For what exactly?"

"For me," she said quietly. "Do you want to negotiate for Ryleigh, Kye, and Opal's safety with me?" And then she would kill him.

Trouble was, she didn't know if she could do it anymore.

If she could leave Tanner. If she'd be able to take down Stefan alone. Because she didn't want to be alone anymore.

"I . . . I can't," she said before any of them could speak. Tears drifted down her cheeks. "I can't go back to him. Please don't make me."

"Like fuck anyone is making you!"

To her shock, the outburst came from Raid. He started pacing. "Damn it, Alec."

Tanner turned her, so her legs straddled his. He cupped her face, wiping away her tears. His face was intense. Stern. "Not happening. Ever. You hear me? Not. Ever."

With a sob, she leaned into him, her face pressed to his chest as she cried.

It was embarrassing, but she couldn't stop. Behind her, voices raged.

"Stop!" Alec ordered. "All of you listen to me. We are not sending her back. And I'm insulted you thought I would allow that to happen."

Oh no.

She hadn't meant to upset him.

"Sorry," she said, turning in Tanner's arms.

He arranged her so she was sitting side-on. Then he grabbed a tissue to wipe her face.

Alec pointed at her. "You do not apologize to me. Understand?" Then he turned that finger to his brothers. "You lot, I'm disappointed in."

"What could we possibly bargain with, then?" Raid asked, pacing back and forth.

"Why bargain with him at all?" West asked. "We should just murder the bastard."

"And how do you suggest we do that?" Alec asked.

"I don't know, pay Regent's contact to poison him?" Maddox suggested.

"He has a poison tester," she said.

"What?" Tanner asked.

"Yeah, someone always tastes his food and drinks first to make sure they're not poisoned. He's a murdering asshole, but he's not dumb. Are you . . . are you planning this arrangement in order to lure him somewhere?" she asked.

Alec stared at her, approval in his face. "You're smart."

She was her father's daughter, after all.

"What? I don't like this idea, either." Tanner frowned.

"Regent thinks it's our best chance," Alec said. "We agree to a trade, lure him out of hiding, and then we kill him."

"And the person you're going to offer to exchange is me," she said numbly.

Alec leaned forward. "Let me make this clear. We are not trading you. You are not going with him."

Lilac nodded, trying to keep her breathing steady. She got it. She really did. And she thought it was the best idea she'd heard.

There was just one problem . . .

"Not. Fucking. Happening."

Yep. That problem.

47

They were all out of their fucking minds.
 Tanner couldn't believe they were even discussing this. Because it wasn't happening.

"I'll do it."

His heart stopped. His head nearly exploded.

"You will not!" Standing, he deposited her on the chair he'd been sitting on and started pacing. "This will not happen."

"Tanner, it's the best idea." She stared up at him with wide eyes.

"No."

"This is our only chance to get him out in the open. I take it you have a plan to, uh, take care of him."

Tanner watched her swallow heavily as she said that. It couldn't be easy for her to talk about killing her own brother, no matter how much of a monster he was.

"That's where Tanner comes in," Alec said. "And Raid. Butch too."

"What?" Tanner asked. What was he talking about?

"We're going to need to scout out a place where we can set you guys up so you can stay hidden with a scope and rifle."

"You want me to shoot him?" Tanner asked. Not that he was against the idea, he was just surprised.

"You're the best shooter we have. Raid and Butch are good too. Maddox, you're on recon." He turned to Maddox. "Need you to have eyes out there, watching for when he arrives. He'll be expecting something."

"Right." Maddox nodded. "I think we should find somewhere open, where he won't expect anything. It might mean you have to take a shot from a long distance," he said to Tanner.

"I can do that if the conditions are right."

"We'll get onto scouting some places," Maddox said, reaching for his phone.

"But there's still a fucking problem," Tanner said.

Alec sighed, looking at his girl, then at him. "We need to use her, Tanner. If there's another way, then tell me."

There had to be another way. Because he wasn't allowing this.

"Fine, we make the bargain, but she stays at the home with the other women."

"We'll need some help to guard the other women," Raid said.

"And Lilac. Because she's staying here," Tanner insisted.

Was no one listening to him?

Lilac got to her feet and grasped hold of his hands. "Tanner, I have to do this. I won't be alone. You'll be there. Alec will be with me." She glanced over at him.

Alec nodded. "Both me and West. Regent said he'd sent Victor and some of his men. I'll probably use them to protect everyone back here.

"That's smart," she said. "I wouldn't put it past Stefan to attack while you were all occupied."

Tanner turned to her. "You are not doing this. I forbid it."

"You can't forbid this."

"I can forbid it. And if you even think of doing it, I'm going to spank you until you can't sit for a month!"

Her gaze narrowed. "I'm doing it."

"Over my dead fucking body."

~

LILAC SIGHED as she watched Tanner pace back and forth.

After their argument in Alec's office, he'd picked her up and carried her upstairs to the bedroom. And she'd let him because she knew he needed that.

He had to protect her.

But if this was the best opportunity, they had to take Stefan out, then she wanted to take it.

She had to. And she couldn't let Tanner stand in her way.

He'd made her get into bed, telling her that she needed a nap.

But there was no way she could sleep when there was so much tension between them. But Tanner hadn't left. He just kept pacing, thinking, muttering to himself.

"I feel bad for doing something that you obviously don't like when I know you're just trying to protect me." She rubbed her belly. "I don't want to argue with you. Or have you upset with me."

"Fuck."

He closed his eyes, looking pained. "I don't want you to do this."

"I know. But I think it's the best idea we have. And you'll make sure that I'm okay."

"I promised you that you wouldn't go within ten feet of him." Opening his eyes, she saw the pain in them. The agony.

God, maybe she was wrong. Perhaps she shouldn't do this.

"If I allow you to do this, then you do everything you are told, understand me?"

"I understand," she whispered. "I'm sorry, Tanner. I'm not doing this to hurt you. Or upset you."

"I know, baby. Fuck, I know." He sat, facing her. Cupping her face, he gave her a stern look. "But you will obey every order. And you will not get hurt."

"I promise."

He drew her to him, rocking her back and forth.

"I love you, baby. Nothing can happen to you."

"It won't." God, she hoped nothing went wrong.

Pulling back, he kissed her gently. "You need to nap."

"I need something else more."

He raised his eyebrows, giving her a stern look. "You've already had your wicked way with me today. Restrain yourself."

Dear Lord. She rolled her eyes at him. "Not that. I, uh, I think maybe you need something else and so do I." She moved from the blankets and placed herself awkwardly over his lap.

He rubbed her ass. "You want me to spank you?"

She wouldn't say want. But she thought that perhaps it would help the guilt in her stomach.

"I think it would help me feel better. And you, as well."

"I'm not your brother, I won't harm you."

She turned to look up at him in shock. "I could never see you as my brother. Ever."

He swallowed heavily. "Good. Because all I want is to protect you."

"I know you do. This has nothing to do with Stefan. I promise."

"Good. But I'm not going to spank you now. You're still recuperating."

"I wasn't sick, Tanner. I'm not ill or injured. Please."

He sighed and lowered her panties. He'd taken her jeans off

when he'd put her to bed for a nap. "This won't be hard or long. Because you're not at a hundred percent. But I will wallop your ass after this is all over for putting yourself in danger. Understand me? You agreed to this plan, but you agree, knowing your butt will not sit comfortably for a week."

"I agree."

"Safeword?"

"Scotch," she replied. The word was barely out of her mouth before his hand landed.

When he said it wasn't going to be hard or long, she misunderstood, thinking it would be soft and quick.

It wasn't.

Yeah, it didn't last for too long, but when he finished, her ass was definitely hot, and she knew she'd be feeling it the rest of the day. She didn't cry, but her breath was choppy as he turned her over and held her on his lap.

"I love you, baby. So, fucking much. Nothing can happen to you. Nothing."

48

Today was the day and Lilac was so fucking nervous. She'd been awake all night, unable to sleep.

Tanner had tried to wear her out, giving her three orgasms with his mouth. But it hadn't helped. Her mind had kept going over everything that could go wrong.

Now it was five in the morning and Tanner was heading out with Maddox, Butch, and Raid to the meeting point. West and Alec were going with her later. Beau and Jaret were staying with all the women and children. Along with Victor Malone and the men he'd brought with him.

He was kind of a scary guy. Silent. Huge. But everyone seemed to trust him to take care of things here.

Alec had called Stefan yesterday afternoon and made all the arrangements for this morning.

It made her shiver, thinking about Stefan, wondering if he was close by.

She hadn't been there for the negotiations. Alec didn't want her getting upset.

Tanner had been kept away too. Which was definitely for the best.

"Be safe," she ordered him, hugging him tight.

She didn't know where the other men were. They must have said goodbye to their loved ones already.

"I will." He cupped her face between his hands. "I'll be fine. We'll all be there to watch over you. You will be safe. You will do what you're told. And you will come back to me."

She nodded, then kissed him, watching him walk out the back door.

"He'll be okay."

She glanced behind her to find West standing there, watching her with serious eyes. He wasn't a happy, easygoing guy. But he had a confidence about him that eased the panic in her tummy.

"I know. Will everyone here be all right?" She didn't think Stefan would come after them, but she couldn't be entirely certain either.

Everyone had moved into the big house during the night with Victor's men helping. Now all of the bedrooms were filled with people.

It was a tight squeeze, but under other circumstances, she might have found it fun. However, no one was in a cheerful mood.

"They will be," West told her firmly. "Beau, Jaret, and Victor are here. Victor's men will patrol the Ranch. Oh, and Linc's here, too."

She could see that filled him with enthusiasm. None of the Malone men seemed to like the way Linc looked at Ryleigh.

"Go get ready," West said gruffly. "Let's get this over with."

With a nod, she moved upstairs.

After getting dressed, she went downstairs to meet Alec and West. Ryleigh and Opal were there as well. Ryleigh threw herself into Lilac's arms. "Are you sure it shouldn't be me going? I feel like it should be. Why you?"

"It's always been me. In Stefan's twisted mind, I'm his. I'll be okay, Ryleigh."

"Promise?" she asked.

"Promise." She hugged Opal next.

The other woman held onto her fiercely. "I'll look after her. But you make sure you come back. Understand?"

"I will." She glanced over at where West and Alec were hugging Flick and Mia.

Victor stood off to one side, watching over them. Alec spoke to him briefly and Victor nodded.

They climbed into a car she hadn't seen before. The windows were tinted. West was driving. She and Alec got in the backseat.

"You're good with what is happening?" Alec asked.

"Yep. I've got it all."

"You stay next to me or West at all times. We lure him out to where Tanner has a shot."

That part made her feel ill. But she had this.

"What the fuck?" West grumbled. "Alec, we've got a tail."

"What?" Alec turned. "Fuck! I need to call Victor."

"Shit! He's coming up fast! I can't outrun him."

Panic flooded her as she turned right as the car behind them smashed into the back of them. She screamed but West held the car steady.

Oh God!

She should have known that Stefan would have a plan. That he'd know they were up to something.

Tanner! He was going to be so upset if something happened to them.

Suddenly, a car pulled out from a side road, crashing into the front of them and sending their car spinning.

The last thing she remembered was a loud screeching, yelling, pain.

Then nothing.

∽

Lilac woke up with a groan. Where was she?

"Hello, sister."

She stared up into Stefan's face. He looked cold. Emotionless. This wasn't good.

But how did he get her? What happened? Why did her body ache?

Then it came back to her. Driving in the car with West and Alec. Someone tailing them. The crash. Then nothing.

"You crashed into us?" She sat up even though her entire body screamed in pain. As she took stock, she could tell she wasn't severely injured.

Well, not unless the shock was disguising the pain of an internal injury.

Numbness filled her as she stared out the window of the car they were in. Where were they?

Oh God.

"I had my men stop the car you were in, yes," he replied.

"West and Alec! What did you do?" Were they all right? Fuck. This is what she'd been trying to avoid . . . anyone else getting harmed.

"Why do you care?" he asked in a soft voice.

Immediately, dread rushed through her. This was Stefan at his most dangerous.

It was like he was trying to lure you into his web with false promises before he bit off your head.

Gruesome? Yes.

Accurate? Also, yes.

She swallowed. "I don't care about them. But if you kill them, it's going to leave things messy. The people of this town won't rest until they find you, including the sheriff."

He made a scoffing noise. "As if I care about a few hillbillies and an idiot sheriff." His gaze narrowed. "You've gotten some attitude while you've been gone. You've forgotten that you're not allowed to lie to me."

Oh God.

Danger. Danger.

"Believe me, I haven't forgotten anything."

Reaching out, he grabbed her by the front of her throat. "You ran from me, Lilac. From. Me. I own you. You do not get to run from me. And then I find you with other men."

"They . . . I . . . they aren't my men," she managed to get out. "They have families."

"I know. And if they weren't related to Regent Malone, they'd be dead."

That meant they were still alive. Thank God.

Stefan drew his hand away from her neck. He watched her closely. "So why were you so concerned about them? Because they're Ryleigh's half-brothers?"

"You knew about her half-brothers?"

"Of course I did. You know I always do my homework, Lilac. I knew her old man's last name before I even met him. I did underestimate you all, though. I never expected you to escape. Or to be able to hide from me for so long."

Was that pride in his face?

Fucking hell.

He was angry at her for leaving him and proud of her for evading him? This was the problem with Stefan. It was hard to best him when he made no sense.

"Why did you do that? Crash into them? They were bringing me to you."

He shot her a cold look. "Were they? Or was it a trap? You forget, Lilac, I haven't lived this long by being stupid."

"I...I don't know what you're talking about. They were going to give me to you in return for you leaving Ryleigh and Opal alone."

"As though I care about those two stupid sluts. No, I couldn't trust those assholes you were with. I don't know them. And I've got enough issues."

"Like what?"

"Well, first, my sister ran from me. Hid from me. I really thought you'd go straight to Ryleigh's brothers. When I realized you were smarter than I'd given you credit for, I drew my men back from watching this hick town. It wasn't until your name set off an alert that my guy found you'd been in the hospital here. Lilac Malone." He leaned into her. "That's never going to happen, by the way."

Oh God.

Tanner.

He'd never wanted her to do this. To be a part of this. He was going to be so upset.

She felt ill at the thought.

"You won't go after Ryleigh and Opal, will you?" she whispered.

He might have said that he didn't want them, but that didn't mean he wouldn't punish them from running from him.

Stefan waved a hand through the air. "Like I said, I don't care about those two sluts. They're not my blood. Ryleigh is tainted and Opal was just a hole to fill."

Gross.

But she thought he was telling the truth.

"And me?"

"You're mine. I'll have to punish you for leaving. Hmm, perhaps I should have grabbed Opal as well. Or maybe even that baby. I could've used either to them to punish you for defying me."

Don't vomit. Don't react.

Her entire body was throbbing with pain.

"You could have killed me, ramming that car into the one I was in," she pointed out.

"My men were told to do it in such a way that no one was harmed. If you'd been killed, they would've suffered my wrath."

Still, she wasn't sure if he'd genuinely care if she died or not.

The real question was…did he know that she was in a relationship with Tanner?

Lilac didn't think that he did, or he would've been on the rampage.

She had to fight hard not to show her fear. Or how much her body hurt.

Showing Stefan any weakness was just asking for trouble.

"Why do you want me, Stefan?" she whispered. "Why come after me?"

He stared at her with vicious intelligence. He was so smart. He could be so charismatic. And yet, he had no empathy, no sense of morality. Of right and wrong.

"I've told you so many times, my sweet sister. You. Are. Mine." Reaching out, he brushed his cold fingers down her cheek. She had to fight hard not to shudder. Not to throw up.

How was she going to get out of this? She'd never be able to escape him again. She'd be lucky if he didn't lock her up.

"What now, Stefan?" she asked.

"Well, I've got some plans for you, Lilac. After I spend a suitable amount of time punishing you, of course. I can't let you get away with this display of disobedience."

No, Lord forbid that she try to do something he didn't want her to do.

A shudder worked its way through her.

"And then I'm going to marry you off, build my empire."

"You . . . you what?" Her mouth was so dry.

Marry her off to whom? Had he decided on someone?

Would they be worse than him? Oh fuck. What was she going to do?

"You've made a decision then?"

"Everything will become clear soon," he said with a drawl as they slowed down.

She looked out the window, despair filling her.

A plane.

"Since when do you own a plane?" she whispered.

"I called in a favor. Don't worry, you're going to help me pay him back. I've been having some . . . business issues. Which is all going to be solved with our new partnership."

With whom? With the person he was going to marry her off to?

"Couldn't you let me go, Stefan? Just let me be free? Isn't there some small part of you that loves me?" she whispered.

He grabbed hold of her arm. Tight. "That's just it. I do love you. I already told you that you're mine."

"That's not love. That's possession."

"Same thing."

Right. Which just proved that he had no idea what love was. Lilac wasn't sure why she'd thought he would understand.

"Come on, come meet your fiancée. We're going to fly home and get you married."

Fear held her immobile. But Stefan just dragged her out of the car and toward the plane. She tried to fight him, to break his hold, but he turned and slapped her across the face. She let out a cry, her face stinging.

"I'm going to have to ask that you don't harm my fiancée," a cold voice said from above them.

She looked up, but her eyesight was blurry, and she couldn't be certain about what she was seeing.

That voice... though...

"She's still my sister and I'll treat her how I want."

Stefan dragged her up the stairs as tears dripped down her cheeks. But she held her shoulders back, facing the person who'd spoken. They'd moved back, letting them have room.

"Here she is. Your new wife." Stefan shoved her down and she fell onto her knees in front of the man.

The man who'd betrayed her.

How could he?

He glanced down at her. His face was icy cold, and she trembled. She wanted to put on a brave front, but it was nearly impossible.

All she wanted was Tanner.

God, she wanted him here so much.

"Yes, well, I've decided not to do that," the other man said.

His words took a moment to filter through the terror surrounding her.

"What do you mean?" Stefan asked. "We're going to form a partnership."

"I'm afraid not. You don't think I know you plan to have her marry me, then kill me? Take everything I own? That's not happening, Stefan. At least, it won't be *you* taking what *I* own. It will be the other way around."

"I don't think so," Stefan sneered. "I'm not going down like this."

Before she even knew what was happening, the man in front of her raised a gun.

"Yes, you are."

This wasn't happening. Lilac stared from one to the other. She saw Stefan tremble. He wasn't used to not having the upper hand, to not being fully in control.

And now . . . oh, God, she was going to be sick.

"I'm a bad person, Stefan. But you're the Devil himself. And you belong in hell."

The gun fired and she screamed, her arms going over the back of her head as she huddled down to protect herself. Her entire body shook, and she knew she was going to be sick.

But she couldn't stop herself from turning to look.

She saw Stefan lying on the floor. He was so still.

So dead.

"Oh God. Oh God."

"Get up, Lilac."

His voice wasn't unkind, but she was too scared to reply as she forced herself to stand.

"Is he . . . is he . . ." she stumbled over her words, her hand over her tummy.

"Oh, he's quite dead." There was almost a cheerful note to Donatello Rossi's voice as he spoke.

Turning back to him, she saw that he'd put the gun away and was pouring himself a drink. How had this even happened?

"You killed him."

"Yes," he replied calmly.

"I thought he was your friend," she said. Well, as much of a friend as Stefan had.

"Stefan doesn't have friends, you know that. And he was no friend of mine. It was only a matter of time until he betrayed me."

"You keep helping me."

He eyed her for a long moment, then he sighed. "I once had a sister who I loved. I couldn't save her. But I could save you."

She swallowed heavily. "It seems too easy. He's been the boogeyman under my bed for so many years and now he's just..."

"As monstrous as I'm sure he seemed, he was just a man, Lilac. A man who got what was coming to him."

Still... she felt all mixed up. He was a terrible person. He would have taken her back to his house and hurt her for defying him.

But he was still her brother.

Who was now gone. And she was free... wasn't she? Or had she swapped one monster for another?

"Where are his men?" she asked worriedly. They'd been just outside the plane. Why weren't they here?

"My men have taken care of them. The idiot thought I wasn't a threat to him because I agreed to be his ally. Don't worry, no one will find out what happened here."

Right. Uh-huh. Yep.

"What... what happens now?"

"Now, my dear, you have a choice. You can come back with me, of course. I'll provide you with a safe place to live. Time and money to do whatever you desire."

She shook her head violently and he smiled.

"Or you can pretend this never happened, you never saw any of this, and you can leave."

"I want option number two. I'll never say a word, Don. I promise."

Please don't let him take her back with him.

"I know you won't, sweetheart. I'm taking over everything he owned, you know. You won't get any of it."

"I don't want it. I just want to live in peace. Please."

Don cupped her face with his hand. "I know you do. I saw that in you the first time I met you. I have no desire for an unwilling woman." He stepped back.

"Some of the people who worked for him... in the house... they're good people."

"If they're good people, they won't be harmed, I promise."

Lilac nodded. She just wanted out of here.

Tanner. She needed Tanner.

"Now, we're going to leave, and you need to get off the plane. But don't worry, I'm sure your man will be here soon."

"You know about Tanner?" she asked.

"Hmm. Tell him Mateo sends his regards."

"You know Mateo?" she whispered. She remembered Alec had talked to him, and he'd said he'd discreetly ask around about her brother.

Why hadn't he mentioned Don to Alec?

"Yes. He contacted me to see if I knew what was happening with Stefan. Mateo wasn't able to get directly involved. But I told him I would do what was necessary to take care of you. He didn't know the details."

Okay. All right.

"I'm sorry, sweetheart, but I'm going to have to ask you to get off the plane. I need to leave now."

Sure. Uh-huh.

Why did she feel so numb? And yet her legs didn't want to move properly.

She had to step over Stefan's body to get out. A sob escaped her. By the time she descended the stairs, the plane was getting ready to leave and she was barely able to stumble far enough away.

Pausing, she heaved up the contents of her stomach, which wasn't a lot.

She wanted to believe she was safe.

She slid onto her ass and waited.

When Tanner arrived with Raid and Butch. He opened the back door of the truck before it even stopped, running toward her.

Crouching down, he cupped her face in his hands. His face

was pale, his eyes wild. "Baby, baby, are you all right? Are you hurt? Fuck, talk to me."

"He's dead, Tanner. He's finally dead." She threw herself into his arms, tears sliding down her cheeks.

She wasn't sure why she was crying, exactly.

Because of everything that had happened? Because he'd nearly taken her? Or because he was dead?

It was all so mixed up in her mind.

"Shh. It's all right. You're safe. I have you. I have you, baby. And you're never going to leave my sight again. I'm going to spank you every night for a year. I'm going to glue you to me, put a leash on you, fucking something."

She let out a sobbing laugh and leaned back to look up at him. "I'm all right, Tanner. I promise I'm safe."

"You better fucking be. Because there's no way I can ever go through this again."

"I love you, Tanner Malone. With all of me. And this . . . this is the start of our happy-ever-after."

EPILOGUE

"Let me play with you."

"No," he said.

The reply frustrated her even as his touch brought her such pleasure she swore she saw stars.

His hands were heavy on her breasts, lips on her nipples. His mouth moved lower and lower. To where she wanted him to touch her.

But she wanted to give him the same.

Wanted to take him. Wanted him to fuck her.

Hard. Fast. With a fierceness their love-making no longer had.

Don't get her wrong, she liked him sweet and slow. Gentle and tender.

But she also liked that other side to him. The man who was in charge. Who commanded her. Who bossed her and teased her. Who flirted and grinned. And yeah, she even missed Meanie Malone.

As he entered her, his dick driving deep inside her, she came.

Her cry of pleasure filled their room in the bunkhouse of the Ranch.

Tanner held himself above her, not giving her his weight, afraid to crush her.

Because he thought she was delicate, fragile.

Ever since Stefan stole her away six weeks ago, Tanner had been broken. He was still here. Still did and said the right things. But he watched her all the time. Every touch was deliberately careful as though he was scared she would break.

She'd long since healed her bruises from the car crash. The mark on her cheek left over from where Stefan slapped her was gone.

The nightmares continued, but they were getting better. She'd only had one this last week. Still, they didn't help Tanner's state of mind. Every time she had one, he freaked out.

Thankfully, Alec and West hadn't been badly injured. After no one could get hold of them, Maddox had gone looking and found them. West had a small concussion, while Alec had a lot of bruises and a gash on his head that had needed stitches.

About ten minutes after Maddox had found them, Tanner had gotten an anonymous message telling him where he could collect Lilac. He'd raced there with Butch and Raid, uncertain whether she was alive or dead.

Yeah, she understood why he was so upset.

Lilac wrapped her arms around him as he continued to drive himself inside her, coming with a muffled groan. Her clit pulsed with the aftereffects of her own orgasm, and he rolled them over until he was on his back with her on his chest.

She didn't know how to get him to see that she was all right now. Yeah, Stefan was dead, and she'd seen it. Yes, everything had gone to crap. But she was okay.

In the end, she'd only told Tanner and Alec the truth of what happened on that plane. She didn't want to talk about it and break Donatello's trust. If that's what it had been. They'd agreed that keeping that to themselves was best.

She'd moved into the bunkhouse with Tanner. They had plans to eventually build a house on the Ranch, but for the moment she didn't mind the bunkhouse.

Ryleigh and Opal were living in the main house with Alec and Mia. Although Opal was making noises about moving into a house in town. It would be closer for her job, even though Alec had lent her a Ranch truck for transport.

She wouldn't be surprised if Ryleigh went with her. If her brothers let her. They'd kicked Linc off the Ranch as soon as everyone had been discharged and gone home. But he now visited the Ranch all the time. Much to the Malone men's dismay. She'd had to talk Tanner out of shooting out his tires.

They were all very protective.

Case in point, the man sliding out from under her to go take care of his condom. When he returned, he tucked her into his side under the covers, kissing her forehead.

"I'm not going to break, you know," she whispered to him.

"I know."

Lilac sighed. She'd tried to talk to him about this, but he wouldn't listen. "You still owe me several spankings. We should get started on those."

"I'm wiping the slate clean."

Damn. She never thought she'd be disappointed about not getting a spanking.

"I love you, Tanner Malone."

"Love you too, baby. Go to sleep. You need your rest."

Right. Because she'd been doing little else these past six weeks. Maybe it was time to get her life back.

∽

"You sure about this, babe?" Opal asked as she pulled up and got out of the truck, handing over the keys.

"Yep. Thanks for meeting me down here at the gate." They were at the entrance to the Ranch. Opal had finished work early today so she could get home and hand off the truck she was using to Lilac.

"All right, but when Tanner and Alec find out I helped you, I'm offering your ass up for a spanking."

She grinned. "That's what I'm hoping for."

Opal grinned back. "That's my girl. Go catch hell." She slapped Lilac's ass as she climbed into the truck.

Lilac rolled her eyes. Then she drove into Haven and into the parking lot of Dirty Delights.

Time to get her job back.

∾

"Please, Devon," she begged.

"Nope. No way. I am not dealing with an angry, possessive Tanner Malone when he comes in here."

And he'd likely be here soon. Would he have seen her note yet? She hadn't wanted to scare him, so she'd left a note telling him where to find her.

She'd just wanted to give him a bit of a nudge.

"I need this job."

Devon pointed at her. "No."

"Just for an hour?" she asked.

"No."

With a sigh, she sat at the bar. "Fine, can I have a beer?"

"You driving?" he asked.

"Yep."

"Then no."

Her mouth dropped open in outrage. "I can have one beer and still drive!"

"Not if you're getting a beer from here, you can't. You're too small to not be a lightweight."

That jerk!

And she'd actually put on a little weight. A tiny bit, but she was getting there. Of course, she had lost some weight after Stefan's death so, basically, she was back where she'd been before he'd taken her.

She was considering talking to someone about everything, though, because it was still a struggle to eat. And sometimes everything would just come over her, making it hard for her to breathe.

All right. Perhaps she was a bit fragile.

But she could handle anything Tanner threw at her.

"What you can have is this." Devon plopped a bowl of fries in front of her.

She sighed. She'd only eaten a couple of fries when she felt him enter. Even though her back was to the door, she knew it was him because everyone went silent.

Turning, she could see why.

Oh, crap.

Perhaps she hadn't thought this through. Getting to her feet, she looked around wondering if she could run.

But then he was in front of her. And suddenly she was flying through the air before she landed over his shoulder.

"Tanner! Put me down!"

Slap!

Holy. Heck.

This is what she wanted.

But not in front of everyone.

Yeah, you really didn't think this through.

"Put me down." She wriggled as he made his way outside.

Slap!

"Tanner, please. I'm sorry."

"Not yet, but you will be."

Well. Hell. That wasn't ominous or anything.

The entire ride home was silent. He'd left the Ranch truck she'd driven into town, using his truck to take them back to the Ranch.

When they reached the bunkhouse, she undid her belt.

"Stay there."

Gulp.

She watched as he ran to her side of the truck and opened the door.

Then she was over his shoulder again.

"Tanner!" she cried. "Someone will see!"

"Should have thought of that."

She should have. She really, really should have.

He slid her down his body once they were in his bedroom, holding her steady until she had her balance. She stared up at him in trepidation.

He was in alpha male mode right now.

His face was tight. Stern. Dominant.

And her insides lit on fire. She didn't know why, but she liked him like this. Not all the time. Just sometimes.

She also kind of wanted to run and pee herself. All at the same time.

"Strip."

"Maybe we can talk about this," she prevaricated as she inched away from him.

But he stood between her and the door. The only place to go was the bathroom and the window in there wasn't large enough to climb out of.

Do you really want to escape?

That would be nope.

"That's not your safeword. Strip."

Holy. Heck.

Deciding she'd have to reap what she'd sowed, she stripped out of her clothes, standing in front of him naked.

A sense of shyness came over her as he took off his own top. He stared at her, studied her. When she tried to cover her breasts, he pushed her hand away. Then he sat on the bed and patted his lap.

"Over you come."

She stepped away. "What are you doing?"

"Giving you a spanking."

"Why?"

He gave her an incredulous look. "You know why. Because you left the Ranch without me."

"Stefan isn't a risk anymore. And I'm safe."

He scowled. "You're not supposed to go into town on your own. I would have taken you in if you'd asked."

"And if I want to get a job? What then?"

He glanced away, his jaw tight.

Lilac walked closer, stepping between his thighs. She cupped his chin, tilting his head up. "It's time to loosen security up a bit. I know you're scared of something happening to me and I'm sorry I left like I did. But I've tried to talk to you about this many times, but you don't want to listen. I'm all right now. I'm safe. You made me safe."

"I didn't, though. You could have died! Right now, you could be with him."

She straddled his legs, and he grasped hold of her hips. "But I'm not. I'm here with you. And I need you to remember that I'm not fragile."

Tanner gave her a look.

"Okay, I'm a little fragile, but I won't break and even if I leave the Ranch, I'm always going to come home to you. Because you are my home."

Leaning in, she kissed him. It wasn't long before he took over, turning the kiss into something hard and wild.

And just what she needed.

Then he drew back, and she whimpered. "More."

"No."

"Tanner!" she cried. "I'm fine!"

"What you are, is naughty. And you need to be punished."

Her heart skipped a beat. Then suddenly, she found herself being moved so she was lying over his lap.

"Tanner?"

"What's your safeword?"

"Scotch."

"You'll say it if you need to. Otherwise, you're going to take your punishment. This is for saying yes to putting yourself at risk with your brother. And it's for leaving the Ranch without telling me."

"I'm never going to sit again, am I?"

"Probably not."

The spanks landed hard and fast. Soon her ass felt like it was on her fire, and she kicked her legs, wanting some respite.

"Tanner, no!"

"A bit longer, baby. You earned this and you know it."

She did know it. At least today she had. She'd felt guilty the entire time about what she was doing, even if she thought it was for his own good.

Tears dripped down her face and she sobbed as her poor bottom throbbed.

When he finally finished, he moved her so she sat on his lap, facing him. Pulling her against his chest, he rocked her back and forth.

"Good girl. You did so well. My brave, beautiful girl."

"That's not your safeword. Strip."

Holy. Heck.

Deciding she'd have to reap what she'd sowed, she stripped out of her clothes, standing in front of him naked.

A sense of shyness came over her as he took off his own top. He stared at her, studied her. When she tried to cover her breasts, he pushed her hand away. Then he sat on the bed and patted his lap.

"Over you come."

She stepped away. "What are you doing?"

"Giving you a spanking."

"Why?"

He gave her an incredulous look. "You know why. Because you left the Ranch without me."

"Stefan isn't a risk anymore. And I'm safe."

He scowled. "You're not supposed to go into town on your own. I would have taken you in if you'd asked."

"And if I want to get a job? What then?"

He glanced away, his jaw tight.

Lilac walked closer, stepping between his thighs. She cupped his chin, tilting his head up. "It's time to loosen security up a bit. I know you're scared of something happening to me and I'm sorry I left like I did. But I've tried to talk to you about this many times, but you don't want to listen. I'm all right now. I'm safe. You made me safe."

"I didn't, though. You could have died! Right now, you could be with him."

She straddled his legs, and he grasped hold of her hips. "But I'm not. I'm here with you. And I need you to remember that I'm not fragile."

Tanner gave her a look.

"Okay, I'm a little fragile, but I won't break and even if I leave the Ranch, I'm always going to come home to you. Because you are my home."

Leaning in, she kissed him. It wasn't long before he took over, turning the kiss into something hard and wild.

And just what she needed.

Then he drew back, and she whimpered. "More."

"No."

"Tanner!" she cried. "I'm fine!"

"What you are, is naughty. And you need to be punished."

Her heart skipped a beat. Then suddenly, she found herself being moved so she was lying over his lap.

"Tanner?"

"What's your safeword?"

"Scotch."

"You'll say it if you need to. Otherwise, you're going to take your punishment. This is for saying yes to putting yourself at risk with your brother. And it's for leaving the Ranch without telling me."

"I'm never going to sit again, am I?"

"Probably not."

The spanks landed hard and fast. Soon her ass felt like it was on her fire, and she kicked her legs, wanting some respite.

"Tanner, no!"

"A bit longer, baby. You earned this and you know it."

She did know it. At least today she had. She'd felt guilty the entire time about what she was doing, even if she thought it was for his own good.

Tears dripped down her face and she sobbed as her poor bottom throbbed.

When he finally finished, he moved her so she sat on his lap, facing him. Pulling her against his chest, he rocked her back and forth.

"Good girl. You did so well. My brave, beautiful girl."

Leaning back, she wiped her face. Reaching over, he grabbed a tissue and did it for her.

"I have something for you," he told her.

He did? What was it?

Reaching over, he opened the nightstand drawer and drew out a velvet bag.

"Hold out your hand and close your eyes," he commanded.

She eyed him.

"Go on," he coaxed.

She felt something slip onto her hand.

"Open."

Tears filled her eyes as she opened them. She sobbed.

"Hey! That was meant to make you happy."

"Mama's rings," she said. "I can't believe you found them." She shakily put them on her fingers. "You got them back for me. Thank you!"

"I'd do anything for you, baby." And then his mouth descended, and he kissed her.

This kiss was filled with hunger. With possession.

Her body heated. "I need you," she told him as he drew his lips away. "Please."

He lifted her off him, and for a moment she thought he would reject her. Then he stripped off his jeans and boxers and sat back, lifting her onto him and impaling her on his dick.

And it was fucking glorious.

Hard and hot.

Fast.

"Fuck. I don't have any protection on," he said through gritted teeth.

"It's okay. Don't stop. Please." Her heart was racing, sweat coating her skin.

More. More.

"You're okay with babies?" he asked.

"Yes," she groaned.

"Christ, that makes me so damn hot, thinking about you pregnant." He moved her onto her back on the bed without slipping out of her. Then he fucked her in earnest.

His finger reached down to play with her clit.

"I'm going to come soon, baby," he warned. "And you're to come with me or I'm going to spank you all over again."

She whimpered. But when she heard him groan, felt his release, it sent her over the edge. She came with a scream, her eyes closing as she was rocked by her orgasm.

When he slid from her pussy, she lay there, unable to move, completely satisfied.

"What's that grin about?" he asked as he lay on his side next to her. He cupped her mound with his hand, and she moaned.

"I just . . . that was so good."

He nipped her bottom lip. Hard.

Her eyes opened and she glared at him. "What was that for?"

"For being a brat." Regret swam in his eyes as he slid his fingers through her pussy, then pushed two deep inside her.

She gasped. Could he feel his release inside her? Why was that so fucking hot?

"I'm sorry I wasn't giving you what you needed."

"Listen to me, Tanner Malone," she said sternly as she cupped his face between her hands. "You always give me what I need. I just . . . what happened wasn't your fault."

She knew that was how he felt.

"I should have been with you."

"And then you might have been hurt. You have to let it go, please. And if you can't, maybe you'd want to talk to someone as well."

"As well?" he asked as he slid his fingers in and out of her pussy.

Her breath hitched. "I think I need to talk to someone about everything that has happened."

"My brave girl. I suppose if you can do that, so can I. Although whoever we talk to might get more than they bargained for."

She grinned up at him as he moved his thumb to her clit, rubbing it. "Now, we're going to talk about your punishment for stealing a truck."

Her eyes widened. "I just borrowed it, though."

"Hmm, nice try. But I think you need to be punished so you remember not to do that again. And I think some time being edged will be just the reminder you need."

Such a meanie.

Her Meanie Malone.

Printed in Great Britain
by Amazon